Steve Cavanagh was born and raised in Belfast before leaving for Dublin at the age of eighteen to study Law. He currently practices civil rights law and has been involved in several high-profile cases; in 2010 he represented a factory worker who suffered racial abuse in the workplace and won the largest award of damages for race discrimination in Northern Ireland legal history. He holds a certificate in Advanced Advocacy and lectures on various legal subjects (but really he just likes to tell jokes). His novel *The Liar* won the 2018 CWA Gold Dagger award while his follow-up novel *Thirteen* was a *Sunday Times* top ten bestseller. He is married with two young children.

To find out more, visit Steve's website or follow him on Twitter.

www.stevecavanaghbooks.com
@SSCav

Also by Steve Cavanagh

The Defence
The Cross (novella)
The Plea
The Liar
Thirteen

TWISTED

Steve Cavanagh

ORION

First published in Great Britain in 2019
by Orion Fiction,
This paperback edition published in 2019
by Orion Fiction,
an imprint of The Orion Publishing Group Ltd
Carmelite House, 50 Victoria Embankment
London EC4Y 0DZ

An Hachette UK Company

9 10

A CIP catalogue record for this book is
available from the British Library.

ISBN (Mass Market Paperback) 978 1 4091 7070 9

Typeset by Born Group

Printed in Great Britain by Clays Ltd, Elcograf S.p.A.

www.orionbooks.co.uk

TWISTED

by

J. T. LeBeau

AUTHOR'S NOTE

This will be my last book. I won't write another. The reasons should be clear by the time you come to the end of this story. That's an interesting word – *story*. Is this a true story? Is it a memoir? Or fiction? I can't say. You may have found this book on the true crime shelf, or in the thriller section of your local bookstore. It doesn't matter. Forget about that. There are only two things you need to know:

1. On my specific instructions my publishers have not edited this text. There have been no editorial notes, structural edits or other outside interference. It's just you and me.
2. From here on in, don't believe a single word you read.

J. T. LeBeau,
California, 2018.

THE BEGINNING OF THE END

August

Paul Cooper waited outside a theater on La Brea Avenue in the hot midday sun with a gun in his pocket and a head full of bad ideas. He took off his sunglasses, wiped the sweat from his forehead onto the sleeve of his tee and went over the plan one more time.

He would wait for the guests inside the theater to leave. Paul had managed to secure a spot close to the barrier, on a fenced-off walkway leading from the theater to the curb. The mourners would have to walk right by him as they made their way to the street and their waiting limos. It gave him the best view of the crowd. The target was here. He was sure of that. More than likely in the theater. Less likely to be in the crowd but he scanned the faces of the people around him nonetheless. He couldn't miss this opportunity. When he saw the target, he would draw that .38 from his pants pocket and pull the trigger in their face.

The lot outside the theater was full. A crowd of two to three hundred people lined either side of the barriers. They were paying their respects to their dead idol. The theater wasn't showing a play that day. No, the space had been booked for a memorial service dedicated to the late J. T. LeBeau.

The service had started late and progressed slower than advertised in the program. Like all memorial services, the speeches went on for far too long. What were the organizers supposed to do? Were they supposed to drag Stephen King or John Grisham off the stage? And while the writers read extracts from LeBeau's work in the air-conditioned theater, outside, the fans clutched books, held aloft signs, sung and supported each other in their collective, unearned grief.

Paul felt sick. Either it was the mass hysteria around him, grown women crying for a dead author, or the heat. Or both. Or the bellyful of vodka. He'd needed a few stiff drinks to stop his hands shaking.

He didn't have a real taste for killing. Not yet. He had blood on his hands – a lot of blood. But this was somehow different. This one was special.

Every time he caught the name LeBeau in the air around him, that knife in his stomach twisted just a little bit more. While J. T. LeBeau was a household name, the author was definitely not a well-known face. The opposite, in fact. No one in the crowd had ever met the writer. They may own every edition of LeBeau's novels, they may even own one of the rarer signed copies of that famous first novel, they may think they know the writer through close-reading of the work, but none of them had ever met their hero. None of them had even seen a picture of LeBeau, much less met him. And now they never would. Dead writers can't do signings.

Four people in the world knew the real identity of J. T. LeBeau. And one of those four people was about to eat a bullet fired from the .38 Special in Paul Cooper's pocket.

The glass doors that lined the entrance to the theater opened and a crowd poured out into the punishing Los Angeles heat. Of course, they'd dressed for it. Pale linen suits hung off the bony shoulders of the men pushing their way to their cars. Most preferred white or cream suits with black ties sufficing as a token of respect. A mournful black suit would be murderous in this heatwave. The women were more formally attired, sacrificing comfort to please etiquette. Somber silk dresses clung to their legs as they adjusted their hats and put on their shades.

Sweat dribbled down his cheek and into his beard. He scooped the bottom of his shirt into his hands and wiped his face, momentarily exposing a pale belly. When he let the shirt fall it stuck to his midriff. The gun felt heavy in his pocket. It also weighed on his mind. He checked the crowd again, putting a foot on the base of the barrier and standing up, craning his neck above the heads of those around him. No sign of the target in the masses. He started to doubt his plan. Maybe the target wouldn't show after all.

And then, without warning, there was no more time for thinking.

There he was. On the red carpet. Five feet away. Walking past, head bowed.

He'd visualized this moment many times. Would he gaze, terrified, at the muzzle of the gun? Would he cry out? Would security have time to react?

There were four armed guards surrounding the target. Moving in tandem, slowly and deliberately. And while the target kept his head down, the security surrounding him watched the crowd on either side of the barrier carefully.

As soon as that shot rang out, the guards would be scrambling for him. He knew he was about to kill someone, in broad daylight, in front of five hundred witnesses. And he knew he would get away with it. No question. Getting away with murder was the easy part. After all, Paul was responsible for at least a couple of corpses. Probably more. It was too easy to lose count.

The hard part for Paul would be pulling the trigger. It's never easy. Gripping the barrier with one hand, his other delved into his pocket and locked around the gun. He told himself he could do this. A ripple went through his guts, sending hot acid into his throat. He swallowed it back down then blew sweat off his lips. His heart jacked up the drumbeat in his ears.

He thought of all that he'd suffered. If anything would get him through the next ten seconds it was rage. He needed it. He had to build his anger into an unstoppable engine that would propel him into this act. For the last few months he'd thought of nothing but revenge. Revenge for the betrayals, the lies, and the pain.

Do it, he thought. *Do it now!*

Paul began to pull the gun. But then he froze. A hand was on his shoulder.

The person behind him leaned forward, and Paul felt their hot breath on his neck as they spoke.

Even with the people tightly packed around him, and the blood roaring through his system, he heard those words as clear as a trumpet blast. And it was a blast. A simple statement. Spoken plainly. Paul felt those words strip the flesh clean off his back.

'I know who you are,' said the voice in his ear. 'You're J. T. LeBeau.'

CHAPTER ONE

4 months ago

The last thing Maria had expected was to fall in love.

And yet she couldn't deny it any longer. Maria was in love with Daryl. Beautiful, thoughtful Daryl. They lay in bed together with sunlight warming their skin. The breeze from the bedroom window an occasional respite from the heat of their passion. Maria caught the smell of the sea in Daryl's hair. His lips pressed to hers. His hands held her body.

And she wanted nothing more than Daryl that afternoon.

She locked her legs around his waist, crossing her ankles, cinching him tightly. His eyes closed. His mouth opened as she felt his body quiver.

When he was done, she eased apart her legs and gently pushed him off. He rolled to the side and slumped down in the bed beside her. Maria turned away and stared out of the full-length window at the sea. It was calm and pure blue. A dog played on the small stretch of sandy beach at the bottom of the hill leading down from her house. She listened but couldn't hear it barking. Too far away. A young couple came into view as they walked along the beach. The girl waved a stick at the dog before hurling it into the surf and linking arms with her lover.

Maria felt a hole growing in her stomach. Her throat was coarse and dry.

She turned over and looked at Daryl. He lay on his back, the rise and fall of his stomach slowing as he caught his breath. She kissed him. That kiss was full of longing. Maria knew she truly loved Daryl. That this was real. And that hole in her stomach came from knowing that she might never walk on the beach with him. Not like that young couple out there on the sand. She drew back, held his face in her hands.

Yes, Maria loved this man, but she was married to someone else.

The thought of her husband felt like someone bumping into a record player, making the needle jump across the grooves in the vinyl, scratching reality into a love song. She had things to do. Had to clean up. She kissed him again. A peck. More of a call to action than a kiss. The real world was threatening to invade her time with Daryl – to steal him back from her and send her crashing to reality.

'You okay?' he said.

'I'm good,' said Maria. 'Just thinking I have to change the sheets now.'

'Give me a sec and I'll help you,' said Daryl.

He got up and walked to the *en suite* bathroom. Maria found her clothes in a pile at the foot of the bed and dressed in her jeans and blouse. She tied up her long black hair with a band and set about stripping the bed. When Maria had a job to do, she did it fast. She couldn't abide laziness. Every task she undertook she hit at a hundred miles an hour. Tidying, washing, cleaning, walking, even making love.

She almost ripped the duvet cover as she tore it off. Then she gathered it in her arms and threw it behind her, into the bathroom. There was a big linen basket in there. After she'd pulled off the sheet, she balled it, but this time she turned and threw it. She went back toward the bed to get the pillowcases and felt something hard underfoot. She'd stepped on something. Daryl's pants. Picking them up, she tossed them into the bathroom too.

'Thanks,' said Daryl.

By the time Daryl put on his blue jeans and came out of the bathroom, Maria was unfolding the fresh sheets she kept in a drawer below the mattress. He switched on the radio on the nightstand. It was tuned to a rock station. Her husband's preference. Daryl hit the search button, found a station that played eighties hits and smiled when the first beats of an A-HA song played. One of Maria's favorites. And he knew it. She could tell by the wry smile on his face. Daryl took one end of the sheet and helped her lay it on the bed. He stuffed the sheet under the mattress without folding the corners. Maria came around to his side of the bed, took the sheet out and folded the corner. Daryl lifted the mattress letting her slip the sheet underneath. Her husband had never changed the sheets. Never helped her with anything. She found herself rocking with the beat, prompting one of those big easy smiles from Daryl. He put his hands on her hips, felt her swaying and drew her to him, gently kissing her neck. She giggled, released herself from his grip. If he planted one more kiss she knew where it would lead. She would be back in bed with him. He was irresistible. She didn't want that – she would only have to change the sheets again.

She'd moved into the house with her husband just after they were married. It would be their two-year anniversary next month. She wasn't looking forward to it. Next week it would be her five-month anniversary with Daryl. She knew which one she was looking forward to most. And it wasn't her wedding anniversary. Maria stood back, satisfied with the bed. Her husband would never know. Although, it was getting to the point where she wanted him to find out. The only reason she held off was because she didn't want to spook Daryl. Things were getting serious, and with every passing day Daryl became more precious. No way she wanted to mess that up.

She hadn't found work since she set foot in the town. There was no great demand for public relations managers in Port Lonely. There was not a great demand for anything. An emptiness hung about the streets even in summer when the sidewalks were filled with tourists and holiday-home residents. This town felt like a rich, shit-kicker's paradise. A handful of decent restaurants, one main street with a dozen stores and nothing in them that she wanted to buy, two golf courses and the sea. That was Port Lonely.

After the first year in town Maria felt herself sliding into a dark place. At first, she flirted with men in restaurants on the rare occasions her husband took her out. She would catch the eye of the best-looking man in the room, then look away, smiling as soon as they returned her gaze. When that failed to provoke a response, she thought about taking it further – maybe having a one-night-stand, but she never did.

Her husband continued to travel for work, leaving her alone. He said marketing was a people business, and face-to-face worked best. Then she met Daryl last December. Things changed. If she hadn't met Daryl, Maria was convinced she would've gone quite mad.

'Would you like me to run you a bath? Or do you wanna smoke first?' said Daryl.

He was only half dressed. His shirt still lay on the chair beside the window, and his pants were slung low. Belt still undone. A thin layer of sweat coated his hard stomach. Daryl liked to workout, dive, surf, and smoke, but not necessarily in that order. The smoking wasn't a problem in the motels they used on the highway out of town, but it was more problematic at home. She often liked to relax in a bath after spending time with Daryl. It soothed her, eased her into a different life.

Maria's throat felt dry, but she wanted a cigarette more than the bath. Never a hard smoker, Maria only felt the craving after sex or a bottle of wine.

He stood there, silently, gazing at his nails and waiting for her response. She didn't want to answer him, and found herself biting her lip, delaying her reply so she could merely look. Maria didn't take Daryl to her bed for his conversation. It wasn't that kind of relationship. He was unlike anyone she had ever met. There was a quiet freedom in Daryl. A handsome drifter quality. He was a beautiful bird that Maria had decided to keep. Not to say that Daryl was dumb, either. He knew about a great many subjects. Or more accurately, he knew a little about a great many things. There was no depth to his knowledge, but Maria didn't care. Daryl had presence. Something in his butter-blond hair and the hard lines on this face that made people look at him. She was happiest wrapping herself in his thick arms and rocking gently in the sun chairs on her porch while they smoked.

'Give me a second, then we'll go out. I don't want the smell in the house,' said Maria.

Slinging his shirt over his shoulder casually, Daryl led her downstairs. The house still looked like something out of a realtor's brochure, albeit a property that had been on the market for a long time. The cream paint job had started to dull and the cracks, covered up by the previous seller, had re-appeared at certain points on the ceiling. Two weeks before, she asked if she could redecorate. That still stuck in her throat – that she had to *ask* her husband. He'd told her *no*. He liked the house just fine the way it was, and she should find herself another project. Preferably one that didn't cost too much money and ideally one that he could control.

Maria followed Daryl through the kitchen, out the glass doorway and onto the back porch. Two rocking chairs were set up. The chairs were painted green, in a *distressed* style, which looked to Maria as if the *guy* who was supposed to be painting the chairs was distressed and this had shown in his work.

'Goddamn it,' said Daryl.

He'd fished a pack of Camel's out of his jeans and was examining the contents. Maria watched him tip loose tobacco and the remains of two broken cigarettes into his palm.

'Oh, sorry. I thought I felt something in your jeans when I stepped on 'em,' said Maria, apologetically.

'It don't matter, honey,' said Daryl, scrunching the pack and the broken smokes in his hand and tossing them into the long grass beyond the porch. A stark contrast to the time spent with her husband. His melancholy gaze didn't draw her in like it used to. She had realized that her husband could not be warmed and opened up like she had imagined. When she'd met her husband, he was a sweet man with a great sadness that clung to him. Maria had recognized something of that sadness in her too, and their relationship seemed marked by each one trying to fix the other. She thought she could change him, make him happy and thereby fix the part of her that was never happy. A bad way to start a marriage. Like two junkies trying to get each other clean. Ultimately, she realized she could not change him, or warm the ice that lay deep inside him like a wound. Daryl didn't need to be thawed, he was warm and open, playful and kind. Maybe a little simple, but the best things in life were exactly that – simple. Somehow, to Maria, sharing that closeness with Daryl, that silence on the porch, was deeper and more satisfying than what went on the bedroom.

'I know where I can get some cigarettes,' she said. And with that, she turned and went back into the kitchen. She could hear Daryl padding after her as she made her way into the hall. Together, they stopped in front of an oak door. Maria reached up to the sill above the frame. Her fingers touched something cold and metallic. She brought down a small key and unlocked the door to her husband's study. Strict about his privacy, her husband had left a key above the mantel on the doorframe for one reason – he kept a revolver hidden behind a volume of Dickens on his bookshelf. If an intruder got into the house, she knew where to find the gun.

Inside the study she saw dark oak paneling. Books lined one wall. A globe in one corner. A solid, wide desk at the end of the room, facing the door. A green banker's lamp on the desk and a laptop and notebook beside it. Maria stood to one side to let Daryl in.

'He keeps a pack around here somewhere. I know he has a sneaky cigarette sometimes. I can smell it on him occasionally. And in the room too. He likes to think I don't notice these things,' she said.

'Then he obviously doesn't know you too well,' said Daryl, placing his arms around her waist and nuzzling her neck. She playfully pushed him away. If she didn't stop him right away she knew she would only end up making love again. The bed was one thing. Having sex on her husband's desk, in his private study, somehow felt a step too far. Her husband was not a bad man. He could be distant and cold, but she knew he loved her and showed as much affection as he could. Two years ago, that was enough to get married. Now, she realized that she had married him for all the wrong reasons. Maria had been in love with the idea of the man her husband could be. She was young, and romantic. She had begun to realize that. Turns out, he couldn't live up to her ideal.

Together they searched the bookshelves, the hidden roll-back compartment in the globe. Daryl moved on to the desk while Maria checked behind the model airplanes, the toy cars, and framed photographs of her and her husband which he kept on the shelves.

She heard a crack of splintering wood and whipped around to see Daryl holding a pack of cigarettes in one hand, and a broken desk drawer in the other.

'Found 'em. Shit, sorry. It came away in my hand. I thought it was stuck so I gave it a tug,' said Daryl.

'Shit!' said Maria.

Papers had fallen out of the drawer onto the rug, and Maria could see a small piece of wood had broken away at the top of the drawer where the locking mechanism had once been housed.

'Jesus, he's going to notice this,' she said.

'When is he due back?'

'Sunday night.'

It was Friday afternoon. The chances of getting a carpenter skilled enough to mend the lock and the drawer in that timeframe looked to Maria about as thin as Daryl's résumé.

'Shit, shit, shit. Don't just stand there, help me pick this stuff up,' said Maria.

They knelt on the rug together, gathering up loose pages that had tipped out of the drawer and onto the rug. Some were merely scribbles, some were draft marketing strategies for his clients, some rough notes probably about one of his campaigns, and some were newspaper clippings – yellowed with age. Once Maria had made a neat pile on the floor, she turned to Daryl to collect the pages he'd picked up and sorted.

Only Daryl hadn't sorted any pages. He was staring at a single piece of paper, his lips making a perfect O.

'I knew you guys were doing pretty good, but babe, I'd no idea you were this rich,' he said with a stupid grin on his face.

Maria's eyebrows knitted, she snatched the page from Daryl. Her husband had his investments, his marketing consultancy which brought in low six figures every year. They had twenty-grand in a savings account. Financially, they were just *okay*. They were *not* well heeled, as her husband continually reminded her.

She looked at the document. A bank statement from last year. Two million dollars had been paid to a checking account with her husband's name on it. The account had their home address in the top left-hand corner. She checked the date on the statement, looked at the amounts. Checked the name again. Then checked the spelling.

Her husband had a secret bank account.

Two payments were made in the last year. Roughly six months apart. One million dollars per payment. And more had been paid the previous year. The balance on the account sat at over twenty million dollars.

A flood of excitement swept through her, capturing her breath, holding it, boiling it into rage. She felt a hot flush on her neck, and sweat broke out on her face.

Her little rebellions in the bedroom were nothing, absolutely nothing compared to this. This liar of a husband.

At that moment, Maria said something she didn't really mean. A statement with no truth in it. Weightless words, spoken in anger. And yet, once she'd heard those words out loud, she was surprised that she'd uttered them.

'I'm gonna kill him,' she said.

CHAPTER TWO

Too angry to object, Maria sat in Daryl's convertible while he drove them into town for a drink she didn't want. She didn't care what the wind was doing to her hair, she just sat with her elbow on the door and her hand pressed to her lips while she watched the sea disappear behind a tall cliff as the car wound its way toward the town. In some ways, she felt glad to be out of that house.

He tried to talk to her, but she couldn't hear him too well over the roar of the engine and the sound of the wind whipping all around them. Eventually, Daryl shut up. The embarrassing silence that greeted each and every sentence had eventually gotten the better of him.

Memories of her short marriage fluttered by like signposts on the road.

That time she bought those expensive designer shoes – the look on his face. Their one-year anniversary – all the complaining he'd done about the champagne. He didn't drink much, and he thought one champagne was just as good as another. So why did Maria have to buy a vintage bottle that cost almost two hundred dollars? She even remembered the way he'd said it – two *hundred* dollars. Like she'd just bought a chateau in the south of France.

When they first met, her husband-to-be had struck her as a lonely man. He'd had that look on his face the night she said 'hi' to him in a basement bar in Manhattan. Before her husband, Maria had a string of confident boyfriends. Talented men, with egos, motorcycles, and most of them with a gift for music. *Troubled* would also have been a good descriptor for those men. Men that women wanted. Barely a night would go by without her catching another woman gazing, longingly, at her man.

That never happened with her husband. He was good-looking, with nice hair and a cute smile. Yet there was a sadness that lingered around his eyes – always. Maybe that was what had drawn her to him that night. Looking back, he had not been so worried about spending money when they first dated. Not so that she had noticed.

Maria shook her head. She couldn't believe she'd been so stupid. All of those times he'd made her feel small about money when all along it wasn't *really* about money.

It was about control.

She had not made love to her husband in months. He was always tired. Always working late at night in his office. Occasionally he would unwind with a bottle of wine, or a joint, and they would make love on those nights, but those occasions had grown more and more rare.

In this last year she had sensed that her husband was keeping something from her. When they talked about their lives before marriage, her husband had barely spoken, and a coldness had fallen on him. As if he had built a barrier between them, keeping certain parts of his life just to himself. Even when they sat together on the couch in the new house in Port Lonely, she would occasionally glance over at him, and find him lost in thought. Distant, even though he was holding her hand.

Now she knew. She had been right all along.

Her husband was not what he seemed to be, her life was not what she had envisaged, and none of it appeared to be within her control. She was on a train, bound for God knows where and she wasn't enjoying the ride. She tried to do other things. Keep herself busy. A pottery class sounded good at first, then she found that she hated the feel of the clay beneath her fingers. There was no gym in town, so she developed a habit of working out at home then going to the country club for breakfast. It was there that she had first met Daryl. He waited tables at the country club, and she'd noticed him but they had never spoken. It was the boredom of Port Lonely one weekend that eventually brought them together. Having ditched her pottery class, she booked a scuba diving lesson instead. When she came down to the marina on that cool December morning, she was surprised, and more than a little pleased to discover Daryl putting on a wetsuit. He was her instructor. She'd liked his smile, and that look in his eyes. They held hands underwater, and he proved to be a patient and careful instructor. She booked another lesson straight away. At the end of the lesson the following week she'd suggested they get a drink, and they'd ended up in a motel that same night.

She knew then that Daryl was something special. That eased the guilt. She wasn't just sleeping around – Daryl meant something. Maybe she had made a mistake to marry. Maybe Daryl was her true love. He made her feel alive when they were together. That life was happening *now*. So much of her marriage was about what would happen in the future – when her husband wasn't so busy, when things calmed down, when he had time. Daryl had all the time in the world for her. He always answered his phone when she called. Always paid the bill at the motel, and never complained when she went days without calling him.

There was a fire in him too. A heat when they made love. A connection in the quiet moments as they held one another. She felt safe and dangerous at the same time. The relationship with Daryl grew. He gave her what her husband no longer did: warmth. He never held back. There was a connection. An instant undeniable, almost cosmic bond. He made her feel like a twenty-one-year-old – silly, excited, protected and loved.

The car rounded a sharp corner, the cliff tops fell away to reveal the ocean. Up ahead she saw the beginnings of the town. Two years ago she'd sat beside her new husband in his Maserati on this same road, headed into town after they'd viewed the house for the first time. As they had driven past the large houses on the edge of town, and the club, and eventually parked up on Main Street, Maria thought she could build a life there. It was peaceful, and quaint and oh so very quiet. He'd laced his fingers in hers, smiled at her and said, *'We're going to be so happy here.'*

For a while it had been true. They were happy. He worked on the house for months – refusing all but the most casual of help – a paintbrush laced with the color of his choosing. Then, when the house was finished, he started spending more time away. Business trips with clients. Golf with the boys on Sunday. Too tired to eat the meals she'd prepared when he did make it home. She wasn't a good cook, but she tried and he didn't seem to appreciate the effort. The quaint, cutesy quietness of the seaside town soon lost its charm. It *was* a new life. A lonely one. To Maria, it felt like she'd been dumped in the asshole of nowhere.

Daryl drove through Main Street, past the spot where Maria and her then new husband had parked and held hands. She closed her eyes and forced the memory away. Maybe she could use a drink after all.

Port Lonely had two bars. Maria had visited each only once before.

One bar called Clarence's charged twelve dollars for a mojito and housed an aging jazz pianist who looked like he was digging his way out of the place through the piano, desperately trying to flee the smell of disinfectant and avocado.

The other bar didn't know what a mojito was, and if they ever encountered an avocado they'd probably shoot it. They served both kinds of alcohol – beer *and* bourbon. Although on ladies' night the bartender had been known to blow the dust off a bottle of tequila.

The locals favored the latter establishment, and normally had it all to themselves. Occasionally a group of young rich kids would stumble into the bar and they'd last around thirty seconds before one or all of them got too scared to stay. The sign outside the bar said, 'Barney's Place.' Barney had been dead for twenty-five years and judging by the smell from the bathroom he was probably buried under the floor tiles.

Daryl pulled up outside Barney's, and Maria held his arm as they went inside, there being no chance that anyone from the country club would see them together. The country club wear-a-tie-on-a-Sunday bunch wouldn't go near Barney's. Port Lonely's locals served the rich, second-home types who didn't tip much and didn't mix with the hired help.

Apart from a few regulars who sat at the bar, the place looked empty. Maria took a table in the corner while Daryl got the drinks. It was dark inside. A neon Budweiser sign buzzed on the wall opposite, and what overhead lamps that still retained bulbs struggled to throw much light in her direction.

After some negotiation with the aging bartender, Daryl brought over two tequilas, each accompanied by a Miller chaser.

'I know it's messed up, but you should be happy,' said Daryl, sitting down on the leather couch beside Maria.

She looked at him, shook her head and thought about her taste in men. They were either good-looking and stupid, or smart enough to be great liars. In her lifetime, she'd experienced both kinds. Her first long-term boyfriend could turn heads, but couldn't turn his hand to earning a cent or working on the house. Her new one, the one she'd married, was a liar. A damn good one. And then there was Daryl. Sometimes he said the strangest things. He had a child-like innocence. Sweet. Cute. Gorgeous. Normally she let Daryl's naivety form part of his charm. This time it was a little much. Her emotions were buzzing and whirling together like the flies around the neon Bud sign.

'Are you for real? Can't you understand what he's done to me?' she said, letting her voice rise.

'Come on, I know it's weird, but look on the bright side. You're rich, girl.'

'No, I'm not. What planet are you from?'

Spreading his hands wide, at that moment Daryl looked unsure about his planet of origin. Maria laid it out for him.

'If he's kept this from me, then there's a reason. He's got something else in his life that's paying him millions – and I'm not part of it. Why? Is he a criminal? Does he have another family, another life somewhere when he goes away on these trips? What the fuck? And he won't let me pay a cent over the odds on anything. I have an allowance. Did you know that? Three hundred a week. And if I go over that allowance he gets mad. Well, *I'm* mad now. Are you getting the picture?'

He nodded, chastised, picked up the shot glass. Maria clinked glasses with him, forced a smile to show she wasn't mad at *him*, then they downed the tequila shots. She'd never liked tequila. That sickening burn began in her throat and she looked around the table for lemon. Daryl hadn't brought any. Instead, she took a long drink from her bottle of Miller.

'Sorry, babe,' said Daryl.

Maria couldn't tell if he was apologizing for not getting salt and lemon for the shot, or just sympathizing with her marital situation. Either way, she waved a hand at him to stop.

The beer bottles were slick with condensation and Daryl began to absently pick at the label. He concentrated on peeling off a section, and said, 'Are you going to confront him with this?'

Before answering, Maria took another sip of beer. In truth, she hadn't really decided. She didn't know what to do. Part of her felt like waving the bank statement in his face. Another part of her just wanted to leave him and file for divorce. Somewhere in the back of her mind she knew that neither of those things were smart. Before she did anything drastic Maria knew she needed more details on the money. She heard the sound of the label tearing off the bottle in Daryl's hand. He still wasn't looking at her.

She knew then Daryl was also worried about himself. She could tell he was nervous. He didn't want to be thrown in the man's face by Maria.

Where did you get this money? Oh, by the way, I've been screwing one of the waiters from the club.

'Don't worry, I'm not going to tell him about . . . *us*,' said Maria.

She'd almost said, *Don't worry, I'm not going to tell him about you*, then changed her mind. This secret money had put a concrete block between her and her husband, and brought her closer to Daryl. Maria was no longer frightened to vocalize the relationship. It was there. Maybe even stronger because of this, but there was no denying it – sometimes they talked about what life would be like together, if she left her husband. She could tell Daryl wanted it, but he was nervous. He told her he didn't have much to offer her. He waited tables, he taught people how to dive, how to surf – he didn't rate his prospects as a financially secure partner, and there was a shame in that for him. At such times, Maria told him she didn't care how much he made – but in truth, she worried about it. Maria wanted security. She needed it. Money had always been a problem, and she never wanted to have to worry about that again. It was the one thing that perhaps made her cling to her marriage. Security. Even if it was just three hundred dollars a week.

Reaching into her hip pocket, she brought out the bank statement. Unfolded it and laid it flat on the table.

All of the payments came from a company called LeBeau Enterprises. Something about that name felt familiar. LeBeau had some resonance to it. Sounding out the name in her head, she tried to remember if it was her husband who'd mentioned it. Nothing came to mind immediately, yet she knew if she thought hard enough about it, she would remember.

'You ever hear of LeBeau Enterprises?' she said.

While he thought over the question Maria watched Daryl's eyes searching the floor. After a few seconds he shook his head gently, creased his forehead but didn't say anything. He closed his eyes, gritted his teeth.

'There's something about that name, isn't there?' he said.

'Yeah, I don't know. It's weird. There's something at the back of my head . . . I just can't bring it to mind. Maybe I'm not thinking straight.'

Maria looked around the dismal bar, her husband's betrayal a knot in her throat so that when she spoke, her words fluttered with emotion. 'Who am I kidding? I *know* I'm not thinking straight.'

'Mind if I take another look?' said Daryl.

He'd said it with a trace of optimism. Enough for Maria to let him have the statement. While looking through the entries, Daryl brought out a cell phone and began typing on the screen, scrolling through the results and checking the statement.

He smiled and said, 'Son of a bitch.'

'What?'

'It matches. Holy shit, it matches!'

'What are you talking about?' said Maria, slipping her phone out.

'Just a sec, let me double check,' said Daryl.

Maria couldn't wait. She typed the words *LeBeau Enterprises* into the search bar, hit return. The screen changed to white and a blue line began to struggle across the top of the page. Signal strength looked poor in the bar. Maria was tempted to ask the bartender if they had WiFi. She glanced over at him, watched him paw at the remote control for the TV then thought better of it.

Reversing his phone, Daryl pointed the screen at Maria and said, 'Maybe you're married to *this* guy.'

Maria took the phone from his hand. On the screen was a web page displaying books by a writer named J. T. LeBeau.

'The date these payments are made on the bank statement tally with the publication dates for the last J. T. LeBeau books,' said Daryl.

She clicked on the image of one of the books that showed a gun and a snake on the cover, scrolled down to the information section and checked the publication date. Glanced at the bank statement. Same date. Repeating the exercise for another two books, she saw the exact same pattern. Payment of one million dollars on publication date.

'What does this mean? What does it have to do with Paul?' she said.

Daryl folded his arms, smiled in a manner that displayed his own self satisfaction.

'Don't you get it? This is *huge*. Your husband, Paul Cooper, is *the* J. T. LeBeau,' said Daryl.

Maria put the phone down on the table, realized her mouth had fallen open and said, 'Who the fuck is J. T. LeBeau?'

The New Yorker, May 2013

Who Is J. T. LeBeau?
by Brian Everett

Everyone loves a mystery. Sales of mystery, thriller and crime novels frequently eclipse that of literary fiction. One author who is clearly reaping the benefits is J. T. LeBeau. His (for we know it is a 'he') books have racked up sales in excess of 75 million copies. Someone in the world buys a J. T. LeBeau thriller every five and a half seconds. He is a household name in most countries. Chances are there's a copy of at least one of his novels somewhere in your home. Readers can't get enough of these page-turners. But a compelling, pacy plot with well-drawn characters doesn't begin to account for this author's appeal. Readers, booksellers and publishers all believe his incredible success is down to one major factor – the twist.

You never see it coming. And when you've put the book down, and gone through multiple twists and turns, the first thing you want to do is make one of your friends read the book so you can talk about it! (Editor's note – 'I've done this with every one of his books.') And his publishers know it. There are no publicity tours, no appearances on *This Morning* on CBS, no bookstore signings, no interviews on NPR. Whatever the opposite of publicity might be – this is it. J. T. LeBeau is a pseudonym. A pen name. For whom? We don't know. Nobody, not even his publishers, knows his real name. All we know is that the author is male. That's as much as his publishers know, or maybe that's all they're willing to say.

In writing this article, I sought to avoid the dozens of pieces that have come before which speculate on the author's true identity. Because that's all it amounts to – speculation. Instead, I want to ask why?

Why does one of the world's most beloved, bestselling and richest authors remain in hiding? Ask yourself, would you? I have been a writer for twenty-five years, I've published four books and nothing would give me greater pleasure than a room full of adoring fans waiting for me to pronounce my genius before signing their books.

Someone once said that being an author is show business for shy people. And that may be true. I'm definitely in the introvert category (I whisper my name to the barista at Starbucks and never complain when they get it wrong), but come on!

How shy do you have to be?

I do not believe that it is shyness. Nor any form of chronic introverted behavior. There just isn't anyone on the planet who could resist the temptation to reach out and accept the love of millions of adoring fans.

My theory, for I recognize that theory it must be, is that there is a darker reason for J. T. LeBeau's anonymity. It could be that J. T. LeBeau is an ex-con with a rap sheet that would make Hunter S. Thompson blush. Or perhaps LeBeau is a guy with two heads and some horrific skin disease who believes that the merest glimpse of his visage would put readers off his books for life. The former, rather than the latter, is my guess. For one reason alone.

At the heart of every good mystery, lies a crime.

And yet I cannot in good conscience accuse an unknown of misdeeds. There is of course a more commercial reason for the success of the J. T. LeBeau novels – the mystery of the author himself. The speculation surrounding the identity of the author feeds his audience just as much as the pace and twists of his stories. On publication of a LeBeau novel you can bet on at least a dozen print media articles, TV news pieces, and furious social media traffic on the continuing mystery surrounding the identity of the author. If all that went away, and we saw the man behind the mask, there is a chance, probably a very good chance, that the sales of the books would suffer as a result.

For now, J. T. LeBeau, the most famous unknown man in the world, will remain a mystery.

CHAPTER THREE

The bookstore on Main Street was virgin territory to Maria. They'd quickly finished their beers and Daryl led her across the street and down a block to Mission Books. On the right side of the window Maria saw a half dozen Christian books with strange titles like *Jesus and Me*, or *Christ in the Digital Age*. On the other side she saw what she supposed were the bestsellers: romance novels with limp-limbed women on the covers who were all being propped up from behind by a ripped guy with no shirt on, mysteries with ticking clocks or silhouettes of men on the covers, and children's books with bright colorful drawings on the sleeve.

However, in the center of the window, in what was the prime position, she saw a number of books with a similar type of cover. The images on the books were all different, but the name on the front cover was the same. Bold type. Inch-high white lettering.

J. T. LeBeau.

Beneath the name of the author was a single sentence. The same one on each book. In the exact same place.

Seventy-Five Million Copies Sold.

'You can't be serious,' she said. 'This is Paul? Paul wrote these?'

'Come on, let's go inside. I need to check something,' said Daryl.

She followed him inside, felt the air conditioning on the back of her neck as soon as she walked through the door and was tempted to stand there for a moment under the cool air. Pine flooring and solid wooden shelves painted pale blue set a neutral tone for the space, allowing the books to be the only sources of bold color. The store had a few customers. Two elderly women browsing in the true crime section. One of them had to be in her eighties. She was eagerly reading the blurb on the back of a book called *The World's Worst Sex Killers*.

A tall, separate stand near the counter housed a display of books by J. T. LeBeau. She watched Daryl grab one of those titles and open it. He bowed his head, scanning the first pages. He stopped. Folded the book, keeping his index finger between the pages as a marker and beckoned Maria to him. He moved further into the store, into the corner dedicated to Christian works. There were no casual browsers in this section. She followed him and stood close. He opened the book and handed it to her.

It was a hardback novel, with a sleeve. He showed her the inside of the sleeve and there were no author photos on either inside fold. The bio for the author simply said, *J. T. LeBeau is a pseudonym. Please respect the author's privacy.*

'Half of the publicity around these books comes from journalists and bloggers who think they've tracked down the real author, but they never did find out for sure. There are theories and that's about it. No one knows who LeBeau really is,' said Daryl.

He then opened the book at the title page. On the other side of that page was the legal stuff. The fine print from the publishers that seemed to be on the inside pages of every book, although Maria had never read a word of it.

While she held the book open, Daryl said, 'Let me check out the statement again.'

She reached into the hip pocket of her jeans, drew out the bank statement and gave it to him. Even though he said nothing, his eyes spoke of some wonderful discovery. He placed the statement on the title page of the book in front of her.

'Look at the fine print,' he said.

Maria read a series of bewildering numbers, probably something to do with the printing of the book, and then read the legal disclaimer. Whatever realization Daryl had experienced seemed to elude Maria, and she gripped the pages tightly.

Whispering through clenched teeth, she said, 'What am I looking for exactly?'

'Copyright,' said Daryl, with a California smile.

Her eyes scanned further down the page. She stopped. Read the line from the page again and then looked at the bank statement. For half a minute she repeated this process, carefully examining the small text of the legal page against the spelling on the bank statement.

There was no doubting it. The deposits in Paul's account had been made by LeBeau Enterprises. There it was again, on the page in the book in front of her.

© LeBeau Enterprises.

She felt sick. Covering her mouth, Maria turned and quickly left the store, ignoring Daryl's calls for her to wait. Not knowing which way to turn, or what to do, Maria stood at the edge of the curb, bent over at the waist, and grabbed her knees. She sucked at the air, closed her eyes, swallowed down the bile threatening to rise up from her stomach. A foul taste filled her mouth and she knew she was going to vomit if she didn't get a hold of herself.

Forcing herself to dry swallow helped. Her throat was still burning. The tequila had proven to be a bad idea. Somewhere, way down inside, she had retained skepticism of Daryl's theory – surely Paul wouldn't lie to her about this. How could he? A secret life as a multi-millionaire celebrity author. A life that he would not share with her.

Maria had grown up the hard way. A brutal father and a mother who loved her but could not save her. There was no money, no security and only small bouts of intermittent happiness. A trip to the movies, or a picnic in Central Park were the only times that Maria remembered being happy as a child. And even then, the happiness lasted no longer than an afternoon and it was always shadowed with the threat of what was awaiting her mother and her when they returned home.

Then at the age of ten, the accident happened.

After that, it was just her mother and her in the apartment in the Bronx. Until she was seventeen. They lived on her mom's salary working six days a week at a deli counter. Times were tough. They didn't have much, but they got by. When her mom died, she did what she could to make a life for herself. A cheap one. She got a job as an intern in an advertising agency in Manhattan that managed publicity campaigns. She wasn't offered a job at the end of the internship – the agency made clear they didn't employ young women who couldn't afford their dress code. Maria managed bands instead, made a little money and blew through some boyfriends, each one worse than the last.

And one night, in a small bar on the Lower East Side, she met Paul. They met by chance. Maria ignored most men that hit on her. She saw him at the bar, and he looked so sad, so fragile. She struck up a conversation with him. He told her the band on stage were awful. They were Maria's band. She told him and he laughed – said they had the best manager in the country, but they were still shit. He bought her a drink and they talked all night. They met up a few days later, and Paul didn't seem so sad anymore. She had given him something, and that made her feel good. He was the first guy she'd met who didn't want anything from her. He was just happy to be with her and, incredibly, also happy to take things slow.

He often said this, but not in a manner that made Maria feel rejection.

Let's take things slow.

It was his mantra. And his escape clause. He knew everything about her. Apart from her father's accident. She hadn't told anyone what had really happened that night. She fell into a well-practiced lie about her father disappearing. He upped and walked out one night, never came back. A bad father walking out on his family was such a common story that no one ever questioned it. Certainly not Paul. Over the course of their relationship in those early days, Maria learned next to nothing about him.

He worked as a marketing consultant. He didn't like to talk about his work. It was boring. No, he didn't have any interesting clients. The only good thing was the pay and the fact that he could work from home. His parents were both deceased. No brothers or sisters. No friends.

When Maria pressed him, even gently, for a story about his child-hood or college or even how long he'd lived in New York – the shutters would come down. He would clam up, say nothing or change the subject. Eventually, Maria stopped trying.

He'd promised her a better life. Maria knew now he could have given her a great life, one where she didn't have to fear how much she could spend, one where she could escape the constant worry about ending up like her mom. But he'd chosen to keep that life for himself.

As Maria bent over the curb, catching her breath, swallowing the bile, she caught sight of her two hundred dollar boots. The heel had cracked a week ago, and Paul reminded her how much those boots had cost. Told her to get them mended.

The memory arrived too quickly and too fully in her thoughts – so fast that her head began to spin. She vomited into the street, dots of tequila and spit sat on her suede boots. Daryl put his arm around her, brought her to his car and into the passenger seat. She felt dizzy and her legs were weak.

'Let's get you back to the house. Tell me if you're gonna be sick and I'll pull over,' he said.

Slouching down into the passenger seat, Maria covered her eyes. A headache was coming – she could feel it. Getting out of the sun would help, and she asked Daryl to put up the top on the convertible. He huffed and muttered to himself while he fought with the vintage roof. The car was a classic, which meant it was a beautiful-looking pain in the ass.

They drove back in silence. She didn't look at Daryl for the whole journey, but she could feel his eyes on her every now and again; the nervous glances of a man who was ready to pull over even it if meant hitting a ditch or a cornfield rather than have her ruin his upholstery.

Even though Daryl's furtive glances were a distraction, Maria had time and silence in which to think. She wanted to confront Paul. At the same time, she knew he would just shut down. There would be no argument, no denials, he would just close himself off and leave the room, like he did whenever she tried to bring up his past.

And she had no moral high ground. This discovery, whatever it was, came through an invasion of his privacy. Basically, a breaking and entering. He could be so defensive when it came to his study. Now she knew why. There was no good way to bring it up. Nothing that would invariably tilt the power balance in her favor. What if he decided to divorce her because she broke into his desk? Would she be allowed to use those documents in divorce court if she technically stole them?

She rubbed her temples as Daryl pulled into her driveway.

'Do you think it's really him? That Paul is J. T. LeBeau?' he asked.

'He reads a lot. Mysteries, detective novels. That sort of shit. I don't know. Could be? He sure isn't getting paid millions of dollars to do marketing.'

Shielding her eyes from Daryl, Maria tried to think. The desk was a big problem. Maybe she could get the desk repaired? Then just take the bank statement to a lawyer and use it against him that way?

One thing she could not do was wait around any longer. He wasn't due back for a few days. Could she sit on this for even one night? It felt like something that would eat into her every waking moment until she confronted him.

And the mere thought of that confrontation sent her heart rate pumping faster, and sweat broke out on her lip.

There had to be another way.

Maria got out of the car, closed the door behind her, and began walking to the front door. Daryl's feet crunched on the gravel as he followed her. She put the key in the lock, opened the door and went straight to the study.

She wanted to look at the rest of the papers in that drawer. She found them on the floor, scanned through them again. The notes and scraps of paper were hard to decipher, but then she saw some words at the top of the page that made her stop and examine them closer.

Notes for Untitled Book Six. Hitchcock plot. Woman sees what may be a murder in an apartment window as she's stationary at a stop light. No. Been done. Theme?

There were more notes like this on the other pages discussing character motivation, plot, timelines. She put these pages to one side, and picked up the newspaper clippings. Some were fairly new, some yellowed with age. They were from the *New York Times*, the *Guardian*, the *New Yorker*, *Time* magazine. They all had a similar headline or theme.

Who is J. T. LeBeau?

Standing behind her, Daryl read over her shoulder. He said, 'It's him, isn't it? Jesus H. I was right. Maria, it's Paul. This is *huge* . . .'

Maria got up fast and said, 'Don't say a word to anyone. We can't let this get out. Promise me.'

Her words calmed him, brought him back down to reality. Daryl was like a ten-year-old kid on Christmas Eve. His excitement threatened to get the better of him.

'We could use this. This could be our way out. We could be together,' she said.

Now she had a chance for a better life. The life she knew she desperately wanted. She just needed to figure out how to best use this lie against him.

And somehow explain what happened to the drawer. Even if she got it repaired, he would notice it. Paul noticed little things. This wouldn't escape him. Maria paused, looked down at the broken drawer. This was a big problem. She didn't want to let him know that she had been in the drawer or seen any of the documents. Not until she could figure out the best way to deal with the situation.

If she confronted him, what was he capable of? She thought about it, and decided that with what she'd learned in the last few hours she didn't know her husband at all. He could leave her, take the money with him and never be seen again. Or worse, tell her that it was his money and she wouldn't see a single dime of it. He could disappear. He had half disappeared already. She didn't know this man. This man who left her on her own for weeks at a time. His cold stare, his pain. And then there was Daryl. Open, loving and devoted to her and she to him.

Whatever else she realized, she knew she was in no fit state to confront Paul tonight. And yet she couldn't let it lie. Resentment and anger at the betrayal were all hitting her at once.

She walked out of the study, through the kitchen and out the back door to the porch. She looked over the dunes to the sea. The wind had picked up, and the surf boiled white. No one on the beach. The sky had begun to darken. A black cloud swollen with rain was rolling in from the coast. She heard Daryl's footsteps on the porch before he came around the corner of the house.

She ignored him. Fixed her eyes to the horizon and knew then exactly how she would handle this.

'You okay? Maybe I should let you process this. He's still your husband, and maybe I'm making things too complicated.'

'No,' said Maria. 'You're not making things complicated. You're all I have now. I love you.'

'I love you too,' said Daryl.

It was the first time he'd said it out loud.

'I'm going to talk to him. Tonight. I can't leave it any longer. I need him to come home, and explain this to me. I have to get him to open up. That's the only way he'll do it. If I confront him he'll just shut down.'

'Okay, do you want me to stay?'

'That would be too much for him to deal with. I have to do it alone,' she said, glancing back at the house, the broken drawer set in her mind. She needed an innocent explanation for the drawer. Something to get her off the hook, and get Paul talking about what was in the drawer.

'Whatever you say. You need anything before I go?' he said.

Maria took a deep breath. 'Yes,' she said and turned to him, her features set in grim determination. 'Before you go I want you to hit me.'

CHAPTER FOUR

Paul Cooper's fingers buzzed across the laptop. He hit the keys confidently. Each stroke had power. This pace always seemed to come when he was approaching the end of a novel. When he was starting out, staring at a blank screen, his keystrokes were slow, light and tentative. His fingers had to feel their way into a story.

He paused, lifted his hands from the keyboard and took a sip of green tea. He brewed it in his little apartment on the east side of Port Lonely where he kept an office. For two days he'd been out on the sea. No WiFi, no internet, barely any phone signal. Just his laptop and a mug of green tea beside him on the boat. As soon as his GPS system had blurted out the storm warning, Paul had saved and backed up his work, closed the laptop and brought the boat back to the marina. Thank God he had his office across the street. He could continue writing in relative peace.

When he was close to finishing a book he required nothing less than total concentration. No distractions of any kind.

At this point it all rested on the final twist.

Endings are a bitch, he thought.

No two writers work the same way. Paul wrote by the seat of his pants. Somehow, he always came up with a twist.

For this book, the final twist had yet to reveal itself. But it would, soon. He just had to be patient.

He put down the mug of tea, returning his fingers to the laptop to dole out more punishment to the keys.

He stopped typing mid-sentence. A buzzing sound in the room distracted him. He reached into his pockets, felt nothing. There it was again, the same sound. He got up and retrieved his cell phone from his jacket. A missed call from Maria.

She rarely left voicemail messages. Not long after they started dating she made him dinner in her apartment in New York. A *proper* date, Maria had called it. Wine, a roast chicken salad and then finishing the bottle on the couch. Paul had gotten up to use the bathroom and passed her telephone, which sat on a small table. It was an old vintage phone. With a cylinder dial. Beneath it was what looked like a tape deck, but Paul then recognized it as a cassette answering machine. To the side of the machine was a box of tapes. Some were blank, some were clearly labeled. They were all labeled with some variation of *Mom*. Like *Mom, Christmas 1985* or *Mom, VCR reminders*.

When he returned to the couch he asked her about the phone and the answering machine.

'I saw your phone set-up. Pretty vintage. You know we have digital voicemail now? And the internet?' he said, jokingly.

She smiled, but there was more behind it.

'It was my mom's. We got the answering machine with some of the money from my father's life insurance. She loved that answering machine. It was kind of like a rite of passage for her – being able to afford our own phone and the answering machine blew her mind. She would call from work a lot, while I was at home alone doing homework. She would make sure I was okay and remind me to set the VCR for *Columbo* or *Star Trek*. That kind of thing. Whenever I felt lonely or scared at home while she was at work, I would play one of the answer phone tapes. No one ever called but her. When she passed I kept the tapes and the machine. I play them now and again to remind me. Just to hear her voice.'

Paul smiled at the memory. Maria was terribly sentimental. When they'd moved to Port Lonely, she had insisted on bringing the damn phone and the answering machine with them. It was all set up, but no one called the house and she never used the old phone, she always called him from her cell.

Paul's eyes fell back to the laptop. The call had distracted him, sent him down memory lane. He tutted – he had work to do.

The phone clock read eleven-thirty. Paul thought it was only around six. He hadn't eaten dinner, and with the blackout blinds pulled on the apartment windows he often lost track of time. In a way, this was a good sign. His head was in the book, not in the real world. Placing the phone on his desk, he returned to the laptop.

This time the phone lit up and vibrated noisily on the table. The jackhammer vibration turning the phone around on the desk. Another call from Maria.

It was unusual for her to call so late.

Reluctantly, he picked up.

'Hi, everything okay?' he said.

He heard her breath first. Hard, panting.

'Jesus, Paul, no! I tried calling you, there's been a break-in at the house. I was attacked.'

'Oh my God! Are you alright?'

'He hit me and I fell. I'm okay. He's gone. I'm scared,' she said, her voice breaking with fear.

'I'll be right home. I just got the boat back in. Lock all the doors. My gun is in a lock box in the study. Get it in case he comes back. Did you call the police?' he said.

She hesitated, and then said, 'No, I called you first. I'll call them right now.'

Before Paul could say anything else she hung up.

He swore under his breath. The thought of some two-bit burglar hurting Maria made him feel sick.

He saved the file, closed the laptop and stuffed it angrily into his bag. He shut off the lights, locked the apartment and ran down the stairs onto the street. The Maserati waited for him in the marina lot. The boat and the car were his toys, his little gifts to himself. The sports car didn't look out of place in a town like Port Lonely. Maria's car was a lot cheaper, but she wasn't into cars. Times like these he was glad he had a lot of power under the hood of that car, although he had bought it for a wholly different reason – you never know when you might need to get away, fast.

He blipped open the car, got in, threw his bag onto the passenger seat and fired up the engine. Five minutes later he was on the coast road, pushing eighty miles an hour, and wishing he'd thought faster when Maria had called him.

Last thing Paul wanted was the police snooping round his house. He called Maria from the car system, but the line was engaged. She was probably still on the phone to the cops.

He pushed the accelerator as hard as he dared. His headlights were the only guide, and the road twisted sharply around rocky outcrops. A glint of flashing lights popped into his rear-view mirror. Red and blue rotating on the roof of a car. He slowed down to sixty, just in time. The police cruiser flew past him in a blur of noise and swirling reds and blues.

Paul swore and thumped the steering wheel.

Ten minutes later he pulled up at the house beside the cop car. Light spilled from every window of the house and the front door lay open. He saw a large man wearing a ball cap, silhouetted in his bedroom window. He was watching Paul.

By the time Paul got out of the car and made it to the front door, he saw the man in the cap standing in the hallway. The cop. He was in his fifties, with a cop-mustache and a little extra weight that made his stomach peek over his gun belt.

'You're Mr. Cooper?' he said.

'That's right,' said Paul, entering the house.

'I figured it was you on the road. Recognized that beast of a car. Sheriff Abraham Dole,' he said, tipping his cap. 'Your wife is in the kitchen. She's pretty shook up, but she'll be okay. The intruder's gone. I'll have another look-see around the house, if you don't mind?'

'Not at all,' said Paul.

While the cop went upstairs, Paul made his way through the living room, down the hallway toward the kitchen. A chill washed over his spine when he saw the door to his study lying open. He glanced inside as he passed. He would check more thoroughly in a moment, but at first sight the study didn't look as though it had been disturbed. Maria must have opened it up, either to get the gun or to let the sheriff check the room.

Sitting on a tall stool at the kitchen counter, he saw Maria holding a bag of ice to her cheek. She'd wrapped the ice in a kitchen towel, but the ice had seeped through, wetting her hair and the left side of her face. When she saw him, she put down the ice and ran into his arms. Paul held her close, kissed her hair.

He whispered to her that everything was alright now. She was safe. Placing a hand on each shoulder he gently eased her back, so he could look at her face. She tilted her head to the left as if she didn't want him to see. Delicately, Paul touched her chin and raised her head.

A red welt on the side of her face. A swollen, angry cheek. Her eyes were red and puffy from the tears. She dipped her head, placed it on his chest and hugged him close, saying nothing, but he felt the gentle rocking from her body as she sobbed. Paul smoothed her hair, then wrapped his arms around her and gave the kitchen the once-over. Nothing disturbed in here. Nothing out of place apart from the ice pack on the counter and Maria's cell phone sitting beside it.

'What happened?' he said.

She held onto him, her voice thick with tears as she spoke. 'I was watching TV when I heard a noise. Like glass breaking. I got up and went to the kitchen. I thought maybe a glass had fallen. There was nothing. I thought maybe I'd imagined it and I was going back to the couch when I thought I heard something in your study. I used your key, opened the door. And that's when I saw him.'

His hold on Maria tightened.

'Who did you see?' he said.

'A man. In black. He wore a hood. I couldn't see his face. He was trying to jimmy open your desk. He saw me. I ran for the phone in the kitchen and he grabbed me by my hair in the hallway. I turned around, screamed. That's when he hit me. I fell and he must've got scared and ran out the front door.'

The desk, thought Paul.

'Did he say anything?' said Paul.

'No,' she said, then, 'Paul, you're hurting me.'

He let go. He'd been holding her too tightly: his fingers had been digging into her flesh.

She stood back and he looked at her face again. Then he turned and ran into his study. The books, ornaments and keepsakes were all where they should be. A laptop lay undisturbed on the desk which faced the door. As he came around the other side of the desk he saw that the window had been broken. Shards of glass lay on the rug behind his office chair. The intruder had gotten in this way. Broke the glass to get at the window lock, then opened it and climbed in. He spun around and checked the desk. The top left-hand drawer had been forced open. Its contents spilled. Kneeling down, he rapidly flicked through the notes, press cuttings and reviews. This was his private desk, in his private study. He looked behind him at the busted window. It was too dark to see the beach beyond the tall grasses. Someone must have been watching him. Someone knew what was in that drawer. The only things in the house that could expose him were in that desk.

The hairs on the back of his neck stood up.

Maria stood on the other side of the desk. She looked confused, and hurt. It wasn't the welt on her cheek that pained her. Something else was wrong, something deeper. He could tell.

'The man didn't take anything that I can see. He didn't go for my jewelry, or my car keys or the laptop. What did he want?' she said.

Paul felt the lie come easy. Even now. Even to someone he loved.

'I don't know,' he said.

The words fell lightly from his lips. No guilt. His conscience had long given up the fight. He loved Maria, as much as he could love anyone. The lies were part of it, and always had been.

'Why did he bust open that drawer? If there's something going on, I have a right to know,' she said.

'He must've been looking for cash, or credit cards. I don't know what he was searching for,' he said.

For a second, he could've sworn he saw a flash of disgust on her face, as if something unpleasant had appeared before her eyes; her lip curled, she looked him over and then burst into tears.

He moved toward her, but she held up her hand and left the room, bumping into the sheriff in the doorway.

'Excuse me, ma'am,' said Sheriff Dole. He tipped his cap again then joined Paul in the study. The big man moved slow, but his eyes worked fast – taking in the room.

'Nothing seems to be disturbed in any of the rooms, 'cept this one,' he said.

He came around the desk, knelt down to take a look at the window while Paul stood back and watched. The sheriff looked at the glass fragments on the rug, switched his attention to the window and stood. He examined the handle of the window, stuck his head out through the broken pane and drew a flashlight from his belt. Paul noticed that the sheriff didn't need to look at his belt to find his light. There were no fumbling fingers either, his hand drew that flashlight in one fluid movement. He imagined the sheriff had done this a thousand times.

'I'll take a look out back in the morning, if you don't mind? This guy didn't land on your porch. He walked there. Might be some tracks in the dirt. Too easy to miss 'em in the dark,' said the sheriff, knocking off the light beam.

'Right, good call,' said Paul.

Sheriff Dole turned his attention to the desk. A messy pile of pages lay on the floor. Above them, the drawer was open.

'Anything missing, sir?' said Sheriff Dole.

Paul shook his head, said, 'Not that I can tell. Looks like Maria disturbed the guy before he had much of a chance.'

'Anyone who would want to hurt you, or your wife?' asked Dole. Paul shook his head.

The law man nodded, looked at the broken lock on the desk drawer. None of the other drawers had been touched. Paul folded his arms, watched the sheriff take another look around the room.

'Aren't you going to take fingerprints or something?' said Paul.

'No need. Burglars wear gloves. Never got a print off a burglar in thirty-five years.'

'What if this one didn't wear gloves? Shouldn't you at least try?' said Paul.

Sheriff Dole's mustache twitched, once, and he said, 'Maybe on this one we will. I'll send a deputy tomorrow. You sure there ain't nothin' been taken?'

'I'll double check tomorrow, but I'm pretty sure.'

'Okay then,' said the sheriff. 'I'll send a car a little later on, just to swing by the property and make sure everything's fine. We won't disturb you. We'll get a statement then, too. Okay then, you folks have yourselves a pleasant evening.'

And with that, the sheriff tipped his hat and Paul saw him to the door, which he closed and locked behind the sheriff. He let out his breath as soon as he heard the sheriff's car pull out of the driveway. He turned around, saw Maria standing at the top of the stairs, watching him.

'It's okay, honey. I'm home now. You get some sleep. I'm going to stay up. This asshole won't be stupid enough to come back. If he does, I'll be waiting.'

Maria said nothing. For the longest time she stood there looking down at Paul. Her hands by her sides, her body perfectly still. Unable to hold her gaze, Paul looked down at the floor, then turned and walked back into the study.

He tried to think about what he'd left in that drawer. He closed his eyes, tried hard to remember if he'd brought anything else from his office to the house. He had brought home a bank statement or two, before he got the safe installed in the marina office. Did he bring the bank statements back to the office? He couldn't remember, not for sure.

For years, Paul had been careful. No outrageous spending. Well, at least nothing he couldn't hide on a tax return. He bought the car through his dummy business account, and the boat he bought off the books. They were expensive, but not millionaire's toys and nowhere near what the average Port Lonely inhabitant had in the garage or at the marina. He didn't stand out. He'd kept his head down. He'd kept his mouth shut.

And yet, he'd been found.

An old familiar feeling clawed its way up from the earth. He could feel it crawling over him, seizing control. The sweat broke like a dam, his tongue dried up in his mouth, his shoulders hunched and he found his fingers had wound into trembling fists.

The fear was back.

He drew out his cell phone, began typing an email and then stopped. He deleted the draft. No need to involve her just yet. What if she was the one who'd betrayed him? No. He was panicking. Not thinking.

There was nothing she could do at this hour, anyway. If he emailed her, she might call him, and Maria was upstairs. She might hear.

Paul shook his head. He was letting fear rule him. His only choice was to wait and see how this played out. Whatever happened, he would be ready. Quietly, he made his way back into the study, removed a thick copy of the collected works of Dickens from the bookshelf and reached in behind it. It was still there. Untouched. Ready for when he needed it.

A Smith and Wesson .38.

CHAPTER FIVE

As Sheriff Dole pulled out of the driveway of the Coopers' house, he grabbed the radio mic and hit the transmit button twice.

'Come on back, Abraham. You catch any prowlers?' said the voice of the dispatcher.

'They were long gone by the time I got there, Sue,' he said.

Sue, along with two full-time deputies, made up the Sheriff's Department of Port Lonely. For a town with little crime it had a well-funded Sheriff's Department. The rich folk who financed the town during tourist season cared about protection. They didn't want the locals going rogue and scratching up their Ferraris or pissing on their roses. And so they contributed to the law enforcement budget through black-tie fundraisers with one hundred dollar plates, bake sales and barbeques. And the money piled up faster than the sheriff could spend it.

Sue had worked with Dole for the best part of twenty years. She was sharp, took no bullshit and even though she was not a field officer, she was responsible for the majority of Port Lonely's crime clean-up rate. This was in part due to her keen intelligence, and the fact that she knew *almost* every living soul in the town and never missed a piece of gossip.

'How's that nice lady doing? She sounded so scared on the phone,' said Sue.

'She's got a mark on her face. She'll bruise, but she'll be fine,' said Sheriff Dole.

'What happened?' asked Sue.

'She said she heard a noise, like glass breaking, in the study. When she unlocked the door she found a masked intruder kneeling behind her husband's desk. He leapt toward her, struck her once while he made for the front door.'

'How'd he get into the study?' said Sue.

Dole's mustache twitched.

'You don't miss a trick, do you?' he said.

'I can always tell when you're squirly about something. Come on, better out than in.'

'Well, there's definitely something amiss in that house. Between Mrs. Cooper and Mr. Cooper. I'd say there's an air of discord.'

The radio stayed silent for a moment, before Sue barked back, 'Come on now, there's more than that.'

'You should teach interrogation techniques, you know that? It's probably nothing.'

'It's something. Don't hold out on me no more, Sheriff.'

'Alright. It just didn't make any sense to me is all. Mrs. Cooper says she unlocks the study door and startles a burglar, catches him red-handed. The burglar just came through a big, open window. Why would he run toward Mrs. Cooper, hit her, and run out the front door when he could just turn around and escape the way he came in, quick as a flash?'

'Burglars are pretty dumb. Could be she's telling the truth.'

'Could be. It still doesn't explain why even a dumb burglar would bust open one drawer in an old desk when there's two-grand's worth of laptop just sitting there in front of him. Easy to move on the black market in Plainsfield. He could get a couple thou, *easy*.'

'*Easy*,' agreed Sue. 'You gonna go back out tomorrow?'

'Probably. I'll take Bloch with me in the morning to get some statements and have a look around. Don't tell her what I said, let her work it out for herself. She's plenty smart and I want to make sure I'm not jumpin' off the deep end. And by the way, don't you go blabbermouthin' none of this either.'

'As if I would? The indignity,' said Sue.

'You would. You *have*. That time I caught old man Peterson in his car, buck-ass naked in a parking lot with an inflatable doll in the passenger seat. The whole town knew about it before I even got back to the station.'

She didn't argue with that one. She was too busy laughing at the memory.

'I'm gonna take a drive around town, see what I can see. I'll be back later,' said the sheriff. Sue signed off, and the cruiser fell into silence.

He reached for the radio, but hesitated when he saw the waterfall on his left.

Ten years ago Dole pulled a body out of the spillway at the bottom of the falls. A young woman. Late twenties. Found at the end of a long, hot summer. Naked, her body swollen by the water. Her injuries were consistent with a fall from the peak. They were also consistent with a violent death. No one had come forward to claim her. No DNA match, not enough teeth left for a dental comparison, and far as he could tell she didn't match the photos of recent missing persons.

She had been buried in the municipal cemetery. Only Dole and Sue at the funeral.

Whenever Dole came out this way, which wasn't often, he took a moment in silence to remember the girl. Most law enforcement would have put the death down to misadventure. No clear evidence of a homicide. They would have moved on.

The file on Jane Doe still sat in the bottom drawer of Dole's desk. He took it out once in a while, checked the updated missing persons databases. The file remained open, and it would stay like that until Dole found out what had happened to the girl.

CHAPTER SIX

Rising at five a.m., Maria showered, dressed, and tip-toed through the living room, past her sleeping husband, out the front door, got into her car and drove away. The newborn sun hit the windshield as she passed through Port Lonely. The next town on the coast was a mere fifty miles away, but she didn't need to go that far. Halfway between Port Lonely and Port Hope, she pulled in at the all-night diner. It was nothing more than a trailer that seated twenty, served coffee so hot it would take the enamel off your teeth and didn't mind if you failed to tip your waitress.

She pulled open the door to the diner, inhaled the smell of bacon and over-cooked eggs. There were two men at the counter. Trawler-men from Port Hope. The diner's profits lay in overpriced, bad food at any time of day. If you just happened to step off a boat at three a.m. and were in need of a beer and a sandwich, you came to the Lonely Hope Diner.

The waitress, a blonde in her forties with a smile that looked in its fifties, stepped out from behind the counter and offered Maria a booth in the corner and a laminated menu which stuck to the table like it was coated in glue.

'Just coffee is fine,' said Maria.

A nod from the waitress was all Maria got in return. Her nametag read, 'Sandy,' and she prised the menu off the table with some difficulty. Eventually it came away and made a sucking and ripping sound while it did so, like somebody tearing apart wet Velcro. A cup and saucer appeared on the table and it was quickly filled from a bun flask with steaming black coffee. Maria asked for cream and sugar, and it came a lot later than it should have. No tip for Sandy, thought Maria.

Just after six a.m., Daryl walked into the diner and took a seat opposite Maria. He asked for a latte, and Maria resisted the urge to smile at the expression on Sandy's face. It is white coffee, or black coffee, or sodas. Nothing else. Daryl settled for white coffee.

'I haven't slept all night,' said Maria.

'Me either. I felt sick. I've never hit a woman. How's your . . .' He couldn't even say it. He let his sentence fall away and simply wiped a finger on his cheek. As he did so, he couldn't hide the look of disgust on his face. He had crossed a line last night, and slapping Maria had left a mark on Daryl too.

Maria reached out, squeezed his arm and forced a smile. 'It's fine. I asked you to do it. Remember? In fact, I had to beg you before you agreed. I'm sorry I made you do it, but I needed him to believe our story. There was no other way. It's fine, just put it out of your mind.'

'I can't. I've never hurt a woman. God, I just paced the floor last night worrying about you. I felt like punching myself in the head, you know?' said Daryl.

'I think it's kinda sweet you feel so bad. I'm sorry. I won't ever make you hurt me again. I'll make it up to you. I promise,' said Maria.

'Did you ask him about the drawer?' asked Daryl.

'He didn't say anything, but I could tell he was rattled. He knows he left something secret in that drawer. The main thing is he doesn't suspect me. The cops came out. They're treating it as a burglary.'

'So you went through all of that for nothing?'

Without consciously registering the motion, Maria stroked the side of her face. The swelling had gone down, but the redness in her cheek remained. Ducking his head, avoiding her eyes, Daryl took a sip of coffee and stared at the table. Maria felt a stab of guilt at forcing him to strike her. For all his physical size and strength, Daryl really was a sweetheart – almost an innocent. Batting down that feeling of guilt, she replaced it with Daryl's warm brown eyes and the knowledge that she was so lucky to have him.

'It wasn't for nothing,' said Maria. 'He doesn't suspect me. He thinks someone broke in and busted the drawer. It was worth it for that alone, but . . .'

She fell silent, shook her head. Her lips trembled and she stared out of the dirty window at the road. Finally, she took a breath, composed herself enough to continue.

'I asked him why someone would break into his drawer. He didn't tell me anything. I dropped enough hints, but he wouldn't say. Damn it, I wanted him to tell me. It was the perfect opportunity to get it all out in the open. And he didn't say shit.'

Maria wrapped her hands around her mug, stared into it. There were no answers on the greasy film that had formed on the top of her coffee. She had loved Paul once. She had felt it early on in the relationship. The more time they spent together, the more Paul had grown. It was like a weight sat on his shoulders and every hour he spent with her it had lifted a little, letting him smile more, relax more, be himself. And yet that weight had never truly disappeared. She had imagined that it might, in time. That love would conquer all. That Paul would finally let her all the way into his life, his past, his dreams. And when that didn't happen Maria stopped trying to shift more of that weight. Paul wasn't around – he was off at marketing conferences, or seeing clients, or out on his goddamn boat. Daryl had nothing weighing him down, no secrets that he wouldn't share. He was open, and honest and . . . free.

Maria realized she could not free Paul. That he had to do it for himself. And when he'd freeze up, bringing those cold barriers front and center time and time again, eventually Maria had simply stopped trying.

She'd realized on the drive over to the diner that morning that she no longer felt any guilt about her relationship with Daryl. It felt more *right* than it ever had before. Her husband was someone else, pretending to be married to Maria. That's all it was, a charade. Now Maria didn't have to pretend to be with him anymore. She'd decided that this bad play she'd found herself in had to end. The sight of Paul lying to her face had sickened her. She had no more will to take part in the performance of marriage.

It had to end.

Daryl shifted uncomfortably in his seat, said, 'What are you going to do?'

Maria smiled. 'For now I want him to believe he's been discovered. Put him on edge. See what he does. He's going to get a shock when he wakes up and steps outside. He drives around in that Italian sports car, and lets me drive a four-year-old Nissan with three hundred dollars a week to keep the house and myself. I used to think that it was fine – you know, it's his money. But that's not a marriage. He's been keeping more than a ninety-thousand-dollar car to himself. Well, that has to change, Daryl. I left him something on that car, and I hope it scares the shit out of him.'

CHAPTER SEVEN

Pain shot up the side of Paul's neck, jolting him awake on the couch. The sun had warmed the living room and as soon as he opened his eyes, it instantly blinded him. Sitting up, he blinked away the sun spots and rubbed at the back of his neck. Some cushions were on the floor beside him. He must've disturbed them in the night, knocking them off the couch. That explained the crick in his neck.

He had slept downstairs in case the intruder returned, but after a few hours he had put the gun back in the study and simply settled down on the couch, too tired to face the stairs.

He still wore his jeans and T-shirt from the night before. They were wrinkled and smelled of his sweat. A bad taste filled his mouth. He hadn't brushed his teeth the previous night. A shower and a change of clothes was in order. Not before he had coffee and a cigarette. He needed both.

A zip compartment in his laptop bag held a soft pack of Camels and a lighter. He brewed an espresso from the machine and took it out onto the porch. It was real early. Maria didn't usually get up till around ten. He had time for a secret cigarette outside. Although Maria already knew he still smoked the occasional cigarette. He always denied it, and she never bought his protestations. He liked it that way. If Maria felt she had outsmarted him about his secret smokes, it gave him more comfort that she would never even dream of discovering his other life. He wanted her to believe she had him all figured out.

As he smoked, he thought over the events of last night. Maybe he had jumped to a conclusion too soon. Everything seemed less sinister in the sunlight. It could have just been a burglar. And if it was just a regular burglar, and even if they did get a bank statement, they couldn't do that much to hurt him. Not yet. They certainly couldn't take his money or do anything with the bank details. The account was in the Caymans, password protected. Safe and secure.

He finished his coffee, went upstairs to see Maria and found their bed empty. He checked the bathroom, called her name and walked around the rest of the house. She was gone. It occurred to him that maybe she'd gone to the beach for an early morning swim. She did that very rarely, and only when she'd had a great night's sleep. She enjoyed being on the beach alone. No one around at that time, she would have the place to herself. From the back porch he looked out on the beach. Three hundred yards away. No towels in the sand. No one sunbathing and, as far as he could see, nobody in the water. Paul walked around the corner to the front of the house and saw her car had gone. He was about to turn and go back inside for a shower when something stopped him. Something in his subconscious. Something odd about the scene in front of him that his mind had taken in, but not definitively processed.

Looking back at the driveway, he saw what had barely registered at first glance.

A white envelope sat beneath the windshield wiper of his car. Paul didn't move. Instead he looked around, examining the bushes and tall grass next to the driveway. Somebody had left the note there. It wasn't Maria. She didn't leave notes. Even if she'd stormed off in a rage, she wouldn't put pen to paper and leave him a note. If she wanted to give him a message she would've texted or called and spelled out her rage in all caps. Strange place to leave an envelope. They could've snuck up to the house and pushed it under the door, or left it in the mailbox at the top of the drive. Instead, the messenger had placed it on his windshield. Paul's mind made instant calculations, based on probability and experience, and then he dismissed most of them in seconds. There were only two reasons to leave the note under the windshield wiper. The first was that they wanted to make sure, as much as possible, that only he saw the note. Maybe they waited until after Maria had left before slipping it under the wiper. The second reason to place the envelope on his car was that they were waiting out there in the long grass and they wanted to watch him open it.

The thought paralyzed him. Only his eyes moved. Slowly, he took in every inch of grass. Every small hill. Every boulder. Nothing. Then he focused on one point in the distance letting his peripheral vision pick up any movement. It didn't work. The breeze that came off the ocean seemed to stir every blade of grass in a soft, gentle lull.

Shaking his head, he moved toward the Maserati. The soles of his feet disturbed the rounded gravel and the sound seemed way louder than it should've been. Like an alarm bell. The grass swayed in the breeze, and no one stood or revealed themselves. He realized such feelings were foolish. His fear and anxiety were rattling his thoughts – sending panic and adrenaline charging after each neuron that fired inside his brain.

He reached the car, stared at the windshield, grabbed the envelope and immediately heard a loud roar and crunch. Before he could think, his body reacted – dropping him into a crouch. Shielding his head he spoke, without even gathering a thought. It was an automaton response.

'What the hell was that?' he said, before he even realized he'd uttered anything at all. The words were as much of a surprise as the initial sound that had startled him.

He looked up, saw the fender of a police cruiser rolling toward him and stopping just a few feet from his head. The driver must have given the pedal a final kick as the V8 screamed once more before the engine died.

Paul got up, using the Maserati for leverage. The driver's door, then the passenger door of the sheriff's car opened.

Sheriff Dole slammed the driver's door closed, looked over the hood of the car at the passenger. A woman in a deputy's uniform. She had short black hair, spiked up in places, messy and yet stylish. She looked a little taller than the Sheriff, but that wouldn't be hard. Paul, at six one, had towered over the sheriff the previous night. Both the sheriff and the deputy wore aviator sunglasses. Both broke off their gaze at each other, began taking in the surroundings.

'Did we scare ya?' said the Sheriff.

Mumbling, 'No,' Paul slid the envelope into the back pocket of his jeans.

'Sure looked like you were scared, way you ducked when you saw us coming,' said Sheriff Dole.

Regaining enough composure to form a decent response, Paul thought he'd better set things straight.

'No, no, you just startled me. I ducked before I even saw your car. It was the noise. And, you know, I'm still a little freaked out about last night.'

'Uh huh,' said Dole.

The deputy strode past him, turned and went into the house through the open front door without saying a word.

'Say, ah, is everything okay?' said Paul.

'Sure is,' said Dole as he came to stand beside Paul at the Maserati. 'That's Deputy Bloch. She's just going to take a look at that window. Is your wife at home?'

'Ah, no. She's gone out.'

'Thought so. Don't see her car. Grocery shopping?'

'Probably. Ahm, shouldn't we go inside and—'

'Nah,' said Dole, 'Bloch will be in and out in a few minutes tops. Just a formality. You don't mind if I just get some details, do you?'

He produced a notebook and pen from a pocket on his belt. Flipping open the book to a blank page, he began to make a new entry in blue ink.

Paul gave his full name, date of birth. Dole wrote down each answer slowly and carefully in a flowing, neat script.

'Where were you last night when your wife called?'

'I'd just brought my boat into the marina,' said Paul. He didn't want anyone to know about his apartment. It might get back to Maria.

Dole glanced up from his notes, his lips parting at the left corner of his mouth and displaying bright dentures. Even with the sunglasses, Paul could tell Dole was struggling to look him in the eye. The sun sat above Paul's left shoulder, burning into Sheriff Dole's face. He could see the bright flare of the sun reflected in those glasses.

'What'd you say was the name of your boat?' said Dole.

'I'm not sure I told you before, never mind, it's *The Clarence*,' said Paul, stumbling over the words.

'What time?'

Paul took a step back, throwing his shadow over the sheriff's face.

'What do you mean? What time did I land the boat or what time did Maria call me?'

Maybe it was the light, but Paul thought he saw Dole's mustache twitch at the corner of his mouth. And even though Paul had asked a question, instead of giving an answer, he watched Dole write down every word that he'd said.

'Both,' said Dole. He wiped his mouth with the back of his hand and returned his pen to the page, ready to note down the response.

'I don't know, exactly. Just a minute or so, maybe more, before Maria called me.'

'Do you have your phone with you?'

'I do,' said Paul, before he could think of anything better to say. He reached into his front pocket for the phone, hesitated, wondered if this was a wise move, then decided he had no choice and he took the phone out and waved it at Dole.

'Let me get a note of the call, and your number,' said Dole.

Scrolling through his phone record he found the call, showed it to Dole who made a note.

'And the number please?' said Dole.

Paul called it out from memory.

'Have you taken a good look around the house? Found anything missing at all?' said Sheriff Dole.

'I did have a look around, for sure. Far as I can tell nothing has been taken.'

The sheriff finished his note, put the book away and said, 'Mr. Cooper, do you know of anyone who would want to harm you or your wife?'

'No. You asked me that last night, I think.'

'Sure did. Could be you weren't thinking straight last night.'

'My answer is still no,' said Paul, folding his arms.

'Uh huh. Well, have you noticed anything out of the ordinary lately? Cars parked on the road? Maybe a new, regular face on the beach?'

He could almost feel the envelope in his back pocket burning a hole through his jeans. He thought for a moment before saying, 'Can't say as I've noticed.'

The sound of a hard sole on gravel approaching from behind made Paul turn. Deputy Bloch left the house, walked past Paul without a word and took her seat in the cruiser.

'Well, looks like we're done here for now,' said the sheriff, tipping his ball cap to Paul. The people of Port Lonely were normally averse to conversation. They said what they had to say and then they shut the hell up. So it didn't come as a surprise when Sheriff Dole got back into his car, reversed out of the drive and made his way east, back to the town.

The V8 engine faded away into the distance like thunder. Paul drew the envelope from his back pocket and opened it. Inside was a single page. Folded twice. In capitals? Handwritten.

I KNOW WHO YOU ARE
MR. LEBEAU

Paul folded up the letter, slid it back into the envelope as he returned to the porch. He'd left his cigarettes on the small table beside the rocking chairs. He lit himself a fresh Camel with trembling fingers, then held the flame from the lighter to the envelope. Watched it burn. He dropped the smoldering envelope in the sand bucket. Waited until it had been reduced to black ash, floating on the breeze.

He knew then there were no coincidences. No mere burglars. He had been found. There was only one thing he could do in response. He would need help. There was one other who knew his secret. She could help.

Paul typed out an email on his phone, hit send.

A feather of ash swept by his face, borne by the zephyrs darting off the sea. He thought of a blue Toyota Camry in flames. The car a red, screaming relief against the black night. He'd watched the gas tank blow, and the inferno die with the dawn. By that time his eyes were burning and the skin on his face felt hard and taut from the heat. He remembered the smell of smoke that lingered long after in his hair and on his hands. Most of all he recalled the noise from the trunk.

Bang, bang, bang.

That night he'd told himself it was the fire cracking glass and the interior plastics which made the sound. Yes, he was sure of it. Or at least he'd convinced himself of this explanation. It couldn't have been the person in the trunk. They were already dead. They had to have been.

His fear had died in the events after that blaze.

Now, it flew back into his body like a phoenix.

If he was going to survive, it was kill or be killed. There was no other way.

Anonymity came with a heavy price.

His phone buzzed in his pocket. He glanced at it. He'd saved the contact on his phone under the name 'Plumber'. Just in case Maria ever got suspicious and decided to check through his contacts list. Paul swiped the screen to answer the call.

'Are you alright?' said the voice. Even though it was a woman on the phone, the voice was deep, and each word sounded slightly cracked. As if there were smoke in her throat. And yet, somehow, the voice always sounded soothing.

'No, I'm not okay, Josephine, I've been found.'

CHAPTER EIGHT

'Mrs. Cooper is full of shit,' said Deputy Bloch.

Sheriff Dole had driven from the Coopers' beach house back to town without Bloch so much as breathing. They had turned left onto Maple Avenue and were approaching the sheriff's office on the corner when Bloch decided she was ready to talk. Shaking his head, Dole parked in the lot out back and pressed his tongue between his teeth. Bloch didn't say much. She took her time to think things through, didn't engage in small talk, never said *hello*, *goodbye*, or *thank you*, but when she opened her mouth to talk you could be damn sure she had something to say. And people listened.

He flicked on the parking brake, turned toward her.

'You figured that much out in the first thirty seconds you were inside the house. Come on, I drove all the ways out there so you could give me something. *Full of shit* I got. What don't I got?'

Bloch stared out through the windshield, avoiding Dole's eyes. He had no doubt she could feel him staring at her. He was doing it on purpose – trying to get Bloch to speak through the pressure of sheer awkwardness. Bloch didn't mind awkward silences. She was a walking awkward silence.

'I checked the tall grass from the porch and again from the upstairs bedroom window. If there had been someone lying out in that grass, casing the Coopers' beach house, you would still see the depressions in the earth, and the flattened grass. No footprints on the grass either. If someone had been out there I would've seen a trace. There was none. No one approached the house from the beach last night.'

'Uh huh, and the rest?' said Dole.

'You knew about the broken window pane in the study. It was broken from the outside. Glass on the carpet. There are twelve panes of glass in that porch window. The intruder broke the pane closest to the latch. That latch is *real* small. You can only see the position of the latch from inside the house,' said Bloch.

Dole hadn't noticed this. It was yet more proof that he'd done the right thing last year by hiring Bloch. He'd interviewed five deputies from five different counties for the job. Melissa Bloch was the least experienced, least qualified, had the poorest recommendations from her senior officers, apart from one glowing reference from New York, and didn't get along with anyone. Least of all Sheriff Dole. In her job interview she'd given short, monotone answers, she didn't smile, and had all the personality of a dead raccoon. At one point, Dole flicked through the pages of the résumé she'd sent over and found the reference from the lieutenant in her current posting. She was in New York, stationed at the Fourteenth Precinct and wanted out. The last line of the reference drew his attention.

. . . *Bloch is a very fine police officer. Smart, hard-working and dedicated, if a little on the quiet side.*

Dole nodded to himself. He'd had better conversations with two-day-old corpses. He had found himself wrapping up the interview ten minutes early just so he could get her out of his office. She made him uncomfortable. Dole guessed she made everyone uncomfortable.

'Well, you'll be hearing from us,' Dole had said, standing and offering his hand.

He remembered that for a few seconds Bloch had just sat there. Then she got up, took Dole's hand in a firm grip and pulled him in close. She inclined her head, whispered, 'The painting behind your desk is upside down.'

She released his hand, nodded and left. Dole turned around and stared at the framed Dali print behind him on the wall. A clock, with roman numerals on the dial, melting on an invisible table in the middle of the desert while strange shapes surrounded it. That picture had been on the wall for the past five years. Birthday gift from his sister in Albuquerque. God knows how many people he'd had through his office. Some of them had even commented on the picture. She was the only one who'd noticed. And now Dole noticed the clock was indeed upside down. He'd been so taken by the striking, misshapen figures around it, he'd ignored the roman numerals. Placing a chair beneath the picture, he stood, took the thing off the wall, turned it around and hung it up again. Standing back a few feet, he gazed at the scene anew. His mustache twitched – goddamn thing looked even weirder the right way up. The picture didn't matter though. Bloch mattered. Never a man to ignore his gut, Dole hired her. She'd spoken maybe five hundred words to him since the day she started on the job.

Every one of those words had been important.

Damn, I should have noticed the latch, he thought. Whoever had broken into that house had been in that room before.

'What do you think about Maria Cooper's story? What's the lie? She disturbs the intruder, gets attacked and then the perp makes a bolt for the front door?' asked Dole.

He didn't need her to answer. She stared at him. Shook her head. None of it was true.

'Uh huh,' said Dole.

They got out of the car and went through the rear security door that led directly to the holding cells. No guests behind bars today. They passed through the cell area via another security door and into the main sheriff's office. Sue was at the coffee machine, pouring herself a cup from the bun flask. She was short, well built, generous waist and tight perm. She managed to be both warm and formidable in a way that disarmed most people. Her pink blouse hung down close to her knees. Dole had ordered her a uniform, of course. It remained in the plastic wrapper, securely stored in her locker. She'd told him she didn't care for it.

'You catch the phantom burglar yet?' said Sue.

'An arrest is imminent,' said Dole.

He glanced over the row of desks until he reached Bloch's. Along with files and mail trays, he saw a J. T. LeBeau novel lying on the desk. The local bookstore sold those things by the dozen every damn day. It seemed that no matter where he went, someone had their nose buried in a J. T. LeBeau book. He didn't care for mysteries. Dole could always see the twist coming.

The sheriff's personal office was nothing more than a boxed-off glass partition. Apart from pictures of McCain and Obama on his desk there was little else of a personal nature. A laptop lay open beside the pictures, no paper lay in his tray, and the Dali print presided over all from the wall behind the desk.

A five-hundred-dollar orthopedic chair took Dole's weight and he hit a button on the armrest to activate the vibration massage on his lower back. He always left his office door open unless he was occupied with a guest. Dole liked to talk to his people, and made sure they were welcome to talk to him. His foot grazed a slim, battered file at his feet.

Jane Doe's file.

It was ten years ago she'd been found by some hikers who'd noticed the body floating in the water below them. They had skirted the ridge, found a cell phone signal and called Dole. He recalled the drive to that scene almost perfectly. The sky had been overcast that morning, with light rain showers every hour or so, but they never lasted long. He thought of the wipers on his old sheriff's truck squeaking all the way there. The local radio station played 'House of the Rising Sun' by The Animals as he hit the coast road. During the drive he'd thought of all the things he might find when he reached the scene. A body wasn't on his list. He was thinking about all of the things that could've found their way in there that maybe looked like a body. Garbage bags. Logs. Old clothes. Pipes. There hadn't been a homicide in Port Lonely in thirty years. Nor a suicide, for that matter.

When he arrived he met the hikers, who took him to a spot where he could look down on the water.

The rain had kicked in again, and the surface of the spillway danced with heavy rain. It soaked in Dole's eyes, covered his glasses, and beat a heavy drum on the back of his neck as he realized the hikers were not mistaken.

The naked body of a dead woman turned gently in the water.

Dole shook off the memory. The office was so quiet it was easy to lapse into bad memories.

The phone didn't ring. No one in the office spoke. The only sounds came from the spoon tinkling against the rim of Sue's coffee cup and the soft whirring from the air conditioners. Dole put his hands behind his head, leaned back and hollered for Sue to come into the office.

She came in, closed the frosted glass door, and took a seat opposite the sheriff.

'No coffee for me?' said Dole.

'Get your own damn coffee,' said Sue through a glorious smile.

'I want you to ask around, find out all you can about the Coopers. You know everyone in this town. Somebody has to be close enough to these people to give us more background. And don't mention the break-in. Far as Mr. Cooper is concerned nothing was taken. That's the quote you give to any newspapers that come callin'. Last thing we need is the press to be all over this. Then you'll have five hundred home owners sleeping with AK-47s on their nightstands.'

'Did you take fingerprints?' asked Sue.

'No point. We'd just get the occupants of the house. No burglar is going to leave behind prints. We'd waste time and resources and be right back where we started.'

Eyes darting to the floor, Sue drank more coffee. A movement that spoke to Dole like she was holding something inside and pouring coffee down her throat lest it came out.

'Talk to me,' said Dole.

He may as well have fired a starting pistol. Sue talked fast. Her diction, perfect. A chain gun of statements and questions delivered in a high-pitched, honeyed Southern drawl.

'Well now, this is just a broken window, isn't it? Nothing was taken and maybe Mrs. Cooper *is* making it up about the burglar. So what? It's not exactly a crime. Maybe it's wasting police time, but hells tits, Abraham, we got plenty of time to waste. And I think that's maybe what we're doing here. It's almost ten years to the day that you found that girl in the spillway. Don't think I didn't notice. I'm worried you're throwing a ball in this broken window case just to avoid thinking about that poor girl. I say we go see the Pastor—'

'No, no, no. Look, it's not about any of that,' said Dole. 'There are things that don't exactly add up. I don't know what went on in that house. I can't be certain there was a burglar or even a real break-in. But I know what I saw. I saw a lady who had been hit in the face. That's enough for me, Sue. And I'm not gonna leave it alone until I find out what happened.'

CHAPTER NINE

The satellite navigation system said the journey would take seventy-one minutes. In fact it took Maria almost two hours to reach her destination. Lomax City was like no city that Maria had ever been to before. If anything it probably resembled a medium-sized town. The casino, the metal plant and the two large Baptist churches fought hard for city status in the seventies. In the end, the casino money falling out of the pockets of the state legislature swung the deal. Not that it mattered now. The metal plant had closed. With the shortage of ready cash the casino soon followed. However, both churches remained packed on Sundays, even if their collection plates were noisier than they used to be. The clink of coins had replaced the quiet shuffle of bills falling into the plates.

Maria stopped the car at a junction, swore at the satnav system that told her she had arrived. Looking around, all she could see was a gas station that looked closed and a strip mall opposite that should've been closed. The strip mall consisted of a dry-cleaner's with white-washed windows, a small bank with a stop sign jutting out of its broken window and beside it she saw a faded sign that just might be what she was looking for.

There was no traffic at noon, and she drove through the junction and parked, got out and walked over to the last unit of the mall. Sure enough, she had found it.

Ezekiel David, Attorney at Law.

The sign would've cost a fair amount of money ten years ago. It hadn't been cleaned in some time. Moss and sun had weathered the lettering badly. Beneath it, the blinds had been pulled in the windows. She couldn't tell if anyone was inside. The door opened and a bell chimed above her head. Maria found herself in a waiting room. Brown tile carpet. Foldable plastic chairs. A table in the middle of the room groaned under the weight of yellowed newspapers and magazines whose pages had curled into fans.

A door at the other end of the waiting room opened and a tall, thickset man came out to greet her.

'Mrs. Erskine?' said the man, in a voice that sounded like it emerged from a tunnel.

'Yes, Janet Erskine,' said Maria. 'You must be Mr. David.'

Ezekiel David had a biblical body to match his biblical name. His head resembled a stone tablet. Broad and heavy with lines on his forehead that could've been a visual representation of the varying layers of volcanic rock in the Grand Canyon. Those massive folds of skin on his forehead led up to a smooth, bald head, which was so perfectly round that it accentuated the ruts of fat that sat above his impressive eyebrows. There was no neck, only a body. And what a body. It looked as though someone had put a beach ball in the middle of a pool table, stood the pool table up on one end and then covered the whole thing in a cheap suit.

Dainty feet in shiny black shoes escaped from the bottom of his gray suit pants. Maria couldn't hide her surprise at how such feet could possibly hold up the huge man in front of her.

'Do please come in,' said Ezekiel.

If she thought the man was big, she wasn't ready for the size of the office chair behind his cluttered desk. It looked more like a throne that could've been used to anoint the crowned heads of Europe. Yet still it squeaked and moaned as soon as he put his considerable ass on it. Maria sat opposite and gazed at him between twin stacks of manila files.

'I imagine you're considering a divorce,' said Ezekiel, in a matter-of-fact kind of way. No hint of sympathy. Maria guessed that he sold divorce as a positive endeavor – something to be coveted and paid for.

'At the moment I just want to know what my options would be. How the assets would be split,' she said.

'That's no problem. I can give you an overview but that's all it is. Each case is different and there are always arguments to be made and deals to be struck. So, I just need to get some personal details first . . .' he said and began writing down the name Maria had given him.

'Address?' said Ezekiel.

'I'd rather not,' said Maria. 'Not yet. This is general advice only and I'm a very private person. I can pay you up front for the hour.'

Opening her purse, Maria took out two hundred-dollar bills and placed them on the desk. Ezekiel put his pen down, folded his hands together and looked over them at the cash on the table.

'Anything you tell me is confidential. Protected by attorney client privilege,' said Ezekiel.

'I'd rather get general advice, Mr. David, but if that's not possible?' She left the question hanging in the air for Ezekiel while her fingers stretched toward the money on the table.

A fat lump, with five fat digits attached, slammed down on top of the bills. Maria smiled, leaned back in her chair.

'I can always give general advice. You're paying up front, so you'll forgive me if our meeting doesn't last the full hour,' he said.

'That's fine, as long as I get the answers.'

'What do you want to know?' said Ezekiel, retrieving the cash and placing it inside his jacket.

'My husband has been hiding money from me. I can't trust him anymore. If he's hiding this . . . well, what else is he hiding? I think I want to end the marriage. Where do I stand?'

A low groan of sympathy escaped from Ezekiel's throat. He shook his head, tutted. That was all the client care he could muster.

'Is there a pre-nup?'

The lawyer's first question had floored Maria. Her mouth moved but no words came out. Before they were married Paul had insisted on a pre-nup to protect her. He said it would adequately take care of her should anything happen and make sure he wasn't entitled to any of her income. At first Maria ignored it, then argued against it and finally signed it and gave it back to him without keeping a copy and hadn't thought about the damn thing since. In fact, until a moment ago she'd forgotten it had even existed. Divorce was the last thing on her mind in those days before the wedding. She'd found *the one.* The agreement protected her, she never guessed it would protect him. Now that she thought about it, that pre-nup felt like a fresh wound. A small cut that she had ignored until it had festered.

'Yes. There's a pre-nup,' she whispered.

'Do you have a copy?'

'No. I read it before I signed it. It's a long time ago, I'm not sure of those details. I'd forgotten all about it until you mentioned it.'

'Who wrote it? Your lawyers or his?'

'His.'

The big man wiped his nose with a handkerchief the size of a pillowcase and said, 'I'm sorry to say that the pre-nup is likely to favor your husband. I'd be surprised if it wasn't specifically designed to protect that money he's secreted in another account. It doesn't look good, Mrs. Erskine.'

Maria was not going to be dissuaded so easily. She'd handed over her last two hundred dollars and now she wanted her money's worth.

'But I've heard of pre-nuptial agreements being thrown out of court. I wouldn't have signed it if I'd known the truth. He lied to me,' she said.

'That's an argument. It probably won't get us too far but it's certainly a point I could make. The problem is likely to be the effect of getting that pre-nup voided. I'm not sure you would be that much better off.'

'What? How?'

'I take it you both reside in this state?' he asked.

'Yes.'

'Kids?'

'No.'

'Is your husband aware of your knowledge?'

'No.'

'Is the money in an account in his sole name?'

'Yes.'

'I see. In this state we have settled laws on distribution of assets. Apart from the money that he's been hiding, what are the assets?'

'The house is in his name. He has a boat too. There's a joint account, of course. Apart from that our cars, but the money that he's been keeping from me outweighs the value of anything else.'

A squeal from the leather office chair startled Maria. Ezekiel swung low in his chair, looked at the ceiling and blew out his cheeks.

'Was the house and that boat bought during the marriage?'

'The house, yes. Not the boat.'

'Do you work and contribute to the marriage financially?'

Maria shook her head, sighed. She knew the guy was trying to give her as much advice as possible, but she wasn't interested. There was only one thing on her mind.

'I did contribute early on in the marriage. Not now. I haven't worked in some time. He pays the mortgage and all the bills. Look, I'm not really interested in this. It's the money he's been hiding that I need to know about. Would I get a share of that in the divorce if we could get the pre-nup thrown out?' said Maria

'I don't want to know where the money came from. I suspect there may be good reason why your husband wouldn't want to have to declare it as single ownership in divorce proceedings. Maybe the IRS or other authorities might have an interest in that money. If that is the case then your husband will want to keep that money on the down low. Could be that's enough of a threat to get a small percentage. State law says that during marriage, any property acquired by a single spouse and retained in their name remains that spouse's property and doesn't fall into *marriage* property, which would be subject to equitable division.'

The lawyer talked fast. Too fast for Maria to follow everything he said.

'I'm sorry, you mean if I divorced him I wouldn't get any of that money in his account? Not one bit?'

'Not a one. Not unless you threatened to expose it. Of course, if the money is legitimately held then you've played your cards and lost and you'll never see a cent.'

'What kind of messed up—?'

'That's the law,' said Ezekiel, cutting her off. 'While you're married, your spouse can acquire assets which they will retain in the event of divorce, just like all the money that they made before the marriage.'

Closing her eyes, Maria pressed her palm to her forehead and took a deep breath.

'This can't be happening,' she said.

The floor felt shaky, like it was moving beneath her even as she sat on the chair. She didn't know whether to throw up or hold on to the chair to stop herself falling off. What felt most strange about it all was that Maria had somehow become aware of it – like she was standing in the corner watching her body go into a full-blown panic attack. She could feel and see the tears on her cheeks, her face paper white and hard as heavy plastic. The shaking legs, the unfocused gaze, lips curled up and dry like they'd kissed pale flour.

As much as Ezekiel's room had now become a rollercoaster, Maria drew some strength from the big man who didn't appear remotely concerned. He looked bored. Most of his days he probably sat there while one divorce client after another came into his office, moaned and cried and left.

'I'll get you some water,' he said, and with some considerable effort he got out of the chair and poured her a paper cup of water from the cooler in the corner of his office. It was one of those cups that looked like a cone. He presented it to Maria and she drank it in one swallow, spilling some of it down one side of her face. The shock of the water trickling to her ear was enough to bring back some measure of control to her voice.

She spoke in a long, fierce breath. Panting in between her words.

'I've . . . been . . . SO . . . stupid,' she said, and more tears came.

'No, you haven't,' said Ezekiel, raising his voice now. 'He's deceived you. He's the one to blame. There would have been signs, which anyone would miss. There always is. Doesn't matter if you're the husband or the wife – a cheating, lying spouse has the cover of your love to shield them. I've seen it hundreds of times before. And the victim always blames themselves. That stops, right here. Look, I'm no Eddie Flynn, but I'm a decent lawyer. We could make a few arguments here and there in court, but I couldn't give you any guarantees. At best, I might be able to negotiate a small percentage, but no more. And maybe not even that. Only right that I tell you up front.'

Maria nodded, though she hadn't heard of Eddie Flynn, she understood the man was telling her she needed a miracle worker to come out well in a divorce. She could feel a fresh flood of tears on her face.

Then Ezekiel said something in an effort to make her laugh. Maria had known men to try and make her laugh when she was upset. It usually worked, calmed her down. Ezekiel's joke strayed over the line into obsidian-black humor.

'Look on the bright side, maybe your husband will have a heart attack and pass everything to you. Bastard deserves it.'

Maria's legs stopped shaking. The floor put on the brakes. The claw of emotion that had held her in that state seemed to vanish like smoke. Maria thanked the lawyer, got up and left. In the few seconds that passed between closing Ezekiel's front door and getting into the driver's seat of her car, everything had changed. She knew her options. Limited though they may be.

There was a long drive ahead of her, back to Port Lonely. Lots of time to think. She drove with no radio playing in the background. A silent car. Only the low rumble of her tires on the blacktop.

She let her mind wander with her emotions. Flitting between two poles.

Two years ago, in Central Park, on a cold Sunday morning in February with Paul. They'd slept late in her apartment. The old radiators didn't give out much heat, and neither of them wished to leave the bed to fire up the electric heaters. Instead they made love that morning and lost themselves in each other for a time. Saying nothing. Just being there. It was the closest she had ever felt to someone. They dressed, ate pancakes at Bloom's Deli on Lexington Avenue and then caught a cab to Central Park. They sat on a bench and watched the ice skaters on the pond, the fingers of their gloves intertwined. All that day they had barely spoken. There was no need.

'This is the best day I've had in a long time. I'm sorry if I'm distant sometimes. Things in my past that I can't talk about, that I don't want to talk about, they take hold of me some days. I'm sorry for that. I love you,' said Paul. There was a look in his eyes that stamped his words with purest truth.

Maria felt love in her whole being. She had lifted this man from his pain, given him a life. She'd fixed him. Now he would be hers, forever. He was a good man. Still quiet, but he no longer seemed to be hiding from life, or from her.

But she hadn't fixed him. Not at all.

Since moving away from New York to the house in Port Lonely, to raise a family, Maria had been alone. Even when he was with her, he was somewhere else in his mind. There was a sense of failure. Her failure. Why couldn't she get him to open up? Why did he have to go away all the time? Why did he need to spend all those hours locked in his study? Those questions now had a simple answer. He had a secret life. There was no great tragedy in his past – that was just a smokescreen so Maria wouldn't ask too many questions.

Paul had lied to her from the very beginning.

She knew she wasn't a failure as a wife. That Paul's distance was not a result of some weakness, or failing on her part. He was being someone else.

And yet that hurt remained. The hurt that had driven her to Daryl.

'Selfish bastard.' She said it out loud. In the car. To herself. She needed to hear it.

Her father had been a drinker and a junkie. He leeched off of Maria's mother for gear, taking her paycheck at the end of every week. He then went out and bought groceries, brought them home and then blew the rest on cheap booze and heroin. Maria didn't know for sure, but she guessed her father could live with himself if he knew his wife and daughter weren't going hungry and he always found enough cash on the street to pay the rent. Maria's mom never asked where it came from. Then, in the last year of his life, he stopped buying groceries. He took the whole paycheck. Nothing for food or rent in return. What little possessions they had went missing. Maria's bicycle, her mom's hair dryer. He stole from them. And he beat them, too. There was always violence in the house, and even in the quiet moments the threat of violence remained. Maria ate meals with the neighbors and at the Salvation Army kitchens. It wasn't enough, and her mom resorted to stealing from the deli.

The night of the accident, she had stolen a whole salami and a loaf of bread. She sat in the living room rocking back and forth and crying at the shame of it while Maria lay at her feet, eating the bread and sausage and staring at the tape holding her mom's shoes together. It was a Friday night. And her mom had hidden her paycheck. Dad came into the apartment, high on something and smelling like chemicals. It was summer, and the air-conditioner had broken. Maria's mom had removed it from the window and lain it on the floor. Better to have both windows open and at least let in some breeze.

He started laying into her mother right off the bat. Closed fists. Hard punches to her head. Told her she was holding out on him.

Maria grabbed him by the hair, managed to get him off her mother, and then he punched Maria, sending her down on the floor holding her stomach. She glanced up, saw her mom swinging a chair. It crashed over his head, but didn't break. Then she pushed him. And he staggered back, high and drunk on booze, black tar heroin and rage. He almost fell out of the window, only grabbing the edge of the frame in time – his ass half out over the street.

Her mom rushed toward him. Instantly Maria felt glad. Her mom was going to save him, and then, a second later, she felt regret. Her father wasn't going to change. He would get his footing back, and then give them both the beating of their lives.

'Get him away, Mommy!' shouted Maria.

'Bastard,' said Maria's mom, and pushed him.

He fell twelve stories.

And they were happier for it.

The autopsy showed he was loaded with booze and heroin, and the cops bought the story of him falling out of the window. They didn't give a shit about a deadbeat junkie.

In the months that followed, Maria sometimes wondered if her mom was going to save him. What would have happened if she hadn't cried out like that? Her mom told her she was glad Maria said it. That she was going to push him anyway, but she was glad nonetheless. When her mom told her this, she didn't look Maria in the eye. She spoke slowly and deliberately over the clicks of her knitting needles, and was always quick to change the subject.

With his life insurance policy payout, Maria and her mom had the best year of their lives – they didn't need to worry about money. Maria could not think of a happier time.

And here she was again, with another selfish bastard.

If she couldn't get the money in a divorce, there had to be another way to get it. She was no chump. She was on to this cold bastard, and he didn't know it yet. Maria wanted to go home, pack a bag and leave town with Daryl. She could persuade him. She knew she could persuade him to do anything. She would leave Paul behind. Let him keep his money.

And yet the hurt remained.

And not just the pain. The fear of starting all over again, with no money, and a partner who barely made his rent through waiting tables, surfing and diving lessons. She had given up her career, such as it was. There was no work for her in Port Lonely other than waiting tables or popping beer bottle caps and pouring bourbon in a Port Lonely bar. Her tears came again, and she felt afraid. Was it worth risking her security for a chance to be happy with Daryl, with a man who *really* loved her? Paul wouldn't leave her hungry, but at the same time, he had hidden a great wealth and would have kept it from her for the rest of her life. She was certain of that.

Maria hit her turn signal, and slowly pulled over onto the shoulder. She stopped the car. The rain fell hard now. It was a deafening sound as it hammered the roof of the car. Maria gave in to the tears. She needed to let it out. The car shook from Maria's sobbing, and the relentless pounding of the rainstorm.

She would be happy with Daryl, but terribly afraid of where the next dollar would come from. A perilous existence beckoned with him, one that she didn't know if she could get through, no matter how much they loved each other. On the other hand, Paul and security and a miserable loneliness.

Perhaps there was a way for her to have Daryl, *and* some kind of financial security. To ask her to make such a choice seemed unfair to Maria.

There had to be a way to have both.

CHAPTER TEN

Paul paced the first floor of his office in Port Lonely. He stopped every few seconds when he heard a car outside and gazed down to the street through the wooden blinds. His office also overlooked the marina. The chop bobbed the boats moored at both piers. Radio said a storm front would arrive at four o'clock. The wind was sure picking up. The waves were gaining height and the sky looked dark with the promise of rain. It was almost four.

A gray Cadillac pulled up outside. A woman with long blonde hair got out of the driver's seat and gazed up at the window.

Josephine Schneider. Paul drew away from the window and heard the intercom buzz. He pressed the button to open the door down-stairs. He never locked his office door. There was nothing below him on the ground floor, only the entrance and a staircase. The store below him had its own entrance and no access to this floor. It had long ago closed down – a 7-Eleven. Paul bought it and shut it a year ago. He wanted quiet when he was working.

Josephine's boots thumped up the stairs. She always wore knee-high leather boots. It was kind of her thing. She came through the door in a cloud of Christian Dior perfume and flowing blonde hair. She kissed him on the cheek, and they hugged. He was always surprised by the strength of her embrace. Releasing him, she stood back, looked him up and down and said, 'You haven't been eating, sweetie.'

'I'm fine, Josephine. Well, actually, I'm pretty far from fine, but it's nothing to do with my weight.'

'Oh, darling, what a total nightmare,' she said.

Moving past him, Josephine dumped a white shopping bag by the couch in his office, followed by her handbag and then her gray cashmere coat. As usual, she was dressed for all occasions. Black skirt, black leather boots, dark blouse.

Keeping a secret was like holding on to a weight. Paul had only ever shared his secret with one other person – Josephine. She didn't know the whole story, but she knew enough. As Paul's literary agent, she had to know. And being able to share that secret with one other person had helped to lighten that burden, just a fraction.

'Thank you for coming down. I . . . there's no one else I can talk to about this.'

Waving a hand at Paul, Josephine tutted. He didn't hear her over the jangle of the gold bracelets on her wrist.

'Darling, you're my most important client. And this is a mess. Of course I'm going to be here.'

Josephine had been raised in a wealthy family on the Upper West Side of Manhattan and she sounded like it – perfect pitch with a hint of sarcasm underlying the tone. And when she spoke her hands did the same amount of work as her mouth. Long pink fingernails flashed and stabbed at the air with almost every syllable.

As Paul spoke he massaged his temples, using his index finger and thumb. He often did this. His skull doubled as a stress ball.

'Just tell me what happened,' said Josephine.

He told her about the break-in at the house. Maria being assaulted by the intruder. His private desk broken up – maybe important documents missing, notes or at worst a bank statement. And then the note that had been left on his windshield.

'You're right on the money. Someone *has* tracked you down. How much does Maria know?' she said.

'Nothing,' said Paul.

'Nothing? Like, *nothing*? You've never told her?'

He shook his head.

'My God, I mean, it's your marriage and everything but I thought when you got hitched and moved out here you would tell her,' said Josephine, her eyebrows shooting up her forehead. She reached for her bag, took out a pack of cigarettes, lit one and then offered one to Paul.

He made a point of not smoking in this office. Occasionally he lit up a cigarette in his study at home, but he'd been trying to cut down and he knew if he started smoking in this room he wouldn't stop. He'd have the place smelling like a 1930s jazz club in a week. All the same, he didn't stop Josephine, and took the cigarette she offered. He needed one to calm down. Lighting him up with the same gold-plated lighter, Josephine settled into the couch and waited for an answer. Paul took a drag on the cigarette and paced as he talked.

'I didn't tell her because I love her. In the beginning I couldn't tell her. I didn't know her. As we got closer I thought about it. By then it was too late. Plus, it's too dangerous. What if she let it slip someday, by accident. Or worse, on purpose.'

'What did you tell her you do for a living?'

'I told her I was a marketing consultant. Good excuse to get out of the house and write. I tell her I'm meeting clients. Then I can go out on the boat, or come here.'

'She doesn't know about this place?'

'No. I'd like to keep it that way. Maria has everything that she needs. I make sure of that. If I'd told her she would've wanted to use some of the money. I know she would. That kind of spending draws attention. May as well hang a sign outside the house. Maria likes to spend money, too. It's important to her. She likes having financial security. Something to do with her past, I guess. She grew up poor.'

They fell into silence. Just the pop and breath of smoke breaking on their lips, and the sound of Paul's heels on the floorboards.

'Two things I need to know. How did this get out in the first place? And second, what the hell am I gonna do about it?' said Paul, fixing Josephine with a stare as he spoke.

'I sincerely hope that wasn't an accusation,' said Josephine.

The thought had crossed his mind.

'You don't trust me? After everything we've been through?' said Josephine.

She hadn't been through all of it. Not like Paul.

She wasn't responsible for the lives that had been taken. She had no idea what that was like. He'd kept some things from her. For obvious reasons.

'Do you have any new staff? Any new computer systems? Any cyber attacks?' said Paul.

Josephine acted not only as Paul's literary agent, but as a buffer. The money coming from LeBeau Enterprises would be lifted by Paul, in cash, in person, and filtered through his client account at Schneider and Associates. The tax advantages alone made Josephine's fifteen percent cut worthwhile.

'No. There's just no way. All your information is stored on my laptop. No one has the password for that laptop but me. It's my secure workspace. My work goes through my office computer. That laptop is for our business alone. It's on a private network with my machine as the only device. It's totally secure.'

'Then how the hell is it that I've been found after all this time?' said Paul.

Josephine crossed her legs, dropped the butt of her cigarette into a coffee cup and blew out a plume of smoke as she said, 'Don't ask me. I'm here because we had planned for this day. I'm going to get you out of here. Get you somewhere safe. I've got your seed money in my bag. Twenty grand. Should be enough to get you started someplace else.'

'What's the point of running if I don't know how I got tracked down in the first place? Someone has been talking, Josephine. Someone at your agency. I don't know who, but it had to come from somewhere.'

'That's not possible. There must have been some other leak along the chain. The bank?'

Like a coin that had been spun on a table, the rotations in Paul's head were slowing down – the coin wobbling, then falling over and settling still and flat. Paul's breath returned, his nerve endings dulled.

It could have been the bank. He shouldn't jump to conclusions. There was really only one way to tell for sure.

'I'm going to take the emergency cash you brought, and I'm going to disappear. Don't take it personally, but I'm not going to tell anyone where I'm going. That okay with you?'

'Fine by me, but what about Maria?' said Josephine.

'If I go, she should be fine. I'm the target.'

Josephine sighed, gave him a look that made him feel ten years old.

'No, Paul. I meant, what the hell are you going to tell Maria? You're married to this girl, remember?'

Their wedding day had been a small affair. Courthouse wedding. One guest. Maria had one friend who acted as bridesmaid and witness. He didn't think she had seen her since. A meal in a high-class restaurant afterward. No speeches, no confetti, no fuss. Just the way he liked it. Paul felt close to Maria. Closer than he was to any other human being. And yet still there was distance. Distance that he'd created and maintained.

'I have to leave. I can't take her with me. We'd be too easy to track. She has access to the domestic account – there's close to twenty grand or so. And she has the house. When I get clear I'll find a way to send her some more money. The house is worth four hundred thou, so I'll clear the mortgage and send her an extra hundred grand. That should be enough for anyone.'

'She won't have you,' said Josephine.

'She never really had me to begin with. I'm not sure anyone can. She won't have to watch her back for the rest of her life either. I love her as much as I can love anyone, and I couldn't bear it if something happened to her. She can't be involved in this. It's too dangerous,' said Paul.

'I understand, but that's cold. You should tell her.'

He rounded on Josephine, an edge to his voice now. 'Tell her what? That she never really knew the man she married? And by the way – *goodbye forever?* I can't—'

'She deserves an explanation.'

'I've given her all I can. I can't tell her. No one can know.'

Josephine sighed.

'When are you gonna split?'

'Tomorrow. I need time to clean up a few things then I'm gone. I'll call again before I go. You need to do a full sweep of your office. I know you don't want to but just indulge me, okay?'

Raising her hands in defeat, Josephine said, 'I'll check things out my end, but I don't think anyone got to you though me. There's no way,'

He was going to go home. To plan. To pack. Tomorrow he was going to walk away from his life and everything in it. He told himself Maria would be okay, in time. He would leave her a note saying she would be safer without him. Probably happier too. Paul had felt her drifting away from him in the last few months. A cold, invisible mist hung between them. This may have been his fault for being away so much. The effect of his absence was not increasing her affection toward him. It was doing the opposite. Perhaps neither of them was suited to this marriage.

When he'd first met Maria, he had been sure she was the woman he'd always dreamed of. The one. There had been others before her whom he'd imbued with that same messianic title. And sure enough they'd proven themselves to be false prophets, with one exception, but she was gone now. And part of Paul went with her. He didn't think he could love again, until he met Maria. He knew it then, and he still felt it now. Perhaps he'd changed. He knew she had changed. The move to Port Lonely had been jarring. She loved the house, and the beach, but hated the town. She couldn't seem to appreciate it in the way Paul did. She didn't see the richness of character in the people. Maria saw only that there was no mall, no nightclubs, everything shut around ten-thirty, including the bars, and she couldn't walk along the street without everyone believing she was an outsider.

Which she was, of course. The chill that had accompanied her classification didn't add to the charm of the place for her. She wanted to leave in the first month. Paul wouldn't let her, and that day he saw in her, for the first time, the look of incredulity. She couldn't believe he wanted to stay in Port Lonely. Paul had spent a little time there, some years before, with a woman he had been seeing. It was special to her, and so it became special to Paul. When he was in the town he somehow felt close to his old self. Maybe that had made him disconnect from Maria, somehow. The rift began not long after they moved here. And in the months that followed the tear in the corner of their relationship began to widen with his work, and distance and time itself. Maybe he was only speeding up the inevitable.

Yes, we weren't going to last anyway, he told himself.

Every exotic bird has to leave the cage at some stage, otherwise it's cruel.

Paul could be cruel. He had to be to survive with his secret intact. He would let his little bird of paradise go free no matter how much it hurt him.

There was simply no other way.

Josephine stood, straightened out her outfit and left an envelope filled with cash on the couch.

'I guess that's it then. I should go. You have a lot to plan,' she said.

He walked her down the stairs to the front door. There was a camera on the wall to the right of the door. He checked it. The screen showed both sides of the street. A few cars were parked along the curb. A few that Paul recognized. He was used to the local cars now. Always kept an eye out to see who was in the neighborhood. If he saw a car that he didn't recognize in the street more than once he would make a note of the license plate. Usually within a week or two he would figure out who the car belonged to. And then all was well again.

He only gave the camera a quick glance. Nothing suspicious on the street this time.

Paul opened the door, and the rain hit them both full in the face. From her bag, Josephine produced an umbrella, spread it open and began to wrestle with it in the doorway as it was caught by gusts of wind. Taking hold of her arm, and helping to steady the umbrella, Paul walked out with Josephine, turned a corner and headed for the rental car parked just off Marina Street.

In some ways he felt like a kid escorting a benevolent aunt to her car after Thanksgiving.

Josephine had promised to look after him. And she'd made good on that promise. Here she was, in a flash, with emergency money and a smile.

The umbrella bowed and swayed in the blustery shower, and didn't provide much cover. Josephine unlocked the car with the fob key, and the lights flashed through the rain. She opened the driver's door, threw her bag in the car, collapsed the umbrella. She gave Paul a hug.

'Be careful. And don't worry about delivering the next book for a while. Get settled somewhere then let me know you're okay. Take a week. Then get writing. That's what you're good at,' said Josephine. She cupped his face in one hand, kissed him lightly on the cheek, then got in the car. Paul closed her door. Watched her drive away and then went back inside, out of the rain.

CHAPTER ELEVEN

Maria drove through the tears and the rain.

When she drove past the sign that read 'Welcome to Port Lonely' she wondered how she'd gotten back so quickly. Her mind had been filled with so many turbulent thoughts that she had little or no memory of the drive. She'd gotten there on autopilot.

Her throat hurt from crying. She pulled over at the gas station, bought some cigarettes and a Diet Coke and then drove to the marina. The Coke helped her throat. It was cold and soothing. Cracking the window, she lit a cigarette, took a drag and felt the burn again at the back of her throat. She washed the pain away with more soda. Fat pearls of rain dripped into the car from the open window, spreading dark pools of water droplets across the knee and thigh of her jeans.

There was no good outcome. No solution that would make things alright again. Her world had tilted and everything would be different from now on. She thought she knew Paul. Trusted him. All along she had felt he wasn't like the others. He was honest. Quiet. Damaged. He had baggage that he couldn't talk about. God knows, Maria had baggage too. In some strange way, for a while at least, they'd made each other whole.

Things change.

She would leave him. She would be with Daryl. Whatever she got in the divorce, it would be enough. Probably half of the money in the joint account. Ten grand, and maybe a small share of the house. She would tell him about Daryl. Explain what happened, tell him she was lonely and that she had fallen in love with someone else. She didn't want much in return. The thought of coming clean, and leaving this godforsaken town with money in her pocket, filled her with a new kind of excitement. Holding hands and kissing Daryl in public – unashamed and unafraid. And in love. She would take ten grand then and there and never look back.

Enough to get started again. And if he said no, then she would pull the J. T. LeBeau card. Threaten to expose him. No way he would risk that for a measly ten grand. Thinking about that confrontation set her skin alive with goosebumps. Excited, and afraid. That was the easiest way to get out of there fast. And yet the thought of Paul hiding all that wealth from her made her stomach turn. She had given up everything to be with him and there was no easy way to build that life again. The soda can screeched and she realized she'd crushed it. Cola ran over her fingers, making them sticky.

She was afraid. And angry. And one fed off the other.

It wasn't fair. Not fair at all.

The rain eased a little, and she looked around the town. Then out to sea. She knew one thing for certain. No way was she going to miss this place. She couldn't wait to get away. That's if she could persuade Daryl to quit his job and move.

Lights flashed. Someone unlocking a car. Maria turned, casually, toward the only activity in view. It was a car, maybe fifty feet ahead of her and on the side street. She saw a blonde woman struggling with an umbrella.

A man walked beside her.

The woman put the umbrella in her car. She wore black leather boots, and a beautiful coat. Women in this town knew how to dress expensively. Maria thought she recognized something about the man with her. She hit the windshield wipers. Once.

Once was enough.

The woman embraced Paul, touched his face. Maria's breath caught in her throat. Such an intimate gesture. One born of a long relationship, trust and naked affection.

She got in her car and drove away.

Paul walked to the end of the street, then turned the corner and disappeared.

She knew then that there was more than one reason why Paul was away so much. From the look of that car, it was brand new. A hundred grand for a new model SUV like that. She didn't recognize the woman. She was richly attired. Pretty. Blonde.

The pounding sound in her ears came from her heart. She could feel it pulsing at her throat. First time she was ever aware of her heartbeat.

Maria put the car in gear, pulled straight out into the road from the parking bay to the sound of a horn behind her. She'd pulled out in front of another car. She saw it now in her rear-view mirror, the driver shaking two fingers and mouthing obscenities. Maria didn't care. She stood on the accelerator, raced to the bottom of the street. No sign of Paul. He couldn't have driven away. In fact, she saw his car, empty, parked across the way in the lot reserved for the marina.

She turned at the junction, drove away fast and kept her foot on the gas until she got to the parking lot at Mariner's Point four minutes later. It was a jagged spike of rock, jutting into the sea, with a path worn by many feet to the end of the rock and the roaring white water below it. Maria's car was the only one in the lot. The rainstorm kept everyone else away. Maria got out of the car, ignored the rain whipping through her clothes, soaking her hair, her makeup, her feet. She threw a leg over the barrier that prevented visitors from walking out to the end of the point. She took five steps, felt the wash from a wave crashing against the rock. Tasted the salt on her lips.

Maria bent over, put her hands on her knees and screamed.

The fear was gone.

Only anger remained.

CHAPTER TWELVE

Four lazy hours into his shift at the country club bar, Daryl saw her.

He'd been uncomfortable since that morning. He didn't like the direction Maria was taking this. She'd told him that morning she was on her way to see a lawyer. Someone in an out-of-town practice. When he'd begun seeing her, the last thing on his mind was Maria getting a divorce, but things change. People change. Maybe he could steer her out of that mindset. Maybe part of him didn't want to do that. It was a delicate situation. That much Daryl could comprehend.

The bar at the club could've been a replica of a hundred bars in a hundred different country clubs. Oak paneling on the walls. Bad oil paintings of golfers. Worse oil paintings of landscapes. And dotted around the bar were antique five-irons, deer heads and dull silver trophies locked in glass cabinets. Leather studded benches and chairs sat around dark tables. Scotch sold well, and the older the better. Wives lunched together – picking over their food and complaining about their terrible husbands. The husbands drank together and bitched about their wives.

The only people of color were those serving the members. An old-school rural American nightmare. And despite the wealth of the members, not one of them would lay out a decent tip even if their knees depended on it.

Daryl pulled down the front of his waistcoat and collected some more glasses from the tables, stacking them tall in the crook of his arm. He leaned over a table, turned when he saw movement at the entrance to the bar and caught a glimpse of a lady talking to Aaron – the deputy bar manager.

He'd collected more glasses than he could comfortably carry, so he set down a stack and began to clean the tables he'd just cleared with a cloth and antibacterial spray. While he cleaned, he watched. She wore a long pink blouse. Maybe too long for a short lady like her. A tight perm made her hair look like a crash helmet she could take off and set down on the stool beside her.

The lady was familiar. Maybe he'd seen her before, maybe not. He couldn't pin her down for a long time. Only when he saw the notebook emerge from her purse as she sat at the bar did he make the connection because only two types of people make notes in that kind of notebook, having that kind of conversation – journalists and cops.

She was no journo.

Sue. Yes, that was her name. Sue. Or Mary Sue. One or the other or both. They all sounded the same to him. She worked with the Port Lonely Sheriff's Office. He'd seen her before, coming out of that building on Main Street and getting into her car. She was leaning over the bar, listening closely to Aaron. Whispering. Making notes.

There had been no incidents at the club. No thefts. No damage to club property and no fights in the bar. Sue was there to find out more about Maria. He felt sure of it. At some moment, Aaron would mention his name to her, and then he'd turn and point at him. His boss never missed a trick – Aaron had caught sight of him talking to Maria a bunch of times. Even made a joke out of it, but it was a joke with a jag at the end.

'We provide a service to the members, Daryl. We're not here to service them.'

Not even a good joke.

He took the glasses past the bar, hiding his face behind the stack, and went into the kitchen and placed them on the bench. Checked his watch. Another eight hours to go before the end of his shift. He heard the bar manager, Tom, talking to the head chef in the kitchen about an order for lemons and limes. Bending low, he opened the dishwasher, loaded up the empties and put it on a cycle.

His phone buzzed in his pocket. Maria. He let it ring out.

It gave him an idea of how to get out of there. Making his way further into the kitchen, he found Tom standing with the head chef at the pass, comparing order sheets.

'Hey Tommy, I just got a call on my cell. Family emergency. You mind if I take a personal day?'

'We're covered for tonight. Go do what you gotta do and I'll see you Monday,' said Tom.

Turning swiftly, Daryl thanked Tom, then took off his bow tie and opened his collar as he cut through the kitchen to the back door. In the back parking lot he found his car, and thankfully there wasn't a delivery truck parked in front of it, blocking his exit. He got into the car and drove out of the lot.

Taking the back streets, he avoided most of Main Street before finally turning onto it and then off it again when he came to a parking lot. The rain came on strong now. Hammering the car. He killed the engine. The rain followed the dark clouds like a promise.

He took out his cell and called Maria back.

'Hi, how's—' he began, but she cut him off. Maria spoke in between gasps of air. Her voice trembling and her throat thick from crying.

'Paul has been seeing someone else,' she said.

There was nothing he could say in return that wouldn't sound hollow and hypocritical. He wanted to go to her. Hold her. Calm her down and tell her everything would be alright, that *he* was there for her all the way.

He didn't get the chance. All he could do was listen to her crying. He tried to talk to her. Softly at first. Then, when she either couldn't or wouldn't hear him, he stopped. And just listened. After a while, her breathing slowed, the powerful tremor in her voice abated.

'I want to come and see you. Where are you?' said Daryl.

The stuttered breath returned. 'No, I can't see anyone. I need some time. I . . . I have to *process* this. Understand it. I don't trust Paul. I don't even know him anymore. I . . . I need you to . . . to . . . do something for me.'

'Anything,' said Daryl, instantly.

'I need you to follow Paul. His car is in the marina lot, but he's not out on his boat. He's here, in Port Lonely. Follow him. Tell me what he does. He'll see my car and he'll know it's me. I need *you* to do this. Please. I can't take this anymore.'

'Okay, okay, just breathe. Take it easy. I'll watch his car. I'll follow him. Keep an eye on what he does. Just please don't do anything stupid, okay? I . . .' He hesitated, but only for a second. 'I need you, Maria.'

She hung up. Daryl started the engine, drove to the lot at the marina and found Paul's Maserati. He parked a good fifty feet away, killed the engine and watched the car through the rain streaming down his windshield. He thought of Maria, and how strong she could be. Some women would have gone straight for their husband's throat, justifiably so. Maria always had a cool head. She wanted ammunition. She wanted to gather whatever she could and then go after the bastard.

Smart lady.

Daryl saw Paul making his way toward the car, his coat gathered up around his neck, an umbrella bending and twisting in the wind. He waited until the Maserati left the lot, then Daryl followed. He kept his distance as the car turned onto Main Street, drove through the town and out toward the coast road leading to the house. Daryl couldn't stop at Paul's house, and there was no cover for the car. He was reasonably sure that's where Paul was headed, so he made a left turn at the beach and parked in the lot. Thankfully, the rain had eased.

Stepping out of the car he caught the scent of rain, the ocean and a face full of sand-flecked gusts. From the trunk he retrieved a weatherproof jacket. He put it on then lifted clear a black leather hold-all and slung it over one shoulder, then the other. Throwing up his hood to shelter from the wind, Daryl set off toward the beach. It was cold now. The wind unforgiving in such an exposed area.

Despite the conditions he trekked up the beach. A half-hour passed before he saw Maria's house. Paul's Maserati was parked outside the house and Maria's car wasn't in the driveway. That was the first thing he noticed. Second thing he saw was Paul through the bedroom window of the house that looked out over the ocean. The beach looked deserted and Daryl took a knee behind the ridge that separated the grassland from the sand dunes. Reaching into his hold-all, he removed an old pair of binoculars he sometimes used for bird watching, and focused them on the house. Paul stared down at the bed, leaned over and adjusted something, then moved away to the closet. He returned with a pile of folded jeans in his hand, bent over the bed and disappeared from view for a second before straightening up again and then leaving the room.

Lowering the binoculars, Daryl scanned the house looking for any sign of movement. The side door opened and Paul left the house, dragging a large suitcase behind him. The automatic lid release on the trunk activated before Paul could walk around the car. He then heaved the case inside, touched a button on the trunk and as it slowly descended Paul went back inside. Soon after, the lights came on in the kitchen. Paul went to the fridge, collected some items and placed them on the counter. He took a chopping knife from a board and started to work.

Daryl had only eaten at Maria's once before. She said she didn't cook. Couldn't cook. Paul must've done the cooking, when he was home of course. Only thing she could manage to put on the table without burning it was spaghetti. He told her he liked spaghetti. She steamed and swore her way around the kitchen and twenty minutes later produced a plate of spaghetti with tomato sauce from a can.

Daryl smiled and ate it and told her it was good. It wasn't.

He fished his cell phone from his pocket. Maria calling. He picked up.

'Hi, where are you?' she said, in a raw, pitchy voice. He could tell she'd been crying again.

'I'm on the beach. Paul's home,' he said.

Right then, Daryl didn't want to say more. She was hurting, and that made her volatile in his mind.

'What's he doing? Anything out of the ordinary?'

He sighed. No choice but to tell her. No easy way to break it. He just had to come out with it.

'He's just packed a bag and put it in his car. Looks like your note on the windshield spooked him. No doubt about it now. He's J. T. LeBeau. Real and in the flesh,' he said.

'I'll be there in twenty minutes. Thanks for this,' she said in a way that didn't sound thankful. He could hear the words catching in her throat – tears and a flood of pain threatening to drown each sentence. Daryl could hear the car in the background. Heard it accelerating, eating up the road. She was on speaker phone. 'You didn't, ahm, *talk* to him or anything?'

'Course not. You want me to wait around in case there's trouble?'

'No. There'll be no trouble,' she said. Daryl could tell by the tone that she wasn't sure.

'You don't have to go home, you know. I could meet you at our favorite spot. I'll bring a six-pack and a bottle of red, and we could stay out all night. We should be together,' he said.

He let Maria take in that offer. Waited for her, patiently. When she finally spoke, he heard her through a fresh blanket of tears.

'No . . . it's fine. Thank you. I love you so much. I'll call you,' she said, and hung up.

Stretching his legs, Daryl pushed the cramp from his calves, and then stood. He put away his binoculars and his cell and started back to his car. He drove to the marina, got into his boat. This wasn't like the cruiser that Paul had, it was smaller and older. Daryl had bought it cheap and fixed it up so he could take people on diving classes, make a little money on the side. The storm prevented him leaving the marina. He'd be risking his life taking the boat into this chop. Instead, he put on his wetsuit, loaded up a fresh tank of air and slipped over the side. The thought of the police asking questions in the bar unsettled him. It could either be a starting point or a finishing point in their investigation. The more he thought about it, the more he came to believe the cop was just getting general background on Maria and Paul. They might want to talk to him, as he served Maria more often than not when she came into the club. And Paul never came to the bar. Maybe that would be a line of inquiry – maybe not. For now, all Daryl wanted to do was be in the cold, dark waters. There was a perfect solitude in the deep. Down where all the monsters lived.

CHAPTER THIRTEEN

A makeup bag in the glove compartment had come to Maria's rescue a number of times. She'd parked a few hundred yards from the house, in the entrance to a disused lane that led to old farm land long since sold to developers who'd done nothing more than let the land run wild. The crying she'd done in the past twenty-four hours had swollen her eyes, and that last statement from Daryl had made the tears flow once more.

She looked in the rear-view mirror, checked her lipstick and eyes – declared it a decent repair job.

Deep breaths. Four or five of them. And then she pulled out onto the coast road and within seconds found herself at the house. All that day she'd been thinking about the place as *the house*. It struck her that she'd nearly always referred to it that way. Not once had she ever called the place *home*.

She saw him through the side window, cooking dinner in the kitchen.

More deep breaths.

She got out of the car, locked it and went into the house.

He was playing music. Classical. Not something to her taste but she'd gotten used to it. It was the kind of music Maria could simply zone out – as if it were background noise. Her footsteps on the wooden floor rang out her arrival. When her heels touched the hard white tiles of the kitchen Paul swung around, startled, the knife in his hand, his face glazed in fear.

'It's me,' she said.

His turn with the deep breaths and a hand on his chest. Paul's lips curled into a smile which quickly faded into a stern expression. Not anger. Concern, maybe.

'You're soaked through. Where have you been all day? I was worried,' he said.

If he had been worried he'd clearly gotten over it, thought Maria. He didn't ask how she was doing? If she was alright? He didn't approach her for a hug, or a kiss. The bastard didn't care about her at all.

The silence sounded like an alarm bell.

'I've been thinking things over, Paul. That was no ordinary burglar in the house last night. What did he really want?' said Maria.

Swinging the knife in his hands, absently, Paul ignored the question at first.

'I'm scared, and I want you to tell me the truth,' she said, firmly. Even with the power of those words, Maria struggled to get them out straight through her fluttering chest.

He put down the knife, came toward her and placed his fingers, lightly, on her shoulders. Maria shrugged them off, folded her arms, set her lips together and bored her gaze into his like she was drilling through steel.

'I don't know who it was, or what they were after. I promise you, I *don't*. It was just a burglar, and you scared him off before he could take anything. That's all.'

'You're hiding something,' she said, softly.

'I would never hide anything from you,' he said, and kissed her.

She could taste the lie on his lips – bitter and salty. She pulled away, went upstairs. Every nerve ending screamed at her to confront him.

Just tell him you know!

She opened their bedroom door, went to the nightstand on her side of the bed and opened the top drawer. If Daryl hadn't told her about Paul packing a case, she probably wouldn't have come home at all. But she had to. She had to check. The plastic strip of contraceptive pills lay on top of her passport. She picked up the strip of pills, and her passport, and saw the bottom of the drawer beneath it where Paul's passport normally lay. It was there yesterday. She'd seen it when she lifted her pills. It had gone.

This confirmed it. He was leaving her. The suitcase in his car, his passport. He was running away and leaving her behind. The money, the blonde who'd stroked his face. That touch wasn't a goodbye – it was a touch that meant she would see him again soon. That their parting was only temporary. He would go back to his house, pack up and leave the wife behind. He had another life to lead.

Son of a bitch.

She bit her lip, too hard, and drew blood.

For a woman as strong as Maria – it hadn't taken much effort for Paul to control her. All of her.

Her finances.

Her house.

Her feelings.

Her body.

She stripped and went into the shower. For a long time she let the hot water sting her skin, willing that heat to empty her mind. It didn't. She got out of the shower, dried her hair with a towel which she then wrapped around her body. Maria returned to the bedroom, threw up the duvet and climbed into bed, covering her head with the pillow. For a long time she cried, and moaned with anger into the soft mattress. She wanted to go downstairs and hit him. Scream at him. Tell him that she knew who he was. She'd seen through all of his bullshit.

He called up the stairs once or twice, asking if she was okay. If she wanted dinner. If she wanted water. Then he told her he was going away in the morning. Only for a few days.

The calls went without answer. And he stopped calling. He didn't come up to see her and Maria was at first hurt by that, and then felt differently. In her mind, Maria began the process of untangling her feelings from Paul. She had given him love. And he had given nothing of himself to her. She had to take that back. Gather those last threads of affection lodged in memories, in time and objects.

She took off her wedding ring and engagement ring. The gold band felt light and cheap in her hand. The engagement ring cost a few thousand dollars – a pittance when seen in contrast to Paul's real wealth. She squeezed the rings in the palm of her hand, as if she was trying to remove the last sentiments of happiness from them.

The night closed in.

Maria waited. In that time, she used her phone to read every article she could find on J. T. LeBeau. She wanted to know everything. Understand who this man was – this man that she had married, this stranger in her life.

At four a.m. she got out of bed, and padded downstairs in her bare feet.

Paul slept on the couch, just as before. A half-eaten plate of food on the floor beside him. Maria stepped lightly into the hallway, gently picked up Paul's car keys from a bowl on the hall table. The table housed stacks of mail, all opened and neatly arranged by Paul. Silently, she approached the front door.

The lock gave only the faintest of clicks as it opened. She slid out of the house, and felt the hard stones on the soles of her feet as she slowly made her way to Paul's car. A flash of light and the metallic thud of the locking system disengaging. She pressed the fob button for the trunk, and watched as it silently rose. Quickly, Maria opened the side pocket of Paul's case, removed his passport. She zipped up the pocket, closed the trunk and locked the car.

She skipped over the stones to the front door, held her breath for a moment. There was no sound other than the sea. Curling her body around the front door, she went back inside and held her breath again while she pushed the door closed. For what seemed like a minute, she lowered Paul's car keys into the basket on the hall table – careful that they made no sound. As she passed the open door to the living room, she heard him snore loudly. He hadn't moved.

Back in bed, Maria lit up her phone and typed out a text message to Daryl.

Once she'd written it, she stared at it for a long time, willing herself to believe it, to let it sink in that this was now reality – this was really happening.

She didn't know her husband. He'd taken her and consumed her and now he was throwing her away. Maria was not going to allow it, and yet it took her a full half-hour before she had the nerve to hit send.

My marriage is over. I'm going to need your help.

The reply came in after five minutes. A low vibration on the mattress.

Whatever it is, I'll do it. I'd do anything for you.

Guardian

Who is J. T. LeBeau?
And why should you care?
by Jeremy Frumpton

The first J. T. LeBeau novel didn't stand a chance, all things considered. It had a bad title – *Twist*. Generic, even for a thriller. The title was one which the publisher wasn't fond of at all, according to anonymous sources from the publishing house that released his first book. They had bought the book for chump change, put zero dollars into marketing or promoting it, the cover looked appalling, and the original editor who had acquired the book, Bob Crenshaw, passed away not long after its initial release, but long enough to see the beginnings of what was to come.

Despite its lack of pedigree, the book started to sell. This was unexpected, as the book came out to no fanfare with an initial print run of only a thousand copies.

What happened was something unpredictable. A few people bought it. And they loved it. And they told people about it. So more people bought it. And very soon the magic thing, which happens to so few books, started to take hold.

Word of mouth.

Nothing sells a book like it. There are certain books which get people talking. That doesn't mean it's a book the reader falls in love with, it's a book which once finished, the reader presses into the hands of their friends and colleagues so that they can talk about it at the water-cooler or over coffee. When that happens, the book spreads like a virus.

Initially, very few bookstores took *Twist*. But the ones that did sold out. And they ordered more. Their customers talked about the book. Discussed it at book clubs, recommended it online and slowly but surely a tiny fanbase began to grow. More bookstores ordered it when they saw the sales numbers increase. And over time the book began to have a life. On its fourth printing of thirty thousand copies, eight months after initial release, the editor who had been saddled with the book after Bob Crenshaw died, finally read it.

They tried contacting the author to see if they would partake in some promotional work – maybe a small tour or a couple of interviews with online publications. The author refused, point blank, and stated that they wanted to maintain their privacy. According to an interview with that editor, they decided the author was a prize asshole who would never make it in the business and they wanted nothing more to do with him.

Word of mouth about the book continued to spread. Readers were careful not to give anything away, but they seemed compelled to press the book into the hands of their friends once they'd finished. There was nothing to talk about when it came to the author, as they had never revealed themselves to the public.

On the tenth time of printing, at one hundred thousand copies, the editor was informed by the publishing director that it didn't matter if the author was an asshole – the house had a hit on its hands and they needed another book.

The editor emailed J. T. LeBeau.

Three months later another book arrived with another killer twist.

The initial print run of LeBeau's second book was two hundred and fifty thousand copies. This one sold better than the first. Same reason.

An article in *The New Yorker* tried to proclaim that the real author of the J. T. LeBeau novels was Ken Follett. Mr. Follett regretfully denied the moniker, but this was just the start. Over the next ten years the novels kept coming, the contracts kept being signed, the author remained a ghost, the sales kept increasing and the press ramped up the conspiracy theories and detective work in an effort to track down the elusive J. T. LeBeau.

The various suspects who were alleged to be J. T. LeBeau included Stephen King, John Grisham, Jodi Picoult, J. K. Rowling, who was eventually revealed to be Robert Galbraith, and even James Patterson.

The speculation continued. The books kept coming. One a year. Each one just as good if not better than the last.

Publishing gold.

Then the lawsuits started coming in – another marker for success.

Half a dozen authors claimed J. T. LeBeau had stolen their books, outlines, ideas and/or characters. None of the lawsuits got anywhere. The publishers were able to produce the time- and date-stamped emails and without fail they were always earlier than the works which claimed to have been copied.

One lawsuit got pretty far, backed by a newspaper. The newspaper knew the lawsuit was bogus, but they fed it long enough to get it to the first day of a hearing because what they really wanted was to see J. T. LeBeau being called to the stand. Didn't happen of course, the lawyers managed to get the case dismissed on the evidence of the editors at the house and the emails alone.

After that expensive mistake, the lawsuits died out.

The interest in the real identity of J. T. LeBeau only increased.

The National Book Award, the Edgar Award, the Theakstons Old Peculier Crime Novel of the Year award, the Anthony award, the Crime Writers Association Gold Dagger, not even a Pulitzer was enough to tempt J. T. LeBeau out of hiding and onto a stage to make an acceptance speech.

He never showed.

So who cares about this mysterious, hermetic writer, anyway? Isn't it enough that we have the books?

Yes.

And no.

You see, the only person in publishing that we know of who met J. T. LeBeau was the late Bob Crenshaw. By all accounts, a man who had a drink and drug problem and was estranged from his family and friends. The sad tale of Bob Crenshaw, who died before he could see his greatest success spring fully to life, was perhaps a salutary warning to the then inexperienced LeBeau. Perhaps he saw the disintegration of his editor, and knew then that he should keep his personal life separate from his writing life.

We can only guess, but untimely demise of Bob Crenshaw must have had an impact on LeBeau.

He wrote about it, in a subsequent novel called *The Burning Man*. Of course, the facts were changed, but the death of the character in that novel bore striking similarities to the death of his editor.

Bob Crenshaw didn't overdose, but it is believed by the NYPD that his death surrounded a drug deal gone wrong.

Bob Crenshaw burned alive, locked in the trunk of his car.

It is perhaps this violent death that pushed the shy LeBeau to become a recluse. We may never know the real story behind the elusive, anonymous writer whose work is beloved by millions of adoring fans the world over.

CHAPTER FOURTEEN

Six-thirty on a Sunday morning seemed as good a time as any for Paul to leave his wife. He'd thought about it over and over. There was no *good* time to do it. He just had to grit his teeth and rip off the Band-Aid.

No choice.

If he stayed, more people would die. And Paul didn't want to kill anyone.

Not anymore. Still, he would take the Smith and Wesson with him. Better to have it close, just in case.

He got up off the couch, stretched and went immediately to the kitchen where he found a pen and paper. All last night he'd debated whether to go up to the bedroom and talk to her. She deserved more. She deserved better. Paul had vacillated over what to put in a note, and even if there should be a note at all.

Eventually he decided he couldn't leave without saying goodbye. He would leave a note. And he would be honest, to an extent, in what he said.

It took a few minutes to write. He left it there on the kitchen counter with the pen resting on the page and closed the front door behind him before the ink was dry. He got into his car, reversed onto the road and drove toward town and the marina. The thought of being away from it all was intoxicating. Simply being on the ocean, in his boat, gave him immediate emotional distance, as well as physical distance. Something happened to his brain on the water – it was as if he was free of the social constructs that would restrain him on land. On the ocean there were few rules, and responsibilities were an island he'd left behind.

Yet he knew that in the weeks and months to come he would feel the weight of what he'd done. She didn't know he had another life. A writer's life. Solitary, insular, shut off from the world completely. She didn't know about the money. She couldn't know.

That was the deal. Tell no one. Keep the secret and everything will be alright.

No one else needed to die. He just had to leave it all behind.

He pulled into the marina car park and got out of the sports car. Retrieving his case, he set it down on the asphalt and pulled the extendable handle while the hydraulics closed the trunk lid. One click from the fob locked the car. The gate to the marina bore a heavy chain around it, secured in place with a fat padlock. Paul had a key, and he relocked the gate behind him, double-looping the chain in place to make it more secure.

He found his boat just where he left it and climbed aboard. He had to leave with his boat. Plane tickets left records. If he could avoid that, so much the better. Plus, Paul loved his boat. He loved the car too, although he would have to leave it behind now. He could always buy another when he got settled someplace else. For now, he wanted to keep moving. The boat was the perfect way to disappear.

Despite the time he spent on the boat in the last number of years, Paul was by no means a competent seaman. He'd completed a survival course and a boat safety and maintenance course but he'd long since forgotten them, and now couldn't even remember which way was starboard.

He figured he probably didn't need to know these things – after all, he wasn't really sailing. The boat had a motor, and Paul had money for fuel. Not much else to it, apart from making sure his tiny kitchen was stocked with the essentials like good cheese, baguettes and plenty of roast ham, bacon and beans. Cooking for himself on the small stove in the galley had proved to be one of the more difficult and unexpected chores to master. He could render half a dozen recipes, but not on a one-ring stove. Things got pretty basic real quick. He didn't mind, as long as he remembered to keep the wine rack full.

Paul completed his checks on the boat. These were done more out of habit than any real effort to discern the seaworthiness of the vessel. Over time, he'd cut down the number of checks because he'd more or less forgotten what he was looking for and why. He made sure his navigation system and radio were working, and that there was plenty of fuel. That was it. Once the engine fired up, and sounded like it should, he kicked off from the jetty and moved out at a slow speed. Maneuvering between boats he soon left the marina and then gradually let out the throttle. The waves remained tall, and he made sure to keep the boat angled toward them, letting the bow break them so the boat would glide over the wall of water. Not the biggest waves he'd seen when out at sea, but large and threatening nonetheless. The cabin cruiser bounced over the largest waves, and once or twice he heard crashing sounds. Like the boat was rising and landing on something hard.

It was dangerous work, and he battled through it most of the day without food and only two bottles of water. He dared not leave the helm for a second. In late afternoon, the waters calmed. The weather conditions precluded speed, and he found that he had not traveled that far from the marina despite his efforts. The tide had been beating him back all day.

He cut the engine, went below and ate a can of beans that he'd heated on the stove, along with some bread. Two glasses of wine and a soda set him up for a few hours at the laptop. The voyage had focused his mind – requiring total concentration. He had not given Maria, or the burglar, a second thought.

Distance.

The fatigue in his back and his shoulders wouldn't stop him writing. Some writers had routines which they'd built up to help them write but Paul's only requirement was solitude. He didn't mind the gentle roll of the waves, the sounds of the ocean lapping against the hull, or the cries of sea birds overhead. As long as he was alone and there was no music other than the sentences in his head.

And the twist, of course. There are many different types of twist. This book would be a snare. Paul knew it. And now he had to lay his rope. He'd had a twist brewing in his mind for the last one hundred pages. Subconsciously he'd been leaving clues – little traces of the trap peeking through the foliage.

Now it came to him fully formed. He could see it all in his mind's eye. The characters and plot laid bare like the inside of a Swiss watch. Ticking along perfectly until it came to the moment to drop the hammer.

The excitement took hold, a desperate need to get the words down on the page before they dulled or fizzed away from his consciousness. This was what Paul lived for.

He just liked writing twists good enough to make the reader drop the goddamn book.

And there was one on the way.

CHAPTER FIFTEEN

He's really gone.

The silent, empty house in a silent, empty town. Maria felt that absence of life more keenly than she had ever done before. It wasn't just her waking present that felt empty. It was as if Paul had sneaked into her life and stolen her past. Three years. Gone. She had never felt so alone. Never felt so violated. The love that she had undoubtedly felt for Paul had twisted, and knotted itself around her pain and transformed into a thirsty wound.

No love remained. She had loved a lie. That man she'd met and laughed with, slept with, held, and loved – he didn't really exist. He was dead to her now.

Maria let Paul's note slip from her fingers and drift through the heavy air to rest on the kitchen counter.

Maria,

I have to go away, maybe for a long time. You won't be in danger if I'm not there. The house is yours, the money in the account too. Don't worry about me.

I'm sorry.

Paul.

Maria went straight to his study, unlocked the door and checked behind the volume of Dickens he kept on the shelf. He'd taken his revolver with him. She trudged back out of the study, poured coffee and sat at the breakfast bar in the kitchen.

The clock on the wall read nine-fifteen a.m. Maria called Daryl. She had to set the phone down on the counter and put it on speaker. Her breath came hard through her nose and she wrapped her arms tightly around herself.

'You okay?' said Daryl.

'No, I'm not okay. He's gone. He really did it. I didn't think he would really do it,' she said, spitting the words at the phone in short, harsh breaths.

'What are you going to do? You gonna divorce the prick?'

'No. It's gone beyond that now. I . . . I don't even know who he is. He's like a stranger that I've just found in the basement. A stranger who's been sleeping in my bed for three years. I married a man I have no clue about . . .' She broke off, choking down the tears.

'It's okay, Maria. Take it slow,' said Daryl, gently.

'No! I'm through with this shit. He's conned me. He's taken years of my life and dumped me in this shithole town. I've lost all of my friends. I've lost my job, my life. I'm not gonna take this, Daryl. I need you.'

'I'll help you in any way I can. You know that,' he said.

'Good. I needed to hear that. I need you. I want a new life. *My* life. *Our* life. I want to be with *you* now. Always.'

She listened for a response. When it came, it filled her body and mind with a calm and reassurance she hadn't felt in days.

'I want that too. More than anything. I love you, Maria.'

'I love you too,' she said, and she felt it then more deeply than she had ever felt it before.

'What are you going to do about Paul?' said Daryl.

For all her ravaged senses, the turmoil rolling through her guts, Maria gave thought to how she was going to respond. She chose her words carefully. It would feel good to say it. It would feel right. This was how she would reset her life and build a new existence in comfort and security with the man she truly loved. She imagined herself on a beach far away. Maybe somewhere in the Caribbean. White sand flecked on her tan legs as they stretched out on a sun lounger. A drink by her side. The sun on her face. Watching Daryl swim in the ocean. A pair of Manolo Blahnik heels buried in the sand beside her. A life of freedom. Away from this trap, with everything she could ever want. Either she could have that life. Or let Paul have that life, with the blonde. The two of them, lying on a beach and laughing at foolish Maria. The stupid wife, who didn't even know she was married to one of the richest, most famous authors in the world. It wasn't just money. Twenty million dollars was more than just money.

It was a whole world.

Maria wanted that world. More than that, she wanted to make sure that Paul couldn't have it.

And so, clearly, slowly and confidently she said, 'I'm going to need you to help me get a slice of the money. I want my fair share. That's all. Can you do that for me?' she said.

'Whatever it takes, I'll do it for us.'

It was Daryl's simplicity that made Maria feel safe around him. In this man, there was very little gray – things were black and white. Simple. He would do something, or he would not.

'I'm going to get him to come back to the house. We're going to ask for ten million dollars or we go to the press and reveal his identity to the world. If he wants to keep his secrets, it'll cost him.'

She heard him blow out his cheeks. Taking in the thought, and then blowing out the tense air burning his lungs. 'Wow,' said Daryl. 'What if he says no? Or calls the cops? It's blackmail. I mean, he deserves it and all – but that's pretty heavy shit.'

'Don't you want to us to be together? Don't you want to have enough money to make a great life?'

'You know I do. With that kind of money we could be . . .'

'What?' said Maria, knowing the answer. She wanted to hear him say it. Needed it. If she was going to do this she had to know Daryl was with her.

'We could be *free*,' he said.

'We have to be so careful. I couldn't bear it if you got hurt,' said Maria.

'What do you mean?' said Daryl.

Maria sighed, said, 'He has a gun.'

'You don't think he'd shoot you, or me, do you? He's your husband, you know him, you think he could hurt you?'

She almost laughed. Daryl's sweetness fed his naivety. Or maybe they were one and the same, she couldn't tell.

'Until two days ago, I *thought* I knew my husband. Today, I've no idea who he is, or what he's capable of. I do know one thing. We need a plan. We have to assume when I get him home he'll be armed and pissed-off like he's never been before. And we have to be ready.'

CHAPTER SIXTEEN

The sky was darkening above the boat. Paul hadn't noticed the time. He was lost in the writing. He checked his phone, found that he still had two bars of signal. He dialed his agent's cell phone. Josephine picked up straight away.

'Hey, Paul, you okay?'

'I'm fine. Did you find the leak?'

She sighed and said, 'There's no leak. I had someone from IT check out my computer. I'm the only one with access to your information. It's not stored on our accounts systems. According to the tech there's no trace of any kind of hack. No spyware, no malware, nothing. The log-in times correlate to my work. I change the password for the computer every three months. There's no leak at my end.'

Standing, Paul's eyes flicked around the cabin as his mind turned the information over. He was back at square one.

'Then how was I found?' he said.

'I have no clue. You sure you didn't get drunk and say something you shouldn't have? It happens, you know . . .'

'No. I didn't. Never. There has to be someone on the inside.'

'The bank. Has to be the bank.'

The bank. Some clerk at the bank maybe figured it out . . .

He shook his head – no. That simply wasn't possible. Nor did he believe that Josephine had ratted him out. A literary agent's livelihood relies on their clients. Paul knew he was a special client. Aside from selling his books to publishers, Josephine had helped Paul to manage and hide the money. She helped to keep Paul's secrets – in exchange for a fee, of course. A huge fee.

It had to be something else.

'Where are you?' she said.

'I left. I'm on my boat.'

'How did she take it? Did you tell her anything in the end?' asked Josephine.

Paul wiped his mouth, said, 'I left a note.'

Silence. A sigh, and then, 'She deserved more than that. I hope you explained things. Some women blame themselves, you know. Doesn't matter if they did nothing wrong, they'll feel guilty about everything. What did you tell her?'

'I didn't tell her anything. I just said I was leaving. And I was giving her the house and the money in our joint account.'

'Twenty grand and a house in the middle of nowhere? If she has any sense she'll come after you.'

Paul looked out at the waves.

'She won't be able to find me. And even if she did, and filed for divorce, she can't touch my money even if her lawyers found out about it. I made sure we moved to the right state for that. No way do I want my money showing up in some court document. I would be found out, for sure. May as well put a billboard outside my house. Look, it doesn't matter, she doesn't know about the money. She doesn't know about me. I prefer to keep it that way. At least there's someone out there who hates me for being Paul, and not for all the other things I've done.'

'Let's not go into that,' said Josephine.

He had never told her the whole truth, but he'd guessed she had already put it together. Josephine didn't want to talk about the murders. She found it . . . unsettling. Distasteful. In her world it was like using the wrong spoon for soup. Maybe her knowledge tainted her somehow, but as long as it was a secret she could deal with it. And Josephine was a lady who took pride in her reputation. If people knew the truth, she may not get invited to the right parties.

'How's the book comin—'

Paul ended the call, and provided the answer to an empty cabin – *the book is fine, Josephine. You'll get it when it's ready. Not before. Screw you and your deadlines.*

For now, he had his walking-away money. Twenty grand. It wouldn't last long. In the next few weeks he planned to go to the bank in Grand Cayman. Take out a large, lump sum, and then switch the rest of the cash to a different account. Maybe somewhere in Zurich. Just to be on the safe side, in case it was someone at the bank who had worked things out. He put his phone down on the counter next to the coffee pot and poured himself a fresh glass of red wine. Raising it to his lips, he heard the faint tremor from his cell phone as it vibrated with a new message.

He drained the glass, feeling the rosy, inky wine against the back of his throat.

The wine helped prepare him for the SMS message. The cell text message alert sounded again. He now had two new messages from Maria.

She must've found the note that morning and she'd been building up to this text for most of the day. All of the moisture left his mouth. She wouldn't understand and Paul didn't want to explain. Josephine was right. Maria deserved more, but at least she would be safe and that was the main thing in his mind. He clung to that like a life raft, but he knew he was sinking in a sea of black guilt.

Maria had saved him. She deserved better.

Between the burning car and the publication of the second J. T. LeBeau novel, Paul had passed the time in a dim, gray haze. He was living in New York. Although you couldn't really call it living. Each morning he got out of bed through habit more than any pressing need or desire to ever leave his sheets. Not that he slept. His dreams were too violent, and filled with vivid red flames. He dressed and left the apartment. It was one hundred and seventeen paving flags, or eight blocks, to the diner. Sixty-seven of the paving flags were broken or cracked. He'd counted them each day.

The floor of the diner was a polished pine, stained with coffee and syrup and God knows what else. The waitresses all wore white sneakers. After a meal it was two hundred and three paving flags to the bar. Once inside it was always too dark to make out the floor clearly. Some kind of hard-wearing rubber that sucked at the soles of Paul's boots. He sat at a bar stool and watched his feet dangling above the rubber flooring until he was too drunk to count paving stones on the way home.

Days became weeks, and Paul still couldn't shift the weight of what he'd done from his shoulders.

Then one night a band was playing in the bar. They had come in early to set up their equipment and do a sound check. He smelled Maria before he saw her. A sweet, citrus smell. Then he saw her boots, her legs encased in tight jeans and he smiled to himself in regret.

Then the most extraordinary thing happened to Paul. To this day he could not explain it, but the lady in the boots hooked a finger beneath Paul's chin and gracefully angled his head up so she could look at his face. And what a face she had. Gorgeous blue eyes set in a perfect frame. She said hello. Paul said hi. They talked. He left the bar with her that night and couldn't find his way home. He didn't recognize the buildings or the storefronts. For a time he couldn't really figure out why. Then he realized the lady in the boots had lifted his head from the ground. Paul had gazed into her eyes without feeling the need to look away in shame. Those eyes held his, without fear, or disgust, or anything other than kindness. She made him feel like himself again. It was a gift he took with both hands. The lady in the boots was called Maria, and she had saved him.

Now she wanted to know why he'd left her. He hadn't given much to her in the marriage. He couldn't. She had fallen in love with Paul. Telling her about the money would change things. She'd want to spend it, live the high life. The life that attracted attention. It wouldn't take long for Paul to be discovered. No, he couldn't have told her about his other life. Too dangerous. Instead he had tried to make a new one. The only life he could have was one he could control. Which meant controlling her, too.

How foolish he had been to believe he could control anything. He wished he had never met her. Things would be far less complicated. His head would still be down, pointed at the street, where he should have left it.

Paul clicked to open the messages. Two of them. One was a picture file, the other plain text.

The picture loaded on his screen.

Oh shit.

His passport. Sitting on the kitchen counter. He clicked the text message.

Forget something?

CHAPTER SEVENTEEN

Sunday afternoon shopping used to be a small pleasure for Maria. Hours spent in record stores on 42nd Street, followed by a beer and a slice of pie with extra pepperoni. Always on her own, never with friends. That way she never felt guilty about taking her time. There was no one else to worry about.

This afternoon was different. She'd driven an hour to the mall and the giant hardware store beyond it. At the mall she'd withdrawn five hundred dollars, and gone next door to the hardware store.

She had a list in her hand, even though Daryl told her to memorize the items she would need and not to write them down. She'd written them down anyway, knowing in her present state of mind she could easily forget to buy something important. Her brain felt flighty – unable to hold onto one thought for very long before a hundred others came crashing through the door of her consciousness.

Dressed in blue jeans, white blouse and a denim jacket, with her hair tied up in a red handkerchief, Maria pushed her shopping cart around the aisles picking up items and ticking them off her list with a pen.

Two gallons of white paint.
Two paint rollers.
Two paint roller trays.
One bag of paint brushes (in varying sizes).
Four bags of strong plastic dust sheets.
Duct tape, three rolls.
Cable ties, one bunch.
Four pairs of plastic overalls.

Two paint masks.
A box of latex gloves.
Three rolls of drawstring garbage bags.

When her cart was full, she made her way to the teller and paid in cash. She kept the receipt in her purse, rolled the cart all the way to her car. Loaded up the trunk, got drive-thru coffee and went home.

The shopping list looked, for all intents and purposes, like a lady about to do some serious redecorating. And indeed she was. Maria got home, opened the paint can with a screwdriver and mixed the paint. Then she poured some into the paint roller tray, dabbed a brush into it and wiped off the excess paint before testing the color on the kitchen wall.

She stood back. Examining the difference. Maybe it was her state of mind at that time – she was way off the reservation and living through a hyper-real, hyper-unreal world, but the paint mark looked more like she uncovered the true color of the wall, rather than applied a fresh coat of paint to the surface.

Her phone buzzed.

Daryl.

'I got everything on the list,' she said. 'I'm going to set up the dust sheets and send him a text message. Come over, I'd say he'll come back late tonight.'

They had discussed the plan at length.

When Paul came home she would wait for him in the kitchen – the passport hidden. The space would look like Maria was starting to paint it. A single chair laid out in the center of the dust sheet, facing the back doors. Maria would get him to sit down, so they could talk. Daryl would come up behind him, grab his arms and hold them while Maria came around the side with the cable ties and fixed Paul's wrists to the chair, then his ankles. Search him and relieve him of the gun if he was carrying it.

Then Maria would lay it all out. She knew he was J. T. LeBeau, she knew about the money. He would wire them ten million dollars or Maria dimed the *New York Times*. It was his choice.

Maria didn't know how Paul would react. If he got violent, she wanted Daryl to have the upper hand and not be afraid to give Paul a slug in the mouth. He didn't want to do it, and it had taken her some time to persuade him that he would only be protecting her. She had thought about Paul going to the police if things got physical. That's why they had the dust sheets – they would protect the floors if anyone got cut. The dust sheets would be lifted and burned afterwards. No blood on the floor. It never happened. With paint cans scattered around the kitchen the dust sheets wouldn't look out of place.

Maria had thought this over again and again.

This was the only way.

It somehow all made sense to her, even though it left a cold feeling at the small of her back. Like an ice cube slowly tumbling down her spine.

CHAPTER EIGHTEEN

The sun was blood orange, just beginning to dip below the horizon when Paul decided to go back and collect his passport. He'd checked the pocket in his case, and found it empty. He was sure he'd taken the passport and packed it.

Lying on the couch in the cabin, he'd stared at the ceiling for an hour or more and ran through all the possible scenarios. There were many, but some were more troubling than others. He didn't want to go back. Someone had found him. What if Maria had been captured, and the text was a trick to lure him back?

The thought that she could be harmed brought a sour taste to his mouth. He closed his eyes, cursed his stupidity. He had let himself believe that he could hide. He should've resisted Maria, suppressed his feelings. Allowing himself to love her had put her in danger. His own selfishness had caused this. Then again, maybe it was Maria who had sent the text? Whatever the real scenario, it made him even more convinced that he had done the right thing by running.

He decided he would go home, wait until it was really late and sneak into the house while it was dark. If Maria was asleep, he wouldn't disturb her. If he thought something else was going on, he would deal with it. He needed to bring the revolver with him. If he saw anyone in the house but Maria, he would go in shooting. Only way to be safe.

Decision made, he inhaled and let out a breath slowly. A creeping unease spread through him, making the hairs on the back of his neck tickle. Something wasn't right. It was then, free from distractions, that he noticed the boat no longer felt like it was rocking.

He raised his back off the couch, swung his feet around and placed them on the floor searching out his boots.

Instantly, he brought his feet back up to his chest, swore. His socks and feet were freezing – like he'd just dipped them in a bucket of ice.

No, not ice.

Water.

He looked down and saw a thin layer of seawater on the cabin floor. *Jesus Christ.*

Those crashing sounds as he'd brought the boat, full throttle, over the large waves. Maybe he'd hit something – damaged the hull.

First things first. Paul grabbed the laptop from the table and pulled it toward him. He checked the latest version of the manuscript had safely uploaded to the USB memory stick, and then removed the stick and placed it in a plastic baggy. He kept a handful of baggies on the table. He'd once made the mistake of leaving the boat with the USB stick in his pocket and he'd slipped on the deck before leaping onto the jetty, falling into the water. He got out just fine, but he'd lost three days' worth of work.

He sealed the bag and put it in his pants pocket.

Wishing he could remember more from his boat safety course, he decided he had to do something at least. He ignored his boots. His feet were soaking anyways. He stood up and his first thought was to try and start the engine.

It failed.

He went below, checked the bilge pump. This cruiser had a wooden hull, built in the fifties and while it looked pretty, it didn't possess a lot of the finer safety equipment that would've helped in this type of situation. It did have an electronic bilge alarm. He checked it, found it dead. There were other back-up safety systems that he was encouraged to fit to the boat, but he figured this beauty had been sailing for sixty years without one and he wasn't going to start messing with that. He regretted it now.

The bilge pump was dead. Oil flooded the pump housing, mixing with the water. There was a hand-crank pump somewhere, maybe on the deck, but Paul's heart was tripping faster than he could think and he had no idea where the hand-crank might be or how to operate it.

The radio.

Paul had a VHF radio. He went back to the helm, found it, turned it on, looked for the book that came with the radio so he could find the correct channel to send a distress signal. He swore instead, and just started talking on the thing. He looked at the GPS system, read his co-ordinates out and screamed into the mic that his boat was sinking.

No answer.

He opened the box marked for emergencies, took out a life vest and a personal locator beacon. This piece of equipment he did know how to use. He switched it on, watched the little red dot flash and then put the life vest over his head just as the boat tilted, throwing him down onto the deck. Paul spread out his hands to break his fall, but not quickly enough.

A dull thud was the last thing he heard before the lights went out.

He woke up choking in the dark.

Four feet of water in the boat and the stern had completely sunk into the freezing black waters. He had almost slipped into that water and been drowned in his own cabin. He felt his way out of the cabin and crawled up the main deck toward the bow. He was slipping and sliding on the smooth boards, and blood poured from a cut on his scalp. Looking around, he saw nothing but black sea, black night and blood in his eyes.

Paul lit the torch on his life vest and jumped overboard. The boat was going down, and unless he got off it he was going down too.

He thought it would be okay. The Coast Guard would be on their way to him right this second. A boat and a chopper. He would be fine. He'd seen it on the Discovery Channel. Soon as he hit the Personal Locator Beacon, the alarms started going off in the US Coast Guard's office. For a moment he felt like he was doing the right thing. Getting off the sinking boat would save him.

He couldn't feel his feet anymore, they were so cold. So he didn't notice the change in temperature until his whole body hit the waves, and his head momentarily went under before shooting back to the surface with the forceful buoyancy of the life vest. *Then* he noticed the cold.

The shock.

It was like something was strangling his entire body, and burning it at the same time. He couldn't get air, and his mouth opened to suck in a lungful and fend off the blaze of agonizing cold that hit his system like a wrecking ball. But there was no air. Just seawater.

He vomited, instantly. But still there was no oxygen, even though his mouth lay open and his body screamed for it. His arms stopped moving. His legs stopped kicking. The cold paralyzed him. For a second Paul thought he'd just taken a dive into battery acid. His skin was alive in agony. A pulsing, searing agony that took everything from him – his voice, his air, his limbs.

But not his thoughts. He could think clearly. The cold-water immersion had triggered shock. Even if he survived that, he wouldn't live long in the water. He knew his body temperature was falling rapidly, his system cooling, shutting down. Strangely, he began to feel warm.

He knew he was going to die before he passed out and the cold really took hold of his bones. The last thing he saw before he closed his eyes was the light flickering on his vest and the last thing he thought of was Maria.

CHAPTER NINETEEN

Paul's eyes opened to black.

He felt a massive pressure on his chest and suddenly his mouth filled with water. It sprang from his throat like a burst pipe, covering his face. He coughed, tried for air, got some and struggled to lift his head, but could not.

Black above him and now something else. Stars.

A noise filled his ears – the roar of a motorboat. His arms fell by his sides and felt something solid. A face loomed over him. A man, with dark stubble and a sharp face. He wore a bright yellow waterproof coat and he was speaking although Paul couldn't hear him at first. Paul's eyes felt heavy, he could barely focus.

'Hey! Stay with me buddy!' said the voice.

Buddy? Paul didn't recognize the man. Maybe the man knew him, maybe not.

Paul felt so sleepy.

Something smacked off his cheek, stinging his face. He opened his eyes and found the man there again, in his face, screaming at him to stay awake. Paul could smell fish. And his hands on the deck of the boat felt slimy.

A fisherman.

A fisherman had rescued him.

Paul smiled, laughed, and felt a sharp pain in his legs and then he was moving. The man was dragging him across the deck. Then the fisherman was there again, close now, wrapping his arms underneath Paul's, hauling him up. Paul could smell the catch on the man's skin. The stink of fish made him gag again and more seawater erupted from his stomach. Then he was inside, out of the cold. The fisherman was pawing at him, removing his clothes, rubbing his skin, putting a shiny silver blanket on top of him. The fisherman had a kind face. His hands felt rough, hard. Paul imagined that years of pulling ropes, hauling nets and gutting fish had worn those hands into stone.

'It's okay. You're gonna be just fine, pal. I'm taking you in. You're the biggest thing I've caught today,' he said, in a pure Southern accent. He followed it with a long, loud laugh. That laugh was reassuring. The danger had passed. He was going to be fine, just as the fisherman said.

Paul felt warm again, and yet he knew he was safe. He always liked fishermen. They were real men, who took real risks with their lives. They lived hard, and there was no give in them at all. Particularly this one. Quick to laugh, and solid. Paul drifted off to sleep.

Only then did he realize he'd left his case on board. Along with his traveling money. His phone. And the revolver. It was all gone.

But at least he was alive.

CHAPTER TWENTY

She opened the front door when she heard Daryl's feet on the gravel. He slipped inside and she closed the door quickly. Taking him by the hand, she kissed him hard. It was part passion, part fear.

'The cops came to the club today. Maybe it had nothing to do with me, but it was scary, you know? I drove around and around for an hour. I wanted to make sure I wasn't being followed. It's fine, it's just me being paranoid, honey,' he said, before embracing her again.

The mention of police gave her another frisson of fear but, like Daryl said, it was probably nothing. He'd been careful, but more than that. He'd called her *honey*. It was the first time he'd used a word like that. A special word, for her. To hear Daryl use a word for her made her stomach flutter. It felt like something he would say to her when they were living together, a year from now, in their home far away from Port Lonely.

It was a glimpse of a new life. And she loved it.

He took her in his arms and Maria knew peace. She loved the smell of him, the feel of him. The strength in his body tempered by the smell of citrus and spice from the scent he always wore. It reminded her of Christmas. She nestled her head in the crook of his chest, felt his hand stroking her hair.

He released her, kissed her delicately, and she led him down the hall. Daryl stopped dead at the kitchen door, taking in the scene. Maria smiled, and hoped he would be pleased with her work. He followed her into the kitchen.

Every surface was covered in thick plastic dust sheets, apart from the far window at the end of the room. The sink and counter below the window also remained uncovered and the remnants of a meal lay there. Spaghetti in a pot, a bowl with the red stains of tomato sauce and a chopping board with a large kitchen knife still resting upon it beside the stains of chopped yellow peppers and basil.

A dining-table chair sat in the middle of the plastic sheets.

Daryl looked around for the rest of the supplies. They were gathered in a neat pile in the corner.

'I got everything. You'd better hurry, he could be back any time now,' said Maria, and she grabbed Daryl by his shirt, leaned in and kissed him roughly before pushing him toward the pile of items.

He smiled, turned away from her and she watched him rip open the sack containing the overalls.

Maria grabbed a handful of cable ties and the duct tape, put them on the counter beside Daryl.

'I opened the paint, left the can on the floor so he'll see it when he comes into the kitchen,' said Maria. Daryl zipped the white plastic overalls up to his chest before covering his head with the hood, and then zipping it all the way up to his throat. He fitted a mask over his mouth and slipped the elastic behind his head.

'It's not too late to back out,' said Daryl.

She wrapped her arms around her body, holding herself together.

'I'm not backing out. I just want to make sure we don't get hurt. I should've bought a taser or something. What if he reacts and we can't handle him? What if he comes through the door with the gun in his hand?' she said.

'I'll be behind the central counter. That way I can move without him seeing me. We'll hear his car in the drive, you check out front then lead him in here, get him to sit down and talk.'

'What if he won't talk? What if he shoots me?' she said.

Daryl looked around the kitchen, saw an open tool box in the corner with a screwdriver lying next to it on the floor. The tip of the screwdriver was covered in paint and it had stuck to the plastic sheeting. Daryl went over to the box, picked up a claw hammer.

'If he threatens you in any way, I'll tag him with this,' said Daryl.

A cold shudder rippled through her.

'Don't worry, I won't let him hurt you none,' said Daryl.

The sudden change in the timbre of his voice made Maria turn sharply. The vision before her was at first confusing.

Daryl was standing right behind her, only a few feet away. He looked scary in those plastic overalls, but now she saw the hammer in his right hand. She knew then that this was a terrible mistake. It could all go horribly wrong. Maria felt a sliver of fear even now, watching her lover stand there before her.

The man who had just called her *honey*. The one she loved more than any man. And yet seeing him dressed like that sent a million goose pimples prickling over her skin. There was no way she could go through with it. Paul had betrayed her terribly. The other woman, the money, the life he denied her. And yet the betrayal did not warrant this risk. What if someone got badly hurt? She couldn't risk Daryl. He was too precious. No way. It wasn't too late. She could put a stop to this. She had visions of Paul shooting Daryl, and then her. It wasn't worth it for all the money in the world.

Yes. Stop it. *Stop it right now.*

The sense of relief swept over her body like cold mist. It *wasn't* going to happen. It felt like waking from a long, terrible dream. Back to reality. Back to safety.

She opened her mouth, and was about to tell Daryl that she wanted to stop when her breath caught in her throat. Daryl's eyes were no longer his own. She saw something hard in those eyes – something empty. A look she had never seen before. He seemed taller. The surfer dude slouch had gone. He held his back straight, head up, shoulders squared. Ropes of muscle stood out in his neck.

'I can't risk this. It's not worth it, let's forget the whole thing and we'll just pack our bags and go.'

Her words didn't soften his stance, or his eyes. From behind the mask he said, 'Sure, whatever you want. Grab the dust sheets. Let's clean the place up and go.'

Maria turned away from Daryl, picked up the dining-table chair. She felt another huge wave of relief. Her mother had put her father through a window to save her. And although they were happy together after, she knew her mother carried that weight even if she never spoke of it. Maria couldn't take the chance that her plan could all go south. She was moving on. Getting out of Port Lonely. To hell with the money, she had Daryl and they would make do.

She began to turn to her left with the chair, ready to put it back behind the dining-table when something stopped her. Maria heard a pop and the world tilted and shuddered before the black took her.

CHAPTER TWENTY-ONE

Watching Maria fall to the plastic-covered floor, Daryl swore and then bit his lip behind the mask. The blow had struck her on the left temple, sending a small yet powerful blast of fine blood mist into the air. He heard the faint pitter patter of the spray hitting his white plastic overalls. He even felt spots of blood landing on his brow as softly as sea spray.

The blow had force behind it. Real power. Yet it landed when she was turning her head, the hammer glancing from her skull.

Crouching beside Maria he saw her eyes closed, her mouth open. Unconscious, not dead. Daryl raised the hammer again and brought it down with a terrible crack on the front of her head. More blood hit him back in retaliation, and Maria's body began to convulse. Her limbs jerked and flailed. One eye opened. Not an accusatory stare, nor one of horror. It was a pitiful eye that had ceased to operate with any intention at all and yet her body continued to twitch.

The plastic sheeting screeched beneath her, and Daryl hated the sound. It reminded him of a kid in school who could run his nails down the chalkboard. That was a noise Daryl felt he wasn't programmed to hear.

He raised the hammer again. Took a deep breath. The twitching slowed, then stopped. Her one visible eyeball stared into space, and her body did not move.

He waited for a few seconds. Staring down at her, the pool of blood collecting on the sheet beneath her head. The hammer hadn't seen much use. It had a few notches on the head and was scraped here and there. It was Paul's hammer. One that he'd used in the house. It would carry his prints and his DNA. He dropped it beside Maria.

He stood up and found the edge of the sheet that Maria lay upon, tore it away from the duct tape holding it to the floor and proceeded to kneel down again and wrap Maria's body, rolling her over and the sheet with her. Wrapping her like a Christmas present. When the sheet had been rolled to the other edge, he stopped, got up and went to the front door and opened it. He ran his gloved hand over his chest then smeared a little on the front door. He went back inside, carefully took off the overalls and mask. Then he placed them in a bag, along with the gloves and put the bag in his jacket pocket.

Daryl turned out the lights before he left the house. He got into his car and drove to the top of the driveway, stopped. From the trunk of his car he took a ten-pound hammer and approached the mailbox at the top of the drive. One swing would do it. The hammer caught the wooden post at the base, and the mailbox went over into the dirt. To the casual observer, a car could've misjudged the road and taken out the box. He put the big hammer back in his trunk, and got into the car.

He felt nothing for Maria at that moment. Dead. Cocooned in plastic. He believed that everything in life happened for a reason. Even murder. Right then, Daryl had twenty million reasons to kill Maria.

CHAPTER TWENTY-TWO

Big Bill Buchanan took the last bite from a pastrami sandwich and washed it down with a cold can of soda. He belched, once, returned the can to his cup holder and looked out at the sea. So far, his dieting wasn't going as his wife had planned. In the six weeks since he'd had the stent inserted in his artery, he'd lost over fifteen pounds. There was no denying that he felt better for it. No longer out of breath on the stairs, and with the benefit of the newly opened artery and the medication, he was almost a new man. He'd gone back to work last week, and must have put three or four pounds back on. As a US postal worker, he had a lot of time on his hands, unsupervised. The walking was good for him, and he no longer took the van up the steep hills on Corbyn Street. At lunch he ate the salad his wife had prepared for him freshly each morning, and drank the bottled water. Every other day he topped off the salad with a sandwich from Pete's Deli, a Coke and a bag of chips. Justifying the pleasure came easy – he felt the hill walks and increased activity balanced out the calories. At least Bill allowed himself to believe that fantasy.

Sitting in the parked mail van, in the old entrance to what once had been the Pearson farm, he balled up the wrapping paper for the sandwich and stuffed it into the door well. He would dump it later. Almost ten-thirty now. He'd been on the job since five a.m. One final stop. He started up the engine and drove the few hundred yards to the Cooper house. He stopped, got out and opened up the rear of the mail truck. A small stack of envelopes lingered in the bottom of a mail sack. He retrieved them, whistled his way to the mailbox and stopped.

The mailbox wasn't there.

Well, it was, but someone had knocked it over.

Maybe some drunk driver misjudged his speed and the slight bend in the road. Big Bill picked up the mailbox, checked it was empty, then made his way toward the house. He'd made his last delivery to the house on Friday morning, and the mailbox had been fine then. Maybe they didn't know it had been hit. He also wanted to make sure the three or four letters in his hand got safely to their intended recipients.

The tune on Big Bill's lips died when he reached the front door. It lay open just a crack, and there was a strange stain on it. Only Mrs. Cooper's car sat in the driveway. Mr. Cooper wasn't home a lot but Big Bill liked to take a moment and admire that sleek Italian sports car whenever he got the chance. Mr. Cooper must have been someplace else.

He hit the doorbell, waited. Nothing. He knocked the door with his knuckles. Again, louder this time. That's when he realized the stain on the door looked like blood.

'Mrs. Cooper?' he called.

'Mrs. Cooper, it's Bill Buchanan – your mailman. Is everything alright?'

The silence ate into his flesh.

Tentatively, Bill touched the door and gently pushed it open. He called out again, asking if she was alright, was there an emergency?

A dread took him when he crossed the threshold. He shouldn't be here. Had no business being here. He could get fired. But what if there had been an accident?

The little hallway led to the living room. Bill placed the mail on the table in the hall, then poked his head around the corner. No one in the living room.

'Mrs. Cooper!' he yelled. This time there was panic in his voice. Bill had already sweated through his shirt, and now he removed his ball cap and wiped the sweat from his forehead onto his sleeve. He was out of breath, and he put out a hand onto the wall, used it as a base to poke his head into the living room. No one in there. And nothing looked disturbed.

He called out again, then thought maybe he was being foolish. He should just leave. Bill had all but made up his mind when he happened to glance downwards. More stains. On the floor. Fine red droplets on the white rug.

If anything, it made Bill more confident in his decision to investigate – that it was okay he'd come into the house. He called out again, with urgency, and was now moving through the living room toward the kitchen. These old houses had once populated the shoreline and Bill knew they were all the same. There were two doors leading to the kitchen. One from the living room and one from the hallway. Bill followed the blood pattern on the floor of the living room to the kitchen. The door lay closed.

He touched the handle, then gripped it and turned it. Opened the door an inch and caught a strange smell and an even stranger sight. The walls, the kitchen floor, or what he could see of it, were covered in dull gray plastic sheets. The smell hit him. It was familiar, but he couldn't place it. Droplets of sweat ran off his nose, falling on his boots. He wanted to shout out again but he didn't have the breath. Nothing he could do but open the damn door.

He pushed it, hard.

And fell to his knees.

A large ball of plastic sheeting on the floor. Blood pooling around it.

The roll of plastic had been ripped open. The glass doors beyond which led to the porch were covered in bloody handprints.

One of those doors lay open.

Pain shot through his left arm, as if he'd been struck with a bat. He looked around, but there was no one there. The pain traveled up his arm, into his chest and his jaw. His hands patted his pockets and he found his cell phone. Dialled 911.

He told the operator the address and said there was blood all over the kitchen, someone had been attacked. Big Bill listened to the dispatcher confirm she was sending police and paramedics. He lowered the phone from his face, took a hit from his inhaler and told the dispatcher to hurry, he needed an ambulance right away. He was having a heart attack.

CHAPTER TWENTY-THREE

Sheriff Dole got out of his police cruiser and ran around it. He got into the passenger seat, closed the door and put on his seat belt. Deputy Bloch shuffled over from the passenger seat. She lifted her right leg over the center console, got into position in the driver's seat and put on her belt. She hit the siren, and the lights, and the gas. Dole picked up the radio, confirmed they were handling and tried to get more information from Sue.

In many ways, Dole was a fine law enforcement officer. Chief among his virtues lay the knowledge of his own limitations. Dole was never going to chase down a purse-snatcher on foot, he could hit a barn door with shotgun but not much else, and he was the worst high-speed driver in the history of the county.

Bloch was a different story. She ran ten miles every morning. He saw her sometimes, on the beach, pounding through the sand. She could also shoot and drive. Probably all at the same time, thought Dole.

Sue didn't have any more information from the caller. It was a tough situation and she was doing her best to keep them calm.

The tires screeched out of Port Lonely and onto the coast road. Dole glanced across and saw the speedometer pass one hundred. He took hold of the handle above the door and thought about what he would do when they arrived at the scene.

Paramedics had to come from county. No matter how long it took Dole and Bloch to arrive, the medics wouldn't get there for at least another ten minutes. In the trunk Sheriff Dole knew he had a medical kit and a defibrillator. Those he knew how to use.

Hitting the brakes, Bloch told him to hold on. No need. Dole felt the seat belt crushing his chest and then, when Bloch took her foot off the brakes, she took a sharp left, down the little road that led to the parking lot. Dole's body was thrown right, and his shoulder cracked against the door.

As he straightened up, Dole pulled on the handle, stopping himself being thrown into the driver's seat.

More accelerator. A thump as the car broke through the narrow wire fence blocking traffic from the beach.

Instantly, Bloch lost control and the car began to skid on the sand. At this point, Dole knew he would've ended up driving head first into the dunes or sliding into the sea. Bloch did neither. She dropped down a gear, using the torque to find grip. After some snaking and wrestling of the steering wheel, which threw Dole around, the car straightened up and Bloch pointed at the windshield.

'There they are, up ahead,' she said.

Squinting through the windshield, Dole could only see a collection of black dots in the sand in the far distance. It seemed like Bloch had better eyesight too. It didn't take long for the dots to become larger, so they looked like a rock formation. The closer they got, the more details came into view for Dole.

The car pulled up, thirty feet from the figures up ahead. Bloch killed the siren, but left the lights flashing. When Dole got out he could finally see the scene clearly.

A man with a cell phone to his ear jogged toward them. Beyond him, someone was lying on their back on the beach. A blonde-haired girl leaned over the body in the sand.

'Where's the paramedic?' cried the man with the cell phone.

Bloch was already halfway to the man. Dole went straight to the trunk, threw it open and brought the medical kit and the defibrillator with him. With so much to carry, Dole only jogged to the nearby figure. Bloch was there already, talking calmly with the blonde-haired jogger beside the body.

'She just came running toward us. She was screaming. There was so much blood . . .' said the blonde-haired jogger.

Dole's legs locked, and he slid to a halt on the fine sand as soon as he saw who was lying there.

One side of Maria Cooper's face was black with blood and dirt. It had caked over one eye, closing it. Her mouth was open, and she was screaming. The right eye was wide and panicking – searching around, fearfully, for the source of some new, unseen attack. She squirmed in the sand, her cries now a raw guttural roar.

Dole called Bloch to him. He opened the medical kit, handed Bloch some gauze and told her to keep light pressure on the gash on the side of Maria's head. While she did so, Dole took Maria's hand. She was bone white. She'd lost a lot of blood.

Gently, but quickly, he wrapped the gauze to the side of her head with a bandage while she dug her nails into the sand, and bucked and squirmed and screamed.

All the while, Dole whispered to her softly, telling her she was going to be alright. Soon as the gauze was in place, he set about checking her vitals.

She was breathing, she was in shock, and Dole couldn't find a pulse. Either it was so erratic he couldn't detect it, or it was her jerking, writhing movements making it impossible to find.

'Maria, what happened?' he said.

She ignored him. He placed his hands on either side of her face, trying to focus her attention, to calm her and get some sense of what had happened. The pupil of her right eye had all but disappeared into the iris. It was a tiny black dot and it didn't move as he brought his face closer to her. Dole pinched her left eyelid, prised it open through the cake of blood. His hands instantly fell away.

Oh Jesus.

The pupil of Maria's right eye had flooded the iris. It looked as big as an eight ball. Dole was no medic, but he knew what that meant. Maria had suffered some kind of brain damage.

'Maria, it's Sheriff Dole. What happened?' he said to her, now more urgent than ever. The sound of sirens in the distance. The paramedics would be here any minute.

'Maria!' he shouted.

She stopped moving, looked at him and spoke. Her voice box was shot to shit with all the screaming, there was blood in her mouth and in her throat, but through all of that Dole heard those two words from her, clear as day. And those words sent an icy needle through his entire body as sure as a shot of liquid nitrogen.

'Who's Maria?' she said.

When the paramedics arrived, they took over after Dole had given them her vitals. Maria was in shock, she'd just become tachycardic and they strapped her to a stretcher and loaded her into the ambulance with great speed.

Dole heard the radio crackle with more from Sue.

Big Bill Buchanan was delivering mail up at the Cooper's house. He'd found a bloody crime scene and called it in.

By the time the paramedics arrived at the house, Bill was dead on the floor.

CHAPTER TWENTY-FOUR

Paul felt the sun on his face. A warmth that spread over his cheeks, and down through his body. The sun was strong. He could see the blazing sphere even with his eyes closed. It burned a circle of light through his eyelids, dim and muted, but there all the same.

After the sun came sensation. He couldn't feel his tongue. Stuck to the roof of his mouth, dry and alien. He swallowed, almost gagged and somehow a sliver of saliva brought it back to life. His arms were heavy, and he found he couldn't lift them. He turned his head and felt like he was spinning. Dizziness made way for nausea, but his stomach was groaning and empty. Nothing to be sick with.

Slowly, memories returned. The room. The fisherman. The boat.

His eyes opened, and he quickly shut them again when the light from the bare ceiling bulb sent a sharp stab of pain into his head. The light went off. He heard movement and opened his eyes again. It seemed to take a long time to adjust to the darkness, and bright spots flickered in the corners of his vision. A rotten smell came next. Sweat and sick. He realized he was catching the scent from his own body.

'Hello?' he said.

A lamp clicked on in the corner of the room. The shade veiled the harshness of the light, and he found he could look around the room without that searing pain in his head.

A dark basement. He tried to curl his arms beneath him to sit up, but found he could not. Someone was holding him down. He glanced left, then right. Swore.

Both wrists were tied to the bed with rope. He pulled his arms toward him, testing the rope, feeling its bite. After a few moments he stopped, exhausted. The fear took him then. It had been a long time since he'd allowed it to overwhelm him, but there was no choice here. His body shivered, and the tears, filled with salt, burned his eyes as they erupted and fell upon his cheeks.

He lifted his head as much as he could and saw a man sitting in front of the bed. He couldn't make out his features. It was the two items on the small lamp table that sent Paul off the cliff edge of fear and into primal, instinctual . . .

Panic.

His legs hammered the mattress, he screamed and swore and tugged at his bonds until his wrists bled and foam sat thick on his lips.

On the table he saw a laptop and a gun.

A hand reached into the light and tapped the keyboard. The laptop came to life. The glare from the screen proved painful at first, but Paul welcomed it now. Pain was good. Pain meant he was still alive.

The screen shifted and changed and Paul found he was watching the live feed from a news channel.

'Remember me? I'm the guy who pulled you out of the water. You're in my house. Been here a couple of days,' said the man.

The man leaned forward, and in the glare from the laptop screen, Paul could just make out the man's face. Dark stubble, tousled hair. A strong jaw and clear, bright eyes. Hard to guess at the man's age in this light, maybe mid-thirties or early forties. Last time Paul saw this guy he was in bright yellow waterproofs, his hands on Paul's chest pumping water out of his lungs.

The fisherman.

'I would tell you to calm down, but I don't much care for you at the moment. They're saying a lot of stuff about you on the news, fellah. I want you to watch. Then I want to hear your side of things. If I don't like what I hear then either I'll turn you over to the cops or I'll shoot you myself. If I save a man's life, I figure I have a right to know what kind of man I saved.'

The panic subsided enough for Paul to know he was in a lot of trouble, and he had to pay attention if he wanted to see his way through this. He switched his focus to the screen.

The news anchor talked about the President's foreign trip, the storms hitting New Orleans and then, finally, local news. Police still appealing for any witnesses who saw Paul Cooper two nights ago. His picture appeared on screen. A photograph of Paul on his boat, taken by Maria the first month they'd moved out here. The anchor continued the report as Paul's picture filled the screen, he said that Paul Cooper's boat had sunk in the bay and he hasn't been seen since. Coast Guard have called off their search. Then he saw Sheriff Dole being interviewed, asking for witnesses who can account for Maria Cooper's movements on the same night . . .

Paul held his breath.

She was stable in the Bay City Hospital, having suffered life-threatening brain damage from a vicious attack in her own home. The sheriff of Port Lonely does not believe this was a house invasion and is urging residents of Port Lonely to remain calm. Sheriff Dole believes the victim was attacked by her husband, the missing Paul Cooper.

Paul didn't believe it was possible to feel any worse – but he found himself tumbling into a dark hole. Maria was hurt. Badly hurt. His mind spun away in a thousand directions, each driven with fear and anger and no clarity of thought. If the sheriff believed he had been the attacker then Maria was obviously in such a state that she couldn't tell them what really happened, or maybe she thought it was Paul, or maybe she was in a coma?

Fresh tears came now. Paul's body relaxed and he gave himself over to the pain. He'd caused this. Maria could have been killed because of him.

Because of J. T. LeBeau.

A hand closed the lid of the laptop as the anchor moved on to other news. The same hand then came to rest on the butt of a .45 pistol sitting on the table.

'Talk to me, goddamn it. I'm gonna count from five,' said the man.

Whatever feelings Paul still held for Maria twisted inside him. This happened often. People will do extraordinary things because of hate, but they will do even greater things for love.

'Five,' said the man.

The love that Paul held for Maria fed his anger – building the adrenaline in his system. Whoever had hurt her would suffer. Paul would make sure of it.

'Four.'

To do that, he had to think, he had to relax and speak, right now, or it would all be over.

'Three.'

Paul dug his fingers into the mattress, gripping it tightly, anchoring himself in the now. The next words from his mouth better be good, and they'd better be the truth.

'Two,' he said, picking up the gun.

'I didn't hurt her,' said Paul.

'One.'

'I love Maria. That's why I left her.'

The gun stopped in the air before its aim had fallen across Paul. The man put the gun back on the table with a slow, graceful movement that Paul considered carefully. This was not a man who acted on instinct.

'I don't understand,' said the fisherman.

Paul's mouth became dry again, his throat burning and constricting, and yet somehow he spoke – his voice broken and cracked. The first thing that came into his mind was the truth. He had to say something convincing or he could spend the rest of his life in a jail cell.

'I have a secret. Somehow . . . someone has discovered my secret. I thought they might hurt me, or someone close to me.'

He managed to swallow, bring some moisture back to his mouth. Enough to say, 'That's why I left.'

For a time, Paul listened to his breath whistling in his throat, his lungs, and kept his eyes firmly on the man across the room in the lamplight. Paul watched him stroke his chin, then lean forward and put both hands on his knees.

Finally, the man nodded and said, 'I don't like secrets, Paul. Not if you're gonna stay here. If what you're saying is true, then there's somebody out there who's trying to kill you. They probably put a hole in your boat, and they damn near killed your wife. Far as I can tell, the cops aren't looking for anyone else but you. You're the prime suspect. If you didn't hurt your wife, and from what you've told me I don't think you did, then you'll need help. Trust works both ways, Paul. Here's your last chance. Tell me what this secret is, and why it matters so much, and don't lie. If you lie I'll toss your ass in the street and call the cops myself.'

One last push. One final sentence. The look in the man's eyes was a laser beam. Paul couldn't lie. He had never been more vulnerable – tied to a bed in an armed stranger's house. A stranger with a look that could cut through bedrock.

It took all of his strength, and he almost vomited as soon as he did it, but Paul managed to sit up a little in the bed, at least getting his shoulders up off the mattress, and hold the man's gaze as he spoke.

'I have money – a lot of money – I have twenty million dollars in an account in the Cayman Islands. Someone found out about the money. They want it,' he said.

When the fisherman picked up the gun again, Paul knew he'd just made a huge mistake.

'You a drug dealer, Paul?'

'No, no, no. Definitely not. It's not what it looks like.'

'It looks illegal, is what it looks like. No straight person I know has got twenty million dollars in an offshore account. Now you want to tell me the truth, or do I gotta call the cops? Because right now I'm thinking I need to give 'em a call.'

There was no choice. Technically, there were two ways to go with this but really one wasn't an option at all. Paul had only one thing he could say which could rescue him from this situation. The ropes pulled at his wrists and his shoulders were barking with the strain, but despite all of that, Paul spoke those words – the words that he had never spoken before.

'I'm J. T. LeBeau.'

No sooner had the name died on his lips than he vowed never to speak those words again.

'The writer?'

'Yeah, the writer. I had my latest novel on a pen drive when I went overboard. I've got a lot of money, and someone has figured out who I really am and they're coming after me. That's what this is all about.'

The fisherman bent over, pulled up the leg of his jeans and came back up with a knife in his hand. The blade caught the lamplight, flickered like flame. The edge was slightly curved and sharp as the devil.

He started walking toward Paul, silently. A death march. He was a big man. Tall and thick with muscle. Paul couldn't read the man's eyes. He could smell the sea and the faint odor of fish as he came closer. Paul felt strangely calm. He'd done all he could. He could say nothing more. The only thing he could wish for now would be to bleed out fast with as little pain as possible. A last tear filled the corner of his eye. Trembling, he shut both eyes, felt the tear bleed on his cheek and waited for the cold touch of the knife.

Instead he felt the rope around his wrists tightening, then freeing.

Paul looked up at his captor who had severed the rope around his wrist. He then cut the rest of Paul's bonds.

'My apologies, but with the news and all . . . I just had to be sure. I'm sorry, Paul, or should I call you Mr. LeBeau? Probably not. I've read your books, like most folks. If I can help you I will. There's a sink over there for you to wash up and fresh clothes in the trunk. Get some sleep. In the morning I'll come get you. Relax, you're safe here. And you're very welcome to my house.'

CHAPTER TWENTY-FIVE

The drive home from Maria's house gave Daryl the chills. He had a bag in his trunk filled with bloody coveralls, bloody gloves and Maria's body wasn't even cold yet. It was unlikely anyone would find the body until the next morning when the mailman would approach the house having found the broken mailbox. Then he would notice the open front door, the blood Daryl had smeared upon it. Enough to entice him inside and find Maria's body wrapped in plastic.

Relax. He had time, he told himself.

The main thing was to drive home safe that night, and make sure he didn't get pulled over. His leg bounced nervously on the gas pedal at every stop light, his fingers trembled if he didn't grip the steering wheel tightly. Passing the sheriff's office, he could feel a tightening of the muscles in his neck, but he didn't glance at the building. Not once. At last, he got through the town and took the old coast road that swept down to the ocean on the other side of Port Lonely. Twenty minutes later he arrived at the water's edge. His boat stood at the private jetty, and his house was quiet and dark. Daryl parked and took his backpack with him as he left the car. He had a burn barrel out back. The backpack went into the barrel, followed by lighter fluid and a box of matches. Daryl watched the flames take hold then left the barrel to do the rest of the work.

The deadbolt on the front door slid open, then the cylinder lock. Daryl flicked on a lamp in the hallway, and stood silently, listening. Every sense he possessed seemed heightened – the adrenaline surge that spiked when he delivered the second hammer blow to Maria's head was really messing with his thinking process.

Daryl took another key from his pocket and unlocked the basement door. He took the stairs at a steady, safe pace. The lamp in the corner of the basement just throwing enough light on the steps for him to see. When his boots hit the basement floor, he paused.

Floorboards creaked as Daryl made his way to the foot of the bed. There lay the sleeping figure of Paul Cooper. Daryl had not yet tightened Paul's bonds. He would do it in time, when Paul had slept some more.

'Hey, you okay?' said Daryl.

Paul stirred, turned and half opened his eyes.

'Where am I?' said Paul, his voice thick with sleep.

'You're safe,' said Daryl.

Paul tried to focus on Daryl and before he fell asleep again, he said, 'You saved me. You're the fisherman. Thank you.'

'Don't mention it. I'm just glad I caught you,' said Daryl.

As Paul slid into another dream, Daryl filled a fresh syringe with a shot of his special mix and injected it carefully into the fleshy part of Paul's side. So good with the syringe, Paul didn't even raise an eyelid as Daryl slid the needle into his vein. The tranquillizer and morphine mix, a special blend Daryl had concocted.

'Sleep,' said Daryl. 'Your troubles are only just beginning.'

Paul wouldn't remember the conversation after that shot.

For a couple of days Daryl kept Paul sedated. Daryl ate noodles, cleaned his gun and watched the news.

He gave Paul sips of water. And plenty of injections.

The latest report from the local news anchor gave him some hope. Maria Cooper was in a stable, yet critical condition having suffered brain damage. He knew if his luck held, she wouldn't remember a thing. He cursed himself, too. She should not have survived. The press liaison officer for the hospital revealed on the news that Maria had undergone emergency brain surgery to remove a massive subarachnoid hemorrhage.

The cops filled in the missing blanks in a press conference. Sheriff Abraham Dole of the Port Lonely Sheriff's Department confirmed that she'd suffered some memory loss and appealed for witnesses to come forward. The Sheriff's Department were also keen to speak to any witnesses who could confirm the movements of Paul Cooper. The State Coast Guard had received a distress signal from Paul Cooper on Sunday evening, the night before Maria Cooper was found on the beach. His boat had sunk, and his life vest had been found several miles away from the shipwreck. Specialist divers were still examining the wreckage.

Paul Cooper was missing at sea. The Sheriff's Department has refused to rule him out as a suspect.

Daryl shut off the TV, finished a glass of milk and set it down on the coffee table. He'd been careful with Paul's boat. The hole he'd made in the hull while diving in the marina was ragged enough to appear accidental. The battery he'd hooked up to the bilge alarm, and the bilge pump itself, had simply shorted the circuits. The marine investigation team would have to use a screwdriver to get a look at the internal circuitry anyway, thus removing any tool marks he'd left on the screws. No, there would be no way to trace the sinking of Paul's boat back to him.

Only Maria could give him trouble. His one loose end. One that he could tie up if she left hospital before he was through. He thought about the look on her face before the hammer fell for the second time. She was terrified. He held that image before him. Savoring it.

It almost made up for the feeling of disgust that hit him when he'd called her *honey*. That left a foul taste in his mouth, like bile. He shook his head, ran his tongue around his mouth, tasting the residue of noodle broth. Anything to take away that taste.

Maria's survival was a significant setback, but one that he now believed he could deal with. Thankfully, she hadn't remembered anything. If she had told the cops the truth, they wouldn't classify Paul as a suspect. No, then the alert would be in full swing for Daryl.

So far, his luck held. It would need to hold for longer. It would require some adjustments, and he would have to accelerate his timeframe, but Daryl knew he could continue with his plans.

He checked his watch. It was coming up on four-fifteen on Tuesday afternoon. He took his empty glass and washed it in the basin then left it to dry. He opened another pack of noodles, placed them in a pot of water and turned on the gas hob. A towel sat on top of the kitchen counter. Spread out on the towel was an array of weapons. A pair of hunting knifes. One with a blade a foot long. Sharp and curved on one side, serrated on the other. Its twin was identical but much smaller. Daryl placed the smaller blade in the ankle scabbard and clipped it around his right ankle. The larger knife he placed in the scabbard and then put it in the lock box at his feet.

That left the handgun. He picked up the Colt, loaded it, chambered a round and engaged the safety before slipping into the waistband of his jeans. The other knife he stowed in the box, which he locked with a key from his key chain. He removed the kickboard from beneath the kitchen counter, slid the box into the space and then replaced the board.

His laptop lay on the table.

He opened it, hit the on switch then turned away and brewed coffee. While the liquid bubbled into the bun flask, Daryl sat down at the kitchen table and opened a blank Word document.

It had been a while since he'd sat down to type.

At first, his fingers failed to find the right keys. He was a little clumsy, and the inaccuracy of his fingers fed into his words on screen. There was no flow in the language, which felt stilted and halting.

He looked at the screen.

He'd typed a couple of paragraphs. Good enough for now.

He poured his first cup of coffee from the fresh batch, and thought about Maria.

She had been struck from behind. He could blame Paul if her memory improved. Feed her a lie that Paul attacked her, then him, and it was all he could do to escape with his life. Whatever happened, he would deal with it.

He slept fitfully that night, knowing he would speak to Paul in the morning. He'd reduced the shot, knowing it would have worn off by daybreak. On the Wednesday morning, he dressed in his old fishing sweater and brought the .45 and the laptop into the basement, woke Paul and did his fisherman routine. He had enjoyed listening to Paul squirm and panic. Even though Paul had been economical with the truth, Daryl had at least managed to get him talking about the money. That was all he needed.

Twenty million dollars was a hell of a prize, and Daryl knew he had to work for it. He'd made a plan, and so far with a few exceptions it was proving its worth. The only thing he hadn't expected was how much he was enjoying it.

CHAPTER TWENTY-SIX

Sheriff Dole stood in the emptiness that invaded every scene of extreme violence. The house wasn't just empty of its inhabitants, it was as if life itself had left the place. The silence spread everywhere, like an infection. Inevitably, the houseplants would die, the blood stains would wash away but the hole in the fabric of the house would remain.

The Sheriff's Department had been over the house a bunch of times. He'd arranged for techs from Lomax City to take away Paul Cooper's laptop and bring it back once they'd overridden the password and opened the damn thing up. He didn't expect to find much, but it couldn't hurt to try. Deputy Bloch had spent half a day at the scene, and had filled a notebook with observations, thoughts, theories and notations describing in detail anything that she considered curious.

True to her nature, Bloch was reluctant to discuss her thoughts. There was so much evidence at the Cooper house and yet so much of it raised more questions than it answered. Dole insisted that they visit the house together, and talk. With some agitation, Bloch had agreed but added the caveat that their conversation should not be documented, lest their theories become fodder for a defense attorney way down the line. Dole accepted this.

Now, at ten-thirty on a bright Wednesday morning, Dole stood in the living room of the Cooper house and stared at the outline of a large body, marked out in yellow tape on the floor in the shape of the local mailman. Poor Bill. By the time the ambulance had arrived, Bill's heart had stopped. The paramedics had worked on him for forty-five minutes, but the clot-buster injection, and the paddles and CPR had all failed to revive Bill Buchanan.

Poor man, thought Dole. An unintended victim. However, Dole knew that in every violent crime there were always more victims. Friends, family, lovers, passers-by. The more violent the incident, the more potent the strain of trauma that infected others. It got into their system through their eyes, or their senses, or in the more fatal cases it targeted the heart and soul. Dole had seen it before in other towns, other cities. A child dies, or is taken, and the parents pass not long after. It won't say so on the death certificate, but Dole knew there was such a thing as death from a broken heart.

He knew because he was a survivor. He'd never married. There were women who'd come and gone when he was a young man in the deep South, before he moved to New York. That's where he had met one who had been very special indeed. Her name was Eden, and she was twenty-five years old when she died of a rare form of cancer. Dole had fallen in love with her first time he saw her, dancing in a bar with her friends on a Saturday night in downtown Manhattan. They had one amazing year together, and then she got sick. The months of chemo, and treatment and pain were the toughest of his life. He knew he would lose her and she refused to marry him. Refused to make him a widower at twenty-six. Not long after she passed he spent a night with a bottle of whiskey, and lost count of the amount of times he'd put his gun in his mouth. He never pulled the trigger.

In Port Lonely, he found himself gazing out to sea from time to time, searching the horizon for ships, ready to walk into the water and disappear. The job held him back. Jane Doe especially. He couldn't leave that case alone. He needed to find her killer, and he needed to give her a name. Until then he would keep on surviving.

So far, Maria Cooper was surviving too but she was in an induced coma, and her chances were fifty-fifty.

Footsteps outside. Dole opened the front door of the Cooper house and greeted Bloch. Forensic investigators had already visited the property. No need for the hazmat suits. Bloch put on a pair of black latex gloves, same as Dole wore, and then she nodded.

Ready.

They took some time to examine the bloodstains on the door. A smear of dried blood, three inches above the lock. Same blood type as Maria – they were awaiting DNA confirmation that it was indeed her blood. For now, both Dole and Bloch worked on the assumption it was hers.

'Killer leaves by the front door. Blood transference from hands or gloves?' said Dole, standing inside the house, with the door slightly open and reaching a hand up to the area of the stain. Easy to see how someone could grab part of the door, swing it open if they were making a quick exit.

Bloch nodded.

Nothing more of interest outside for now, they went indoors.

Droplets of blood on the floor. The staining looked circular, with tails dotted around the outside in an even pattern denoting the drops fell vertically, probably at ninety degrees.

'Funky old answering machine,' said Bloch, pointing at a black cassette deck that sat beside the house phone.

'I used to like those machines. If someone left you a message and you didn't want to return their call, you could always say the tape got chewed up,' said Dole.

The cassette in the machine was new, and unused. No messages. There was also a record player in the other corner and a stack of vinyl records beneath it. Dole figured Maria or Paul Cooper were into their retro devices. He turned away from the living room, looked down the hall.

The kitchen held all of the secrets.

Going in first, Dole made his way around the kitchen toward the refrigerator to give Bloch space to examine the area where they guessed Maria had been attacked. The ripped-up dust sheet which contained most of the congealed blood had been removed and preserved as evidence. Dole had watched it being taken away. That's when he'd found the hammer when it slid out of the plastic. One set of fingerprints on the handle. By taking comparison prints from the house, and the door handles of Paul's car, they were reasonably sure the prints on the hammer belonged to Paul Cooper. As well as the hammer, two of Maria's fingernails fell out of the plastic as the techs took it away. Dole insisted they be placed in the evidence bag too.

With the bloodied, ripped dust sheet removed they found some blood-mist staining on the sheet behind it, covering the back wall, some staining on the floor, and blood on the porch doors, but apart from that this was a scene of someone who had just begun to redecorate. Cans of paint in one corner, with one of them opened and a test patch on a wall, rollers, brushes, everything you might expect to see. A toolbox lay in the corner of the kitchen, a screwdriver beside with a paint-stained tip.

After a few minutes of Bloch looking around the kitchen, they both went upstairs. They looked through closets, they looked under the beds, checked every drawer. Satisfied, they headed back to the kitchen.

Sliding open the porch doors, Bloch went outside and shielded her eyes from the sun as she gazed down toward the beach. She came back in, nodded and said, 'I think Paul Cooper is our man, but I don't like it.'

'It's nearly always someone close to the vic. A dollar gets you two that's his fingerprints on the hammer. DNA should confirm it,' said Dole. 'What's not to like?'

She shook her head. 'I know there's no real need for a motive in a domestic, but this feels planned.'

Dole folded his arms, leaned against the kitchen counter and said, 'Uh-huh.'

'We know from the receipt in her purse she bought all of this. And we have her shopping list left on the counter. It could be redecoration, but it's a hell of a coincidence. The dust sheets will keep paint off the surfaces, but they'll also keep a crime scene clean from forensic traces. It's too . . . convenient.'

'I don't like convenient,' said Dole.

'I can tell,' said Bloch.

'There's a toolbox over there. Maybe they argue, it gets way out of hand and he picks up the hammer? What's planned about that?' asked Dole.

'The plastic sheets make it the perfect opportunity. And he uses them. Wraps her and the weapon in a sheet.'

'Why leave her here?' said Dole.

She sighed, looked out the window toward the clear blue ocean and said, 'He got waylaid. He wasn't planning on leaving her here. If he was going to get rid of the body there are only a couple ways to be sure. He takes her out to the car, puts her in the trunk and drives somewhere remote. Risky. Even with the dust sheet there could be leakage in the trunk leaving more forensics. Look out there. You want to dump a body – there's a million miles of ocean on your doorstep.'

The storm had passed, and the water looked inviting.

Dole said, 'If he put her in the trunk and drove to the marina, he still has to get her from the car to the boat. Lot of ways that could go wrong. All it takes is one passer-by. Easier to bring the boat out here. The shelf only goes out about three hundred yards then there's a deep channel. He could swim ashore, but how does he get her to the boat?'

'The dead float,' said Bloch. 'He could tow her body from the back of the boat if he didn't want to risk taking the sheet on board, then dump her in the deep blue nothing. Nobody will find her except the fish.'

'If he does it at night, no one will see him. The house is clean and this is just an accident at sea.'

There were no security cameras at the marina. They had no information as to when Paul Cooper left in his boat, or why it sank.

'There was no distress radio call,' said Bloch. 'If your boat starts sinking, first thing to do would be to get on the horn. Cooper didn't. He trigged an emergency beacon, but that might have happened accidentally if he was putting on a life vest. Plus, there's a suitcase missing from a set of three matching luggage items upstairs in the closet and his passport is sitting on the counter. Maria's passport is still in the drawer upstairs. Only one person was leaving,' she said.

'The plan fell apart big time when his boat sank and Maria woke up?' asked Dole.

'Like I said, it makes sense of what we have here but . . .'

'But what?' asked Dole.

'Bill Buchanan,' said Bloch.

Dole hung his head. He'd wanted this case wrapped up. Husband attacks wife, husband has an accident at sea and is found dead. No trials, no media – a simple form of natural justice. Nothing would have given him greater satisfaction. Trouble was, he couldn't help but see the flaws in this story. Now Bloch had seen them too. Perhaps that's what he'd needed. If one person has an idea it can remain in an ill-formed cerebral fog. When two people have the same theory it begins to take more of a physical shape; it's tangible and much more credible.

Pushing off the counter with his arms, Dole curled a finger at Bloch and she followed him out of the house, up the driveway to the mailbox. He didn't wait for Bloch to spell it out, he spewed that fog of ideas straight from his head and watched them solidify in her eyes.

'Bill Buchanan has blown the case wide open. The mailbox post has been knocked over. A passing car, right? No, I don't think so. To hit the post so cleanly, it would have to be either a blow to the box or to the post. The wood is split low down on the pole, which could only happen if the car drove straight over it. Happens all the time. Except there are no tire marks on the grass.'

He watched a light bulb flare behind Bloch's eyes, and her gaze then fell to the grass and scanned the area. No tire marks.

'When we were here the other day, and you talked to Cooper, the mailbox wasn't damaged,' said Bloch.

Dole led her back to the front door.

'How did Bill get inside? This is what bugs me,' she said.

'Exactly. He didn't get in through the porch doors, because there was no blood on his shoes. Paramedics found the front door wide open. If the mailbox hadn't been damaged Bill wouldn't have any cause to go near the front door,' said Dole.

'If Paul Cooper thought he'd killed his wife, and was coming back to remove her body, you'd think he'd close the damn door so no one could wander in and find her. The door is in good condition – no sign of forced entry. The window is still broken in the study, but first responders found the study door locked. Bill didn't get into the house that way. Only way he gets inside is through the front door and there's not a scratch on it,' said Bloch.

Shifting his weight onto one leg, Dole put his hands on his hips and said, 'Only reason the killer would damage the mailbox and leave the front door open is because they wanted Maria Cooper's body to be found.'

For a time, they said nothing. The only sound came from the wind in the grass, the muted tumbling of the surf and the occasional car passing on the coast road above them.

'Our attacker may be alive?' said Bloch.

'Uh-huh. I've asked a Bay City forensics team to look at the mailbox. I doubt they'll get anything from it, but they'll be here sometime this morning to pick it up. Let's wait inside. For now, Paul Cooper is still our main suspect. We just need to be open to the possibility that it might be someone else. Or maybe we're reading too much into this,' said Dole.

'Maybe. What's the plan for the rest of the day?'

'Once the Bay City team has left, I say we go see Maria. God, I hope she pulls through. Maybe she can tell us something.'

CHAPTER TWENTY-SEVEN

Paul never much cared for noodles. They certainly never featured on the menu for breakfast. In his weakened state he didn't complain.

The fisherman had introduced himself as Daryl that morning. He asked Paul if he was hungry, and then set him down a bowl of steaming instant noodles in pale brown broth. He didn't even taste the first bowl. They were hot and soft and they slid down his throat all too fast. The second bowl followed the first just as quickly, but this time he tasted chicken from the broth. He sat over the third bowl for some time, enjoying the taste. Four glasses of water didn't even touch his thirst.

'Take it easy. You've had a serious knock on the noggin. You'll throw up if you don't slow down,' said Daryl, taking away the empty bowl from the table and refilling Paul's water.

Sure enough, Paul felt an uneasy sensation in his gut. The hunger pains had gone. The nausea remained in a mild form. He turned his attention to the laptop, opened on the dinner table in front of him. Daryl had signed him into the laptop as a guest user. Paul hit the back button, and read the next news report about him and Maria. The Google search had thrown up over a thousand relevant entries. He'd narrowed the search terms and was on the fifth page of the results.

With every news item he read his gut felt tighter.

Tentatively, he touched the bandage on the side of his head and felt a sharp stinging sensation. The walk up the basement stairs had been precarious. Until he'd tried to stand he had no appreciation for just how weak he'd become. With deep breaths, and a rest stop halfway up the staircase, he'd managed to make it to the dining-room chair, and the noodles, and the laptop and the water.

He was dressed in a pair of baggy sweatpants and an old white tee that was worn thin from too many wash cycles. Eventually he would have to ask about his clothes, but that morning he couldn't face it.

What if the memory stick had fallen out of his jeans?

He suspected the worst. Until he was feeling more like a human being, Paul didn't want to face another blow. A year's worth of work on a novel was no easy thing to lose. Still, it was the least of his worries right now. He didn't give it another thought.

Not after reading about what happened to Maria.

Some of the articles, from the more low-end tabloid news sites, described her injuries in greater detail. Fractured skull. Blunt instrument believed to be a hammer. Severe brain injury.

Wrapped in a plastic sheet and left on the kitchen floor to die.

Two of the articles claimed to have unnamed sources inside the Port Lonely Sheriff's Department, and those sources said that Paul's fingerprints were on the hammer. Of course they were, he thought. It was his hammer.

Reading it made him feel like he was drowning; that he'd fallen into black water and everywhere he turned it filled his mouth, his throat, his lungs and his mind. A cold darkness that suffocated him. He thought maybe that's what he deserved. Perhaps he should never have gotten off that boat. Maybe he'd be better off in the deep. In the dark. This was why he'd wanted to stay quiet, stay hidden. And when he'd been exposed he knew he needed to run.

If only I'd gone sooner, he thought.

Daryl interrupted his thoughts. 'Mind me asking what you're planning on doing about all this? Maybe talking to the cops ain't such a bad idea.'

Oh, it was a real bad idea from where Paul was sitting. He was the number one suspect. He would be arrested and probably charged with murder one.

For sentient beings in the US of A, there were three things they feared above all others. A terrorist attack. A school shooting. And the American justice system. Not necessarily in that order. Because Paul was missing, even if he handed himself in he probably wouldn't make bail. He could be locked up with America's most violent criminals for two to three years before he even saw the inside of a courtroom. And the cost of a lengthy criminal trial could run into seven figures even with a mediocre law firm. The best representation might save him, but at what cost? And how long would he have to sit in a cell with a murderer while his lawyers ate lunch on him and charged him six hundred dollars for the hour plus the tip. He could be free in two years, if he survived custody, and the man who hurt Maria would be long gone.

'The cops think I did that to Maria. I can't go to the police. It's way too risky. I need to find the man who did that to her on my own,' said Paul.

'How are you gonna do that?' said Daryl.

'I have plenty of money. I can buy information. A private investigation firm would cost a fraction of what I'd pay a team of lawyers just to try and keep me out of a life sentence for attempted murder.'

The timer on the coffee machine clicked, and Daryl poured a cup for Paul and then made one for himself. He put the coffee on the table in front of Paul and stepped back, leaned against the counter and said, 'I think you're forgetting something.'

'What's that?' said Paul.

'You don't *have* any money. Not no more.'

At first, Paul thought this was some kind of bad joke. Or something more sinister. A threat maybe. He sat very still and watched Daryl's passive expression. The silence became uncomfortable. Paul dared not break it. This was a man who only hours before had held a gun, which he was willing to use.

'Don't you get it, Paul?' said Daryl. 'You're basically dead. They're calling off the search. You'll be declared deceased and your money will go God knows where.'

He relaxed, at first, but for an instant, as he realized Daryl wasn't issuing a threat. Then the reality kicked in. If he didn't go to the cops, or the Coast Guard, and thereby avoid arrest, he would be allowing himself to be declared dead. That had consequences. Daryl was right. And it wasn't like Paul could transfer the money remotely. The account had strict security protocols. Not a single dollar could be moved without a personal signature and a twelve-digit code entered manually at the bank itself.

'If I go to the bank, I could be arrested. The cops are looking for me. If they find out about the money, then I'm done. The police will set an alert on the account. Monitor it. The bank will report me as soon as I set foot inside the place. They have to.'

'Cops are pretty smart,' said Daryl. 'You can assume they'll find the money.'

Paul pushed the coffee aside, placed his hands on either side of his head and smiled at the ridiculous fucking mess that was now his life. Nothing he did was without consequence.

Come forward – preserve the money and take his chances in court.

Stay hidden – Maria inherits twenty million dollars she knew nothing about and he has to trust that Maria could give him enough to track down the bastard who attacked her. A lot could go wrong with that plan. Too many variables. He had hurt her enough. Whatever happened, he had to keep his distance from Maria. She was too precious. His presence in her life had been a black mark – one that nearly killed her.

A third option – stay hidden and leave the money.

No, no way. Option three wasn't any kind of option at all, the way things were going – he had someone on his tail, someone willing to kill. If he was to go into hiding, and then try to find out who hurt Maria, he needed that money. The money was life. For him. For Maria. How long would she live before the attacker came back to finish the job? He had to end this to save Maria, and himself. He couldn't let another die because of him. It was essential he get that money. There was no way to finish this and outrun the law without it.

'You're in some kind of fix, pal,' said Daryl. 'Hard to know what to do.'

'I need to get that money, I know that,' said Paul.

Daryl sipped his coffee. Paul held his head together with his bare hands. Neither spoke. The sound of the water lapping at the shore outside became a clock, ticking rhythmically. A metronome of water and concrete, and time, with birdsong high above it like a clarinet on an opening movement.

'You know, there might be a way around this,' said Daryl.

Paul's hands fell away from his ears and settled softly on the table while he gave Daryl his full attention.

'Only thing is, it ain't exactly legal,' said Daryl.

'Go on,' said Paul.

Whatever was about to pass Daryl's lips came abruptly to an end as he clamped shut his teeth, shook his head.

'No, on second thought it probably won't work. Too risky,' said Daryl.

'I've taken risks before. Whatever it is, let's hear it. I need options here. I don't have much choice.'

'No, I meant it's risky for me,' said Daryl.

'Just tell me, please,' said Paul.

The two men exchanged a look. Daryl's skeptical eyes met Paul's eager, pleading stare.

'Fine, but I'm telling you it won't work,' said Daryl.

For the next five minutes, Daryl laid out a possible way out of the situation for Paul. One where Paul got his money back.

When Daryl was done, Paul reappraised him anew. Here, he thought, was one smart son of a bitch.

'It just might work,' said Paul.

'Nah, like I said, too much of a risk. I got a good life here, man. No hassle. I sell what I catch and it just about pays the bills. I got no one coming after me, and I don't owe nobody nothin' so . . . you know . . . I feel real bad about what happened to you and your lady, but I'm not about to risk the little I have. No offense, but I don't really know you well enough to put myself in that kind of situation.'

Paul nodded and said, 'I understand. I'm not asking you to do this out of the kindness of your heart. I'll pay you . . .'

Waving away the offer, Daryl stopped Paul mid-sentence and said, 'No, look, I couldn't—'

Paul wasn't taking no for an answer. He cut off Daryl's protest at the knee.

'I'll pay you two million dollars, cash,' said Paul, and instantly regretted his timing as Daryl spat a fountain of coffee over Paul and the table.

'You serious?' said Daryl, wiping his chin.

'I'm serious,' said Paul.

'I'm in,' said Daryl.

CHAPTER TWENTY-EIGHT

The hospital wouldn't let Sheriff Dole and Deputy Bloch into Maria's room. He stood in the corridor, staring through glass with the smell of alcohol-based disinfectant in his nose. The odor didn't seem to bother Bloch, but it always made Dole's eyes sting just a little. On the other side of the glass Maria lay in bed, her head wrapped in an impossibly large bandage, making it look as though her skull was egg-shaped.

A skinny nurse with sharp cheekbones had given them an update.

The swelling in Maria's brain had subsided following both the injury and the surgery. Her vitals were good, the steel plate in her skull would take without rejection, there were no signs of infection and barring the scars on her head where surgeons had taken off the top of her skull, she would come out of this with no visible damage.

There was no telling what would happen when she woke up. They wouldn't know if she would remember anything, or everything, or most things, or if her memory would ever function again. Her speech, balance, temperament, even her personality could all be adversely affected. In the next few hours the affects of medical sedation would wear off.

She would wake up in the next six to twelve hours, or next day, or next week, or in six months, or never, and any time in between.

There was just no way to tell. They would have to wait and see.

All of these things ran through Dole's mind again and again as he stood beside Bloch, gazing upon the serene face of Maria Cooper.

'Not much we can do,' said Bloch.

He nodded, without looking at her, then turned and together they made their way down the corridor toward the nurses' station.

If there was any change in her condition, Dole wanted to know. He wanted to be there when she woke up. The nurses had his cell phone number and the number for Port Lonely Sheriff's Department already, but it didn't hurt to pay them a reminder.

Dole stopped at the nurses' station and saw the angular features of the skinny nurse again. It said, 'McCutcheon,' on her name badge.

'You'll let us know the minute there is any—'

'Of course, Sheriff, we already have your contact numbers. There's not a lot we can do until she comes round. Oh, do you want to take her clothes? I saw them in the lockers this morning when I came on shift. No one has collected them yet.'

'Sure, we'll take them.'

'There's quite a bit of blood on them. When she was brought in we didn't know what had happened to her, so the nurse put her clothing in a clean bag. You know, for evidence. We had to cut the clothes off of her, but they're all there. I'll just get them for you,' said Nurse McCutcheon.

Dole had come across this new procedure once before. If the hospital suspect the injuries occurred as a result of an assault, they preserve the clothing in sanitized bags in case it has any evidential value. In this case, Dole couldn't rule that out. He would take a look at the clothes back at the station then seal them in evidence bags and get them to the forensics lab in Bay City.

The nurse went into a private room behind her station, and was gone for almost a minute before she returned with a large yellow plastic bag, sealed at the top with a cable tie.

'Here you go. And don't worry, soon as there's any change you'll be the first to know,' she said, handing over the bag. Bloch reached out, took the bag from the nurse and thanked her.

'Let's go,' said Dole.

In the Port Lonely Sheriff's Department, way in the back in one of the interview rooms, Bloch spread out a sheet of plastic on the desk, put on a pair of latex gloves while Dole watched her carefully. She placed the bag they'd picked up from the hospital on the plastic, then took out her notebook and began making an entry. Documenting the chain of evidence, thought Dole. He took the department camera from its leather case and snapped a couple of establishing shots – just to be on the safe side.

There was probably nothing very important, but he needed to be careful. Every cop knew a story about a perp walking away because a five-hundred-dollar-an-hour defense attorney had taken a cleaver to the police evidence. He put down the camera, put on his own gloves and asked Bloch to take a picture of the seal on top of the bag, and to snap one of Dole breaking the seal.

She put down her pad and pen and took two shots of each action.

While Dole held the bag open, he asked Bloch to remove the first item of clothing. What had once been a white tee, now appeared to be a burnt blood-orange color. The dark, deep hue of blood on cotton. A color he had seen before. Many times. Bloch held the tee by her fingertips, and slowly, reverently, she placed it on the plastic and tugged the edges until it had spread out its shape. The camera flashed on the tee, and he watched Bloch lean over to get a close-up of the darkest stain, on the right shoulder. She turned over the tee, photographed the back. Satisfied, Dole put the shirt in a separate evidence bag, sealed it and logged the exhibit number on the bag while Bloch made notes.

They would do this for each item. Bra, socks, underwear. Dole still found himself noticing the respect, and solemnity in Bloch's careful touch of each item. The blue jeans were the last item in the bag. Same drill. An establishing shot of the clothing coming out of the bag, spread on the table, facing front, with close-ups of staining, then flipping the item over. This time, when Bloch turned over the jeans to photograph the backside, she called a stop.

She'd spotted something. Dole leaned in, squinting. There was a lot of blood on the back pockets, probably from the way Maria had been rolled in the plastic and then left. Few areas of the body bleed as much as the scalp. The blood had run right down her back. Dole felt his lip twitching.

'There's something in her hip pocket,' said Bloch.

Without further instruction, Dole gently picked at the top of the hip pocket, on the left side while Bloch snapped away. His fingertips took hold of something, and with his other hand he used his index finger to pry open the pocket further. The sound of dried blood cracking was audible over their breath, but no other sounds could be heard save for the occasional digital click of the camera.

With great care, Dole slipped a piece of paper from the pocket. It was folded in two, and one small corner had been exposed over the lip of the pocket, staining it dark red. Dole placed the paper on the plastic sheet, stood back for the establishing shot, then returned to the paper in the wake of the camera flash.

The stained corners were holding the piece of paper together, binding them in blood. Very slowly, Dole tested the paper, pulling it apart millimeters at a time, listening to the cracks as it separated.

He opened the single page, and put it down on the plastic. Bloch got her shot. They both leaned in.

A bank statement belonging to Paul Cooper.

CHAPTER TWENTY-NINE

The plan.

For an hour Paul lay on the bed in the musty basement and sifted through the finer details in his mind. He often did this. In his novels, his characters' actions had to be credible, something that definitely *could* happen. In other words, could it happen once in the real world and would it work?

If the answer was yes, then he had to look at it again from a different angle. If it could really happen, then what could go wrong? What are the chances of everything falling into place at just the right time and people behaving as you expect them to in that situation? Human error had to be factored into every scenario. No one was perfect. Things went wrong all the time.

Paul played the game in his head. Ran through all the pros and cons, the slips, the what-ifs, the likely outcomes and the fallout.

Man, it really could work.

He rose, went upstairs to the ground floor of the old wooden house and found Daryl on the phone. Paul said nothing. Daryl waved a hand at him, telling him to be quiet.

'I'll be by later,' said Daryl. 'Ten o'clock. Got it. I'll bring cash. Just have everything ready to go,' he said, then hung up the call and gave Paul a thumbs-up.

'You found somebody?' said Paul.

'Sure thing. My buddy in the city knows a lot of the wrong kind of people. He did a nickel in state a while back and made some friends on the inside. You ever been to jail?' said Daryl.

'No, thank God. Hoping I never do,' said Paul.

'Me neither, but it pays to have contacts who've done some time.

My guy says this dude has the skills and he can hook us up. I'll go see him tonight. Probably best if you stay put.'

Paul knew he was right, of course. His picture had been all over the news for days. The Port Lonely Sheriff's Department must have struggled to find a picture in the house. Paul was always careful about photos. There was nothing of him online. In the end, the Sheriff's Department had given the media Paul's photo. All it would take would be one person to notice him sitting in a car and it would all be over.

'Okay, I'll stay here. You know, I think this is going to work,' said Paul.

Daryl smiled, said, 'I know it will.'

CHAPTER THIRTY

It wasn't very often that Sheriff Dole lost his cool. Several things were likely to set him off, none more so than listening to 'hold music' with a phone pressed to his ear.

He put his feet up on the desk, and scrolled down on his mouse, revealing more of the text on his screen. All of the deposits listed in Paul Cooper's bank statement had been made by LeBeau Enterprises. The public company information was sufficiently wide to allow the company to undertake every kind of business from sustainable fishing to fracking.

An internet search for LeBeau led only one place. The Wikipedia entry for J. T. LeBeau made interesting reading. He knew he would need to read it again. With some kind of electronica version of a Scottish ballad playing in one ear, he wasn't quite taking it in.

Checking his watch, Dole said, 'Eighteen goddamn minutes I've been on this call. And I've only spoken to some guy in a call center. I don't think there is anyone at the bank. If there is they must all be deaf 'cause they're not answering the frickin' phone any damn time soon.'

Bloch didn't look up from her iPad. She flicked her little finger across the screen and read more. They'd both noticed that the payments into Paul Cooper's account had come from LeBeau Enterprises.

'You think it's something to do with this mystery writer?' said Dole.

Bloch shrugged. She was back to her chatty self.

'You read books, don't you? Ever read this guy?' said Dole.

'Most of 'em. He's pretty good. Lots of twists, but I prefer Lee Child and Michael Connelly,' said Bloch.

Blowing hot air through his lips, Dole tried to relax. The soothing sounds of Celtic ballads played on a synthesizer made him want to punch a hole in the wall.

He had a pile of reports on his desk compiled by his team over the last two days. He couldn't delay reading them much longer. Anything important had been relayed to him already, but nevertheless he wanted to read the reports – make sure no one, including him, had glossed over any potentially important details.

When he was done with this call he would read the reports. Nothing else for it.

The music died, and Sheriff Dole swung his feet from the desk and sat up straight as if the person on the other end of the line had just walked into his office.

'Hello, can I help you?' said a voice.

'Yes, thank you for rescuing me from that hold music. I've been waiting a long time to talk to you – time I don't have, frankly. My name is Abraham Dole, and I'm Sheriff of Port Lonely, USA. An account in your bank has become relevant in a serious criminal investigation and I need your help,' said Dole.

'Of course, we will assist in any way we can. My name is Mr. Alleyne. I'm one of the account managers here. What is it you require?'

Dole found a photocopy of the bank statement, and he read out the account number, sort code and personal information.

'There's a lot of money in this account. I need to know how it got there. Plus, there's a chance that the money in this account might be moved somewhere else. I believe the account holder may be deceased. If a single cent is removed from the account we need to know about it, immediately. Nothing is to leave that account without my prior authorization.'

'I'll need a warrant which is valid for this jurisdiction,' said Mr. Alleyne.

'We're going to email a letter from my department soon as you give me your address,' said Dole.

'We don't work on email, I'm afraid. There is no WiFi system in place in this facility. Too much of a security risk. We have a fax machine to deal with urgent matters.'

Dole found himself longing to work in Cayman International – no email, no WiFi, just the low-tech stuff he felt more comfortable using.

'Okay, we'll fax it. The warrant comes from a State judge, but I am assured from the consulate there is mutual respect for our laws,' said Dole.

'That goes without saying. Security is our number one priority,' Alleyne said, and disconnected the call.

Dole called Sue and asked her to fax a letter of authorization to Cayman International. He dictated the letter on the phone, and the warrant, and asked Sue to set up a meeting with Judge Caplan to get the warrant authorized.

'Have you read my notes yet?' asked Sue.

Working his fingers into his forehead, Dole said, 'No, not yet. Anything you think is important in there I should know?'

'I didn't go to all the damn trouble of typing up my notes so you could just ask me on the phone. I'm at the front desk if you want to speak to me. You remember where that is, Abraham?' she said, and hung up.

'Shit,' said Dole.

'Coffee?' said Bloch.

The voice startled Dole. Most of the time Bloch was so quiet he forgot she was there.

'Sure. In fact, I'll get it myself. You should take the clothes and the statement over to the Bay City lab. We've held onto it long enough.'

As Dole stood his knees gave him a reminder that he was north of fifty-five and not in the best shape to handle a major criminal investigation.

The Nespresso machine in the modern kitchen extension spat an espresso into a designer glass mug, which Dole then handed to Bloch. She poured it into a go-cup and left. Dole made two more espressos and then poured them all into a porcelain mug embossed with the Port Lonely Sheriff's Department logo. He walked back to his office, settled in his chair and started to read the pile of reports on his desk while Sue worked on the warrant.

Two hours later he'd reduced the pile considerably, and had skipped a few reports to find Sue's. It was spiral bound, around ten pages in length with closely typed text and sported a burgundy card cover. Bloch returned to the office and went straight for the coffee. She had something in her arm, a package in a Styrofoam box. He opened Sue's report and began reading. At the bottom of the fifth page he got distracted. Dole removed his reading glasses and let them fall to his chest, secured there by a cheap gold chain around his neck.

Dole stood. He came around his desk and opened his office door.

Dole saw Bloch had set up a laptop on her desk. It must have been Paul Cooper's. The techs at Lomax City must've been able to bypass the security and let Bloch inside. She had another laptop hooked up to Cooper's and she was standing behind her desk, hands on her hips, staring at the screen. Her chair was a good ten feet behind her, like she'd stood up suddenly and sent the chair rolling away behind her.

'I think you need to take a look at this,' said Bloch.

'What is it?'

'More on J. T. LeBeau.'

Dole pulled up a seat at her desk so he could see the laptop. Deputy Bloch explained she had found several thousand images. At first, Dole didn't understand how so many images had been stored on the computer. That is until she told him that once an image appears on screen, it is copied and saved to the hard drive. Like a ghost. That image is there forever more even if the computer operator didn't consciously make a copy of it.

Bloch explained she had used a justice department program to extract the images. They were then broken down into thumbnail-sized blocks so she could quickly scan fifty at a time on screen. It was easy to tell most of the images were perfectly ordinary stock images from news sites and research sites.

One image had struck Bloch immediately. When she'd clicked on it, she knew it was important. It was a screenshot. In fact, there were two of them. Taken over ten years ago. It was a conversation on some kind of private messenger service – maybe Facebook or something like that. The images had been stored on a file labeled 'J. T. LeBeau'. The computer program labeled the shots as exhibits.

EXHIBIT DB4
Screenshot 11th November 2008

I know your name.

Whatever you think you know is wrong. Don't test me.

My name is Linzi.

So?

I was the moderator in the Facebook group. I helped you.

I think you're confused. I don't know you.

I helped you with that book. I know you. I want to be paid for my services. 100k. Cash.

No, you didn't help me at all. Keep quiet and I'll pay.

Meet me on the South Ridge, Port Lonely. Friday at midnight.

What you're doing is very dangerous.

Pay me or I'll tell everyone who you really are.

EXHIBIT WS3
Screenshot from 8th January 2009.

I know who you are . . .

Sorry, you must have me mistaken with someone else.

I read your WIP. Remember?

No.

The group. Remember now? You shared some of your WIP for comment.

> You're confusing me with someone else.

NO, I'M NOT. I know who you really are . . .
Mr LeBeau.

> You're wrong. I'm going to report this conversation.

I have Linzi's messages. I'll call CNN, The New York Times?

> Who are you and what do you want?

You know what I want. Tell me where she is . . .

Dole's lip twitched. He leaned back in his seat, waiting for Bloch to speak. He folded his arms, watched her work through the possible scenarios in her mind. Even though she didn't talk much, she had an expressive face. A slight raise of her eyebrows. A nod. She had made up her mind.

Bloch got up, went to the coffee machine, refilled and went out back, through the secure door into the lot. Dole followed her. He found her sitting on the hood of a patrol car, looking at the night sky.

'You know if this investigation is going to go anywhere you're going to have to talk to me,' said Dole.

She nodded, blew the steam off her coffee and took a sip.

'If I didn't know you any better, I'd say you were afraid to say something in case you turn out to be wrong. But you know you're nearly always right. There's no shame in giving a theory,' he said.

Bloch went over to her own car, opened the trunk and came back with a hardback book in her hand. 'I haven't read this book,' she said, turning it over in one hand.

The flap copy said, '*The Hanging Tree*: the latest from the multi-million-selling author, J. T. LeBeau.'

'Why has this author's name come up twice in this investigation? There are no coincidences when it comes to crime. Come on, you said so yourself.'

'No one knows who J. T. LeBeau really is. It's a pen name, for an anonymous author. And no one knows why. It's kind of its own mystery,' she said.

'You think Linzi solved this mystery?' he said.

'The first message is from Linzi. My best guess is she's messaging Paul Cooper, saying she knows he's J. T. LeBeau. She wants money. They arrange to meet. Then, the second message – that's from someone unknown. Whoever that person is they know Linzi. Probably from that writers' group they mentioned. Linzi's missing. And this guy knows she met LeBeau. He wants to find her.'

Dole nodded, said, 'So Linzi and person unknown are in a writers' group with Paul Cooper. Paul hits it big time with the pseudonym of J. T. LeBeau, and Linzi calls him out. She says she helped him with the book. Maybe she critiqued it before he sold it to his publisher. She wants money to stay quiet. Blackmail. Nasty business.'

'Maybe she got paid and disappeared?' said Bloch.

'I've been reading up on LeBeau,' said Bloch. 'If two people know who he is, why haven't they come forward to the newspapers before now? They could sell a story like that for a fortune. Definitely more than a hundred grand.'

Dole looked at the sky. The clouds were threatening another storm. He couldn't see the stars, and the moon was partially hidden behind fast-moving cloud.

'We'll run searches on missing persons with the name Linzi. See what comes up,' he said. 'One thing is clear – there's a lot more to this LeBeau character. And I don't like the feel of it. There's something else about those messages. Something sinister. Something I'm not seeing clearly.'

'Whatever happened, it was a long time ago, almost ten years,' said Bloch.

Dole froze, he turned and ran back inside.

Two things had just collided in his head.

Linzi's meeting on the South Ridge. Ten years ago. He burst open the door to his office, and found the Jane Doe file. He flipped it open, checked the dates on the inside cover. He didn't need to check them. He knew them off by heart. It didn't matter – he wanted to check the dates. He wanted to be sure. Needed to be sure. Taking the file with him, he sprinted to Bloch's laptop, scrolled up and read the first message again. Bloch followed him, stood behind him as he opened the Jane Doe file again.

'Ten years brings it close to the Jane Doe case. Look, it's right on the timeline. The first message. Cooper was going to meet Linzi on the South Ridge, in Port Lonely. Look at the date. November 11th, 2008. On Sunday November 16th we pulled Jane Doe out of the spill well, at the bottom of the *South Ridge*. She'd been in the water a couple of days. Jesus, if he met her on Friday the 14th, then that's her. That's Linzi. The son of a bitch killed her and threw her over the cliff.'

Dole could no longer see the screen. The screenshot of the messenger conversation blurred into white and blue smudges. He felt Bloch's hand gripping his shoulder. Only then did he realize he was crying.

CHAPTER THIRTY-ONE

Paul opened the plastic baggie, felt inside. The memory stick was wet. The bag had a small rip in the lower corner.

'Do you have any rice?' said Paul.

'I think there might be a box in the cupboard above the coffee machine,' said Daryl.

'Thanks, I'll just get changed then I'll check.'

The sun had gone down, the heat had stayed up, and Paul had finally managed to pluck up the courage to ask about his clothes, and the memory stick. Thankfully, Daryl had checked the pockets of Paul's jeans before throwing them in the washing machine. The stick had evaded a rough time in the machine, but it still had been exposed to seawater. He had no idea if it would still work. He took his folded jeans, T-shirt, underwear and socks into the bathroom and changed out of the baggy sweats that belonged to Daryl.

He then returned to the kitchen and checked the cupboard. An old supermarket brand box of rice lay open. Paul found a bowl in another cupboard. It wasn't hard to find a clean bowl in this house – noodles seemed to be the dish of the day, every day. Paul supposed that they were a cheap food source for a fisherman who didn't like eating fish and struggled to make ends meet on his haul.

The bowl was soon filled with dry rice, and Paul stuffed the memory stick deep into the grains. A few months before all of this, he'd dropped his cell phone in the toilet bowl and found a thread on reddit about how to dry out cell phones that had water exposure. Uncooked rice seemed to be the preferred method. Sure enough, a day later he turned the phone on and it worked just fine.

With no idea if it would work for USB sticks, Paul just had to wait for another day. He had bigger things to worry about, but writing was his life. It kept him sane when all around him was chaos.

Daryl opened the laptop, and Paul glanced over. He was checking out the street view of some location that didn't look at all familiar to Paul. A digital chime sounded on the computer – a prompt to confirm an update with the option of restart or shut down. Daryl hit the return key, closed the computer, put on his black denim jacket, threw up the hood of his sweater and looked around for his keys.

'On the counter,' said Paul, pointing to them.

'Thanks,' said Daryl. 'I won't be that long. Four, maybe five hours tops. Relax, just don't go outside.'

'Trust me, I have no inclination to set foot outside this house. It's not worth it.'

'Fair enough. If there's a problem, my cell number is programmed into the house phone. It's the first contact. Okay?'

'Okay,' said Paul.

Taking a large brown envelope from the hall table, Daryl stepped out onto the porch and closed the front door behind him. Within a minute Paul heard the rumble of a car with a hole in the exhaust pipe grumble further and further away from the house, up onto the dirt road and into the trees – headed for civilization. Headed to a meeting somewhere shady to buy Paul a way out of his current, extensive problems.

There was nothing on TV. Evangelical preachers, advertisements for anxiety meds and orthopedic folding mattresses, three hundred more channels all showing crap that nobody wanted to see.

He turned off the TV, sighed, and got to his feet. There was too much rolling around in his mind – Maria, the money, the cops, and the certain knowledge that someone had found him. Someone who wanted him dead. His head felt like it was filled with hornets, stinging his brain with every image that flashed before his eyes. Most of those scenes involved Maria.

He felt the urge to write. To escape this life for a couple of hours and delve into someone else's world, someone else's problems. It could never be cathartic for Paul. Maybe it was for others, but when

Paul closed the laptop or put down his fountain pen, his life came rushing back in just like the tide. It always returned.

In the time he'd spent at Daryl's house, he hadn't noticed a notebook lying around, or even scraps of paper. He liked to start a story the old-fashioned way. Pen, paper, lamp and a pot of coffee.

At least there was coffee. He filled the machine with ground beans, topped up the water and switched it on. While it brewed, he took a look around the house. A two-story painted house. Downstairs there was a kitchen and lounge. The house had been set back off the water and heavy concrete walls poured on top of the foundation to make sure the basement didn't allow the bay to seep through the walls. Upstairs there was a bathroom and two well-appointed bedrooms. None of the furniture looked as though it had been made this side of the millennium and it showed.

In the basement he'd seen a couple of rows of bookcases, and there was one in the living room. Paul made for the books. He eased open the door, walked past the silent TV and clicked on the table lamp that sat beside an armchair which in turn was positioned close to a bookcase which had probably been built into the wall when the house was first constructed.

The set-up with the armchair and the table, the lamp, it looked like a reading corner. Paul put his hands on his hips, took in the bookcase. There didn't appear to be any order to the arrangement. Nothing was in alphabetical position, the books ranged from small, yellowed paperbacks to fairly new hardbacks. The lack of arrangement made for a disorderly shelf, and Paul knew if he had to stay in the house much longer the sight of a tall hardback side by side with a paperback would drive him crazy enough to re-arrange the entire bookcase.

Scanning the titles, he saw biographies, thrillers, romances, historical novels, three Jane Austen books, a few more Dickens, hard-boiled crime and the rest were a myriad collection of non-fiction. The non-fiction seemed to have a particular slant. There were half a dozen books on police and FBI forensics. More on the history of the FBI, a large number of true crime books on serial killers and many more on the academic side of serial murder varying from criminologists, psychologists, FBI profilers and more.

While researching his novels, Paul had flicked through a couple of books on serial killers, checked out the information on the FBI website, and read a few more articles online. He'd not come across these books before. Reaching for a tall hardback on the middle shelf entitled *The Killer Next Door: the Sociopath and Modern Living*, he suddenly stopped, his hand hovering in the air. He realized then that he couldn't concentrate enough to read. He really needed to write.

Stupid. There was no paper and pen, but he had the next best thing.

The laptop.

Paul returned to the kitchen, poured some coffee and opened up the laptop. This was the first time he'd opened up the computer by himself. The screen came up with Daryl already logged in. Daryl must've hit the wrong prompt before the update kicked in. Instead of a restart or a shutdown, the laptop had remained on and logged in. There was an option to switch user. Paul did so. He had no wish invade Daryl's privacy any further than staying in the man's house.

He clicked on the Windows icon, but there was no option to open a Word Document. Paul switched users, clicked on the icon again and this time he saw the option for Word. He clicked on it. The screen changed to show the program loading. Then it opened.

Paul moved the cursor over the icon for a new blank document. Then stopped.

There was only one document on the system. It had been opened the day before. Paul wiped his hands on his thighs. He thought about whether he should click on that document, or not.

He guessed it wouldn't do any harm. It looked intriguing.

The title said, 'Twisted.'

Paul clicked on the document.

It opened. He read it.

Then he stood, fast, knocking over the chair.

He began to tremble. It was uncontrollable. He felt the warm urine trickle down the inside of his leg. His body wouldn't move. It was as if liquid nitrogen had flooded his veins.

Trapped in pure terror.

The bastard had found him.

TWISTED

by

J. T. LeBeau

AUTHOR'S NOTE

This will be my last book. I won't write another. The reasons should be clear by the time you come to the end of this story. That's an interesting word – story. Is this a true story? Is it a memoir? Or fiction? I can't say. You may have found this book on the true crime shelf, or in the thriller section of your local bookstore. It doesn't matter. Forget about that. There are only two things you need to know:

1. *On my specific instructions my publishers have not edited this text. There have been no editorial notes, structural edits or other outside interference. It's just you and me.*
2. *From here on in, don't believe a single word you read.*

J. T. LeBeau,
California, 2018.

For ten years Paul had had to run and hide from one man. The man who had undoubtedly killed Linzi. The man who had tried to kill him. The man he'd watched burn Bob Crenshaw to death.

And now, he was in the man's house.

Daryl had been the one who'd attacked Maria. Paul knew it now as clear as he knew anything.

Daryl wasn't who he claimed to be.

And Daryl knew Paul had lied to him.

But now Paul knew Daryl's real name. And he knew the name that Daryl used for the world.

Daryl was J. T. LeBeau.

CHAPTER THIRTY-TWO

The highway stretched behind Daryl like a neon river.

Bay City traffic lay ahead. He pulled off the interstate the first chance he got and drove though the docklands. Towers of shipping containers, stark and colorful against the night sky, gave the false sense that there was some life to the city. There was not. Unemployment was high, crime was up, businesses were closing at their fastest ever rate and there didn't seem to be anything anyone could do about it. He hit industrial sites next. Apart from a couple of businesses, the ghosts of large abandoned factories loomed over the area like a warning to any haphazard visitor – there is no life here. Beyond this were the suburbs and finally the city itself. Making sure to take the long way around, ducking stop-light cameras and the more highly populated areas, Daryl eventually got through the main streets with their empty tourist traps and came to the oldest part of the city.

The buildings weren't so pretty on this side of town. Most stores were boarded up, and apart from small groups of drug dealers huddled around blazing oil drums on the corners, the streets were all but deserted. This suited his purpose.

He found the old cigarette factory without difficulty. The building opposite stood alone. A long-closed liquor store with an apartment above it. Daryl saw a light on in the apartment. The directions he'd been given had worked out just fine.

He thought about Paul, lying in wait back in Port Lonely.

Idiot.

He cracked a smile when he thought about Paul lying to him – telling him that he had twenty million dollars in an account because *he* was J. T. LeBeau.

The balls on the man.

Before Daryl had taken the name J. T. LeBeau he had read Paul's work in their writers' group. Daryl had a different name then. A name he'd left behind a long time ago. Paul's work was good but not great. Second-rate mysteries at best. They lacked the . . . authenticity that Daryl brought to his work through his research.

The twenty million was many things – blackmail money, a means to incriminate Paul, and a trail of breadcrumbs that had taken Daryl ten years to follow to the end. Paul knew Daryl's real identity, and because Daryl couldn't find him, he paid him. For the last ten years he'd searched for Paul, trying to trace him through the money, through his books. It had been a long struggle. One that had finally paid off. And now he was going to get his money back. And he was going to get a new book out of it.

Daryl always knew Paul could never go to the cops claiming he knew who J. T. LeBeau really was and that the mystery author was a killer. No way. No way to prove any of it. Daryl couldn't let Paul go, he needed a way to make sure he didn't cause trouble, keep him at the end of a long string. It was a good story – and Daryl was getting ready to write it all down.

And then Paul was going to suffer for what he'd done.

Maria had been a way in. A pawn. An excuse to send Paul on the run for Maria's murder. Only she had survived.

He almost admired that. She was resilient. Smart too. She had needed some careful nudging in the right direction. He'd managed to get Paul's bank statements by intercepting the mail to his secret office in town. He copied them, then returned them to their envelopes, resealed them and delivered them. As well as the office, he knew Paul would have something secret in that study of his. Otherwise there would be no need to keep it locked. Daryl had stayed over in the house a few times when Paul was away. He'd crept downstairs while Maria slept, used the key to get inside the study. The desk drawer was locked, and there was no key around. Paul must've kept it with him. This had given Daryl the idea – how he could set Maria and Paul against one another. He'd brought the bank statement with him on Friday, Maria hadn't noticed him slipping it in amongst

Paul's papers when he'd broken the drawer. His manipulation of Maria had, however, served both his purposes. Spooking Paul into running and making him a suspect for police. Forcing him into a situation where he needed to get hold of money. A situation that Daryl would exploit.

Whatever else spiraled from the investigation was fodder. It would all end up in the new book. Or some of it, anyway. He liked the title – *Twisted*.

For now, Daryl focused on the task in hand. He needed to get his money out of Paul's bank. For that, he needed Paul alive. And he needed some documents.

He left his car in the abandoned lot of the cigarette factory, walked to the side door of the building with 'Cal's Liquor' in peeling white paint on the bricks.

There were no streetlights on this side of the building, and he let his eyes become accustomed to the dark before he knocked on the cold steel door.

In the distance he could hear a car engine. Probably at least two blocks away. A car was yet to pass him on this street. Quiet like this unnerved him. He was used to having to blend in with people on the streets, keeping his head down and his mouth shut. Somehow he felt safer in a crowd. The quiet of the country life was different because he'd expected it to be quiet.

Cities are not quiet. At least they're not supposed to be.

He waited. Another ten seconds. No sound of footsteps on the stairs. He knocked again. Waited. Stared at the peephole.

The clank of metal on metal and the door was wrenched open fast.

At first, Daryl thought he had imagined the door being opened. Or maybe there was another door on the inside, because only tips of light at the uppermost corners of the doorframe shone into the dark. He shielded his eyes, blinked and looked again.

This time the image in front of him made sense.

The door had been opened by the biggest man Daryl had ever seen. His girth extended beyond the doorframe. This man would have to walk sideways to come outside. He looked up, and readjusted his thinking. Not only would the man have to shimmy in sideways, he would also have to duck. The top of his head was shielded from view by the top of the frame. Daryl could only see a massive jaw.

The mountain bent his knees, looked at Daryl and said, 'You Daryl?'

Only then did Daryl notice the man was holding something. A fist that could've enveloped Daryl's entire head held a sawed-off shotgun. In this man's hand, the shotgun looked like a kid's toy.

'Ye-yeah, I'm D-Daryl,' he said, making sure to inject some nervous tension into the sentence, breaking up the cadence in an affected stutter. Daryl didn't want this man to believe he was a threat of any kind.

'Then get the fuck in here, you late,' said the man.

He stepped back and to the side, and Daryl managed to squeeze past him. As he did so, he saw the glee in the man's eyes. The man enjoyed inspiring fear in others. Daryl played along, for now. He would pretend to be afraid. It put men like this at their ease.

Beyond the man was a short hallway that led to a set of stairs. A bare light bulb hung high above the staircase. He heard the door slam shut as he ascended the stairs and then, moments later, he felt the vibration from every step the giant took up the stairs. The thud of each footfall shuddered the staircase and pulsed into Daryl's body – shaking the bones in his feet.

At the top of the stairs he found an open door on the right shielded by a curtain. He pushed it aside and stepped into a cloud of smoke. In front of him he saw somebody sitting on a couch – a man with long dirty hair wearing a dirty silk bathrobe that lay open, exposing a patch of sweat on his chest. Beneath the robe he wore canvas shorts, and flip-flops on his pale feet. The smell of weed, sweat and booze was almost too much for Daryl.

He thought about taking a step back behind the curtain, just to get a breath, when he felt a hand the size of a hubcap on his back, pushing him further into the room. Looking around, he saw a digital camera mounted on a tripod and pointing toward an empty stool. A big-screen plasma TV had been pointed toward the man on the couch. Daryl wished that the man on the couch had pointed himself toward a shower a bit more often. The stench of sweat came again, stronger this time, as the man got up from the couch and moved to the farthest corner of the room. At this end, beside the large window overlooking the street, there was a bank of monitors and four or five computer towers. There were black cables snaking to the floor, some of which led across the room to another desk, upon which he saw half a dozen printers and two scanners.

'I'm Bunny, you're late,' said the man in the silk bathrobe as he began to tap at the monitor screen.

'I-I'm sorry I'm late,' spluttered Daryl.

'SIT DOWN!' screamed the giant behind him. Daryl jumped, held up his hands then immediately moved toward the couch.

'No, not there. On the stool,' said Bunny.

Daryl stopped, moved toward the stool and sat down facing the camera while Bunny and the giant exchanged a low murmur of laughter. He knew some people thought causing fear in others was funny. Something that had never amused Daryl. He never found it funny.

'Take off your jacket. Sit up a little bit, don't smile, and look at the camera,' said Bunny.

Daryl followed the instruction, placing his jacket at his feet. The flash on top of the camera clicked, charged and then clicked again.

'That's fine,' said Bunny.

While Bunny worked on the computer, Daryl looked around the room, and tried to ignore the huge, threatening stare from the giant. Every time his eyes scanned that side of the room, he saw the giant looking at him like a great white shark looks at a seal.

Daryl leaned forward and fixed his eyes on the floor.

After a few minutes, one of the printers began to whirr and click and a small sheet of plastic spat out of the back.

Bunny got up, moved to the printer and began to break the plastic. It looked to Daryl like there was a perforated break in the center of the plastic, which Bunny was pushing through. Once he'd worked the center of the pink plastic card free, he took a pair of scissors and snipped off any jagged corners. He placed the card in a black wallet and turned to face Daryl.

'Pay the man,' said Bunny, gesturing toward the giant, who stepped forward on cue and stood beside Daryl, looming over him with that sawed-off shotgun held low.

Hesitating at first, Daryl leaned back on the stool, dove into his pocket, removed a roll of dollars wrapped in an elastic band and dropped it into the massive hand. The big man unwrapped the roll, counted and checked the bills before wrapping them up again and nodding toward Bunny.

Bunny opened a drawer, took out a US passport and bundled it together with the wallet and handed them to Daryl. He examined Bunny's work and could find no fault with it.

'You had a lot of balls, coming here,' said Bunny. 'You'd best not come back. Don't matter who you know that got you in the door. Don't come back no more. You hear? I see you again I'm gonna kill you.'

'Okay,' said Daryl, putting the wallet and passport in his front jeans pocket and then holding his hands up, placating the men looming over him. The giant and Bunny smiled at one another. Power was intoxicating. Daryl leaned forward to stand up, as he did so he let his hands sweep low as if to pick up his jacket, but instead his right hand brushed against his ankle and then, with his weight over his feet, he stood up.

He stared up at the giant and waited for half a second. Just long enough for the big man to meet his eyes. Soon as those huge eyeballs met his own, Daryl's right arm flashed forward.

The big man's expression changed. His smile died. His eyes grew wider and the cavernous mouth opened silently. With his left hand, Daryl casually took the shotgun from the giant.

Bunny didn't have time to react to Daryl's sudden movement. He didn't know what had happened until the giant's round stomach opened and the first roll of gray intestine emerged from the wound, and flopped out of the giant's shirt like an alien.

The sight was so horrific, so visceral, that Bunny was instantly paralyzed. His gaze transfixed on the big man's stomach erupting. He didn't even see Daryl pointing the shotgun at his head.

'What are you doing?' said Bunny, his eyes still fixed on the intestines slipping from his partner's wound. It seemed like a stupid question.

'Research,' said Daryl. Bunny didn't look at Daryl. Didn't see the slab-dead expression on Daryl's face as he pulled the trigger. Bunny's face disappeared.

Daryl swept the gun to his right and put the other shot into the giant's scream.

He dropped the shotgun, wiped the blood off his blade and replaced it in his ankle strap. There was blood on his shirt, jeans and boots. Not much, all things considered. He put on his jacket, which had survived the spatter, then stepped over Bunny's twitching corpse.

Two blasts from a shotgun was a sound as regular and routine as bird song in this neighborhood. No one would call the cops. Even if they did, Daryl suspected the cops probably wouldn't show up.

Though he probably had all the time in the world, he worked quickly, ripping off the aluminum covers of the desktop computers and removing every hard drive. Once he was finished, he found three bottles of developing fluid and other flammable chemicals in the bathroom and took his time soaking the entire apartment. He then found a cigarette lighter lying beside a bong in the corner. He lit some printing paper, tossed it and watched the room go up in flames.

Last things he took before he left were the camera and the five grand he had given Bunny.

He changed at the back of the car, putting his bloody clothes into a black garbage bag. There was a wheel brace in the trunk, which he used to destroy the hard drives. He put the remnants in the garbage bag along with the pieces of the camera that he could find. The memory card in the camera he snapped in two. It all went into the bag.

Daryl found a couple of homeless guys drinking around an oil drum twenty blocks away. He gave them fifty dollars each, told them to go find another spot. They left, and Daryl dropped the garbage bag into the drum and stayed for a few minutes, making sure it burned up real good. He thought about the look on the giant's face when he'd split open his belly. Some men would become aroused at such a sight. Others would glory in the savagery, the power of taking life. Most psychologists put it all down to sexual desire – especially the influence of violence, or pornography, or abuse during puberty.

Daryl had never been abused, and his parents couldn't have been nicer people. He'd been a good football player, an A-grade student and an obedient son who was popular in school. He'd dated girls, gone to parties, made memories and done everything a young man could want to do. Apart from drinking. Daryl never saw the attraction of alcohol. He did take a glass or two of wine nowadays, but never more than that. The thought of not being fully in control seemed so repellant to Daryl.

He felt the flames on his face and tried not to breathe in too much of that odor of burning plastic and thought about the men he'd killed that evening.

In truth, when Daryl murdered those men, he'd felt absolutely nothing at all.

It had been the same the first time he'd killed someone. All those years ago.

Fifteen years old. His weekly visit to the local library. His parents had brought him once a week, from a young age, and he'd fallen in love immediately. He could take out books, any books he liked, from the children's section, read them and then bring them back two weeks later. For free. He'd read the entire children's section by age nine. At fifteen he wandered into the non-fiction section with interest for the first time.

He wasn't interested in space, or science. People – that's what he loved. He sometimes felt like Holmes did – that people's behaviors and mannerisms could be examined, determined and predicted if you paid enough attention. He stopped at one shelf, labeled 'True Crime'. He picked the first book off the shelf. It had a picture of a woman on the cover. She was scared. Tied to a chair. The ropes binding her were tight, stretching across her midriff, just beneath her chest.

He opened the book and found more photographs. Men. Women. Dead. Mutilated. Shot. Stabbed. Beaten. As well as the photographs there were descriptions of the crimes. Analysis from cops and psychologists (or *head* doctors) as his mom called them. He didn't like the head doctor. His mom insisted he had to go. She said he sometimes had a problem making the right choices. On Mom's orders he'd been a few times to talk about what he'd done. Earlier that summer he'd corralled a herd of ants coming out of their nest in the back yard, and burned them in a small fire. Then he'd set fire to the nest.

His mom had warned him not to do it. That he shouldn't harm any creatures. And it wasn't the fact that he had disobeyed her which had made his mom so mad. No, it was that he had felt absolutely nothing. When his dad found the neighbor's dog buried in the back yard, that had been the catalyst for sending him to the head doctor. His name was Dr. Carson. He was easy to fool. All Daryl had to say was that he felt sorry for the ants. And he felt sorry for the dog. Remorse, Dr. Carson called it. He pretended to feel all of those things. His parents kept sending him until he left home, and he kept on pretending, and kept on lying to Dr. Carson, never revealing the truth, especially about Isabella.

Isabella arrived at his school a week before his sixteenth birthday. She was introduced to the class by the teacher, and told them all her father was in the army. He got transferred around a lot, and this was her third school in the United States. He liked her long blonde hair and her smile. He wrote a story about her that night, his first, and kept it hidden from his parents, under his mattress. The other girls were jealous of the newcomer. A week after she arrived at school he met her, alone, by chance, in an abandoned lot down by the old hospital. He told her he was looking for a cat. There were posters all around the neighborhood from locals who had lost cats. There seemed to be an epidemic. One owner promised a reward for the safe return of her cat, a ginger Tom called Bernard. He persuaded Isabella to come with him to the old hospital, so they could look for it together. Isabella found Bernard, and a good many other cats in various states of decay, in the basement incinerator of the old hospital. She was a little older than him. She didn't scream like he expected her to. She just stared at it, in disgust. Then turned and looked at him, and that disgusted look remained on her face.

'I wrote a story about you, Isabella,' he said.

'Let's get out of here, this place is creeping me out,' she said.

'Don't you want to know what happened in the story?'

She moved away from the incinerator, nervous, on the verge of panic, and said, 'Sure, let's just get out of here.'

'But the story happens in here. You can't leave. Not ever.'

The whole neighborhood searched for Isabella for weeks. Most of the search took place on the highway and the swampland surrounding it, because that's where he told the police he last saw her, talking to a long-haired man in a red truck parked by the side of the road.

They never found her, and the cats stopped going missing in the neighborhood. For a while, at least.

CHAPTER THIRTY-THREE

The station house was finally empty past midnight. Dole told the dispatch clerk, Sherry, to leave him in peace and that he should not be disturbed under any circumstances. After he'd said this, he felt bad about it, went back to the desk and talked to Sherry again, telling her that if the building was under attack, or on fire, maybe she should come and disturb him for that, but pretty much everything else could wait and preferably could be dealt with by the night shift, currently out on patrol.

The investigation had yielded a lot of new information in the last twelve hours. And Dole had not yet assimilated all of it. It would take a while to percolate in his brain. If anything, he had more questions now than answers.

A yawn pulled his jaw open, closed his eyes, and when it was done he kept his eyes closed and leaned back in his chair. He could sleep there, no problem. It wouldn't be the first time a cleaning lady had woken him at six a.m. with a vacuum cleaner.

'Go home,' he told himself.

Nodding his agreement, he got up and made his way out of the building to his personal vehicle – a seventeen-year-old Toyota pick-up with two hundred thousand miles on the clock and no intention of giving up.

If only he could be more like his Toyota, he thought.

By the time he pulled in to his driveway his right knee was really barking. Slowly, he worked it free of the pedals and got out of the vehicle. The little house in Spring Hills, a working man's suburb of Port Lonely, lay dark and neglected. The house could do with a new paint job, a new boiler and if it wasn't for his neighbors mowing his lawn he would have to fight his way to the front door with a machete.

His key slid into the lock, and he put his shoulder to the door to open it. The wood had swollen in the summer heat. Taking a quarter-inch off one side of the door with a sander was still on his list of priorities, just like last summer and the summer before.

He tossed his keys on the kitchen table, turned on the lights and made himself a sandwich with pastrami, pickle and mayo. A bottle of beer helped it go down that bit faster. Too tired to switch on the TV, or read a book, he went straight upstairs, brushed his teeth, stripped and got into his cold bed.

A half-hour later he was still tired, and still unable to sleep.

He reached out an arm and found his cell phone on the night-stand. Disconnecting the charging cable he turned over in bed and brought up the image that Deputy Bloch had taken from Paul Cooper's laptop. The two exhibits she'd talked to Bloch about earlier. The messages.

He read them through, let the phone fall on the bed and ran every piece of evidence through his mind.

The messages from Linzi were chilling. Here was his Jane Doe, chatting to Paul Cooper, arranging for the meeting that would kill her and send her body over the ridge, into the water where he'd found her all those years ago. He still didn't know anything about Linzi. Bloch had spent the rest of the evening with him, running database searches on missing persons. Each database had a different search function. Some you could search under 'Linzi,' some you had to search under the initial 'L'. None of them looked like the woman he'd found dead. They would keep looking.

Tomorrow Bloch said she would search Facebook. Linzi and LeBeau had met through a Facebook group, maybe some kind of creative writing thing. The second message to LeBeau had been from someone who knew Linzi was missing, and knew LeBeau's real name was Paul Cooper. Why didn't this person report Linzi missing? Were they still alive?

And why did Paul Cooper feel the need to hide behind a pen name?

It felt like he was close to something. He just needed to make a little leap forward, and he was there.

Deputy Bloch had searched the laptop and apart from the images, she'd found no evidence of any files relating to LeBeau, no manuscripts, no social media, nothing to suggest he was about to try and murder his wife, nothing incriminating and certainly nothing illegal, but the internet history did make interesting reading.

Paul Cooper did a lot of research on sociopaths, and psychopaths. He regularly checked out the FBI's Most Wanted list, and read a lot about the Bureau's Behavioral Analysis Unit – the department that tracked and hunted serial killers.

Dole decided then that Paul Cooper was alive. Maria had found out her husband was J. T. LeBeau from the bank statement in her pocket. She confronted him, and he attacked her. That's how it played out, even with the broken mailbox. Paul knew a lot about how the FBI track a wanted man, and faking your own death, particularly just after your wife has almost been killed, counted as a good way to disappear. The FBI don't hunt dead men.

'The Port Lonely Sheriff's Department does,' said Dole out loud.

CHAPTER THIRTY-FOUR

Daryl closed the front door to his house, moved to the kitchen and switched on the light. He drank a glass of water and looked around. With the exception of the light in the kitchen, the house was silent and dark. He listened. Trying to catch the faintest noise to make sure his guest was still at home.

Nothing.

He put down the water, moved to the hall and saw the basement door stood open an inch or two. With great care, he slowly opened the door and took hold of the flashlight that lay on the shelf just inside. He switched it on, pointed it at the stairs and crept into the basement.

Step. Wait. Listen.

Step. Wait. Listen.

Nothing.

The old boards creaked with his weight, but the sound didn't carry. He reached the last step, and sat down.

He angled the beam to the wooden flooring that sat on top of the concrete. Tilted the flashlight. The beam hit the bottom of the bed.

Daryl hesitated. If Paul had decided to run then all his efforts would be for nothing. If Paul Cooper had left, Daryl would have to hunt him down and kill him, and he would never get his money back.

He flashed the light upwards and saw Paul asleep in the bed. He stirred, and Daryl swung the beam into the corner of the room. The light settled on Paul's jeans, spread out on a clothes rack.

'Uh, Jesus Christ . . .' said Paul.

'Sorry, I didn't mean to wake you,' said Daryl.

'You scared the life out of me,' said Paul. 'Did you get everything we need?'

'Sure did. What happened to your pants?'

'Oh, just me. I'm so clumsy. Dropped a cup of coffee all over my crotch. Thank God it was nearly cold. Otherwise I'd have boiled my nuts.'

Both men laughed. Daryl sensed the laughter from Paul was not genuine and this bothered him.

He clicked off the torch, said, 'Sorry to wake you. Goodnight.'

'Goodnight,' said Paul.

Daryl went upstairs, using the light from the kitchen to find the steps. He put the flashlight back on its shelf, went into the hallway and closed the basement door. He couldn't wait to get back to his laptop. Back to the story he'd been brewing for ten years. Maybe the last story he would tell. He knew that paying Paul all that money would eventually lead to a good novel.

It was time to get started on it properly.

He fetched a key from the chain attached to his jeans, and locked the door. In the morning he would need to be up early to unlock the door. Paul mustn't be allowed to suspect a thing.

Returning to the kitchen, he reached up above the kitchen cupboards, found a box of pills stashed behind the lip on top of the cupboard. He took one of the pills, swallowed it with more water and replaced the pack in its hiding spot. The pills kept him level – even. In control. Anti-anxiety meds helped him to take the edge off. Without them, he found it harder to manage his urges, and bring the adrenaline down after a kill.

He found that he was staring at the floor. Looking for the wet patch where Paul had spilt his coffee. His dirty mug sat beside the sink, so he guessed it must have happened in the kitchen, and he looked again.

There was none. He checked the hallway, living room. Bone dry. He peeked into the waste basket in the kitchen, and saw there were some used paper towels.

He tried to put it out of his mind. Brewed some coffee and opened up the laptop. He hit the power button, waited for it to load up then entered his password. He clicked on Word and then selected his work-in-progress document. He smiled when he read over the author's introduction. He didn't intend it to be a confession – he wanted to muddy the waters so the readers wouldn't know what was true, and what was fiction. He liked it that way – it kept them guessing. The author's note was nowhere near as bad as he thought it was the day before. He left it alone. This was going to be his greatest work. He always knew there would be a book in Paul Cooper's story once he tracked him down. It would make for a great twist. He thought about the title – he liked *Twisted*. It was a callback to his first novel, which was called *Twist*. The publishers would probably hate it, but they wouldn't change the title. *Twisted* had a nice ring to it. He thought this new book should have more than one twist by the end. It would be his last, probably. Lots of people might come looking for him after this book. That was okay.

They would never find him. Not like Paul. It had taken Daryl a long time, but now he had him.

Daryl couldn't be sure, but he felt Paul had been lying about something tonight.

He simply knew he had to be more careful. Paul Cooper was not a man to be underestimated. And he forced himself to remember that Paul was many things. A man who had eluded him for a long time. A writer, with imagination and a certain amount of intelligence. A devious husband who had kept his secrets even from his wife. And above all, he told himself, Paul was smart.

Daryl knew he just needed to stay focused and watch his back. Paul was not a man to be trusted. He was desperate.

And desperate men can kill.

CHAPTER THIRTY-FIVE

Paul lay on the bed, wide awake, and listened to the footfalls of Daryl above him. Eventually, he must have gone to bed, and silence enveloped the house. Paul's heartbeat slowed, and he closed his eyes. The sins he had committed were coming back to haunt him.

It all started with a writers' group in New York. They would meet up once a month, critique each other's work, drink beer and eat pizza and then go home feeling lousy about what they'd written. That's where he'd met Linzi and they quickly became friends. She was from Iowa, and had moved to New York to make it as a writer. Her parents had both passed, she had a small bank of savings, motivation and talent. She also found she had a gift for mentoring writers and she was the one in the group whose opinion mattered the most. Pretty soon people stopped coming to the group meetings. They just fell away. It was tough to get published and more and more people quit. Paul didn't quit, but at that stage he was going to the meetings to see Linzi more than anything else. They had a brief fling, but Linzi broke it off, not wanting to ruin their friendship. She was unsure about her feelings for Paul, and wanted time away to think. Linzi moved to Bay City as it was cheaper and her savings were running low. She wanted to keep going with the writing group, and she loved having Paul involved, so she decided to set up an online writers' group on Facebook. Writers could pay for feedback from Linzi and Paul who at that stage each had a novel published, to little acclaim and virtually no sales. They had met up in Port Lonely, six months after she moved to Bay City. It was Paul's first time in the town. Linzi had visited a few times, and loved the place. They spent the weekend, and talked and laughed and held one another. When Paul went back to New York, he knew he had spent time with a true soul mate. Linzi still wasn't sure about a relationship, but they agreed to let things stay as friends, for now. The writers' Facebook group grew over six months, and gained maybe two dozen members. Most of them couldn't write for shit.

Except one guy. He submitted the first half of a novel to Paul and Linzi, and it was just unbelievable. The memory of that first reading was strong with Paul. It was a scene Paul had read a thousand times. Police discovering the body of a murder victim. It was like nothing else he had ever read. It was as if you were right there. The sights, the smells, the visceral details – all burned into his psyche. Both Paul and Linzi gave the writer feedback; just some simple suggestions to improve the piece – shifting some sentences around, shortening a paragraph here and there. Nothing major, but nevertheless it improved the work.

Soon after the writer who had written that scene left the group. About a year later Paul had published his second novel, and he came upon an advanced review copy of a debut novel by J. T. LeBeau. His agent, Josephine, had been sent it, and she passed it on. The first chapter was word for word the same scene that he'd read a year earlier from the guy in the Facebook group. A veteran cop discovers the body of a missing girl in the basement incinerator of an old abandoned building, surrounded by the bones of dead cats. He called Linzi, sent her the book, she read it and confirmed it was the exact same one. They tried to get in contact with the guy, to congratulate him, but he wouldn't return any of their messages.

Paul thought nothing more of it, until the book was published and began to sell well. The book grew and grew and when it finally went stratospheric the first article appeared in the *New York Times* discussing not just the sensational success of the book, but the elusive author J. T. LeBeau. It was a mystery that gripped the country, at first, and then the world.

Only Paul and Linzi, it seemed, knew the truth. They'd talked about it endlessly, pondering what to do and whether they should talk to the press. Paul had traced him through the Word document license for the piece he'd uploaded to the group. He had his real name.

Linzi was broke. She called Paul, asked him for a loan. He didn't have anything to spare. Paul suggested, as a joke, that she tap-up J. T. LeBeau. He could afford it. The initial joke wore thin when Linzi said she would do just that. She had helped him, he could afford to throw something her way. Then Paul had told her to try it. It couldn't hurt. Plus, they had his real name. He could pay to keep it quiet.

Linzi messaged LeBeau, arranged to meet up.

They had both helped with his book. The changes they had suggested made the final draft. LeBeau was set to make millions and Linzi was on her ass. At that time Linzi lived on the coast, and she arranged to meet him in Port Lonely. Paul had waited all night, desperate to hear what had happened. Had he given her some money? Eventually, he got tired of waiting and he called her. No answer. Days went by. Then weeks. He tried texting, emailing, Facebook, left repeated voicemail messages.

Nothing.

Sick with worry, Paul messaged LeBeau and told him he knew who he was, and asked what happened to Linzi. LeBeau asked for Paul's number, and Paul gave his cell number. He called straight away.

He used some kind of voice distortion device. Paul heard an electronic voice – cold and inhuman.

'You talked about me with Linzi, didn't you. You know who I am?'

'That's right, I know. That doesn't matter – where is she?'

'She made a mistake, Paul. She threatened me. I met her on the cliffs of Port Lonely. Nice little town, close to Bay City. I gave her the money, and she said that was just a down payment. She could get more from the press. Said CNN offered her half a million dollars for an exclusive. That was her mistake – greed. I caved in her head with a rock, stripped her clean and tossed her over the cliff.'

He'd said it casually, like he was describing the weather.

'She should have taken the money, Paul. She begged me in the end. She realized she'd made a mistake. She talked about living in Port Lonely with you some day. Setting up a home, having a baby. She won't be doing any of that now.'

'You're an evil son of a bitch. I'm going to the police,' said Paul.

'Don't do that. I'm going to make you an offer. I don't know where you live, or how to find you, but I will someday. And I'll kill you. Only way out of that is for me not to have to worry about you, Paul. Here's what's on offer. I was a wealthy man before I published, I'm even wealthier now. So here it is – one million a year for the first three years. Then it goes up to two million a year. That's enough money that you won't be tempted to go to the police, or the press, and I won't miss it that much. Do we have a deal?'

'Fuck you,' said Paul, and hung up. Paul called the police, but with no record of the call, and no evidence of anyone missing, he soon got the run around. They thought he was a crackpot. He called LeBeau's editor, Bob Crenshaw. Told him he knew who J. T. LeBeau really was.

Paul arranged to meet Bob Crenshaw beneath the Manhattan Bridge. Bob said he would be driving a green Toyota. Paul found the car on fire with Bob still in the trunk. Maybe alive, maybe not. He had tried to black out that part of his memory. He couldn't get to him, the flames were too hot. He stood there and a couple of seconds later the gas tank went up. Paul knew then, as sure as he ever knew anything in his life, that he was responsible for Bob Crenshaw's death. LeBeau killed him to keep his secret safe. Linzi too. Paul had caused all of it.

The secret was the strange life of J. T. LeBeau. Paul had done his homework before he'd met Crenshaw. He knew everything that there was to know about LeBeau. People around him had a habit of disappearing. Classmates. Neighbors. Work colleagues. Even his parents.

He tried to kill Paul that night under the bridge. LeBeau must have tracked him down, somehow. He knew he was meeting Crenshaw and had taken care of that problem.

Paul saw him from afar. A dark shadow. Paul ran through the lot, hid in an old dumpster filled with rats. He watched that car burn all night through a hole in the side of the dumpster. He got out by morning, before the fire department arrived. Commuters on the bridge saw the smoke, called the cops. No one was going to call the cops in the middle of the night for a fire on a lot. The fire department wouldn't be interested either if it was just a car in an old lot. No hazard. They would put it out in the morning.

That morning Paul knew he had to run. He figured LeBeau already knew where he worked, knew all the names of his friends – probably even where he lived. Paul ran. Hid in Manhattan. But he couldn't work.

He needed to end it. He knew that much. The police would never believe him. LeBeau had managed to avoid suspicion. The only way was either to kill him, or make him believe that Paul was not a threat.

He got a call from the same anonymous number the night after Crenshaw died.

'Did you hear Bob calling out as he burned? Take the money then I don't have to worry about you. It's almost over, Paul, you're going to be rich.'

Paul did take the money. He knew that it had two purposes for LeBeau.

First, if LeBeau was ever caught, he would tell the police Paul knew everything and he was paying him to be quiet, making Paul an accomplice after the fact. The money had to be substantial for this to work. The cops would figure that a payment of over a million dollars a year had to be to hide something more important than an author's real identity. This was the kind of money someone was paid to cover up a murder. Second reason, LeBeau would try to trace Paul through the money. Digital banking had so many pitfalls Paul hired an ex-con who'd done time for money laundering to help him move the cash with the sole purpose of hiding it from the original payee. That only worked for a short time, and he had to change the system in advance of each payment. Then he'd confided in his agent, Josephine. She acted as a barrier between him and LeBeau Enterprises, and filtered the money through her accounts, but the payment still went into Paul's bank, minus Josephine's commission, with the payer's name on the deposit – LeBeau Enterprises.

After a while, Paul felt safe. The money came in regular from LeBeau Enterprises. He made sure not to flash it. Any big purchases left a trace. Most of the money he kept. And he hid in New York.

With time, Paul stopped being afraid. Paul knew LeBeau's real name, but he'd never met him, and there were no photographs, anywhere. Paul didn't know what he looked like. Any man on the street could have been LeBeau. All he could do was hide. Eventually he told himself that he could not be found.

Years went by. Paul started writing again. His agent knew he was in hiding. He'd told Josephine the truth. And for a fee she'd kept his secret. LeBeau continued to publish. Each book a nightmarish retelling of a real murder.

Even if he could spend all that money – Paul never wanted to. It was blood money. Then, he met Maria. He didn't think he could love anyone again, but she had proved him wrong. They moved to Port Lonely after they were married. Paul figured it would be the last place LeBeau would look. Linzi was gone, and that broke his heart for the longest time, but he wanted to fulfill her last wish, he wanted a life in Port Lonely, only it had to be with Maria, not Linzi. In a way Paul told himself it would help him move on, help him deal with his guilt. In some ways it made it worse, and he had thrown himself into his work.

Paul knew the break-in was LeBeau. He'd gone for the private desk, where Paul kept the articles and press clippings on LeBeau, trying to track his movements and relate the murders in the novels to real cases. The day after the break-in, Paul had seen the message on his car.

I know who you are. Motherfucker even signed it, *Mr. LeBeau.*

Paul had been found. He had to run again. He was afraid LeBeau would harm Maria. That's why Paul never told her the truth. The last person he'd told about LeBeau had died in agony. He could not poison her with that knowledge. Josephine needed the split from the LeBeau money, and she would never tell a soul. He knew now he should have taken Maria with him, but he'd figured she would be safer if he left her behind, after all, LeBeau wanted Paul, not Maria. He had been wrong about that. And then LeBeau fooled Paul into thinking he was rescuing him from a sinking boat. Paul guessed LeBeau was likely the one who sabotaged the boat in the first place.

He fought down the pain. He would deal with it later.

LeBeau had found him through the money, somehow. Probably the bank. And now LeBeau wanted the money back. That much was clear. He had come up with the plan to help Paul get the money out of the bank. If it was solely about killing Paul, Paul would be dead already. LeBeau could easily have killed him half a dozen times.

Coward.

He let that word sit in the forefront of his mind. Paul was a coward.

He had let people die to protect himself. Paul knew LeBeau would not stop the killing. He couldn't have gone to the police about Linzi, or the theories he had about LeBeau's real-life murders. There was no real evidence. The wild accusations from a jealous author, most likely. He knew he couldn't go to the police now. They wanted him for the attack on Maria, and he was an accomplice – there was twenty million dollars worth of evidence to convince any court of that.

Paul decided there was only one course of action. He wouldn't run anymore. He would get the money first, and at least then he would have a chance of making things up with Maria. He would tell her everything, give her the life she truly deserved.

LeBeau wouldn't try to kill him until the money was out of that bank. Paul had the advantage of this knowledge. He realized then, that he had always known this day would come – that he couldn't run forever. That someday, LeBeau would find him. Maybe that was why he couldn't fully commit to a life with Maria. There was always something dark and terrible on the edge of the horizon.

He sat up in bed, opened his eyes and made a promise to Maria.

He would get the money.

He would give it to her.

He would kill LeBeau.

CHAPTER THIRTY-SIX

Lying in bed wide awake before sun-up was not an unusual occurrence for Sheriff Dole.

He found sleeping ever more difficult as he grew older. Never marrying and rarely sharing a bed with a partner meant he had picked up some bad habits. He drank too much coffee. He snored. He sometimes left the TV on in the corner of the bedroom, and he had no routine. Didn't much feel like starting one, either. Sure, some warm milk, a little soothing music, reading a novel, or even meditating – all of these things he knew could help him sleep. He just couldn't get the hang of any of them. Meds were out of the question. No way was he gonna let a doctor give him so much as an Advil. Word got around town fast. Soon people would say the Sheriff was past it. No, he told himself he didn't need any pills, or routines, and he definitely did *not* want to meditate.

In this job you sleep when you're dead.

That's what he told himself. Increasingly, he thought his advice sucked.

He thought about the message that Bloch had taken from Cooper's computer once again, then decided to get up. The one thing he allowed himself as a little luxury was a damned good coffee machine. It was older than his car, made a hell of a racket in the morning and if the coffee didn't jar him awake, the noise from the goddamn machine surely would.

The sun began to rise behind his house, and he sat on the front porch and drank an espresso. His third of the morning. He'd often sat there while thinking about the Jane Doe case. Now she had a name, but no past, and no identity.

Dole felt the familiar tug of guilt. It was a weight that he fitted around his own neck. Sometimes he carried it okay, other days it took him right down to the floor.

Dole had known Linzi had been murdered. He didn't believe the medical examiner's conclusion – suicide.

Who takes their clothes off, hides them so they can't ever be found on top of a ridge and then jumps off?

He didn't believe suicide then. He had not come closer to doing so since.

He blamed himself for not getting to the truth sooner. Paul Cooper was J. T. LeBeau, Paul Cooper had killed Linzi then moved to Port Lonely years later. Dole told himself he should have seen something about Paul. He should have been able to spot a killer right in front of his eyes. It was ridiculous. Nevertheless, he felt that guilt. And that made it real.

Beneath a plant pot, beside his porch bench, he'd stashed a box of small cigars. He moved the pot, took a cigar from the box and lit it with a match. Unlike his father, who always put the cigar in his mouth to light it, Dole simply held a match to the cigar and turned it. Soon as the tobacco began to glow, he blew out the match then took a puff on the cigar. A poker player from New Orleans had shown him this technique. He said it made sure the flavor of the cigar was not ruined by inhaling the chemicals from the naked flame.

He drank his espresso. Puffed on his cigar. Watched the sky. Listened to the creaking of gutters and stucco from the houses across the street as they were warmed into life by the new morning sun.

In the distance he heard the screech of tires.

Then an engine, revving high.

The Sheriff's Department vehicle came over the rise at fifty miles an hour, catching air and landing with a thump on the blacktop. It stopped outside his house in a scream of tires and smoke. Deputy Bloch got out and ran up his porch steps.

'I'm not on duty until I put my pants on,' said Dole, taking the last drag on his cigar before sending it flying over his porch rail and into the next-door neighbor's rose bushes.

Bloch watched the flight of the cigar butt, then turned back to Dole with a scowl.

'His cat shits on my lawn. What are you gonna do? Arrest me? Christ on a bike, Bloch, it's only seven in the a.m.'

'I wouldn't be out here if you'd answered your damn phone.'

He'd left his cell on the bed. Still, he was only a ten-minute drive from the Sheriff's Department anyway.

'Is somebody in imminent danger?' asked Dole.

Momentarily confused, Bloch said, 'No, but have you read—'

'Then it can wait. My brain doesn't start work until at least nine-thirty, and not before I've had more coffee and some bacon and eggs.'

'This can't wait,' said Bloch.

They moved inside, and Dole fired up the coffee machine just as Bloch started talking. Moments later the coffee made its way into Dole's cup, he made one for Bloch then the machine fell silent. He turned to face her.

'Are you always so talkative in the morning?' he said.

'We have a new suspect,' said Bloch.

Dole ran a hand over his face.

'It's in Sue's report. Maria Cooper got friendly with a waiter in the country club.'

'That's it. That's our new suspect? Some waiter she was *friendly* with?' said Dole.

'No, not just some waiter. I called the club this morning. The waiter hasn't shown up for work in a few days. He went home early the day before Paul Cooper went missing. Hasn't been seen since. His name is Daryl Oakes.'

CHAPTER THIRTY-SEVEN

Paul had never seen the point in meditation.

In the summer there were more yoga classes running in Port Lonely than bars. He'd read articles, even went to some of those classes and bought an online video masterclass on transcendental meditation. The idea behind it seemed solid enough, and he craved the serenity, peace of mind and anti-anxiety qualities of the practice.

It had never worked for him. He couldn't switch off that brain of his. A writer's brain, where every piece of information is fed into the conscious and subconscious and is liable to be spat back out at any moment in the shape of an idea for a story or a line of dialogue on the page.

Only thing that had proved moderately useful were the breathing exercises. Paul had learned to gain control of his breath. Sometimes it helped take the edge off his anxiety, but as soon as he closed his eyes he would see visions of burning cars. He couldn't change that channel in his head – no matter how hard he tried.

Standing at the edge of the bed in Daryl's basement, Paul opened his hands, spread out his arms and took a huge intake of breath. Held it. Let it out slow. Repeated his mantra and started all over again. After ten minutes, all he could see was that car and the flames licking out of the windows. Even so, his heart rate was down. He found he could speak without stuttering over every word, and he was no longer shaking.

It didn't take the fear away. It did help slowing down his body, the first step in being able to manage his fear. He felt better. He would need to be.

Maybe meditation wasn't so bad after all, he thought. This was the first time he'd gotten results like this. It could've been the fact that if he didn't act normal around Daryl he would be in serious trouble, or it could've been the lack of stimulants – no booze in Daryl's riverside palace.

He told himself he was calm. He had to be calm.

If he didn't cool it, he would be dead.

He knew then that the imminent threat of being murdered had provided the only incentive he'd ever had to really giving meditation a try. His life depended on it.

The thought made him smile, in spite of his situation, but he supposed that if more people were in immediate danger of being murdered they might be open to trying new things. It had a freeing quality that morning, for which he was grateful.

His jeans were still a little damp by the time he put them on, but he could live with it. The sock was still damp. He didn't need it; Daryl had left him a few pairs the day before. He put on fresh socks, then made his way slowly up the staircase to the door. It was open, just a crack. He dragged it open quietly then stopped when he heard a knock on the front door.

The front door sat around six feet from the basement door. He heard Daryl's boots in the hallway and closed the door over instinctively, leaving only an inch or two of a gap. Daryl's face appeared in the space.

'Somebody at the door. Keep down and don't come out. I'll get rid of them,' he said in a low voice.

'Who is it?' said Paul.

Daryl turned around, glanced out of the hall window.

'Sheriff. Don't worry. Just stay down.'

As Daryl turned around Paul noticed the gun tucked into the back of his jeans. Daryl reached around, took the gun in his hand, checked it and then placed it beneath a kitchen towel on the hall table.

Paul held the door handle and pulled it toward him, narrowing his view, but at the same time allowing him to see Daryl, unobserved.

There was no kind of bullshit meditation that could stop his heart punching that beat in his chest. He felt the sweat form on his forehead and he clamped his jaw shut to stop the tremors reaching his teeth.

Daryl opened the door, leaned into the gap to fill it, put his boot on the other side to stop the sheriff pushing it open any further.

'Hi there, Mr. Oakes?' said the sheriff.

Paul couldn't see him, but he recognized Sheriff Dole's drawl.

'That's me.'

'Mind if I call you—'

'Mr. Oakes would be just fine,' said Daryl. 'Can I help you?'

'We're hoping so. Mind if we come in?'

'I'm not accepting company at the moment, all due respect, Sheriff. I ain't been feelin' too good these past few days and I've neglected the house.'

Silence. Then the sound of Dole's boots on the ground outside.

'Uh-huh,' said Dole. 'Well, I suppose we can talk here. It's not like there's neighbors to worry about, now is there?'

'Nope.'

'Could you tell us where you've been the last few days?'

'Here. I maybe went out for groceries once or twice, but like I said, I've been pretty sick.'

'I can see the sweat on your lip, son. Fever, is it?' said Dole, in a way that appeared to hint that the sweat on Daryl's face was for some altogether less innocent reason.

'Somethin' like that,' said Daryl.

Another pause. Deliberate. Even though Paul couldn't see the sheriff, he knew this was not a man who had any trouble dreaming up questions.

'Do you know Maria Cooper?' said Dole.

'I saw it on the news. Poor woman. She came into the club every now and then. I'd wait her table, pass the time, you know – I don't like seeing a lady sitting on her own drinking. And she always tipped good. Not like those other cheapskates who wouldn't give you the shit off of their shoe leather.'

'What did you folks talk about?'

'Not much. We talked about the weather, the news, I don't know. Just small talk, I guess.'

'You ever meet each other outside of the club?'

It was Daryl's turn to pause. A dull ache came from Paul's jaw and his teeth squeaked. He let go of the door handle. It took everything Paul had not to attack Daryl. This murdering son of a bitch had almost killed Maria. Beaten her skull to a pulp. He told himself to cool it. Keep calm. He thought of the money, dug his fingernails into his palm and shook with the rage boiling up inside. It was confirmation of what he had already known, deep down. He bit his lip to stop himself screaming and punching the walls.

Daryl stared at the ground, his fingers barely touching his lips. It looked like he was trying his hardest to remember – careful about his answer.

Paul knew Daryl was in trouble now. If Daryl said he'd never seen Maria outside of the club, and Sheriff Dole knew otherwise, then Daryl may as well cuff himself right then and there.

'I don't believe so,' said Daryl.

As he waited for his answer to drop, Daryl's left hand slid out, flipped away the kitchen towel and rested on the gun on the counter. The sheriff and whoever was with him wouldn't be able to see it. Not until it was too late.

Paul bent his knees. If Daryl moved the gun one inch then Paul was going to burst through the door and charge him. He might get there before the first shot, but probably not. Still, if Daryl went for it then he would have to try. Paul couldn't let anyone else die because of Daryl.

Or because of him.

'You sure you never met up outside of the club?' said Dole.

'Pretty sure,' said Daryl, keeping his arm straight, ready to whip the gun into Dole's face if this went south.

With the blood roaring in his ears, Paul didn't catch the sheriff's response.

Daryl's arm tensed. Paul shifted his weight, ready to spring forward off his right foot.

Bird song. The wind in the pine trees. The fragile murmur from a TV in another room. And the soft, internal drone of Paul's body churning adrenaline. Nothing else.

He assessed the distance between him and Daryl again. He definitely wouldn't make it.

Paul crouched down further and opened the door.

CHAPTER THIRTY-EIGHT

Dole had been keeping one eye on Bloch the whole time he'd stood on the porch. She would turn when Oakes was distracted enough by Dole, and holding her camera by her side she got some pics of the side of the house and part of what lay at the rear.

She'd had long enough to get some pics and Oakes was giving them nothing. At the same time, Dole felt uneasy as soon as he'd laid eyes on the man. For a waiter at a country club, Oakes looked incredibly fit and muscular. There was almost zero fat on the man, and his bicep stood out like a softball under a washcloth.

This was a man who kept in shape.

It wasn't the physicality that unsettled Dole. No, it was the eyes. The expression. Clearly the man was hiding something. His behavior spoke volumes.

Right then Dole didn't know exactly what Oakes was hiding. He sure didn't like the question about meeting Maria Cooper outside the club. No, sir. He'd taken his time to answer – probably weighing up whether Dole had something in his back pocket like a statement saying Maria Cooper and Oakes met every Tuesday afternoon in the diner for skinny lattes and Bridge.

Dole readjusted his stance, trying to save himself from the dull ache that was springing to life in his knee. He put his hand on his hip, straightened his other leg and shifted his center of gravity, taking the pressure off the bad knee.

Soon as Dole's hand went for the hip, right behind his gun-holster, he saw Daryl's arm tense.

That's when Dole sensed something badly wrong with Oakes. The man at the door was ready to attack. He probably had a two-by-four on the table next to the front entrance, or maybe a gun. A frightening thought even without the shark-dead eyes.

He asked him if he was sure. Oakes thought about it. Or was he thinking about whipping out a knife or a gun instead? Eventually, Oakes said he was pretty sure.

Dole let a good many things slide. He'd never gotten around to joining the digital revolution, there was a broken plank on his stairs, his shoes could do with a polish, but he put these things off – said he'd get around to it eventually. Eventually he would, too.

One thing he didn't let slide was his gun handling. Dole shot fifty rounds every two weeks. All of them wound up just where he'd intended them to go. Every month, he did draw-fire training. A hang back to his first days on the force when he'd undergone close protection training. He could draw his weapon from the holster, fire three shots. All in under three seconds. He'd gotten it down to just over two seconds in his youth. Now he was content with a two-point-five second average. Bloch was about the same.

If Oakes did make a play – Dole was ready.

Dole didn't ask any more questions. Now was not the time. He just let the moment breathe. With any other potential suspect, Dole would search their face carefully, especially the eyes. Oakes had dead eyes. Almost black in this light.

Remaining quiet and watchful for most of the conversation, he could sense Bloch's unease. She shifted her feet, then took a step forward.

'Do you know Maria Cooper's husband, Paul?' said Bloch.

'No, can't say that I do,' said Daryl.

'Maybe we should be getting back,' said Deputy Bloch.

Never taking his gaze from Oakes, Dole took a step backwards, said, 'Maybe you're right. You've been helpful, Mr. Oakes. We'll leave you in peace, for now.'

When Dole and Bloch were safely in the car, and Oakes had closed his front door, both of them breathed a sigh of relief.

'That guy is intense,' said Bloch.

'Sure is, did you see the boat out back?' said Dole.

'I sure did. Got a sneaky pic on my phone, too. That's a hell of a boat to run on a waiter's salary.'

'We'll head back to the station, do the paperwork then get it to the judge. You think it's enough for a warrant to search Daryl's house?'

She nodded, put the car in reverse and got back on the road.

CHAPTER THIRTY-NINE

Daryl shut the front door, locked it with the deadbolt then turned and saw Paul on his hands and knees in the hallway.

'Have they gone?' said Paul.

Pulling back the blind, Daryl watched the sheriff's car reverse back up the driveway, out onto the road, stop and then drive back toward town.

'They've gone,' said Daryl, lifting the kitchen towel away from the gun. He picked up the weapon then put it back into the waistband of his jeans. At the front this time.

'You were supposed to stay in the basement,' said Daryl, in a flat, casual tone.

Paul stood up and said, 'I thought you were going to shoot. You might have needed an extra pair of hands to make a quick exit.'

Shaking his head, Daryl said, 'Nah, that would have been a last resort. Thanks, anyway. Did you hear what we talked about?'

As Daryl asked the question he took a moment to study Paul. If this man had begun to suspect Daryl then he needed to know. They were about to take an incredible risk, and Daryl knew he couldn't pull it off if Paul was not to be trusted. As Paul took in the question, Daryl saw his neck flushed red. Maybe it was a reaction to the cops being here, or maybe it was something else.

'I heard a little. I didn't know you worked at the country club,' said Paul.

Ah, maybe that was it, thought Daryl.

'I worked there part-time. Fishing don't pay the rent on its own. I saw your wife there a couple times. And what I told the cop was the truth – that's why he left; I only talked to her for a few seconds. Just passing the time of day. That's all. I didn't know her.'

Again, Daryl brought all of his attention and concentration to focus – zeroing in on Paul's every movement, gesture and word.

'Fair enough. I mean, why would you know her, right?' said Paul.

Daryl nodded, 'Right,' he said.

Daryl knew there would always be a wrinkle of doubt in Paul's mind. Had to be. The only uncertainty would be whether that wrinkle got mostly ironed out in time or just got bigger and bigger. That was beyond Daryl's control. He would just have to wait it out and see. No way to second-guess it. The only thing he could do was to keep a closer eye on Paul, make sure he was thinking about other things.

There was a lot to think about.

'I think we have to move up our schedule,' said Daryl. 'That sheriff is a fool. Same with his deputy. They can't find you so they're running around chasing their tails. They want to make sure they've got their man.'

'So when do we leave?' said Paul.

'We'll get loaded up now, aim to be out of here in two hours flat.'

'That soon?'

'Yeah, your money is not going to wait there forever. If you're declared dead you'll never see it again. Let's go get it.'

CHAPTER FORTY

In most novels and movies, people wake up from comas by sitting bolt upright in bed and screaming.

It's dramatic. Visual.

It just so happened that Maria Cooper woke up that way too.

But Maria didn't really wake up. Not fully.

Her eyes stirred beneath her eyelids. Her heart rate went up. Breathing rate intensified, her chest filling with air then blowing out, faster and faster in time with her heart until she was panting. The nurses would have seen the spike in her vitals if they happened to be in the room. In the case of the nurses being engaged in other activities, the only way they might know if she was awake was an alarm.

The heart rate got close to sounding that siren.

In the end, there was no need. The nurses came running when they heard the screams.

Maria's eyes opened, startled by the noise. The terrified scream. It took her a few seconds to realize it was her that was making that noise. And then she really let go.

A junior doctor was paged, and he came and administered a sedative to calm her while the nurses held her down.

She didn't say a word. She just screamed.

Maria's mind had reset. She had vague memories of a kindly woman in New York working barefoot behind a deli counter, a man with a sad face who spoke softly to her and held her close, and a house on the beach with the wind whipping the long grasses around it.

She didn't know if this was her life, or a dream.

The sedative kicked in right when Maria felt a scorching pain in her head.

The last thing she saw was a wall of plastic, drenched in blood.

CHAPTER FORTY-ONE

In the Port Lonely Sheriff's Department, spread out on a normally cluttered desk, was a line of hardback books. Ten novels.

The complete works of J. T. LeBeau. Bloch had been to the bookstore.

'Make sure you write it up on expenses,' said Dole.

'I've read most of them. We need to get inside Paul Cooper's head. See how he thinks.'

'And the search warrant for Daryl's place?'

'Sue is typing it up,' said Bloch.

For almost ten minutes she briefed Dole on LeBeau's work. Each novel was a different thriller – different characters, different settings, different plot. All of the novels were global number-one bestsellers. And no one was really sure why.

'Why would one of the most successful authors on the planet, adored by millions of readers, not want to come forward and accept that recognition?' said Dole.

Dole had sat in his chair, listening intently to the potted history of J. T. LeBeau. It had been the longest, sustained time he'd heard Bloch talk. He hadn't interrupted. He could tell that at various points during her mini-presentation she had become conscious that she was talking for a long time. Dole said nothing. His attention and silence willing her on. Bloch was beginning to open up, and he wanted more of that. He liked her. Even admired her. In time, she would be a much better officer than he could have ever hoped to become.

It wasn't so easy bouncing ideas off Bloch. They tended to hit her, then slide off her forehead like Jello. She didn't talk much at all, but when she did you could be damn sure she had something worth saying.

'Come on, you must have thought about this, no? Why would the guy stay anonymous when the world loves him so much? Who could resist that?' said Dole, finally breaking into her speech.

'I could,' said Bloch.

Nodding, Dole said, 'I could believe that, but you're—'

'I'm what?' said Bloch.

'You're not the type that talks or socializes much, are ya?'

'I socialize, but not in Port Lonely. Are you kidding me? If I want to meet somebody I'd prefer it if they weren't carrying a cane and standing on their new hip.'

'Yeah, I get it. We're all old. There are a few your age. Paul Cooper and Maria aren't that much older than you.'

'True, but they're not my type. Anyway, I get out and see people. And I talk to them. So what? I'm quiet, and I know that.'

'There's nothing wrong with telling me a theory,' said Dole.

'I don't like to speculate. I like to look at the evidence – I like to *know*,' said Bloch.

'We don't *know* much, but there's nothing wrong with healthy speculation. Use your imagination. Let's say LeBeau isn't a mute hermit. Let's say he's an ordinary guy. Why doesn't he put his hand up and claim all the credit and adoration?

She pulled at the flesh on her chin, said, 'That's the wrong question, Sheriff.'

Tapping his finger along the spines of the books on the table, Dole said, 'He wrote all of these books. I don't have time to read them so you'd better cut to the chase if you know something I don't. What *is* the right question?'

Bloch picked up a book entitled *Twist* and gave it to Dole. He took it in both hands.

'This is his first book. I read it when it came out, but I don't remember the plot. I'll need to read it again. First books are often autobiographical, whether the author intended them to be or not. It just kind of comes out. There might be a clue in this book. See, the real question is why did Cooper kill Linzi to keep his LeBeau identity a secret? When she was murdered, the book had done really well, but it wasn't a global bestseller just yet. That wouldn't happen until later.'

'He already had something to hide. He didn't want anyone to know who he was from the get go. Success didn't feature in it. There was something about Cooper that was rotten from the start. What could that be?'

'I couldn't find anything linking Linzi or Paul Cooper to a writers' group on Facebook. I'd say all the accounts are deleted. My feeling is Cooper was trying to hide his past. Yet his record is clean.'

Opening the first page of *Twist*, Dole shook his head and said, 'Whatever it is he's hiding, it was worth killing Linzi to do it. At least to him.'

'Has to be something big, doesn't it?' said Bloch.

'Sure does,' said Dole. He scanned the first line of *Twist*, written ten years ago, and let the words sink in.

There is little in this world that is more fascinating than a dead body. Especially one that has had its head twisted around the wrong way.

CHAPTER FORTY-TWO

Paul had watched Daryl pack a small bag. A shirt, jeans, the items he came back with the night before, a ball cap, a .45 and two knives. And his laptop.

All set.

They loaded up the boat with bottled water, some baloney sandwiches, and that small bag. Paul brought two items. The memory stick was the first. It felt dry to the touch, but he still had no idea if it would work. It didn't seem to matter much when he thought about it as a novel. It was more about Paul's motivation. He was about to do something that could get him arrested or killed. He had to believe that there was a life after all of this was over.

The memory stick was a symbol of that life-to-be. He wanted to keep it.

In the afternoon they set off on the water. Daryl piloting. Paul sitting in the rear of the boat, behind the cabin. After an hour or so of silence, Daryl said, 'We should be in Miami in another three hours. We'll refuel and head off from there. Should reach the Caymans by dawn.'

Staring at the back of Daryl's neck for hours set Paul's mind into focus. He needed Daryl to get the money. No way he could get it without him. At the same time, he occasionally leaned forward and felt the paring knife in the back pocket of his jeans. His second item. A secret addition to his otherwise sparse luggage. He'd been quick and quiet in the kitchen, whispering open the drawer and selecting a sharp, small knife which fit easily into his pocket. Daryl didn't see a thing – he'd been out at the boat, making his checks.

Paul thought about Daryl sabotaging his writing boat, and then showing up as his savior. He thought of the life he could have had with Linzi, and her last minutes on this earth. His teeth ground together, making a squeaking noise and his jaw muscles pulsed. He thought about Maria. She would've been terrified, and all because of this man. He thought about drawing the little knife from his pocket and slamming it into the base of Daryl's skull. Twisting it.

Twisting it again.

Feeling the warm blood run through his fingers.

The salt on his lips tasted like blood in that moment of thought. And tears followed. He wiped them away, quickly.

The money stopped him killing Daryl. And the fearful weight of what would happen if he missed with the knife . . .

No, Paul decided he would wait. One more day. Soon as they had the money, and they were going back to the boat, Paul would find a way to kill Daryl.

He had to.

Because as soon as the money was out of that bank, and in Paul's hands, Daryl would try to kill him too. Daryl had the gun, the knife, the weight and height advantage. Plus he was a smart son of a bitch. But with the money on board, Daryl would relax. He didn't know Paul was alive to his real identity. That gave Paul the advantage. He could play it cool. Get the money, wait until Daryl is distracted driving the boat, then he would strike. If Daryl was going to attack Paul, which he clearly was, then he would wait until they had the money and the boat was in open water. That would be the time to pull the gun. As long as Paul got to Daryl before that, things would be okay. He couldn't run without the money – he'd never make it.

The boat skipped along the coastline, riding the waves from haulage ships and cruise liners. A whine from the engine, the splash of the hull on the bed of the waves, the smell and taste of the sea all took on a dark tinge for Paul.

Tomorrow one of the men on that boat would kill the other. Taking a life was no small matter. Paul had never been in that situation. Now he wanted nothing more than to stop this killer. He imagined kneeling over Daryl's body, the life slowly bleeding from the killer's eyes. He would lean over Daryl then, and whisper to him that he knew all along about his plan. He knew who he was, and he was going to kill him.

For Maria. For himself.

For Linzi.

As alien as the thought felt, it also made him feel strong. He needed that strength of belief if he was to survive. Before they'd left, he'd asked Daryl if he could do one last news search and see if there was any update on Maria's condition. Daryl relented, and Paul searched and found nothing more.

He needed Maria to pull through. Something good had to come from all this darkness. Paul stared again at Daryl's back.

Tall, lean. The muscular valleys of Daryl's back were a perfect target. Paul started to plan it out. How he would do it.

Where he would put the knife.

The sun began to set. And the lights came on in the distance. Miami. A pitstop.

By the time the boat approached the mooring, Paul had a plan.

CHAPTER FORTY-THREE

Judge Griffiths, a seventy-four-year-old man who signed whatever law enforcement put in front of him, authorized the warrants and orders that Sheriff Dole put on the judge's desk. He was in the judge's house, in the judge's private study, on the judge's own time, and his Honor didn't even read a goddamn word of what Dole had written.

Nor did he look at the photographs Bloch had taken at Daryl's house.

The judge didn't listen to him either. After leading him into the house, and then the study, the judge had seemed only too glad to have some respite from his wife. Dole had met her a few times, and he'd been pleased to leave her company on every occasion. Mrs. Griffith talked. She talked a lot. Never saying anything *to* you, just *at* you. And she did so at great volume. For a small, slight bird of a lady she had a tongue on her like an industrial wind machine. Thankfully, Mrs. Griffith was upstairs for the moment.

'Now, now, there's no need, Sheriff. I'm sure this is all absolutely necessary and just fine. There you go, all done,' said the judge, handing the executed paperwork back to him. Just at that moment, Dole wondered what would happen if he ever found himself on the wrong side of the law. With Judge Griffith showing no inclination toward his professional duties or even a moment's thought toward the constitution, Sheriff Dole imagined that being on trial in front of the judge could be a difficult problem for any defendant. Unless you were accused of murdering Mrs. Griffith – in that case you might get an easier ride out the door than expected.

'Thanks, Judge,' said Dole, making his way to the study door.

'You gotta leave so soon? I was hoping you could stay a little while, have some coffee and say hi to Mrs. Griffith,' said the judge.

Dole increased his pace, practically running out of the study and toward the front door, answering the judge over his shoulder – 'Sorry, Judge, I have to go right now. Urgent police business.'

He shut the front door behind him. At that moment he felt a little sorry for the judge.

Back at the Sheriff's Department, Dole locked the search warrants in the safe. The order freezing the account of Paul Cooper in the Caymans he faxed and emailed to the bank, requesting an immediate response. Two hours later an email landed from the bank's chief legal officer confirming the recognition of the court order by the bank under international money laundering regulations. Not a penny could be taken or removed from that account. The twenty million was going to stay in the account, and no one would be allowed to touch it. In the morning, he planned to hit Oakes with the search warrant. Dole closed up his office and saw Sue at the dispatch desk, filing her nails with a level of concentration that amazed him at this late hour.

'I read your report,' said Dole.

'I'm honored,' said Sue, neglecting to lift her gaze from her nails.

'Now don't be getting on your high horse. It was good work. All of it. I wanted to ask you something.'

This time she looked at him.

'What do you make of this whole J. T. LeBeau business? You think it's Cooper who attacked his wife? Or the other fellah, Oakes? Maybe he had something to do with Cooper's boat sinking?'

Sue took off her earpiece mic, folded her arms and said, 'It's sure suspicious that Oakes has been sick since the night of the attack. You need more before you could pin it on him. Lot more. I think Cooper was afraid of something. Maybe he was afraid you'd find out he was that author fellah LeBlue.'

'LeBeau.'

'Whatever. Any which way you look at it, Mr. Cooper didn't want the Sheriff's Department wriggling around in his business. That's for sure.'

'What makes you say that?'

'Honey, you may be the sheriff, but I take the calls. We've had four breaking and entering reports over the last three years. Every one of 'em was a pain in the ass for me. Those people were never done callin' and complainin', *why ain't you caught that burglar? When am I gonna get my grandma's necklace back?* Now I know there was nothin' taken in the Cooper break-in, but Mrs. Cooper got a slap for her troubles. Any man in this county would be breakin' your balls to catch the bastard who broke into their house and assaulted their wife—'

'But not Cooper,' said Dole.

'Right. I wouldn't be surprised if he knew exactly who broke in.'

Dole's mind ticked over. Everything seemed to be pointing at Cooper for Maria's attack, and Linzi's death.

'Thanks,' said Dole.

'Now was that so hard to say?' said Sue.

On the way back home, Dole pulled over. Stopped. Closed his eyes and repeated the thought pattern in his mind.

Cooper's cover had been blown. Someone broke in and either they discovered Cooper's identity as LeBeau, or they already knew it. It makes sense that the intruder would also know why Cooper was hiding behind LeBeau in the first place.

It was Oakes. He somehow worked it out. Could be that he attacked Maria, maybe sank Cooper's boat too. Maybe he was after the money in the Caymans. All Dole needed was a solid link between Oakes, Cooper and LeBeau.

He fired up his cell phone. Called Bloch. He was bumping up the time of the raid. Told her to meet him at the station at five a.m. At five thirty a.m. they were going to break down the front door while Oakes was still asleep, arrest him, search him, and then search the house. Daryl Oakes had a lot of questions to answer.

Tomorrow this case would be blown wide open.

He could feel it.

CHAPTER FORTY-FOUR

Miami proved to be a longer pit stop than Daryl had expected.

For most of the day he'd gone over the plan in his mind. Trying to find weaknesses. Probing the possibilities. Paul had said little that day, but as they approached Miami he cracked the silence.

'I need a suit,' said Paul.

'What for? We're not going to a fancy dinner anytime soon,' said Daryl.

'I've been to the bank maybe eight or nine times. I've always dressed well. It's that kind of place. Don't think I'm being ungrateful and I sure as hell don't mean it as an insult, but these jeans and this shirt kinda make me look like I'm on the run.'

Looking over his shoulder, Daryl gave him a look up and down.

'We get one shot at this. Everything needs to be perfect when we land in Grand Cayman.'

'Okay,' said Paul.

They moored the boat at the marina, and Daryl paid the harbormaster in cash for the docking fee and the fuel, and even threw in an extra fifty for the late arrival. Paul stood behind him, saying nothing, his face hidden under one of Daryl's ball caps.

Within ten minutes they were on a strip filled with bars, restaurants and nightclubs. The heat was worse in Miami, the wind off the coast didn't seem to bite into the humidity one bit. They were sweating through their clothes, tired and hungry. Sweet spices and cigar smoke caught the air outside every restaurant, the patio tables filled with diners. They would eat later.

Daryl hailed a cab, which took them to an all-night shopping mall. After a day in the sun, and the Miami juice that filled every particle of air with water, the air-conditioned mall was delicious. Together, they found a department store – not too flashy, but not too shabby either. Paul took his time, selecting a blue cotton shirt, light gray single-breasted suit. He found a cheap pair of brown polished-leather shoes that looked fairly expensive at first glance. A pair of gray socks finished the ensemble. No need for a tie. Smart casual was just fine.

He took the items into a changing room, tried on each one. In the mirror he caught sight of his face. Almost a week without a shave. Several months ago he'd tried to grow a light beard to follow the current fashion trend. Maria said he looked dirty. He would need to pick up a razor and some foam. Maybe a hair product too.

Satisfied with the suit, he undressed and carefully rehung the items and left the fitting rooms.

Daryl sat on a stool outside, like he was waiting on a partner.

Paul picked out a pair of black jeans, black sports coat, a Stetson hat and a white shirt for Daryl who took all of the items to the counter, paid in cash and they left together. They ate a meal in silence in McDonalds with their shopping bags around their ankles. Instead of a cab back to the boat, they walked to allow Paul to stop at a pharmacy and pick up a pack of disposable razors, hair gel and some shaving foam.

Ninety minutes after they docked, they pulled away in Daryl's boat into the night with the light streams of Miami reflected in the water. They would hit Grand Cayman before midday. Paul took himself to the back of the boat, curled up on the bench and tried to sleep. He was exhausted, and with every passing mile he felt further away from himself. This reality appeared both dreamlike and yet hyper-real. All of his senses were on high alert. He could smell everything, his eyes had grown accustomed to the darkness and his body to the roll and bang of the boat as it caught a wave. This was not Paul's life. This was a test. A strange, deadly game that he had found himself playing. He didn't dare think of the consequences of messing up.

His thoughts drifted to Maria. Now, in the dark, alone and with the knowledge of all that had happened, he knew then that he had wronged her. She had been the one great thing in his life, tainted only by his lies. He couldn't be with her again. No way to square that circle. If he lived through the next twenty-four hours he would try and make amends. He swore it. And he meant it. If she hadn't met Paul, then Maria would not have had to go through that attack. Praying was not something Paul had even entertained for the last twenty years. Yet he found himself clasping his hands together and mumbling the Lord's Prayer for Maria. For himself.

He wondered if he could pray for the death of the man steering the boat.

If there was a God, he prayed it was a vengeful one.

CHAPTER FORTY-FIVE

Dole knew he didn't need to give a warning.

Didn't matter much to Dole. He did things by the book. Even if they were pointless matters of protocol, you never knew when the smallest slip might come back to bite you in the ass.

'Daryl Oakes, Port Lonely Sheriff's Department, we've got a warrant to search this property. Open up or we're coming in!' cried Dole.

He waited. Counted to ten. Gave the nod.

Bloch picked up the Big Black Key. This was the name Dole had given to the thirty-five-pound steel battering ram that the department had used only once or twice since they bought it. Bloch had used it on every occasion. Dole didn't have the strength. She swung it away from her body, stepped forward, reversed the momentum and guided the impact sphere to the point on the front door right beside the lock.

The wooden door gave way, the lock punching out and hitting the back wall. Sidearms ready, Dole and Bloch went in. They'd already scouted around the property. No back door. And the boat was gone.

They cleared the first floor. Then the upstairs bedrooms and bathroom. No one at home. Just the basement. The most dangerous room in the house. No easy way out, no way to clear the corners before you found you were standing in the middle of the room, an easy target.

Bloch and Dole lit up pocket flashlight and took it slow on the basement stairs. They paused every fourth stair to allow Bloch to crouch down and check through the slats of the steps at the area behind and beneath them. While she shone her light through the gaps, dipping her head down low for a better look, Dole crouched down too and kept his torch moving, hoping to catch any movement over Bloch's shoulder – covering his partner.

Descending in this manner was the only safe option. It took three minutes to get down. Dole didn't mind. He had three minutes to spare.

They checked the basement. Nobody there, but there were signs of recent activity. Circular grooves in the dust covering the table where someone had placed a cup of coffee. The bed sheets smelled relatively fresh, while everything else had the faint odor of mold. It was in Bloch's nature to be meticulous, and Dole found himself watching her work. She checked the places that Dole had already searched, just to be sure. They took their time. It felt like there was something in the house. Something there to be found. A strange feeling, but one not unfamiliar to law enforcement.

They found nothing of great interest in the basement, and after a half hour they went back up to the ground floor.

Without saying so, Bloch turned left out of the basement and made for the kitchen. Dole guessed he should check the living room. The door to the living room lay open, letting out a sliver of light. Dole couldn't remember if he'd closed the door behind him or not. He knew he'd left the living room after Bloch, so it must've been him.

Even so, he drew his weapon once more and nudged the door wide with his foot.

He let out his breath, lowered his Glock. Just his imagination.

Bloch came in behind him, said, 'There are spare charging cables for a computer, but if there was one I guess he took it with him. There's a gun locker under the kitchen units, but no gun. I found gun oil and some brushes, still wet. He cleaned a weapon recently. Anything in here?'

The living room didn't look like much to Dole. A bookcase seemed to be about the only thing of interest. Dole took a walk to the window and stared out over the water, as if he might still see the ripples from Daryl's boat. There were none. He'd missed him.

He turned and saw Bloch studying the shelves.

'Lot of true crime books, mostly on serial killers. The rest are mostly manuals on police procedures and forensics,' said Bloch.

'I'm sure he's got a DVD box set of *CSI Miami* somewhere too,' said Dole.

'I don't think so,' said Bloch, reaching for a large volume on the second shelf. 'This is a book on FBI profiling in the Behavioral Analysis Unit. It's not a memoir, or a true crime gory history of that place. This is an academic work. It's been read a number of times, too, look.'

She held up the book, and pinched a yellow Post-it note that had been attached to a page, marking it. When she flicked to that page it was a chapter on profiling serial killers though their signatures. This didn't mean analyzing their handwriting, but examining the crime scene and the victims to establish a pattern of violence in each murder, which the FBI called a signature. There was a note in the margin. Handwritten.

Weapons, victim selection, victim type, location, overkill/rage wounds.

'If you were a serial killer, and you knew the feds were looking for a pattern in your victims, it's the easiest thing to change weapons, tactics, alter your victim selection and vary the amount of violence inflicted on the victim pre- and post-mortem. If you did that, it would be almost impossible to link two murders together,' said Bloch.

Nodding, Dole flicked through the rest of the book, looking for any more pages that had been marked. He found none.

'Strange reading material for a waiter and diving instructor, don't you think?' said Bloch.

Dole didn't acknowledge her. He didn't hear her too well. His mind was taking in the bookshelf, and the little yellow flags that protruded from those books on the shelf.

Daryl had been doing some serious study.

Dole's phone began to vibrate. He picked it up. The call came in from Bay City forensics.

'Sheriff Dole,' he said.

'Hi, it's Max McAllister, forensics. I got something that might be of interest. We managed to hack into Maria Cooper's phone. I've got call history and text messages. I'll send it over in a zip file asap,'

Dole thanked the man, and ended the call. Only when the call disappeared did the thought occur to him that he had no idea what a zip file was, and he stared at the phone, about to call McAllister back.

He didn't call McAllister back. Before he could press redial, his phone started to vibrate. A number he didn't recognize.

He answered the call, listened, thanked the caller and said, 'We'll be right there.'

Bloch waited, expectantly, cradling an armful of books from Daryl's shelf.

Dole said, 'We're getting a zip file with Maria's phone records on it. Better yet, that was the hospital – she just woke up.'

CHAPTER FORTY-SIX

Of all the times he'd been to Grand Cayman, Paul had never once arrived there by boat. It took a hell of a lot longer than hopping on a plane, but it was a lot more low key. He'd used the time wisely, washing his hair and body in the little cabin sink, then shaving and running the gel through his wet hair.

He looked and smelled like a human being for the first time since his boat sank. He couldn't wait to put on the suit, add the finishing touches when they docked. Until then he admired the view. Despite the situation, he couldn't help but marvel at the beauty of the place. To Paul, this was paradise – the colorful island birds circling overhead, the school of dolphins that seemed to usher the boat to the harbor, the smell of fresh fish and roasting meat on the grills right beside the water.

They'd landed in George Town, and Paul felt a familiar tinge of excitement.

Paul changed clothes in the cabin while Daryl tied up the boat. It would feel good to be outside, away from the stench that came off his deadly companion. And Daryl was always on his mind. Even while he changed his clothes, he made sure to keep Daryl in sight at all times through the cabin windows. He put the small knife in his jacket pocket.

Soon as Daryl set foot back on the boat, Paul moved away from his bag, away from the view he'd had through the cabin window. It must've been noticeable, because Daryl's demeanor seemed to alter afterward. He appeared to be just as interested in Paul's movements as Paul was in his whereabouts.

They were circling one another. Each reluctant to put the other out of sight. Paul was fully dressed now. Suit and button-down shirt, and hard, leather-soled shoes. He exited the cabin, giving Daryl some privacy.

Paul walked around the cabin, holding onto the safety bars on the roof, and made his way to the port side of the boat. He put his back to the cabin, so Daryl couldn't see him from any of the windows. He listened to the thump of Daryl's boots hitting the floor, then casually flicked all of the cartridges he'd taken from the .45 into the water. They made a soft plonk as they sunk below the surface. When his pockets were empty, he went back inside.

Just in time.

Daryl unzipped his bag, drew out the Colt .45 and gripped the slide, ready to jack it back and check the load in the chamber window.

'Wait, leave that here,' said Paul, with authority. Daryl froze, looked at him.

'You can't take that into the bank, and there's nowhere safe to stash it outside. Leave it here.'

Daryl sighed, stuffed the gun back into his bag like a surly teenager and stood, adjusting his jacket.

'How do I look?' he said.

'You look . . . perfect,' said Paul.

They took a cab to the First National Bank of Grand Cayman on Elgin Avenue. The island authorities knew banking tourism was one of their main attractions – so the banks mostly put up shop on Elgin. It was a wide street, with four lanes of traffic and palm trees whispering above the roll of Bentleys and Ferraris beneath. The sound of the wind in the palm leaves reminded Paul of the whisper of thousand-dollar bills fanned out from a stack. There was a sweet dryness to the sound. Something calming, and yet exotic.

Paul went up the steps first, Daryl trailing a few feet behind.

Marble pillars framed the glass doors. Even from outside, Paul could see the ornate mosaic floor spread out in the shape of the island. He thought he could smell the vanilla-scented air freshener, the leather seats and the faint aroma of sweet decay which seemed to permeate every part of the island.

Paul had chosen this bank carefully, all those years ago. He thought about it now as he pushed open the glass doors, holding one open for Daryl.

His new shoes echoed on the floor. And he was reminded of the first time he'd set foot in the bank. He knew then that he'd chosen wisely.

First National Bank of Grand Cayman had a diverse spread of clientele: Hollywood movie moguls, property developers, hedge fund managers, twenty percent of the world's drug lords, most of the illegal arms dealers and three of the biggest charities on the globe.

Absolute privacy. Total security. And zero tax.

The three magic beans in banking for the super-rich.

You couldn't hold an account here unless you deposited five million. The bank had reasonable charges, and in return you were accountable to no one. A limo would pick you up from the airstrip, bring you to the bank, and remain at your disposal until you decided to leave. No limo for Paul this time.

This time he was slumming it.

There were no cashiers' desks, just a reception, with a manager behind it ready to greet you, and five heavily armed guards positioned around the room.

He couldn't help but notice those men with black suits stretched over tactical vests, cradling assault rifles in their arms. They stood out. Even in the corners. He knew Daryl would notice them too. Paul raised his head, looked around the domed, gold-leaf ceiling.

The one thing he loved about the bank was that it put its faith in assault weapons for security, and not cameras. There wasn't a single security camera on a wall, anywhere. Paul had to confess he saw the logic. An AR-15 is better protection than a Kodak. And the bank's customers were keen to maintain their privacy in all of their dealings. He heard Daryl's footsteps behind him, veering off to the left towards the leather couches against the wall.

Paul approached the manager. She was tall and rather severe in her appearance. Her black hair pulled tightly away from her forehead, and her large brown eyes looked as though the hair band was stretching her entire face into a demented, and yet delighted smile. She wore a purple tweed suit, lilac shirt beneath. The bank's colors.

'Greetings, may I help you?' said the manager.

'Yes, I'd like to make a withdrawal,' said Paul.

'Certainly, sir. Please enter your security code into the pad.'

In front of Paul was an iPad type device. He entered his security code using the touch-screen keypad. His account information came up.

Paul tried to swallow, but found that he couldn't. His throat had closed, and a flood of sweat hit his back.

'I'm afraid there is a problem, sir. I must call the account manager. He will come and see you,' she said, picking up the phone.

Thirty seconds went by without Paul realizing his foot had been tapping out a beat on the floor the whole time. He couldn't force down the nerves any longer, they were making him crazy.

He knew he had to be calm. That was the only way this would work.

A bank manager came through an oak door behind the reception and approached the desk.

'Sir, there is a little problem,' said the account manager. He introduced himself as Mr. Alleyne. 'I'm afraid we received an injunction, mandating the freezing of this account. We can sometimes be flexible in these situations, but not this time. There is nothing I can do to help,' he said.

'Oh, but there is,' said Paul.

Inside he was screaming, on the outside he looked little more than mildly amused as he turned and beckoned to Daryl for help.

The eyes of the security guards were melting into his skin like hot lasers.

He remembered that when he was very young, things seemed to take forever. An escalator took two years to get to the next floor, when he lay in bed and couldn't sleep he counted the seconds to an hour but when he checked the clock only ten minutes had passed, and the time spent doing homework seemed to take all night instead of half an hour.

But nothing, absolutely nothing, took longer than it took Daryl to walk twenty feet from the couch to the reception desk.

And Paul's life lay in the hands of the man he hated most in the world.

CHAPTER FORTY-SEVEN

'That was kind of a bust,' said Bloch as she flipped on the siren and flashers in the patrol car. They were on their way to Bay City.

It was the first thing she'd said for an hour.

And Sheriff Dole knew it didn't need to be said at all.

They'd torn the house to shreds. Apart from the books – they got zip. Nothing. Not a single trace of evidence, or even a lead that could connect Oakes to either Paul or Maria Cooper. The books were interesting, and Dole could tell that Bloch was still churning them over in her mind. She'd taken half a dozen in evidence bags, but of course, on their own, they were not evidence of anything other than perhaps poor taste or an unhealthy obsession. If they got something solid, a decent prosecutor could put a spin on those books for a jury.

'Maybe there's something on Maria's phone,' said Dole.

He was reaching, and he knew it. Dole put a hand on the dash as Bloch hit the brakes. Stop light. She slowed, then rolled through the traffic on Johnstone Avenue amidst the blare of car horns.

The hospital loomed in front of them. Dole didn't know if Maria was medically fit to be interviewed.

Not that this mattered to Dole. The doc couldn't stop him speaking to Maria. There were advantages to being a sheriff, one of which was professional courtesy from his Bay City counterparts, and there was no way they would bar him from the hospital.

Dole didn't want to push Maria. He knew she would be fragile. Maybe even delirious. The memory of the attack might never return to her and Dole had accepted this fact. He'd heard of it before. Some things are just too painful for the human mind to hold onto. They have to be expelled or their poison will spread, destroying the host. Human memory was designed to remember and to forget. A fact that was never lost on Sheriff Dole. He could no longer remember Eden's face before the sickness took her. Yet he remembered the pattern of tile on the hospital floor, the smell of the chemicals that they'd pumped into her, the sallow pitted cheeks that would draw her lips into a smile when she noticed him by her bedside. He could not forget Linzi's bone-white bloated body floating in the water, and the nights he'd spent searching for her. Memory could be a curse.

They pulled up in the lot opposite the hospital. It was too damned busy to try and get a space any closer. And if by chance they did find parking in the multilevel lot, they could get stuck in there if they tried to leave at shift change. Safer to stay across the street and walk over, which is what they did.

There was a crowd of people waiting outside the bank of elevators on the ground floor of the hospital, but despite his eagerness to speak to Maria, Dole decided to wait for the elevator. Eight floors of stairs would put his knee on ice for week. He needed to be mobile. At least for a while longer.

By the time they got to the right floor, visitors had begun to arrive on the ward. Bloch spoke to the nurse who'd been so friendly to her the other day, and she showed them both to Maria's private room. They let the nurse go in first. Bloch approached the glass, peered inside. Dole did the same. It was important they didn't scare her. Taking things softly and slowly with trauma victims came as second nature to good cops. Bloch and Dole both.

The ceiling lights in the room had been turned off. The only light came from an extendable lamp attached to the wall above the bed, pointed toward the corner so it didn't shine directly into Maria's eyes. Other than the muted lamp, the machines surrounding Maria gave off a faint glow. There was enough light from the corridor to reach her face, but again it was shaded through the tinted glass window.

Maria sat up in bed. A vast bandage around the top of her skull. She was talking to the nurse, and the nurse in turn was caressing the back of her hand, calming her. With Maria's other hand, she shaded her eyes from the lamp.

The nurse reached up and moved the lamp out from the wall by two or three feet. This increased the light in the room, and Maria tightened the fingers over her eyes. Dole could see Maria's teeth clench against the intrusion, her jaw muscles bunching, a faint hiss as she took in a sharp breath. This must've been because of the coma, or the head injury, Dole wasn't sure which. Light sources were a problem for Maria in her current, weakened state, and Dole knew he would just have to deal with it as best he could.

The nurse left the room, said, 'You can go in, but please don't upset her.'

Dole nodded, asked if she'd been told what happened to her.

'No, not yet. She's been told she had a traumatic brain injury, and that's all. Go easy.'

Dole held open the door for Bloch. She went in first, just a few feet, allowing Dole to come inside and close the door. They left distance between themselves and Maria's bed. Maria watched them come in, but said nothing. It was hard to read the expression on her face. At first it appeared blank, but as Dole's eyes became accustomed to the gloom he saw wrinkles in her forehead, creases in the center of her brow. Her pupils were still unbalanced. One fat black pupil in her right eye, the other pupil a small dot in a paddling pool of electric blue.

'Maria, it's Sheriff Abraham Dole. This is Deputy Bloch. How are you feeling?'

'The pain isn't so bad. They gave me drugs,' she said, softly, and as if to explain she held up her right hand, showing them the butterfly line into her vein, and a tube leading from her hand off the bed and ascending into clear bags of liquid hung above her.

'May we talk with you?' said Dole.

She didn't nod, she closed and opened her eyes with a fleeting half-smile that disappeared as quickly as it had arrived.

Dole took this to be a *yes*.

They approached the bed, reverently, and both sat in the low vinyl chairs that had been set out on the left side of the room.

'If at any point you want us to stop, just say so. We can come back another time. Okay?' said Dole.

'It's fine.'

Dole and Bloch exchanged glances, unsure. Dole didn't want to get his hopes up.

Licking his lips, Dole thought about a question. Something to get her talking. Something wide open. He didn't want to jump straight in.

'What do you remember?' he said.

Maria closed and opened her eyes, turned to Dole and spoke carefully and confidently, her voice a dry branch cracking in a forest.

'Some things are foggy. Some aren't,' she said.

Dole nodded, but didn't say anything more. He wanted Maria to open up. The silent prompt worked.

'I found something out about my husband,' she said.

'What did you find out?' said Dole.

'It's hazy. He has money. I remember that.'

Bloch brought out her cell phone. She cycled through her email, recovered the picture of the bank statement she'd saved. Showed it to Maria.

'J. T. LeBeau. He's an author,' said Bloch. 'We think your husband might be the man who wrote those books. It would seem to explain the money.'

'Yes. Yes, he lied to me. We argued. I remember that.'

'You argued about him lying to you?' asked Dole.

Her eyes began to sightlessly search for an answer.

'It must have been that. I remember I was in the kitchen. I was thinking about him. I thought about how much I loved him. Then he must've hurt me.'

Dole took a breath, waited, then asked, 'Do you think that you confronted your husband? Is that what happened?'

'He hit me. From behind,' said Maria. 'It must've been him. It could only have been him. I was in the kitchen. Waiting for him. I didn't see who it was. I felt something hit the back of my head. He must've snuck in through the front door.'

Dole didn't know if she was voicing memory, or convincing herself about what happened.

She paused, then stared at Dole and said with absolute conviction, 'My husband hit me on the head. He tried to kill me.'

CHAPTER FORTY-EIGHT

Twenty sweat-soaked minutes.

That's all it took.

Daryl spoke to Mr. Alleyne for three minutes. Showed him ID. Paul showed Mr. Alleyne ID as well. Mr. Alleyne smiled. Then he told them to wait.

Seventeen minutes later two large leather satchels appeared on the heavy shoulders of two big security guards.

Nineteen point three million dollars. There were some local taxes and bank fees to be paid, which totaled six hundred and ninety-eight thousand dollars. The two grand was a service charge for secure transport. Paul signed a chit allowing the seven hundred thousand dollar deduction. The guards came with the cash to a town car parked outside, put the cash in the trunk and ushered Daryl and Paul into the back. The car was fully loaded with champagne, still water, whiskey and gin. Paul didn't dare touch any of it, no matter how many times the guard up front told them to pour a drink and relax. The bank's security team drove them to the marina, loaded up the boat with the satchels. Daryl tipped the harbormaster ten grand to make sure there was no record made of his short docking.

Paul felt like he hadn't drawn breath since he'd walked into the bank. Soon as Daryl fired up the engine and took them out of the dock, Paul knelt over and gasped for air, felt his heart quickening and his eyeballs bulging out of his head.

They had done it. Daryl's crazy-ass scheme had worked. He'd anticipated the bank freezing the account, and he'd dealt with it smoothly. Paul sat behind Daryl and laughed.

Daryl, at the helm, started laughing too. He took off his jacket, rolled up his shirt sleeves and gunned the engine.

The euphoria lasted until they broke into open water, leaving the island in the distance. Daryl eased back on the thrust, placed his hand on his bag of clothes, which he'd put on the floor beside him. Neither of them spoke, the giddiness simply passed without comment. The fat leather satchels lay below. Safe. Secure. The relief swept over Paul like soft, cool ocean spray.

But it didn't last long. This was the moment. No going back. Paul let the anger build. He felt it in his closed fists, his tense shoulders and the tightness at the base of his neck. For some time, he didn't know how long, he saw Linzi's face very clearly. The picture dissolved into Maria – lying in the hospital, her head almost caved in. He saw the flames licking around the trunk of a car, and he could smell something or someone cooking. He didn't know if the noise came from the fire eating the car, or if it was the scream and banging of the fire eating the man in the trunk. These images and sounds flew away as quickly as they had come, revealing the man with his back to Paul. The man who was about to pay for all the hurt he had caused. As Daryl looked out at the horizon, behind him, Paul slipped the knife from his jacket. The dock was still visible, but barely. They were headed out into deep water. As soon as the Caymans were distant, and they were alone, Daryl would make his move. Paul could wait no longer. The time was now.

At first he was unsure how he should hold the knife. It felt small and flimsy in one hand. He stood, quietly, got the feeling of the boat under his legs. He moved forward slowly, and holding the blade like a dagger, he told himself he could do this.

It was a beautiful day. Virtually no wind. The sea a magnificent blue. No clouds above them.

Paul moved forward. This man had ruined his life. Paul was going to rid himself of LeBeau forever.

Outside the cabin, a frigatebird rode alongside the boat, catching a thermal, with two white-tailed tropicbirds dancing below it in interconnecting spirals.

Another step. Quiet. Slow. He opened the cabin door, moved inside with Daryl still focused on the course ahead.

The boat passed a flock of gulls resting on the surface of the water.

Paul raised the knife above his head. Arched his back.

A brilliant sun cast silver pearls of light on the tips of the rippling current.

The only sound came from the engine, and the somnambulant beat of the sea against the hull.

His back stretched, his teeth clenched, eyes wide and focused on the back of Daryl's neck.

A seagull cried out.

Paul whipped his arms and torso forward as fast and hard as he could, plunging the knife into Daryl's back like a piledriver.

He'd been aiming for the back of Daryl's neck. In between his shoulder blades. Using his core, his back muscles and his shoulders to give additional force to the blow, he'd hoped to put the knife through Daryl's cervical spine, severing the central nervous system and dropping Daryl like a puppet who'd had its strings cut.

The speed and force deployed shook his aim. Half an inch to the right of the spine, the knife plunged into Daryl's flesh. Such was the force of the downward momentum of the blow, that the knife entered the skin and slid into the muscle up to the hilt then carried on, cutting down through the muscle and opening a three-inch gash in Daryl's back.

Letting go of the steering, Daryl's arms flailed out, his back curved inward and his legs gave way.

He fell to his knees.

He didn't cry out.

Paul pulled the knife from the wound and as he raised it over his head for a second strike, he felt a fine, warm spray of blood on his neck and chin. He leaned back, winding up for the blow and this time as the knife came down he aimed for the top of Daryl's head. An involuntary, high-pitched roar escaped from Paul, gaining in volume as he sprung forward and pulled the knife down toward Daryl.

He missed.

Daryl's arms shot up, and he lurched to his left. It was enough to deflect the blow and the knife clattered against the back of the seat, Paul's wrists hitting the headrest.

Paul couldn't breathe. The knife felt slippery in his hands. Daryl had almost knocked it from his grasp. He knew he had to make the next move and it would need to be decisive. He was not a fighter.

He stood back, grabbed Daryl's left ankle in one hand and began to drag him away from the seats and the console, into an open space, so he could jump on top of him and hold him down with his knees and then put the knife through Daryl's eye.

At first, Daryl resisted, holding onto the seat as Paul tried to drag him.

'Let go,' said Paul, slashing at Daryl's ankle with the knife.

Daryl let go. Paul leaned back and moved his feet, dragging Daryl, leaving a bloody trail in his wake.

Paul let go of Daryl's ankle and lunged forward, leading with the knife, ready to knock the wind from his victim and finish the job.

He didn't see the heel of Daryl's boot coming. He simply felt it crack against his jaw and then his body hit the deck. He got up, scrambling, his feet slipping on the floor. He'd lost the knife. He looked around, couldn't see it. It must've skidded away, under a seat. He dropped to all fours, looked left and right.

It was gone.

He raised his head and saw Daryl standing back at the helm, opening his bag. He came up with a gun in his hand. Paul got to his feet and stood facing the barrel.

Click.

Daryl's expression changed. From a pained yet impassive look his face collapsed into confusion. Paul had a decision to make. Take the chance and charge at Daryl, get his hands around his throat and squeeze. Or back off. Fight or flight.

Paul always wondered what it would be like to have that primal surge of adrenaline soaking through his bloodstream. Would he charge forward, or run? In everything he'd read about it, he'd come to the conclusion that it was not a choice, exactly. Your body almost took over, in a certain respect – it decided to fight or flee, and conscious decision-making didn't factor into it at all.

Except this was not what happened to Paul. His body was trembling, and he felt that flood of adrenaline, but instead of it spurring him into action it rooted him to the spot. Like his body was an over-tuned Camaro and some whack job was standing on the gas pedal, sending the wheels spinning but far too fast and with too much torque to be able to put the power down.

Daryl pulled open the breech, checked the magazine.

Empty.

Paul stood there – his tires squealing and shredding themselves on the asphalt.

Daryl bent low to the bag again, came up with a knife in his hand. Paul had lost his chance. Fear and indecision had chosen his path for him. There was no way he could take on an armed man. Even a wounded one. And this was no ordinary man. He was a killer.

He had but one choice in the moment of clarity that mercifully came back to him. He turned and ran for the cabin door, lifting both satchels as he went. He swapped both bags into one hand so he could open the door, but the weight was too much.

He dropped one bag, opened the door and stepped onto the back deck. He waited for Daryl and slammed the door on him just as he was coming through. Daryl had been expecting it, leading with his foot raised, ready to kick back at the slamming door. The force of Daryl's kick bucked the door back into Paul's face. He stumbled backwards, blood gushing from his nose. The back of Paul's legs hit the rail and he tumbled over it. He was going to fall head first into the water.

Then, he felt a wrenching at his shoulder, arresting his fall.

Daryl held onto the satchel with one hand. In the other, he raised the knife over his head, ready to bury it in Paul's stomach.

Paul let go of the satchel, threw himself backwards, took a big gulp of air and hit the water. Just as his head went under, he saw Daryl swinging the knife like a dagger. The blade embedded itself in the outside of the boat. He'd missed.

Turning in the water, Paul swam down and away. Kicking his legs, pumping his arms. His body was crying out for air, but Paul didn't care. He knew he needed to get as far away from the boat as possible or it wouldn't matter. Drowning might even be preferable to letting Daryl get hold of him.

His eyes were stinging from the salt water, and his lungs were bursting. He began to cramp in his legs, his stomach, his shoulders, and he kicked hard, turning and heading for the surface.

He broke the top of the water, his mouth open and his eyes popping wide.

He'd traveled thirty-five, maybe forty feet from the boat. He didn't see Daryl on the back deck. At any moment he expected the engine to kick into high gear, and the boat to change direction and come after him. Running him over in the water.

He turned, got his muscles working again despite the pain and he went under once more.

It would take him an hour to get to shore, at least. If he kept going under, and swimming left and right at angles to the shore, maybe Daryl would miss him.

He'd fucked up, badly.

No money. No help. No boat.

He couldn't think of that now. One thing was keeping him alive, driving his arms and legs.

Fear. The fear of not making it to the shore. Paul was not afraid of drowning – he was afraid that if he didn't survive then there would be no one to stop Daryl. The man had to be stopped. The man had to be killed. Paul couldn't allow Daryl to hurt Maria again. She was a target because she had survived his attack. He would try to kill her if she ever woke.

Paul had to stop him. So he swam, and ignored the pain, the exhaustion, and the urge to let himself sink to the bottom of the sea.

CHAPTER FORTY-NINE

Daryl pulled at the knife lodged in the back of the boat rail. He'd already hauled the satchel of cash back over the side and into the boat without dropping it in the ocean.

The knife seemed altogether more difficult. It wasn't stuck, the knife moved up and down in the fiberglass rail and he couldn't understand why he was unable to pull it clear.

He tried to give it a good hard tug this time, but he found he couldn't even grip the hilt. His body slumped over the rail. Suddenly dizzy, Daryl's feet tried to find purchase so he could stand, but the soles of his boots were sliding around the deck. He managed to right himself, glanced down and saw the blood beneath his boots. His back was soaking in sweat and blood.

Daryl vomited once, over the side. Then slowly and carefully, panting all the time, he made his way back into the cabin.

He wanted to kill Paul right then. Gut him. Slice him up slow. Make it hurt so bad.

But Daryl knew he could do none of those things. He felt weak, light-headed and so very, very thirsty. The medical kit was under the driver's seat. Daryl pulled it out, opened the box and found some gauze and bandages.

He took a guess at maybe a minute, a minute and a half since Paul had put the knife in him. That was reassuring. If Paul had hit an artery Daryl would already be dead.

If he hadn't nicked an artery, there was still a chance. Daryl knew he had to be fast. He picked up all the gauze from the box, then reached behind his head with his right hand. Soon as his elbow was past the horizontal, the pain turned up a notch and kept increasing the further Daryl stretched his arm backwards.

The wound couldn't have been in a more awkward place.

Eyes closed tightly, teeth grinding and his chest heaving as he tried to get air, he managed to drape the gauze over the wound by leaning forward. He threw the roll of bandages over his shoulder, keeping hold of one end. He reached around to the small of his back with his left hand and found the roll, brought it around and up to his shoulder, threw it over again.

In this way he was able to get two loops of the bandages over the gauze. He pulled the ends tightly, fought down the urge to vomit again, and then tied the bandages.

The pressure on the gauze would help staunch the bleeding, but it wouldn't stop it. Daryl threw up the thrust on the boat, pointed it at Miami.

He felt the blood soaking the seat, and his pants.

Nothing else for it.

He would've loved to turn the boat around and run over Paul, but that would waste time. Time he didn't have. No chance of going back to Grand Cayman. The authorities there no doubt already knew of the purpose of his visit. If he went back they would hold him after he was treated – question him.

No, Miami was his only hope. Four or five hours with the wind behind him like it was now. He could make it. There were any number of quacks in Miami who would stitch him up, give him some antibiotics and painkillers without saying a word.

That's if he made it.

Daryl pushed his back against the seat, trying to keep pressure on the wound. He felt the flow of blood again, resisted the urge to scream and concentrated on piloting the boat.

He could make it, he told himself.

He had the money and that was what mattered for now. He'd tracked down Paul Cooper before, he could do it again.

Gripping the wheel, Daryl forced his eyes open and focused on the horizon.

He felt a sharp pain on his forehead, then realized he'd passed out and hit his head on the wheel. He couldn't have been out for very long, seconds only, but it scared him.

No way he was getting to Miami alive. No way to stitch the wound. He was in open water and if he went back to Grand Cayman there would be questions, and police, and jail.

He had to think. There was no margin for error. Think or die.

Pulling back on the power, Daryl let the boat cruise and slow. He cut the engine, got up and made his way to the back of the cabin. Sweat dripped into his eyes with the effort. Once he reached the bench, he lifted the seat to reveal an SOS emergency kit in the well. He took it out, put it on the table and opened it up.

Daryl selected a flare, then went out onto the back deck. He untied the bandages, then slipped off his shirt. He stood on the deck, feet spread apart. Letting his body find the rhythm of the chop. He reached up, over his shoulder. The effort made him cry. Tears rolled down his cheeks as he lowered his arm. The flare would attract any nearby vessels. And they would come if they saw it. That's the way it worked at sea. Everyone helped each other, no matter what.

'Fuck it,' said Daryl, popping the flare cap.

There were no ships or boats in sight. He wasn't calling for help.

The bright sodium flare began to burn. He reached over his shoulder again, and, best as he could, he held the head of the burning flare against the wound. He had to stop the bleeding, and cauterizing the wound was the only option. The sound of his skin sizzling, and the smell of burning flesh came to him all at once and he screamed into the sun like only a dying man can.

CHAPTER FIFTY

'How in the name of Almighty God do you open a *zip* file?' said Dole.

He got up from behind his desk. Bloch took his place. Dole folded his arms, shook his head and blew out his cheeks. The adjustment to some forms of technology just wasn't as smooth as others. Bloch gave him a withering look, then she took hold of the mouse. Made a few quick clicks, then said, 'It's printing.'

The printer beside his desk whirred to life. Started spitting out pages. Dole picked up the first one, looked at it, then threw it down on the desk in front of Bloch.

'I can't even make sense of this. What the hell is that?' he said.

Bloch picked up the sheet, scanned it.

A list of SMS messages. All from Maria to another number. You didn't get both sides of the conversation. Just the messages to that number and the date and time they were sent.

Bloch got up, lifted the pages clear of the printer as it continued to spit more out. She flicked through them, found another page.

'Okay. So they go through the phone and the computer program lifts the messages sent. Then another part of the program finds messages received. We have to piece it all together. Like a jigsaw,' said Bloch.

Rolling his eyes, Dole then raised his hands to the heavens and said, 'I thought technology was supposed to make all this shit easier. I hate jigsaw puzzles.'

Bloch fought back a smile. They waited until the printer had finished the job. It took twenty minutes and two paper reloads but when it was done they had a stack of pages. Maybe six hundred.

Together they cleared Dole's desk and divided up the pages. Maria's cell phone had been dissected – so they had to put it back together to see the whole story.

A stack of pages at the back of the bundle revealed the call logs. Dole selected the calls from the day before the break-in, right up until Maria was attacked, and put them in a separate pile.

Working together, they made neat piles of message dates and put them together with the corresponding replies. It didn't take that long to divide up the evidence.

After another ten minutes, Dole said, 'I can't read this. The way it's laid out – just a jumble of messages and numbers. Why can't we just take a look at the goddamn phone?'

Bloch nodded, said, 'Let's just check the recent stuff first. While we have it. We can get the phone later.'

Reluctantly Dole agreed. He tried again to look through the messages. There were contact names on some sheets, which must have corresponded to the contact listings on Maria's phone. Dry cleaners. Charity appeal lines. He ignored these, and skipped through them until he found a text message history with a cell number that had no contact listing. At first he thought there was nothing there, then he saw, in the small printing, a date and time for a single text message.

It had been sent the day after the break-in.

My marriage is over. I'm going to need your help.

'Look at this. Check your pile of responses, see if you have one from a cell number with no listing in the phone memory – just the number,' said Dole.

After a few minutes to sifting, Bloch found it.

A single text. The only one recorded.

Whatever it is, I'll do it. I'd do anything for you.

The date and time corresponded. This was the reply to the message.

Before Dole could say anything, Bloch picked up his phone and called the forensics team at Bay City, asked them to trace the cell number for this exchange.

'They've put me on hold,' she said.

'For the love of sweet Jesus,' said Dole. 'I hate this hacker bullshit.'

'I can tell,' said Bloch.

'I prefer real police work. Knocking on doors. Looking someone in the eye,' said Dole.

After a few anxious minutes, Bloch came to life. Grabbing a pen she made notes. Asked a few questions then hung up.

'It's a burner,' she said.

'A what? I thought it was a cell phone?' said Dole.

Bloch shook her head, said, 'A burner is a cell phone. Like a disposable phone. You top it up with a card. It's kind of anonymous. All we know is it had two hundred dollars put on it when it was bought in a store in Manhattan a couple of years ago. Could be it's changed hands since then. Those type of phones are ten bucks in any second-hand shop in the country.'

'Who was she texting?' said Dole.

'From the sounds of it, someone who is trying to let her know that they love her. She doesn't have family. Not that I could trace. Sounds like Maria was either leading somebody on, or maybe she was having an affair?'

'Daryl?'

'That could be our link.'

Dole's upper lip twitched, and he said, 'The burner was bought in Manhattan, you say?'

'Yeah, I've got the address. You want me to call them, see if they have records?'

Dole checked his watch.

'No, let's go knock on their door. We can make New York this afternoon. There's a couple of things we can check out.'

'Like what?' said Bloch.

'Like the address for LeBeau Enterprises. Like that cell phone store. Like . . .'

'Like what?'

Dole stood, turned around and picked up a copy of a LeBeau novel. Opened it to the legal page and said, 'Like the publishers of J. T. LeBeau. Flatiron District. New York City.'

Ten minutes later, Sue had booked Dole and Bloch on the next flight to JFK, and Bloch was doing eighty-five miles an hour on the road to the airport.

With time to think, Dole thought he should call ahead to the local police in Manhattan. It was only courtesy. He called Sue and asked her to do the honors.

'Call Detective Mick Long in the 71st precinct. Tell him it's a courtesy call – I gotta go and talk to some people and I don't want any jurisdictional bull. He'll understand. We go way back, Mick and I. But whatever you do don't call the publishers. I don't want them turning us down. This is too important for some flake in a suit to get uppity about appointments.'

He hung up. Told Bloch to ease up on the gas. Dole knew he was more likely to die on the way to the airport than on a plane. Especially with Bloch driving.

'I'm glad you've still got friends in New York. I burned my bridges before I left.'

'Really? Your sergeant didn't think so. He gave you a great recommendation when you left. I saw it on your file.'

'That's because he wanted to get rid of me,' said Bloch.

An unpleasant look crept over her face, as if she had tasted something sour and wanted to spit it out. She did, in her own way, by changing the subject.

'Think Maria will hold up in court?' asked Bloch.

Dole thought she would, just as long as Bloch didn't drive her to the courthouse – the poor woman would be a shivering wreck if she had to spend time as one of Bloch's passengers.

'That woman is tough. Her recollection isn't the best it could be, but I'd say by the time she's due on the stand she'll be solid. I'd bet on Maria Cooper over a defense lawyer any damn day of the week.'

'She'll need a medical,' said Bloch.

'That's up to the DA. She sounded shaky at the start, but by the time we left I thought she was pretty convincing. I know she was all messed when we saw her on the beach, but she had a brain hemorrhage back then. She's getting better every day.'

'So Oakes is off the hook?' said Bloch.

'Looks like it. We got nothing from his house. He didn't show up for work for a few days, and he says he was sick. That's it. Not enough for an arrest. Maybe we'll get something else on him.'

Could be that burner belongs to him. I don't know, I don't buy it. I don't think Oakes is the romantic type. The fact that Maria thought her marriage was over only puts the heat on her husband, but . . .'

'But what?' said Bloch.

'Maybe Oakes didn't attack Maria, but it could be that he's been helping Cooper?'

'Why would he help Cooper?' said Bloch.

'I think a man with twenty million dollars in his bank account can be assured of help if it became a requirement, don't you?' said Dole.

Nodding, Bloch said, 'Even so. Hell of a risk what with the TV coverage and all.'

Dole held on while Bloch took a corner, clipping the edge of the sidewalk as she made a left turn.

'I get the impression Oakes isn't opposed to taking a few risks if the payday is right,' said Dole.

'Payday? Hang on, what if we're looking at this the wrong way around?' said Bloch.

A fleeting image of the painting in his office swept before his eyes. Bloch telling him in her interview it was upside down, and Bloch rehanging it, the right way up, moments after she left.

'What if Maria was having a casual thing with Daryl Oakes? Then she discovers her husband is LeBeau and he's got twenty mil in the bank. She tells Daryl. Maybe he was encouraging her to confront Paul, and take a share of the money? Maybe he promised to elope with Maria and some of Paul's millions? When in fact Daryl was using Maria to get to the money. *That* sounds more like the guy we talked to at his property,' said Bloch.

'Okay then. But who hurt Maria? It still looks like Cooper, doesn't it?'

Bloch said nothing. She increased the pressure on the accelerator, and wrung the steering wheel in her hands.

Bloch made the airport in thirty minutes – parked in the closest lot on a No Parking grid, daring someone to hand out a ticket, and together they made their way to Bay City terminal one. Their tickets were waiting at the desk and they checked their firearms into the hold through the police air travel system.

The TSA didn't bother Dole or Bloch, and they went straight through security and boarded the plane first, ahead of the line. Three and a half hours of flight time to New York. Bloch had brought the phone records with her. She would get through them on the flight. Dole brought something else. He was about to read his first J. T. LeBeau novel. It wasn't the first book, which he had meant to read after Bloch's recommendation. Nor was it the most recent. Something from the back catalog he'd chosen at random – a book entitled *Angel Falls*. As the plane's tires left the runway, he opened the book. Before he got the bottom of the first page he'd fallen asleep.

CHAPTER FIFTY-ONE

Paul Cooper hauled his sorry ass onto a beach in front of two bemused fishermen. Locals checking their nets, ready to head out in a catamaran for the day. Paul lay on the white sand for a time, getting his breath, letting his overworked muscles rest, but not too much. If he let himself stay there much longer he would cramp up and then he wouldn't be able to move for several hours.

He forced himself to his feet, brushed the sand from his wet clothes and saluted the fishermen as he made his way up the beach toward the highway. He could tell the locals had never seen a white guy wash up on the shore before. There was a first time for everything.

This wasn't Paul's first time starting from scratch. He'd wiped out a couple of times in his life. Lost an apartment once in a foreclosure. Had his car repossessed. Even had to give his dog away because he lost a job.

All of that changed, of course, when J. T. LeBeau came along.

The beach led directly to a stretch of two-lane highway. To the right he could see a strip mall in the distance with a gas station tacked onto the side. He turned in that direction and rung out his shirt on the way. The heat helped. And what the sun wouldn't fix, the humidity would disguise.

By the time he arrived at the gas station he didn't look too much worse than anyone else who'd been outside all day. Except he smelled of the sea, and his shoes squelched with each step. The gas station had a bank of pay phones on the back wall. The first phone had been ripped out of the wall and the cord hung loosely down from the receiver as it lay in the cradle. Second station didn't have a receiver at all. Third one was the charm. Paul picked up the phone, dialed the operator and asked to make a collect call to New York. He gave the operator the number for his agent and waited.

It took a good minute or two before he heard a click, and the operator told him he was connected.

'Jesus, Paul!' said Josephine. 'I thought you were dead. It said on the news that you were missing. Do you understand? Didn't you see that? Where've you been? I have been going out of my mind with worry. I called the cops here and asked them to liaise with Port Lonely and . . . you know how useless cops are? They did nothing. Maria got hurt too. There was a sheriff on TV saying you did it, but I don't believe it. Please tell me you're alright and this is all a big mistake.'

'I didn't hurt Maria. I'll explain later, but you gotta help me. I need you to wire me some money. There's a Western Union on Parade Street, Grand Cayman. Can you manage five grand?'

'Sure, I can do that, but . . . I almost don't want to ask. Paul, what happened to the travel money I gave you, and the money in your account?'

Paul held his head, said, 'It's gone. All of it. There's not much I can do about it. Things have changed, Josephine. I was right, LeBeau found me.'

'Oh my God! Where are you? I'm coming to get you and we can go to the police and straighten all of this out.'

'No. I can't go to the police. I'm wanted for attempted murder. And I have no evidence. It's always been that way, this guy leaves no trace. I have to take care of this myself.'

'You can't do this on your own.'

'I need to. I should have ended it long ago. I have to end it now.'

CHAPTER FIFTY-TWO

For a small, quiet Sheriff's Department, the Port Lonely officers who served that community could be devastatingly efficient. Dole discovered that Sue had already made a booking for a car rental, and an escort was waiting for Dole and Bloch when they got off the flight. The escort was a young man of no more than twenty-five, holding an iPad with 'Sheriff Abraham Dole' lit up on the screen. At first Dole thought the NYPD were cock-blocking his investigation, then he took a good look at the young man holding the computer tablet. He was no cop. And when they approached him he introduced himself as Martin, from Avis. He led Dole and Bloch to the luggage department where they collected their guns, and then took them outside and onto a motorized cart. Ten minutes later he dropped them off at their rental. A gray sedan. Dole signed the paperwork, tipped Martin twenty bucks and waved him on his way.

He waited until Bloch reversed the car out of the space before he got into the passenger seat. The car smelled of fried chicken and lemon air freshener.

'This must be the car they give to all the visiting cops,' said Bloch.

Bloch had driven in New York before. She'd lived in New Jersey for a spell, and had been stationed on the Upper West Side of Manhattan for almost a year. Too expensive to live in the city, she made the commute every day. Her father had served in the same precinct, Dole knew. He'd never asked why she had left, and in truth he didn't want to. He guessed she didn't get along with people – it was all too plain. She put in for a transfer from New York, and hadn't settled anywhere until she came to Port Lonely, which at first seemed like a staging post. Another place that she would use to get to the next place. Only she stayed. Dole knew her record inside out. He wanted her to stay forever.

They took Grand Central Parkway to Randall's Island then the FDR until the exit ramp for the park. Bloch asked Dole to give her the address again. He called it out from his notebook, she nodded and got onto 2nd Avenue headed downtown until they hit 85th Street.

Dole parked and they got out and wandered east on 85th until they stood outside a brick building, with wide glass windows and an American flag flying over the door.

Bloch asked the address again. Dole repeated it and watched Bloch check an app on her phone. She entered the address on 'Maps', and it told them they were in the right place.

'Goddamn it,' said Dole.

'You didn't think it was going to be that easy, did you?' said Bloch.

'I sure didn't, but I was expecting more than this.'

The address they'd traveled to was the same address registered for LeBeau Enterprises. Two hundred and twenty-nine East 85th Street, Manhattan. Only this wasn't a business address. Large aluminum lettering jutting from the brickwork above the door read, 'United States Postal Service, Gracie Station.'

They went inside and Dole let Bloch do the talking. Even though they were both in law enforcement uniforms with side arms strapped to their belts it didn't stop five people calling them out as they walked to the head of the line and Bloch asked to speak to a manager.

Dole missed New York City. When he'd moved there to join to the police force, fresh from his home in rural Alabama, he thought he would never leave. In the end, he had left because of Eden. After she died, he became haunted by the life they had both been denied. He saw her face everywhere: at the window tables of coffee shops they used to frequent, in the neon glow of rain puddles on Times Square, at night on the subway when he would catch her reflection in the glass as another train thundered by. And then there was her smell. It was still in his apartment, on his sheets, on his clothes. He saw her face in the polished surface of his police issue .38 Smith and Wesson. He had to get out, and he knew it. Coming back felt like stepping into someone else's life. The memories not quite his own, not quite as painful, but familiar nonetheless. He realized he had missed the city. There were fond memories here, too.

After a short time in the Post Office, a pale balding man in a stained shirt came forward to talk to them. He confirmed the Post Office held a number of mail addresses for businesses. The particular mailbox for LeBeau Enterprises was in the office. Every month a different courier service arrived with a mandate and emptied the box. That was it. A bust.

'You still think knocking on doors is the way to go?' said Bloch.

'You hit busts all the time. At least it feels like we're moving. Let's try the store,' said Dole.

Twenty minutes later Dole and Bloch entered what looked like a 7-Eleven.

'You sure this is the right address?' said Dole.

'This is it,' said Bloch.

Inside, they realized they were right – it was a 7-Eleven. The clerk behind the counter was in his fifties, pale and sweaty with a straggly beard and an old yellow Arnold Palmer sweater with a polo shirt beneath it. He looked like he was about to tee-off at a golf course in Chernobyl.

'Excuse me, police officers,' said Dole, flashing his badge, but not quick enough for the store clerk to see they weren't NYPD badges. 'Wondering if you could help us. Did this used to be a cell phone store?'

'You're not NYPD,' said the clerk.

'No, we're not. We're officers from out of state, but we're here with the authority and co-operation of the NYPD. So, was this a cell phone store a few years back?'

'No, it's always been a 7-Eleven. Ever since I bought the place in ninety-two.'

'You're the owner?' said Dole.

'Yes, I am.'

Bloch stared at the man's sweater and said, 'You should give yourself a raise.'

'What my colleague here means is that this store is obviously doing well since you've been here so long. Tell me about cell phones. We have records which show you sold a burner a couple of years ago.'

'We still sell them,' said the man, pointing down toward the glass display below the counter top.

Dole stood back, looked at the display and saw a couple of small cell phones in plastic vacuum wrapping.

'Don't suppose you keep any records of who you sell those to? The buyer put two hundred dollars on the phone with a prepay card he probably bought in this store,' said Dole.

'Not a chance. Lot of people buy prepay cards when they buy their phones. No records.'

Bloch looked around the store, pointed to a security camera behind the man and said, 'Would you have any security footage from that time?'

'No, it's busted. Camera hasn't worked in years.'

'What about credit card receipts?' said Dole.

'This is a cash only store,' said the man, pointing to a sign to the right of the counter that read, 'CASH ONLY. NO CREDIT.'

Last chance, thought Dole. 'Do you remember a man coming into your store and buying a cell phone, and a two hundred dollar prepay credit?'

'I don't remember the last customer. Sorry. No clue.'

Dole and Bloch exchanged a look.

'If you're not buying anything you can take your asses back to Tallahassee Land,' said the man.

'I've missed New York,' said Bloch.

At four thirty-five Dole and Bloch entered an office building in the Flatiron District. The lobby was pale pine, stone and bookshelves covered in hardback books facing outwards. The receptionist sat behind a marble desk with a list of companies behind her on a board. There were only a handful of names. This was the real reason for their visit, but they couldn't resist checking out the business address while they were in the city. After all, it was on the way.

A receptionist made a call, told them to take a seat and someone would be right with them. A few minutes later a tall blonde lady in jeans, a black sweater and a false smile came into reception and said that they could have ten minutes with Mr. Fullerton, but she needed to know what it was in connection with first.

'J. T. LeBeau. It's a serious matter, ma'am,' said Dole.

The name dropped the fake smile off her face and she said, 'My name is Sarah. Come upstairs with me and then you can talk privately with Mr. Fullerton.'

She led them to an elevator which took them to the fourteenth floor. An open-plan space with desks, stacks of manuscripts and books everywhere. Most of the employees seemed to be young women. At the far end of the floor, in the corner, was a glass-walled office. Sarah held open the door. Bloch went in first and Dole followed her. Seated behind a granite-slab desk was a very tall man in his early sixties, neatly attired in navy cargo pants, a blue shirt and charcoal waistcoat. He had gray, wavy hair and an easy smile. Once they were all inside he got up from behind his stack of pages and came around the desk to shake hands.

'Theo Fullerton, publisher. Pleased to meet you both. I know Port Lonely. My wife and I used to summer there with the kids when they were young. Beautiful place. What brings you out here?'

'I'm Sheriff Dole, this is Deputy Bloch. We're hoping you can help us with a case,' said Dole. 'A name has cropped up, and we need to find some information. The name is J. T. LeBeau, sir.'

Watching Fullerton carefully, Dole noticed the slight crease in his brow at the mention of that name. Fullerton looked once at Sarah, then at Dole, and the crease got ironed out in a New York smile.

'He's our golden boy, Sheriff Dole. I take it you've done your research, so you probably know as much about the author as I do. Please, take a seat,' he said.

Settling himself into a leather armchair, Dole bit down to disguise the pain shooting from his knees. Fullerton took his seat behind the desk, leaned back and cocked his head, ready to listen.

'We can't go into every detail of our investigation, you appreciate that, but my department may have information which tends to identify a resident of Port Lonely that we believe to be J. T. LeBeau.'

'You know his name?' said Fullerton. As he spoke he sat upright, and then leaned forward placing his elbows on the desk and clasping his hands together. He looked like a kid about to receive a birthday present.

'We have a name. Unfortunately, that individual is currently a missing person. I got to tell you that this person may be dead. I can give you more information, but I need to know your relationship with LeBeau,' said Dole. He thought it best not to mention to Fullerton that if Dole did find Paul Cooper then he would be arrested and charged with attempted murder. Fullerton might not be so helpful if he thought Dole was set on putting his golden boy behind bars for thirty years.

'My God, of course, I'll help in any way. Ahm, well, I've never met LeBeau. No one in the company has. We don't know much about him. He delivers his manuscripts by courier, paid in cash. The envelope is addressed to me, personally. Once the book is edited, the manuscript is sent to his mailbox. He'll make changes and it comes back. That's as much contact as we have with him.'

'What about contracts, payments, all of that?' said Dole.

'Email. He will send an encrypted email to me. And before you ask, it's a dead end. Some of our IT people once tried to trace the IP address for the email – it's rerouted through multiple countries. Anyway, once I have the manuscript, we negotiate and when we have an agreement the contract is mailed out, he signs and returns it and we pay the first part of the advance to the company, LeBeau Enterprises.'

'Where is the company's bank account held?' asked Bloch.

'I'm afraid I can't divulge that information without a warrant. As you can imagine there is a strict confidentiality clause in the contract. I can't give you that information even if I wanted to, although I don't see how that would help.'

Fullerton's eyes were drawn to Bloch and her pen moving across the notebook.

'Why wouldn't it help? We're trying to trace this man.'

'The address for the bank account is the same as the company address – the mailbox.'

'Yes, but there may be more information than simply the address for the account,' said Dole. 'Look, Mr. Fullerton, there has to be somebody in this company who has met him. Come on . . .'

'No, there really isn't. Not anymore.'

'But there was someone, once. I remember now, maybe his first editor?' said Dole.

'Yes, Bob Crenshaw. He's no longer with us.'

'But you must have something on file – an address or something about this man,' said Dole.

Fullerton looked at Sarah while he tapped his fingers on the desk and nodded.

With that, Sarah left the office.

'I'll show you the only information we have on LeBeau,' said Fullerton.

Sarah came back into the office holding two letter-sized pages and handed them to Dole.

They were still warm from the printer.

It was a simple questionnaire. As an address LeBeau had given the mailbox number which Dole and Bloch had just visited. Date of birth, personal history, real name if writing under a pseudonym – all left blank.

'As you can see, this man was never very forthcoming,' said Fullerton.

'You're telling me,' said Dole. 'The editor who first worked with LeBeau, Bob Crenshaw, you say he left the company?'

'Yes, it was very sad.'

'Did he have any family, any work colleagues he might have talked to about LeBeau?'

'No, Bob kept to himself. He was divorced, no kids, and he didn't have any contact with his ex, although I don't know what he did outside of work hours. I already went through all of that with the police at the time,' said Fullerton.

The soft, scratching sound of Bloch's pen moving across her notebook ceased abruptly. This was new.

'What do you mean you told the police at the time?' said Dole.

'When they told us about Bob,' said Fullerton.

'When they told you what? You're not being clear,' said Bloch.

Turning his head, Fullerton stared out of the window at the Manhattan skyline beyond. Dole followed Fullerton's gaze and took in the view: the prow of the Flatiron Building sailed over 5th Avenue, and Madison Square Park beyond. It was as if Fullerton wanted a stark, visual image of life teeming beneath him as he answered the question. Perhaps, thought Dole, it was Fullerton's way of lessening the somber weight of his words.

'Bob Crenshaw burned to death in the trunk of a car in an abandoned lot down by the Manhattan Bridge. Bob was murdered.'

Sarah bowed her head. Dole said nothing. He just listened to Bloch's pen moving across the page again.

'Was LeBeau a suspect in that murder?' asked Dole.

'No, of course not. Why would he be? Bob had a lot of problems. The case was never solved, but there was no animosity between LeBeau and Bob, or LeBeau would've changed publishers. Look, I've tried to help out, but there's not much more I can tell you.'

'You've worked with this guy for years now. There must be something you can tell us about him that we don't know,' said Dole.

Fullerton cast his eyes down, said, 'You know how hard it is to write a twist in a novel?'

'Can't say that I do,' said Dole.

Fullerton leaned forward, gave Dole his full attention, and said, 'It's the most difficult thing an author can pull off, in my opinion. LeBeau knocked them out of the park, every book. You never saw it coming. Now, I edit his manuscripts, lightly, but even with a light touch I get pushback. This guy loves his anonymity, but in a strange way I think he's very proud of his work.'

'Proud?'

'I know, it's crazy. But unless I made a real case for changing anything in the manuscript, he just wouldn't entertain it. I got the impression he was protective of his work. As he should be. He knows just how good he is. I know it's a paradox, but that's just the impression I get. If you've created something really great, why would you shy away from taking the credit for it?'

'Last question, does the name Paul Cooper mean anything to you?' said Dole.

'I think I've heard of him. He's a mid-list mystery writer. Think he's one of Josephine Schneider's clients. She pitched me a book by him some years ago and I turned it down.'

CHAPTER FIFTY-THREE

The sun came up as Daryl passed his house for the second time in the boat. His limbs were lead, and if it wasn't for the adrenaline and morphine floating through his system he knew he would've fallen unconscious before he'd reached home.

He'd hit the throttle and gone past the house soon as he saw his front door lying open. Not wide open. An inch or two. Enough to see the door didn't sit flush with the frame.

The cops had been inside. He knew it. All the same, he needed to check it out – make absolutely certain. If he had heat on him it would affect his movements. Only one way to find out.

All he wanted to do was lie down and go to sleep. He hadn't closed his eyes for two days. He'd spent the night in a friendly doctor's office in Miami, swallowing antibiotics with warm Scotch and then biting down on his leather belt while the doc stitched him up. By the time he'd reached the doctor he was in bad shape. Pale, a fever running him down and it still felt like he had that knife in his back. No time to wait for the morphine to really kick in. The doc had been paid up front, as was customary, and once the doc had counted the bills, and locked them away in a secure box, he then felt compelled to act immediately.

Daryl's back had been cleaned with surgical alcohol – breaking the scab and allowing fresh blood to flow. Then the doc set about stitching the wound and applying a gauze pad, which he strapped in place with a bandage around Daryl's torso. Nausea swept through him, and the morphine tapped out the pain just as the good doctor tightened the bandage. Too little too late. Daryl passed out for a few minutes and when he came to he was on the floor, the doc struggling to lift him.

Somehow he made it back to the boat, and he took it out into the harbor and fought through the dizziness, the sickness and raging fever. He'd taken enough antibiotics to fill his stomach and he knew if he threw up he would be in serious trouble by morning. Through sheer will, he battled on through the night and the waves back to Port Lonely. Back to his house.

And the open door.

Daryl shut down the motor half a mile west of his house, on another jetty belonging to a private house. A holiday home. Thankfully, the owners weren't there to disturb him. That could have been awkward.

Unwilling to leave the money in the boat, he took the leather satchels, climbed onto the wooden pier and made his way to the trees at the edge of the property. The damn bags were pulling on his stitches. He could feel the wound weeping. A trickle of blood running down his back. At least he hoped it was blood. The doc in Miami didn't look like the most hygienic medic. For all Daryl knew it could have been pus running down his shoulder blades.

Instead of thinking the worst, Daryl forced his mind into believing the probable truth. The satchels were stretching the wound. It was just blood. He decided to put his faith not in the doc, but in alcohol used to clean the wound, and the massive dose of antibiotics.

The trees in this part of the county provided great cover. Enough for him to pass unseen by road to his house. The terrain had proved difficult though. It had taken great effort to get over the rough ground carrying the satchels, which continually became snagged in the lower branches, wrenching his back as he moved forward.

And after twenty minutes he reached the edge of the tree line. He could see his house. The front door. He put down the satchels, hunkered down and waited.

Rested.

Listened.

No cars on the nearby road. No vehicles parked anywhere on his property. All was quiet save for the birds and their song.

Daryl found a large oak, and behind it he saw a hollow log. No one was going to see him place the bags in there, and no one would come along checking an old log in the meantime. Safer than the boat, he thought. He carefully placed the satchels inside, then made his way along the edge of the trees until he was as close as he could get to the house without breaking cover. Sitting still, listening and watching, Daryl decided the house was empty. There had been no movement visible from the windows, no lights on inside, no steam from the boiler chimney to show there was anything going on.

Taking small steps at first, crouched low, Daryl made for the house. Soon as he was out in the open he realized how vulnerable he was. His adrenaline kicked in and he jogged, with his teeth clenched against the pain, to the house and the front door.

Pinned to the door was a copy of a bench warrant. His records, his phone, his house – the Port Lonely Sheriff's Department could examine it all.

Goddamn it.

He hated the thought of cops swarming over his stuff. Behind the warrant was a list of items they'd taken. Just books. Didn't matter. He didn't need them. He was about to swear at the cops for leaving his front door open – then he saw that the lock was busted. They couldn't close the goddamn door. And they hadn't taken any steps to secure the house after the search.

As he stepped inside, he found the air thick with their presence. No, not their presence, but the remnants of their visit. A faint smell of dust. Shards of broken wood on the floor. Plates and cups spilled out of the kitchen doorway. Looking in the other direction, he saw books lying on the floor. They had ransacked the place in the way that cops always do. The basement door lay open. His mouth felt dry. He eased the door open a little further, then winced at every step he took, down into the darkness of the cellar. A flashlight lay on a shelf at the bottom of the steps. He took another deep breath, clicked it on. Then scanned the basement.

Bed still in place. Furniture moved around, cupboard drawers lying on the floor.

The floor. It had not been disturbed. He took the flashlight around and found one corner of hard packed earth at the rear of the basement, still undisturbed. He went upstairs, clicked off the torch. Breathed a sigh of relief then went up another level.

In his closet, he found his clothes lying in a pile at the bottom, the hangers limp and empty on the rail. The sheriff had been thorough – and messy.

He laid out a shirt, pants and fresh underwear on the bed. Daryl stripped, washed and dressed. He left the house open, went back the way he'd come, grabbed the satchels and quickly made his way to the boat. This time he mostly dragged the satchels on the ground, making sure he didn't stress the wound. The pier was as quiet as when he'd arrived. A low mist hung over the water. The golden haze from the sun illuminated the mist. It looked like fine white silk masking a candle.

He stowed away the satchels, fired up the motor, cast off from the pier and left Port Lonely behind. A few hours before he'd docked, Daryl thought this would be his last visit to Port Lonely. He knew now it might not be.

He needed to go away for a while. Somewhere quiet. Somewhere safe. To rest. To heal. When he'd begun this task, he thought he would've been done by now. Soon as he got the cash, he could leave. Yet Paul and Maria were still alive. And now the cops were looking into him.

Thank God they hadn't looked under the basement floor. He knew now that they wouldn't be going back to tear the place apart any further. They had done their search. And they had missed the jackpot.

Still, the job wasn't finished.

By the looks of things, Daryl had a lot more work to do.

CHAPTER FIFTY-FOUR

'Hi, Maria, my name is Chad, I'm part of the brain injury team. Don't you look cosy in that bed? Oh you *so* do, missy. Mind if I sit? Thanks. Okay. If I'm going too fast, or if you find yourself drifting off while I'm speaking, or if there's anything you want me to go over, just holler, *Chad, I'm having a moment*, okey-dokey, honey?'

Chad wore a bright yellow tee and blue jeans, he had a sticker on his shirt that read *Jesus Saves* and between his red hair and his blank-white-screen teeth, his cheerful smile and his sing-song voice, Marla couldn't decide if she was awake or dreaming. Chad had entered her room in a flurry of color and mock concern and now he was sitting on her bed. Talking to her like she was in kindergarten.

'Now, honey, you've had a big bang on the head. I'm sure that's been explained to you, but I'm here to tell you about some of the things that you might experience because of this nasty bang, and what we can do to help.'

Maria stared at Chad. A blank expression on her face.

'You may experience some memory issues, some speech issues, some co-ordination issues, even nightmares. Yes. Now, honey, with our program we can make all of those things a lot less troublesome. We're going to be trying some physiotherapy tomorrow, there will be some tests too. Did you know the paramedics and the doctors here thought you'd died? Turns out you have a little something called vasculitis. It's a pre-existing condition. Don't worry about it, this bang on the head means they've caught it now and they'll be treating you. It's nothing to worry about, but we're going to be liaising with the medical team to find out the root cause, okay?'

Vasculitis. The doctors had mentioned it. Like Chad, they said it was nothing to worry about. Maria wasn't worried. Her blood pressure was always on the low side, and doctors pricked and bruised her skin a lot whenever they had tried to take blood. Her mom had been the same – bad veins. What she didn't need was Chad explaining it all in his Disney Channel voice.

'Now, don't fret about those beastly questions we're gonna ask – they're not designed to trick you. It's not like you needed to go to college or anything, they're just some regular questions – nothing to be concerned over,' said Chad, almost purring.

Maria said nothing.

Chad reached out, touched Maria's hand, stroked it gently.

'Oh, honey, you remind me so much of my big sister. I can tell we are going to get on like a house on fire. Now, come on, what's the matter, sweetie, cat got your tongue?' said Chad.

'Get out of my room or I'll give *you* a fucking brain injury. Although judging by the way you're dressed you might already have one,' said Maria.

She stared into Chad's open mouth for a moment. He really did have good teeth.

'Chad?' she said.

'Yes?' he managed to squeak.

'I can't help noticing you're still here. Do you want me to slow down? Is there anything you need me to go over? Are you having *a moment*?'

'I might be,' he said.

'Get out of my room and have it somewhere else.'

She thought Chad might burst into tears as he left. She didn't regret what she'd said. Not one bit. Matter of fact, she enjoyed it. Chad, with his high voice and positivity, struck her as one of life's victims. Someone who could be bullied, walked over, and trampled underfoot. The fact that Chad would allow this to happen sealed his fate that it would happen, at least in Maria's mind. Destined to be last in line, last in love, the one who was always taken advantage of, and then left behind.

Maria had no time for victims. She was through with that shit. Her left side felt weak. She had no strength in her left hand. It took all her willpower to move her left leg. One side of her body felt like it was full of lead. Deadened, slow, numb.

No amount of gentle encouragement was going to help her. She knew that much. Positivity could fuck off out the door behind Chad.

Maria set a course in her mind. A clear objective. She would go through physio. She would work hard – harder than anyone. She would sweat and push and fight through the pain, because nobody wanted it more. Happy faces and applause wouldn't be enough to get her there.

No.

Maria knew then she had an infinite power source in her arsenal. Something deep inside, burning its way through her body.

Hate.

Maria had hate, and rage. That would be enough. That would be better.

Given a few months, she wouldn't just be back to normal. She would be better. Stronger. Faster.

She'd let Paul into her life, and he'd betrayed her. Hurt her. She should've killed him when she had the chance. At home, in the middle of the night with one of his fucking kitchen knives. She shouldn't have relied on Daryl. He was too soft. She thought about the head of that hammer coming down, Paul wielding that hammer. She couldn't see his face clearly, but she knew it was him. He must've found out about her and Daryl.

Then a darkness. And all the while she had that smell in her nose. One she would never forget. The smell of fresh paint and blood.

CHAPTER FIFTY-FIVE

Dole was marching through the Bay City airport when Bloch grabbed his arm, yanking him to a halt.

'We have to do something. Cooper has disappeared. There's no leads, no way to get to him. How the fuck are we going to catch this guy?' she said.

Before they'd left New York, they had tried to talk to Josephine Schneider, Paul Cooper's literary agent.

Schneider wouldn't see them. They never got past the doorman at her office building. She wouldn't talk on the phone, and her secretary point blank refused to take a message. Port Lonely Sheriff's Department had no jurisdiction in New York. Dole had contacts in New York. Detectives who would pull a favor for him if he asked, but he knew there would be hell to pay if he brought an NYPD detective to Schneider's office. According to Fullerton, Cooper's agent was a serious player with friends in the mayor's office. No go. Nothing else to do but go home. This didn't sit easily with Bloch, and she'd been sullen and quiet on the plane. Now, in the airport, Bloch's frustration had bubbled over.

Dole stared at her large, questioning eyes, then over her shoulder. There was a burger joint behind her. An airport restaurant, but still, Dole figured it was pretty hard to fuck up a hamburger.

'I'm starving. Let's eat,' he said.

He walked past Bloch, feeling her gaze on the back of his neck like the afternoon sun.

'We can talk while we eat,' he said.

They ordered cheeseburgers, onion rings and baked potatoes from the bar and took their side salads and Cokes to a table. Bloch looked tired and pissed off. She was a rarity in law enforcement. Smart, on the level, and she gave a shit. There are any number of reasons why someone would become a cop. Some folks want to help their community. Dole had seen his fair share of those officers. Not enough of them, but they were still out there. Others join up because they want the power trip, or their family are cops, or they see it as the beginning of a path to something else, like local politics, and then there's the last kind. It was still something which gave Dole the creeps, but he'd seen it too often to deny it – some people joined law enforcement so they could get the opportunity to kill somebody.

'Why'd you become a cop?' asked Dole.

Bloch finished chewing some lettuce and tomato, wiped her lips on a napkin and took a long slug from her Coke. She put down the drink and said, 'Family.'

Dole's glass hovered close to his lips, he took a sip, put it down and said, 'So you were forced into it?'

'My father was a cop. Thirty-five years. He got busted with five other cops. They were running a protection racket and decided to branch out on their own. They were running girls, coke, guns, you name it.'

Dole was careful to stay quiet in case Bloch wanted to say more, but after a minute he realized he needed to prompt her. Bloch sometimes made statements which were clear to her, but not everyone else followed.

'So you signed up for . . . what reason?'

'My dad had nothing to do with the other five cops. They were his friends, and he had no part in the racket. They all said my dad knew about it, and did nothing. It's not like they paid him off. I think they tried, but he refused. He just turned a blind eye, you know?'

'Did he get time?'

'He died before the trial. Heart attack.'

'Shit, sorry, Bloch. So you're clearing the family name with your service?'

The waitress arrived with the plates, halting the conversation. Dole took a bite on a crispy onion ring and waited for Bloch to answer. It was hard for her to talk about this. A sore subject. He could tell. She was even more difficult to engage than normal.

'At first, sure. I wanted people to remember my dad for who he really was – a good man. Then when I joined up I found out the cops didn't think the same way. Superiors would tell me Dad was a great cop. So did the regular beat cops. My dad didn't rat out his fellow officers, and that was the most important thing to them. Things changed then for me. I wanted to know what it was like to be part of a group where no matter what you did, you were covered. I moved around a lot. It was always the same. Cops look after cops. My dad talked about his cop pals like they were his family. Maybe I wanted to be part of that. I . . . I don't get along with people so good.'

Dole didn't respond.

'How are we going to catch this guy?' said Bloch, changing the subject.

Dole sighed. When Bloch first raised the question, ten minutes ago, he already had a bad feeling that he knew the answer. Now, there was no way to avoid it.

'The money is our best shot. He'll make a play for the twenty million,' he said.

'But we got the court order, he can't touch it,' said Bloch.

'Doesn't mean he won't try. I'll check in, see if there's been any requests for transfer of funds.'

Dole looked at his watch, found the direct line number for the bank in Grand Cayman and dialed it on his cell. The receptionist connected him to Mr. Alleyne.

'Is there a problem, Sheriff Dole?' said Mr. Alleyne.

'I hope not, sir. Just wanted to check in and see if you've had any requests for the money in Paul Cooper's account to be transferred?'

'I'm sorry, I don't understand, Sheriff.'

'The court order we sent you. You remember? We discussed this. I know it's not exactly in your legal jurisdiction, but I thought the bank were going to honor the order to freeze the account.'

After five long seconds of dead air on the line, Mr. Alleyne said, 'Is this Sheriff Dole?'

'Yeah, of course. I thought you already knew that. Is there a problem?' said Dole, who was feeling a tightening in his stomach.

'I think there must be some kind of misunderstanding, Sheriff. Please tell me again how I can help you?'

'I want to know if there have been any requests to transfer the money in Paul Cooper's account.'

'Ah, I see. Well, since the account is closed we wouldn't keep a record of any requests relating to the account. It would not register on our system.'

'Closed? You mean frozen, right?'

'No, closed. Mr. Cooper closed the account once he made the withdrawal.'

Dole's stomach hit the floor. Bloch was staring at him. She'd picked up on the vibe from Dole's side of the conversation.

'Paul Cooper withdrew the money from his account? All twenty million?' said Dole.

Bloch's chair screeched on the tile floor, she stood up, closed her eyes and put her hands on top of her head like she was watching a car wreck.

'Yes, sir. It was under twenty million by the time he'd paid the bank's fee and we'd collected local taxes.'

His blood was up now, and Dole didn't hold back. 'Mr. Alleyne, tell me why I shouldn't fly over there and arrest you right now?'

Mr. Alleyne wasn't in the least concerned.

'Because, Sheriff, I was authorized to release the money.'

'Who authorized this?'

'You did, of course,' said Mr. Alleyne, with some considerable satisfaction.

'I authorized you?' said Dole.

'Yes, you came in with Mr. Cooper, showed us your ID, explained that the freezing order was all just a misunderstanding, and that as a show of goodwill you were there to escort Mr. Cooper and make sure he got home safely with the cash.'

Dole spoke for another twenty minutes, then hung up the call.

'Please tell me he's sending over security camera footage from the bank,' said Bloch, taking her seat again, opposite Dole.

'There is no security camera footage. The bank doesn't have security cameras covering customer areas,' he said.

'Shit,' said Bloch.

'And before you ask, no, they didn't keep a photocopy of my ID. Some prick waltzed in there pretending to be me. It must have been a good fake. Goddamn it.'

'Then he's gone. We're never going to see this guy again, are we?'

They ate their cold cheeseburgers in silence. Dole went over the case in his mind. Step by step. There was nowhere to go from here. He watched Bloch do the same.

'Unless we can make him come to us,' said Bloch.

The Port Lonely Sheriff's Department vehicles were maintained to an exemplary standard. No expense spared. The cruiser that Bloch parked in the lot had had four new tires fitted two weeks previously. She'd burned through Bay City, the freeway and the narrow streets of Port Lonely, back to the department, and parked up to the smell of burning brake disks and two bald rear tires. She'd left a lot of rubber on the streets of Bay City.

Dole and Bloch entered the department office and found Sue typing furiously on her laptop. There were no phones ringing, no one in the cells and Deputy Shanks was still working on Cooper's laptop.

'You got that draft ready, Sue?' said Dole.

'Go get coffee and I'll bring it right in. I couldn't make out every word you dictated in the car. Engine was too loud,' said Sue, firing a disapproving look at Bloch.

Bloch shrugged, said nothing and followed Dole to the coffee machine. They filled up from the bun flask and Dole led Bloch to his office.

They sat in silence, both of them working the coffee. Dole felt revived. He needed the caffeine. He opened his desk drawer, took out a bottle of Advil and dry-swallowed three pills. Sue came in with her notebook and three letter-sized pages. She handed one page to Dole, one to Bloch, then sat down with her copy. She put her notebook on the edge of the desk and took out a pen, ready to make corrections to what she had typed.

They read in silence. Bloch made a few notes in the margins of her page and swept her pen through the odd word.

When they were done, all three of them sat in silence for a moment.

'Send it to New York,' said Dole.

Sue got up, left. Dole got on the phone to Fullerton, gave him a heads up about the draft press release he'd just sent. He wanted to break the news to Fullerton on the phone.

It's not every day a publisher hears that their golden boy is dead.

They waited for a half hour, Dole and Bloch discussing the finer details, then the phone rang. Fullerton. He was on board.

Sue came back into Dole's office with three pages of copy stapled together. She handed them to Dole and said, 'Mr. Fullerton emailed through these changes.'

Dole read the pages, handed them to Bloch. She read them and nodded, said, 'We're good to go.'

Sue scratched her head, said, 'Why are you putting out this press statement, Abraham?'

'We don't want to let this guy get away with it. That's why we're doing this press release,' said Dole.

'But it ain't the truth, Abraham. I have issues with misleading the press,' said Sue.

'Look, far as Fullerton in New York thinks, we're telling the truth. He thinks LeBeau is dead. This isn't about lying to the press, Sue. It's about catching a potential murderer,' said Bloch.

He took the pages back from Bloch.

The Port Lonely Sheriff's Department in conjunction with the World Publishing Group regrets to announce that one of America's finest mystery writers has died. J. T. LeBeau is believed to have died in an accident at sea. To mark his passing, the world's most popular authors will be invited to attend a memorial service in Los Angeles to honor the life and work of J. T. LeBeau. There will be readings of his work, speeches honoring his contribution to popular fiction and the press will be invited to report on the ceremony for his millions of fans across the globe . . .

'I still don't see how telling a pack of lies is any help,' said Sue.

'Pride,' said Dole. 'If Fullerton is right about that, then LeBeau will be there in the crowd. There's no way he would miss this. Fullerton came through with the memorial, and that should be enough to draw him in. There ain't no one on this earth who would pass up the chance to be at their own funeral. He'll be there, I know it.'

'He's right,' said Bloch. 'Plus it gives us some time to get to know this guy better.'

'You mean we should read his books?' said Dole.

Bloch nodded. Dole sighed. He never did care for thrillers. He always saw the twist coming.

Before Dole left for the night, he and Bloch sat down and finished going through the text messages and calls. Some calls were made to the burner the day of the attack. With no way to trace the owner, it was impossible to interpret. They decided to put out an alert on the burner, so that when it was used it would ping a location alert straight to the Port Lonely Sheriff's office. It was likely the burner would never be used again, but at least they were covering their bases.

One thing that they did need to interpret were the two text messages Maria had sent to Paul on the day of the attack. Bloch found them in the print-outs.

A picture of his passport, and then a text message.

Forget something?

What was she playing at? thought Dole. He had to find out.

CHAPTER FIFTY-SIX

Paul was eating shrimp salad cocktail in a seafood shack in South Florida when he heard it on the news.

The local news anchor said a man believed to be the mysterious author J. T. LeBeau had died in a freak boating accident.

He finished the bowl, running his fork around the edge to gather the last of the sauce. Paul ordered another beer, drank it slow and watched the news, waiting for the news cycle to run through and replay the story.

Fifteen minutes later he saw the news item again. He thought about Maria, and the article he'd read earlier that morning. She was making a recovery, and police said she had identified her attacker. The news channel focused on the LeBeau story this time, and he saw a couple of talking heads with a panel discussion. The volume was low, but he followed the debate alright. He knew somewhere Maria would probably be watching too.

She never understood Paul's need for absolute privacy. For protection.

He paid in cash, left and walked to the bus station. Paul bought a ticket for the first bus headed west. The memorial would be in Los Angeles, hoping to attract not just authors but movie stars and directors. It was all about the publicity.

He checked his wallet, and counted out what he had left. Paul wondered what the hell he would've done if it hadn't been for Josephine. She'd wired enough cash to see him through the next month or two, if he lived frugally, even after he paid five hundred dollars to Luis, the fishing boat captain who got him from Grand Cayman to Miami with no passport checks and no questions asked. And an extra five hundred to Luis had bought him a gun.

Paul had some time. He need to plan this out carefully. If he was right, he would get one more shot at Daryl. A chance to end this.

Before he left, he had one last thing to do.

Bus stations were one of the few remaining places where you could be pretty much guaranteed a pay phone. And a working one at that.

Paul filled up the phone with quarters, dialed Maria's cell phone number from memory. Before the phone finished dialing, he slammed the receiver down and listened while his change tumbled into the coin reservoir at the bottom of the pay phone. He fed the phone again, and this time he dialed the house number. Chances were the cops had Maria's cell. He didn't want them to hear what he had to say. Maria might tell anyway, but he wanted to give her that chance. He had wronged her. Lied to her. And he hadn't loved her enough.

The phone began to ring.

Paul pictured Maria's face. The softness in her gaze. The gentle spark that came alive in her eyes before he kissed her.

The ancient answer service kicked in. Paul imagined he could hear the tape turning in the deck. He started talking. There was so much he wanted to say. So much he needed to say. And it all came out in a glut of guilt, tears and anger.

'I've lied to you. I kept things from you. Things I should never have kept secret. I was afraid, at first. Afraid that if I told you who I really was he would come for you, too. Stupid. I've been so stupid. I'm not J. T. LeBeau. It's Daryl, the guy from the country club. Do you hear me? If you get this message, it's Paul. I'm so sorry, Maria. I love you. And I'm sorry. I blackmailed Daryl. Got him to pay me to keep quiet about who he was, and what he had done. After I got to know you I couldn't tell you. I didn't tell you the truth because I was ashamed of what I'd done, and I didn't want to lose you. In the end, when Daryl found me, I had to run to save you. I got it all wrong. I fucked up everything. It's all my fault. I've lost the money. Daryl took it. Do not trust him. Don't go near him. He's a killer. I'm going to try to end this. For both of us.' He paused. 'I love you.'

Paul hung up the phone, wiped the tears from his face and walked toward the stands. He boarded the bus, sat at the back on his own. No other passengers around him. He checked the revolver in his pocket. A full load. He put it away. Sank into the seat for the long ride.

Soon, it would all be over for good. One way or the other, Paul had to finish it this time. There was no going back now.

CHAPTER FIFTY-SEVEN

Maria stared at the screen of her cell phone. It displayed the photograph she'd taken of Paul's passport sitting on the kitchen counter.

'Do you remember taking this photograph? It was taken with the camera on your cell. You sent it to Paul with a message,' said Dole.

She looked at the photo again. Looked away, closed her eyes and concentrated. Her mind felt like a picture puzzle with lines that didn't quite fit together. There were spaces in her memory where there should be none. And yet Maria knew those memories were in there, somewhere. Nothing had been erased, but it wasn't visible right at that moment. It was as if some memories and feelings were sitting just out of reach, shrouded in a dark veil.

Shaking her head, she said, 'At this moment I can't bring this to mind. I don't know why I sent that message.'

Dole nodded.

He flicked his finger across the screen, brought up the text message. Showed it to Maria.

'Does this help?' he said.

Bloch put her pen down.

'I don't remember the text message to Paul, no. I'm sorry. I remember an argument. I don't know what it was about,' said Maria.

It was at this point, Maria knew she would recover. She would get better, and return to her old self again. A welcome relief. She knew it when she had found herself able to lie about the photograph and the text message. No way did she want to let the cops know she had been planning to confront Paul with her lover, demand her share of the money and if he refused – blackmail him. And the passport was the lure for that trap.

That kind of information the police didn't need to know. All they needed to know was Maria's memory of that hammer falling on her head. Every time that image came to mind, she felt a shooting pain in her skull – sharp and violent. She had her back turned, the hammer hit her from behind. It must have been Paul. It could only have been Paul. Daryl couldn't do that – he loved her – he wasn't capable. She didn't understand why the police were asking these questions. Hadn't she already told them everything she knew?

Dole nodded, said, 'Maria, we don't want to put you under any pressure when it comes to these questions. It's just us for now. We just want to know if you remember anything important. If not, that's fine. Do you think maybe your husband was going to leave you? And you found he'd left a passport behind? Something like that?'

Maria closed her eyes slowly, then opened them again. It was her way of signaling agreement. She was conscious of not moving her head. The pain was bad that morning. She was due her next set of painkillers when Dole and Bloch arrived. The drugs made her drowsy. Maria wanted to have whatever wits she had left to be on full power and she'd told the nurse to wait until after the police had left.

'Maybe, I'm not sure. I don't know.'

'Maria, do you know a man named Daryl Oakes?' said Bloch.

'The name is familiar,' said Maria. It was as non-committal an answer as she could think of.

Bloch took the phone, swiped backward a couple of times and brought up the text messages to and from a number which wasn't listed under a name in her contacts. It was just a number.

'Is this his number?' asked Bloch.

Maria drew her fingers across her brow, her eyelids fluttering.

'I-I'm not feeling too good, today. The pain. Can we do this some other time? I just can't think straight,' said Maria.

She watched the cops exchange glances through her fingers. She couldn't swear to it, but she thought she saw Dole's lip quiver – his mustache twitching.

'Sure, some other time,' said Dole.

CHAPTER FIFTY-EIGHT

Dole followed Bloch down the hospital corridor. She took long, elegant strides. He had to up his pace just to keep in time with her. She was taller than him. And with each step his knees sent a little shot of acidic pain through his system.

They made it to the parking lot and the patrol car. Bloch opened the driver's door, stood there for a second then slammed it shut without getting in. Dole stood on the other side and they looked at each other over the roof of the car.

'Damn it,' said Bloch.

'Look, I don't see how it changes much,' said Dole.

Placing her elbows on the roof of the car, Bloch took her head in her hands and said, 'It changes everything.'

'No, it doesn't. So maybe Maria was having an affair with Daryl. So what? She learned that her husband was going to leave her, she texts him and says he forgot his passport. Paul hadn't booked any trips, he was out on his boat. There was sass in that text message she sent him. She wasn't reminding him he'd left his passport behind in order to be helpful.'

Bloch nodded.

'She is still adamant that it was Paul who attacked her. Maybe now that makes a little more sense. She discovers his secret life as an author – confronts him, he tries to leave her but forgets his passport, he returns to the house, there's an argument, probably over the millions in his account and then he hits her on the head with a hammer. That's our story for the moment.'

'I think Daryl was the one who slapped her,' said Bloch.

Dole looked up at the blue sky. It was hot, and he was tired.

'Could be. We knew that burglary call was a dud. Only thing damaged was that drawer. I'd say that's where she found his records, the LeBeau account statement. She used Daryl to cover for her and help her create a story that explained the drawer. Gives her time to think before she confronts him about it.

'Look, we've got time to read those damn books, look into LeBeau some more and get ourselves ready. Paul is going to show at the memorial. I'd bet my life on it.'

Bloch nodded, but that sour look on her face remained.

'We have a case against Paul. We don't have any kind of case against Daryl. Adultery is not a crime. So what's eating you?' said Dole.

She looked at him, and he already knew what she was going to say.

'The mailbox. That's what's bugging me and I can't reckon it with our case. It just doesn't fit.'

CHAPTER FIFTY-NINE
THE BEGINNING OF THE END

August

Paul Cooper waited outside a theater on La Brea Avenue in the hot midday sun with a gun in his pocket and a head full of bad ideas. He took off his sunglasses, wiped the sweat from his forehead onto the sleeve of his tee and went over the plan one more time.

He would wait for the guests inside the theater to leave. Paul had managed to secure a spot close to the barrier, on a fenced-off walkway leading from the theater to the curb. The mourners would have to walk right by him as they made their way to the street and their waiting limos. When Daryl walked past, he would draw that .38 from his pants pocket and pull the trigger in his face. He had no choice. He had to save Maria.

The lot outside the theater was full. A crowd of two or three hundred people lined either side of the barriers. They were paying their respects to their dead idol. The theater wasn't showing a play that day. No, the space had been booked for a memorial service dedicated to the late J. T. LeBeau.

Paul felt sick. Either it was the mass hysteria around him, grown women crying for a dead author, or the heat. Or both. Or the bellyful of vodka. He'd needed a few stiff drinks to stop his hands shaking.

Every time he caught the name LeBeau in the air around him, that knife in his stomach twisted just a little bit more.

Four people in the world knew the true identity of J. T. LeBeau. Two were already dead. Bob Crenshaw burned to death locked in the trunk of a blazing car. One was beaten to death – a young woman named Linzi. Two remained. And one of them was about to eat a bullet fired from the .38 Special in Paul Cooper's pocket.

The glass doors that lined the entrance to the theater opened and a crowd poured out into the punishing Los Angeles heat. Of course, they'd dressed for it. Pale linen suits hung off the bony shoulders of the men pushing their way to their cars. Most preferred white or cream suits with black ties sufficing as a token of respect. A mournful black suit would be murderous in this heatwave. The women were more formally attired, sacrificing comfort to please etiquette. Somber silk dresses clung to their legs as they adjusted their hats and put on their shades.

Sweat dribbled down his cheek and into his beard. He scooped the bottom of his shirt into his hands and wiped his face, momentarily exposing a pale belly. When he let the shirt fall it stuck to his midriff. The gun felt heavy in his pocket. It also weighed on his mind. He checked the crowd again, putting a foot on the barrier and standing up, craning his neck above the heads of those around him. No sign of the target in the masses. He started to doubt his plan. Maybe Daryl wouldn't show after all.

And then, without warning, there was no more time for thinking.

Daryl was on the red carpet. Five feet away from him. Walking past, head bowed.

Paul had visualized this moment many times. Would Daryl gaze, terrified, at the muzzle of the gun? Would he cry out? Would security have time to react?

There were four armed guards surrounding Daryl. Moving in tandem, slowly and deliberately. And while Daryl kept his head down, the security surrounding him watched the crowd on either side of the barrier carefully. He hadn't planned for this, but it didn't matter.

The hard part for Paul would be pulling the trigger. He wondered if he could do it. Gripping the barrier with one hand, his other delved into his pocket and locked around the gun. He told himself he could do this. A ripple went through his guts, sending hot acid into his throat. He swallowed it back down then blew sweat off of his lips. His heart jacked up the drumbeat in his ears.

Do it, he thought. *Do it now!*

Paul began to pull the gun. He stopped when he felt the hand on his shoulder. Someone standing behind him. He froze.

The person behind him leaned forward, and Paul felt their hot breath on his neck as they whispered to him.

Even with the people tightly packed around him, and the blood roaring through his system, he heard those words as clear as a trumpet blast. And it was a blast. A simple statement. Spoken plainly. Paul felt like those words stripped the flesh clean off his back.

'I know who you are,' said the voice in his ear. 'You're J. T. LeBeau.'

It wasn't just words.

Paul recognized the voice.

He felt the hand on his shoulder applying pressure, turning him around.

Sheriff Dole had lost weight. Slimmer, harder. Still had that stupid mustache. It hadn't seemed to lose any weight. In fact, it looked thicker than before. No sheriff's uniform. Plain clothes. To blend in with the crowd. His small black eyes focused on Paul as he shook his head.

'It's over, son. You have to come with me now,' said Dole.

Paul swallowed down a bitter taste. He still had a hand on the gun. If he drew it, Dole would shoot him dead. Not that he had any intention of shooting Dole. He thought if he could draw the gun and fire it over the heads of the crowd he could get away, disappear in the mass of people. That was his plan from the start. Fire, make sure to hit Daryl. Head shot. Then duck and run like everyone else. The crowd was too thick. Too tightly packed for anyone to make a good ID.

'Whatever you're thinking about doing, don't. Just show me your hands,' said Dole. Paul hadn't noticed at first, but he saw now that Dole had drawn a weapon, which he held down by his side.

A fat bead of sweat started a run from his hairline, down over his forehead, curled around his cheek and settled on the end of his chin. He didn't move. The gun heavy and hot in his pocket, his hand wrapped tightly around the hand stock.

'Don't make me put a bullet in you, son,' said Dole.

Paul let go of the gun. Slowly, he began to raise his hands. As he did so, the sheriff's words replayed in his mind. The sheriff didn't threaten to shoot him. Didn't threaten to kill him either. When he'd spoken, it was a plea for himself. Dole didn't want to take a life. He didn't want to have that on his conscience. A strange thing to say, given the situation. It rung true for Paul.

As much as his life was now forfeited, he didn't have anything to live for bar revenge. The pure satisfaction of knowing that he would've gone on breathing for longer than Daryl. There was satisfaction in that thought. It caught his imagination, made him feel powerful. Helped him to regain some of the confidence that had been stripped away, layer by layer, day after day, through living in fear.

In some ways a bullet would not be a bad way to check out. If it had been another cop, barking threats, gun pointed at his head, Paul might have pulled the revolver and fired at his target.

Dole was different. He had reminded Paul that every action he took made an impact. His death would destroy that part of Dole which he had managed to hold onto as a long-serving law enforcement officer. He'd actually *asked* for that not to happen.

Paul respected that. As much as he hated Daryl, he would not take another life other than his. Nor would he ruin a life by taking his revenge. It was too high a price.

'There's a gun in my right pocket. I'm gonna leave it there, and take my hands out slow and put them on top of my head,' said Paul.

He did so, and Dole watched him carefully, ready to raise that gun and fire if Paul made the wrong move. Keeping his fingers splayed open, he slowly raised them and then placed them on his head.

'Turn around, now, Paul,' said Dole.

Paul turned to face the red carpet. He was aware that at least one woman on his left, and two women on his right had realized he was being arrested. No one had heard the exchange between him and Dole over the noise from the crowd. A space began to form around Paul, making him stand out. He looked to his right at the steady stream of people leaving the theater. He looked left and saw Daryl staring at him.

Dole took hold of Paul's left wrist. He pulled it off his head and down around behind his back.

A dark suit, blue shirt and dark navy tie covered Daryl. Not in mourning, then. There was no anger in his eyes, and his expression seemed, if anything, to be one of pity. Paul knew that Daryl, the actual J. T. LeBeau, would not miss this service. The chance to attend and be anonymous in a sea of celebrities and fans celebrating his work.

His bloody work.

Paul felt the cold metal from the cuffs snaking around his left wrist. His right hand was still free. He could reach into his pocket, grab the gun and fire before Dole could stop him. But then Dole would likely put a bullet into the back of Paul's head.

The cuffs began to click as Dole squeezed them closed around his left wrist.

Daryl said, 'Look who it is. The great writer himself.'

There was a keen anger in Daryl's eyes. Paul felt Dole touch his right wrist and he knew Dole no longer had the gun drawn – one hand holding Paul's left wrist tight against his back, the other reaching for his right wrist. Perhaps this realization freed his body to react. Perhaps not. He could not know, would never know whether he acted consciously or unconsciously in those next moments. He certainly didn't think about his actions.

They just happened.

He felt Daryl's eyes touch a cold place in his chest. A place where he had lived for so many years. A fearful place.

Paul whipped his hand down, avoiding Dole's grasp. He couldn't help it. Fear had claimed him. His body reacted as if he was standing in front of a predator. All thought abandoned. The brain disconnected from the body. Only survival mattered. An instinctual, primal mode had kicked in and taken control of Paul's body. His reactions were not his own. They were automatic. He did not decide to make the move – and yet the move was made. The body took charge to rid itself of this danger. It could not trust Paul's mind to make the decision.

His fingers reached the lip of his pants pocket.

Dole realizing what was happening, grabbed hold of Paul's lower arm and with his other hand, he twisted the cuffs. The pain felt sharp and welcome. It did not deter Paul. It could not, and Dole didn't have the leverage to stop him drawing the weapon and firing.

Paul's hand gripped the gun, his index finger finding the trigger. It was a snub-nosed revolver, with no hammer so that it wouldn't get caught in his pocket when he drew it.

Paul began to pull the gun. From somewhere far away, he thought he heard Sheriff Dole's voice. It appeared faint, as if Paul was at the bottom of a deep well. Unable to hear, or think, or feel, just act.

The gun came free of his pocket. He began to raise it.

Daryl didn't move. Didn't flinch. There was no one between Paul and Daryl. No security now. A clear line of sight. A clean shot.

Paul saw some movement behind Daryl.

And Paul's front brain switched on the brakes. His conscious thought took control. It was as if the sight before him operated like a switch, instantly flicking on his brain. And he dropped the gun.

Maria stepped out from behind Daryl. He turned toward her and held out the crook of his arm. Paul watched Maria's delicate fingers wrap around the sleeve of Daryl's jacket as she moved closer to him.

She caught Paul's eyes. Clutched Daryl tighter. Huddled into his side. She wore a black dress and she'd changed her hair. It was a short bob, ink-black. It shone as it caught the dying sun. She looked pale, and scarlet lipstick emphasized her new ivory skin. It was Maria, but not Paul's Maria.

There was no emotion in that face. It looked more like a mask to Paul.

Dole had lost patience with him – he had been shouting in Paul's ear, but Paul had been unable to hear him. Both of his hands were now locked in the cuffs and he felt pressure on his back, forcing him down onto the ground. A woman in the crowd must have seen the gun as she was the first to scream. Within seconds, the crowd were billowing away from the security fence in a mad scramble to get out of the theater lot. Panic had taken hold. People would be hurt in the stampede. Paul knew this, accepted it. After all, it had been part of his original plan.

His chest hit the concrete, then his cheek. He felt Dole's knee in his back, forcing the air out of him. Heard the scraping sound of gunmetal on concrete as Dole picked up the weapon.

Paul had a vague idea that Dole was reading him his rights. He didn't listen. Every sense he possessed set its sights on Maria.

Paul screamed. His voice was raw and guttural, but he had to shout over the crowd, he needed Maria to hear him. And he shouted the only thing he could think of that would have a chance at saving her.

'Maria! Your mom called,' he cried.

Daryl held Maria close, kissed her and turned, and both of them walked away. Paul couldn't tell if she'd heard him or not. He had barely heard himself over the crowd, but it didn't stop him screaming it out.

Paul realized he couldn't even hear the sheriff's voice because he was screaming. His throat felt like a hot skillet, the force of his voice erupting from him – shouting, shouting, crying out.

CHAPTER SIXTY

She heard the commotion and knew it had to be Paul. Daryl had stopped, turned to look at the crowd as they left the theater together. Maria took a moment before she brought her gaze to the source of the disturbance. She didn't know how she would react to seeing Paul for the first time in months. Her heart beat faster. Her neck flushed red. A flutter began in her lower jaw. Breath quickening.

Fear.

There was nothing to physically fear from Paul. She was surrounded by armed security. Her apprehension came from self-preservation. Would she feel something when she saw him? This was what frightened her. That the mere sight of Paul would touch some part of her old self. Awaken it.

Maria had survived an attempt on her life. She hated Paul for that. And she hated herself for living with a man who would do that to her.

In truth, the Maria who had been attacked in her own kitchen did not survive. That Maria had died on the cold tiles.

This Maria was a very different person.

It started with the physical training and physiotherapy. The hospital found a physiotherapist more in tune with Maria's personality. The work had been tough. She had a weakness on the left side of her body. It took a week before she could use a fork properly. The gross motor skills took longer. Walking had been like learning to ride a bike. What had been automatic before had taken thought, massive physical effort and mental processes. She had to deliberately move her left leg: actually think about it before it would obey. There was a corridor outside the gym. One side of a square surrounding a small peaceful garden. Each corridor was ninety feet long. Pale tiled floor. A wall painted leaf green on one side and a long window on the other with a view of the garden. Step by step, using a rollator, covered in sweat, Maria managed twenty feet the first day. Thirty feet the day after. On the third day she had a fall at ten feet. That was not a good day, but she didn't cry. She came out fighting. By the end of the week she'd managed two thirds of the corridor. After two weeks she could manage the entire length of the corridor and half of the next one.

A month after she'd been admitted, Maria could walk around that square unassisted. The weight training helped, and the co-ordination came back. New neural pathways were built, and she had learned to compensate for any difficulties. Not a hundred percent. But not far off.

The psychotherapy lasted one session. Too raw. Too early to process. The therapist talked to her about brain injury – and the effects on the mind. She said it was like a fire that momentarily blazed across the surface of a sponge. The flames would damage the sponge, create holes where it had found air pockets, and in other parts it would melt things together. He told her she might experience gaps in memory, and because of the trauma, her mind might try to fill those gaps in memory. False memories, he called it. Transference. Maria felt a searing pain in her head every time the counselor spoke, so she told him to shut the hell up.

He told her she wasn't ready for counseling. Not just yet.

Apart from the physical therapy, Maria wasn't interested. The head doctors made her teeth hurt. She ignored the neuropsychologist. His name was Brian. She mostly liked Brian. He was tall and had an athletic aspect. Thin, muscular, and long-limbed. He always wore a yellow necktie so bright and garish that it made her eyes pop. That part she didn't like so much. He showed Maria her brain on his computer. The scans were frightening. She couldn't look. Brian explained that he and his colleagues had to do some tests. Most of them Maria thought were stupid or had stupid names. There was a Wisconsin Card Test, or something like that, where he showed her cards and asked her to match them. It wasn't like playing Snap, which she remembered playing with her mother. These cards didn't quite match each other, and some not at all. She had to look at flashing lights while they measured her eye reactions. There were more scans, and the next week she did more tests. One of them was about gambling. Maria liked that one.

On the third time she saw Brian she was bored. And he wore that tie again. Maria only heard snatches of what he said.

'Frontal lobe injury . . . changes in behavior . . . memory impairment . . . disinhibition . . . risk taking . . . impulsivity . . . attention fatigue . . .'

The hospital let Maria go home but she didn't want to return to the house. Instead she got a hotel room in Bay City. Paid in advance for the week. She wasn't just ready to cook and clean for herself – not yet. And in fact, she didn't want to. The sheriff had been good to her. He'd kept in contact, visiting her in the hospital often. And now she was out, he sent regular emails. She always answered him. Had to keep him on her side. Yes, she believed that Paul had tried to kill her. She had never told Dole that she had once planned to blackmail Paul.

On the third night of her stay she got a telephone call.

Daryl.

It was good to hear his voice. Something inside her was soothed by it. Like pouring cold water on her hot, sore feet after a long walk through the city.

Daryl wanted to meet. She told him to come to the hotel and sure enough, the next night he came. Maria opened the door to Daryl, put a hand over his lips and took him to her bed. They talked afterwards and she answered all of Daryl's questions.

No, she hadn't told the police of their plans to confront Paul.

Yes, the police told her that they believed Paul was really the author known as J. T. LeBeau. Sheriff Dole explained it all, in detail, on his last visit to the hospital. On that occasion, while they sat in the little garden, he told her that although the world believed Paul to be dead, Dole did not believe it. There would be a memorial service for LeBeau, and Dole felt strongly that Paul would show up at the memorial. Maria had been invited by the publishers, and whilst she had no wish to honor the man who had tried to kill her – she felt it was important to build a relationship with the publishers. They wanted to come to some arrangement with her about book royalties. She stood to make a fortune. There would be extra security laid on, just for her.

Dole warned her that if Paul got in touch she must call him immediately. The sheriff had done some digging into J. T. LeBeau, and he didn't like what he found. Her husband was a very dangerous man and had likely been responsible for a number of deaths, including a young girl called Linzi. Even in the serene garden, with the sound of gently running water from the fountain and the smell of the roses enveloping her, Maria felt afraid.

Maria lay beside Daryl in the hotel bed, and just looked at him. She had told him everything that had happened and felt better for it. They were both naked, holding each other. Maria enjoyed the familiar touch of Daryl's skin. As her hand grazed his back, she felt something unnatural and recoiled.

'What is that?'

'Paul gave me that. In your kitchen, remember? I heard something, went outside to check what and when I came back in . . .'

'What?'

'You were lying on the floor. I thought you were dead. That's when he put the claw hammer in my back.'

'My God,' she said, covering her mouth.

'I fought him off, got away. I didn't want to go to the emergency room. Everything had gotten so crazy. I was worried out of my mind. Then I got a fever. I was sick, and by the time I came out of it you had woken up in hospital. I almost died. We almost died. I'm so sorry, honey. I went out of my mind for a while. I thought I'd lost you.'

She drew close, and they kissed and embraced for a time.

'How did you find me?' she said.

'The hospital said you'd left. I wanted to give you some time before I called. Given everything that happened. I should never have opened that drawer in Paul's desk. I'm sorry. I felt responsible,' said Daryl.

She placed a finger on his lips, quieting him, said, 'It's not your fault.'

'Do you think Paul found out what we were planning? Is that why he attacked us?'

She fell silent, stroked the fine hairs on his chest, then said, 'Maybe. Probably. It doesn't matter. But how did you find me here?'

'I went by the house. Still closed up, so I knew you were probably staying in Bay City. You always hated Port Lonely and I knew you liked this hotel. We stayed here before . . . well, it was one night. We had dinner in the restaurant downstairs. Paul had been away on a trip. You said you wanted to go someplace where we didn't have to hide, where we could sit together and have a meal as a couple. We ended up staying over.'

Maria had only the vaguest memory of this. She recalled Daryl in a dinner jacket, but couldn't place the location. These gaps in memory were something she was becoming accustomed to. There were dark holes in her mind. Some things were vivid and clear, some were almost there but shrouded in mist, other memories were simply gone. Erased clean. She could remember the smell of her mother's perfume – the only bottle she ever had. Yet she could not remember the day she married Paul, or whether she'd eaten yesterday.

'I don't remember,' she said, then threw a leg over Daryl, got up on top of him.

'Let's make new memories,' she said.

Her life in the weeks leading to the memorial service became filled with days in bed with Daryl, dinners together, movies, and lazy Sunday mornings spent over endless coffee in local diners. They were together. And Maria felt something close to happiness.

Now, in Daryl's arms, on the red carpet leading out from the memorial service, she turned and looked at Sheriff Dole kneeling on top of her husband. She met Paul's eyes. And she found herself feeling something after all.

Pity.

Just pity.

She listened to him screaming at her, but she couldn't quite make out what he'd said. Something about *Tom called* . . .

Whatever love she'd borne him belonged to that other Maria. The Maria who died in Port Lonely.

CHAPTER SIXTY-ONE

The LAPD had been more helpful than expected. They'd co-operated fully with Dole's requests, they'd even gotten Bloch an unmarked pool car on the agreement that she came back in a few months and helped teach a refresher course to their advanced driving instructors. This had been desirable since they escorted them in a rental car from LAX and the escort had been unable to keep up with Bloch.

Dole knew Bloch was much more than a gifted driver.

They stood outside the interview room going over their notes. There was a box of exhibits lying on the floor at Dole's feet. Bloch had prepared for that day in minute detail. She had over one hundred pages of notes, a list of questions which she'd memorized, and two bags full of evidential exhibits which the LAPD had helped them catalog and store. The arrest was made in LA, so the interview had to take place in LA. After Paul Cooper was interviewed he was to be brought to court. The ADA had been instructed by senior police to request the transfer of the case to Port Lonely. They were all set, and they'd managed to keep the case out of the line of sight of the FBI. They could not be more prepared.

'You think we should have arrested Daryl at the memorial?' said Bloch.

'No, I stand by that decision. All the evidence points to Cooper, for now. Maria has some money coming to her. My guess is Daryl will stick around for that.'

Bloch nodded.

'You ready?' said Dole.

She nodded again, sniffed and wiped a thumb across her nose like a boxer.

'Okay then,' he said, and Bloch opened the door, holding it for Dole while he picked up the cardboard box, brought it inside. They stepped into a small room with a table and chairs that had been bolted to the floor. In the middle of the table a steel ring protruded through a hole. Paul Cooper sat in one of the chairs, his hands cuffed to the ring. One of the LAPD techs had already set up a digital video recorder in the corner, which waited idly, prepared and set to capture the interview in its entirety.

Dole put the box on the floor, took one of the seats opposite Paul. Bloch the one beside Dole. There was an empty chair beside Paul Cooper. He'd said he didn't need a lawyer. He just wanted out of there.

Bloch explained she was going to record the interview. She got up and switched on the digital recorder. Dole reminded Paul that he'd already been Mirandized.

The questions had been carefully prepared, edited and rewritten.

'Mr. Cooper, your rights have been explained, and you already know why you're here. Let's cut to the chase, shall we? You want to tell us why you tried to kill your wife?'

'I did not hurt my wife,' said Paul. 'You've got the wrong man.'

As much as they had prepared this interrogation, Dole was still surprised by Cooper's manner. He was obviously scared. That was a given. He'd been arrested for a number of serious crimes – including two counts of attempted murder and an alternative charge of conspiracy to murder. Dole had charges to add – but he was keeping those in his back pocket for now. The conspiracy charge and the second attempted murder charge would probably fall away to a simple illegal possession of a firearm: these charges arising from the incident at the memorial. But even considering all of the circumstances, and Cooper's natural apprehension following arrest – there was something in the way he spoke that gave Dole pause. Cooper sounded as if he meant what he said.

The guy probably had even more time than Dole and Bloch to prepare for this interrogation. Dole told himself the guy had rehearsed for this moment – practiced it. Only natural in the situation. He knew Bloch would feel this too – and suspend her judgment until the end of the interview. She wouldn't allow herself to be thrown by the perp so easily, and so early in the process.

'We have a lot of evidence connecting you to your wife's attack, Mr. Cooper. It would be better for you in the long run if you didn't waste everyone's time. You had to have a good reason to attack Maria, right? Well, now's the time to tell us,' said Bloch.

'I told you, I didn't touch her. It was Daryl Oakes.'

'What makes you think he attacked your wife?'

There was a pause. No answer. Cooper took a big breath, held Bloch's gaze for a three-count then turned his head away and breathed out in one long, pained exhalation.

This man has something he can tell us, but he won't or believes he can't, thought Dole.

Or he's leading Bloch into a trap.

'I'm sure you know, Mr. Cooper, that as police officers we have to pay careful attention to the evidence. That is what guides us, Mr. Cooper. You should know that. You've done your research for books. Don't you write about murder and police detectives?'

He sat up a little straighter, said, 'What have my books got to do with this? Surely it's LeBeau you should be talking to?'

The statement was a gut punch to Bloch and Dole. They couldn't show it. Suspects often said unexpected things in interviews. All they could do was stick to the plan, for now. Plenty of time to listen to bullshit excuses later.

'We ask the questions in this room, Mr. Cooper,' said Bloch. She didn't want to go there yet. But these initial questions were all about destabilizing Cooper – softening him with a few well-timed jabs.

'Do you really want to play it this way? We know it was you who attacked Maria. Tell us why and we don't have to go through this. It will make things better in court if you confess now,' said Bloch.

'It wasn't me. Just ask her,' said Cooper.

Bloch exchanged a look with Dole. It was time to get into it.

Dole handed her the first exhibit. It was a cardboard box. About fourteen inches long, five inches wide. One side of the box was clear plastic. Inside was a hammer. Dark bloodstains still on the handle and the head. They had crusted and dried.

'This is your hammer, used to attack Maria Cooper. We found fingerprints on it. Only one set – yours,' said Bloch.

She put the hammer to one side, brought out a thick typed document, which was stapled together in the top corner.

'This is a transcript from Maria's deposition. She says she found a bank statement in your desk drawer.'

Dole handed over the next exhibit bag. A clear, sealed plastic bag containing a bloodstained bank statement.

'This bank statement. It says you're worth twenty million dollars. Maria knew nothing of this money and she confronted you . . .'

'No,' said Cooper.

'You viciously attacked her. Cracked her skull and rolled her up in plastic ready to take on your boat.'

'No,' said Cooper.

Dole brought out a set of photographs showing a hole in the side of a boat, slapped them on the desk.

'You were going to sink the boat. Fake your own death, and hers. But something went wrong. The boat took on water too fast. You couldn't get to her. So you left her and disappeared,' said Bloch.

'No.'

'You wanted everyone to believe you were dead so you could disappear with the money. We know you emptied the bank account.'

'It was my money. I'd earned it.'

'So why didn't you come forward?' said Dole.

'Because I knew you would think I hurt Maria. He wanted it that way,' said Cooper.

'Who wanted it that way?' asked Bloch.

'Daryl Oakes,' said Cooper.

Bloch leaned back, folded her arms. She was tagging in Dole.

'Deputy Bloch told you we look at the evidence. That's all we do. So tell us, where is the evidence that Oakes attacked Maria and set you up?' said Dole. As he spoke he thought of the mailbox, broken and lying in the grass at the top of Cooper's drive. He was beginning to soften to Cooper. But he had to go where the evidence led him. Right now, there was nothing tying Oakes to any of this.

'If I told you . . .' said Cooper, then shook his head.

Holding his hands wide, Dole said, 'If you told us . . . what? Come on, this is your chance. You won't get another.'

'You wouldn't believe me.'

'Try me,' said Dole. 'Because right now, Maria says you attacked her. If she's wrong, tell us why. Tell us the truth.'

'I can't,' said Cooper.

'Why can't you?'

'Because then you'll die,' said Cooper.

Bloch had had enough. She bent over, picked up a stack of books, started piling them on the desk. Pounding them on top of one another, making some noise with her point. The books piled up. The complete works of J. T. LeBeau. Bloch picked up a copy of *The Burning Man*, slapped it down in front of Cooper.

'The character in your second novel. The victim who is burned to death in a car because he knew too much. Sounds a lot like what happened to your first editor – Bob Crenshaw.'

Cooper shook his head.

'We want to know about the woman in your third novel, *Angel Falls*. She was found in a spill well, naked, no ID was ever made and in your book you say she was murdered by her former lover. She knew a secret about him. That he was really a wanted serial killer living under a false identity.'

Cooper said nothing.

'Her real name was Linzi, wasn't it?'

Tears formed precarious pools in Cooper's eyes. It was the name that had stung.

Cooper cupped his face in his hands, leaned forward and put his elbows on the table. The chain at his wrists straining.

'Then there's your fifth novel, a man—'

'Stop,' said Cooper.

'Oh, I can go on, Mr. Cooper. It's just that we've read these books, and some of the murders bear a striking resemblance to real, unsolved murders. I think you're a killer. And I think you write about your crimes in your books. We've seen the message on your computer. Linzi worked out who you really are. They found out you were J. T. LeBeau, and the reason you keep your identity secret is because you're a killer. I think you're going to death row, Mr. Cooper, unless you start co-operating with us right now,' said Bloch.

Nothing was said for a time. They were waiting on a response. Slowly, Cooper's shoulders began to shake. He'd hidden his face in his hands, so they couldn't see an expression. Then a sound came.

Laughter. Yet there was no warmth in the sound. It was empty and fearful.

Cooper drew his hands away, and revealed a wide, desperate smile.

'You've got it all wrong,' said Cooper. 'I don't have a choice now. I'm going to tell you what really happened. I'll go to jail for my part in it. For keeping quiet. For taking the money. I was a coward and I deserve that. But at least you'll know the truth. I am not J. T. LeBeau. Daryl Oakes is LeBeau.'

'Let's take five,' said Dole.

Cooper leaned back, took a breath. Dole and Bloch paused the video, and exited the interview room, closing the door behind them.

Dole put his back to the wall, focused on the ceiling tile.

'Don't tell me you buy this bullshit,' said Bloch.

'The mailbox,' said Dole.

'What about the fucking mailbox?' said Bloch.

Kicking off the wall, Dole started down the corridor.

'Where are you going?' said Bloch.

'I'm going to see Maria. I want to talk to her. I said I would give her a call after we interviewed Paul, anyway. Maybe I'll just drop by her hotel instead. You keep going with Cooper. You're better at this than me.'

CHAPTER SIXTY-TWO

Daryl had been surprised at how well Maria had taken the events of that day. She truly was a different person. Strong. Uninhibited.

So much more like himself.

He enjoyed her even more now than before. Before she was just a pawn on the board. Now she was a queen.

They took the elevator to the tenth floor. An extensive refurbishment of the hotel was well underway. That morning, as they'd left their room, Daryl and Maria had watched staff carefully removing the pictures from the walls of the corridor, wrapping them in muslin and handing them to the bellhop who then stacked them in the luggage carrier.

That night, as the elevator opened its doors, Daryl caught the smell of fresh paint. The corridors on that floor had been repainted that day. A dark, wholesome green. Maria could smell it too, she was holding her fingers against her nose.

They reached the door, Maria found her key card. Stopped. Took a long sniff of the air. The paint smell seemed stronger down there, at the end of the hallway. She looked at Daryl, and he didn't like the way she did it. There was something unspoken in her eyes. She swiped the card, went into the room and said, 'I need to take a bath.'

It looked more like a suite than a room. Extended bathroom. Two sinks, large tub and wet room. Desk, couch and television in a separate room, just off the bedroom. Sliding glass doors to a small balcony with a little table and two chairs for an alfresco breakfast with a view of the Hollywood sign, LA fog permitting.

Maria went straight into the bathroom, dropped her purse on the bathroom tiles and turned on the faucet. He sat on the bed, watched her undress as the tub filled. Daryl got up and went to the desk, opened his laptop, and fired it up. He entered the hotel WiFi code. There were no other sounds in the room, no TV, no piped music, just the sound of the bathtub filling up.

Daryl remembered the smell in the kitchen of the house in Port Lonely, on that last day. Maria had cracked open a can of paint, and she'd put some on the walls just to make things look a little more convincing. That smell was the same as in the hallway. Odor can be a memory trigger, just like any sense, perhaps even more powerful than sight or sound.

That look she'd given him in the hallway. Sense memory was a powerful thing. For some it could be the odor of a familiar perfume, for others the smell of a particular brand of cigarette, or a flower – that's all that was needed to send the mind reeling into memory and nostalgia.

She knew.

He checked his email account on his laptop. The purchase of the property in Medina had gone through. The keys were waiting at his realtor's office.

Perfect timing. Maria had proved useful, but it was no longer wise nor safe to let her live.

Daryl got up and checked his overnight bag. He'd packed everything bar a fresh shirt, which was still in the closet. He fetched the shirt, folded it and placed it in his bag.

Ready to go.

He could hear the tub still filling. Maria had closed the door without him hearing it. The sound muted now. She'd always enjoyed a long, hot bath. Often, before he left her on those clandestine liaisons, he would run her a hot bath, and watch her slip into it. He knew when the tub had filled and she got into it, he would have at least a half hour before the temperature fell low enough for her to get out.

He hollered at Maria through the door. 'I'll have some wine waiting for you when you get out of the tub, okay?'

'Sure. The red, please,' said Maria.

Instead of getting the wine, Daryl couldn't resist using the time he had to write. He was coming to the end of the first draft. He opened the Word document on his laptop that contained his work in progress – the latest offering from J. T. LeBeau. He began to type. It was a new scene, set in a hotel just like this one. When he'd finished the scene, he read over his work, making small adjustments as he went through it. He would change the names later, so as not to make the truth of the matter too obvious to the authorities who might read the book. He wanted the truth to be there, but clouded, just in case they ever caught up with him.

After ten minutes Darren heard the water sloshing, dripping onto the bathroom tiles. Martha was getting out of the tub, early. She stepped into the bedroom behind him. He turned, and saw the steam coming from the bathroom. She wore a white robe. Her hair looked an even deeper shade of black when it was wet. And now she had removed her lipstick, her pale face merely enhanced the color of her hair further – a lily contrasting with a black rose.

Each was beautiful.

'I'll get the wine, shall I?' said Martha.

'Sorry, I forgot,' said Darren.

The suite boasted a fully stocked bar, hidden away in a dresser. She selected a bottle of Rioja and two glasses. From a drawer she picked up the wine opener, used the small blade at the side to cut away the plastic top. Then she used the automatic machine left in the minibar to uncork the wine. Leaving the bottle on the dresser, she let it breathe.

Darren turned back to his laptop screen, saved the file. That's when he felt Martha's touch on his shoulder.

'What's this you're working on?' said Martha.

He got up, turned the chair around, said, 'Take a seat and I'll let you read it.'

Martha returned to the dresser, poured the wine into two glasses and gave one to Darren. She reversed into the office chair, glass of wine in hand, and Darren gently turned her around to face the screen. While she read, Darren stood to the side so he could watch her expression.

Her eyes followed the text. He could see the rectangle of light from the screen reflected in the large black iris of her right eye, the convex surface distorting the image and bending it into a strange shape.

Tiny muscles in her forehead twitched as she read the third line. Her eyes continued to travel across the screen, and down, and across – following the trail of the text.

She began to tremble. Darren took the glass from her hands without resistance, placed it on the desk.

Tears formed in her eyes. Her lip quivered. She was reading a narrative that described her own murder.

And then, all at once, shock took her. Her hands reached for her face, her body taking in a huge gasp of air – an instinctual response to ready the muscles for escape.

But there was no escape. She couldn't move.

'You're J. T. LeBeau,' she said, in a whisper.

Darren stepped behind her, slipped his arms around her body and lifted her into the air.

'I should have finished you in Port Lonely,' said Darren.

He began walking backwards, her legs kicking, her hands fighting his grip. Darren dropped her onto his hip, but kept one arm locked around her midriff. With his free hand he pushed the sliding balcony doors further open.

She almost wriggled free, but he took hold again. Both arms encasing her waist and he hoisted her high.

Darren took two steps onto the balcony, heaved, twisted, and threw Martha over the edge. He saw that look on her face as she fell, her arms outstretched, her voice only catching into a scream right then.

He didn't wait for her to hit the ground. The screaming and the car horns from below were enough.

Darren went back inside, closed his laptop, put it in his bag. He found Martha's phone sticking out of the top of her purse on the bathroom floor, typed an email to Sheriff Cole saying she couldn't deal with the thought of a trial. She couldn't stand up to her husband, Saul. It was all too much. He had won. She thanked him for what he had done for her, and told him he shouldn't feel guilty for what she was about to do. She had had enough. Darren hit send on the email, and left the hotel.

Daryl finished typing and stood up from his laptop. He walked over to the balcony doors and opened them.

It was time for Maria to come out and have a glass of wine.

CHAPTER SIXTY-THREE

Maria listened to the rhythmic tumbling of water falling into the bathtub and stared into the bathroom mirror.

She stood in front of the mirror in her underwear while she carefully removed her makeup with a cleansing wipe. Tossing the wipe into the trash can by her feet, she looked at the wash basin to find the rest of the pack. The rim of the basin looked very clean and tidy. Only her toothbrush, toothpaste and cleansing wipes remained. At first she thought nothing of it, then she looked again. Daryl must've packed his toothbrush. Stepping to the right, she stared into the trash and saw her wet wipe sitting beside Daryl's disposable razor.

They were due to stay in the hotel for at least another week.

Why had Daryl packed his things?

An image flashed before her mind. The passport. Paul's passport. Sitting on the kitchen counter. The smell of paint was strong now. Almost making her gag. And yet the redecoration crew had not been in their room. Nothing had been repainted in the bathroom and still that smell was in her nose.

Maria closed her eyes. And then saw Daryl, standing in a white plastic coverall suit. His eyes were dead.

Her knees suddenly gave way, and she gripped the sink to steady herself. Managed not to fall.

What the fuck is happening to me? she whispered, clasping her hands to the side of her head as if she were trying to prevent her skull splitting.

Then she saw it again, the image was strong. Clear. There had been no noise outside distracting Daryl, drawing him away from the kitchen. The only one in that room when she was attacked was Daryl. A tremendous stabbing pain brought her to her knees.

She gasped. Grabbed for her purse on the floor beside her dress. She took out her phone, selected the number for Dole then stopped.

Daryl was at the door, asking if she wanted wine. She said yes, the red. It was all she could do to stop a scream erupting from her throat.

She shook her head. Panic was setting in. She thought of Paul that day. He was going to try to shoot Daryl. Not her. It was Daryl all along. She had messed up. Let a monster into her life.

And what had Paul shouted at her? Tom's calling.

She repeated the phrase over and over.

No. Not Tom's calling. Tom called.

Tom called. Tom called. Tom called.

All of the air left her lungs. She shot out one arm to steady herself and almost dropped the phone.

Not *Tom called.*

Mom called.

She dialed the answer machine. Her mom's machine back in Port Lonely. It was one of the first of its type that allowed you to access your messages remotely. She keyed in the code. Listened.

You have one new message.

Five minutes later Maria hung up the call. She took the towel from the radiator next to her, put it in her mouth and cried and rocked back and forth as her body convulsed in tears and shame.

After a while, she put the towel down. Water hit the back of her neck. She turned around, shut off the faucet for the tub. Then let some of the water out so it wouldn't flood the bathroom.

She stared at the door.

Maria knew then that there was a killer on the other side. There was no way out. He had watched her closely that night when they returned to the room. She suddenly felt very afraid and noticed that her body was shivering violently.

She dialed Dole's phone. No answer. She left a muffled message, then put the phone back in her purse. She was shaking so much now that she couldn't even speak.

Guilt. Pain. Fear.

She had wronged Paul.

Maria knew there was only one thing she could do. It was clear in her mind. She had had enough of this mess. Paul had been stupid to take the money. Stupid to hide it from her. But no one had been more stupid than her, she thought. Not only had she fallen in love with a killer, but she had taken him back into her bed after he had attacked her. She felt the vomit rise in her stomach, and swallowed it down.

What have I done?

No way out. No way out. No way out.

She'd had enough of men. Her father, her husband, her lover. They had all hurt her, used her, and left her to die.

She'd had enough pain. She'd had enough of this fear. This guilt. This shame.

This life.

CHAPTER SIXTY-FOUR

Daryl opened the bathroom door. He couldn't see Maria standing in the bathroom, she must still have been in the tub. The lights had been turned low. It was a tranquil scene. He thought about how he would describe it in the book, then stepped inside.

'How about that glass . . .'

His words died in his throat.

Daryl looked down at the tub.

The water was a dull shade of red. Like someone had dumped a pot of red ink in the water. Maria's pale body rested in the tub, her dead eyes staring at the muted light bulbs in the ceiling. One wrist lay on the side of the tub, her fingers still curled around Daryl's disposable razor that he'd tossed in the trash that morning. He saw a deep gash on the wrist, with blood leaking into the tub. He leaned over, saw a cut to the other submerged wrist.

The bathwater was red with her blood. Blood on the razor. Razor in her hand. Cuts to her wrist. He knew he shouldn't disturb this scene, if he could help it. It worked just fine for his purposes.

He took a cleansing wipe from the pack sitting on the basin, wrapped his finger in the wipe and then touched her wrist. He altered the position of his finger several times – feeling for a pulse. None.

She had been dreading the memorial. She was afraid of Paul, and what he might do. Daryl had been anxious as well. Fearful that seeing Paul might trigger some memory that had been submerged in pain, and blood on her brain. He had not expected this. He picked up her purse, took out her phone and checked it. The memory showed no recent calls. It didn't show any calls – so perhaps she had deleted them. He couldn't tell. Perhaps her phone did not store a call history. He typed out the email to Sheriff Dole, a goodbye note, then wiped the phone clean and dropped it on the floor. He turned, walked out of the bathroom with the wipe in his hand.

No time to waste. Daryl packed up his laptop, put it in his bag along with the wipe, which he would dispose of later, and cursed as he left the room.

His teeth grinded. His jaw working hard. Furious.

He really liked that scene. The description of Maria reading about her own death, moments before it happened. It was a moment of pure pleasure that he would now never have. He felt cheated. Robbed of the kill.

And he would have to go to work on the book that night. He couldn't let that anomaly sit in his manuscript. That would eat away at him like a tick chewing his flesh.

He would have to rewrite the whole goddamn scene.

She'd beaten him.

CHAPTER SIXTY-FIVE

Dole pulled up a few hundred feet from the hotel entrance. It was the closest parking space he could get. There was a valet service, of course, but Dole hated the thought of paying some kid to park his car.

LA didn't agree with Dole.

He'd been parking his own damn car for over forty years. He wasn't going to go changing that shit now.

He turned off the engine of the LAPD pool car. A green Pontiac that felt like it was on its last legs. Cracking open the driver's door, he paused. Closed the door and hunkered down beneath the steering wheel.

Daryl gave a ticket to the valet outside the hotel. He had a bag with him. He stood on the sidewalk, taking care to keep his head down. Not looking anyone in the eye. Making himself inconspicuous.

Dole wanted to talk to him, but something held him back. He wanted to see where Daryl went, and if he was staying in another hotel. It would be good to know where he might need to find Daryl in case they decided to pick him up in the morning after he'd spoken to Maria.

While Daryl stood on the sidewalk, Dole took out his cell phone. He thought it might have been vibrating in his pocket while he was driving over here. The old pool car didn't have a phone system, and Dole didn't want to get caught on a traffic camera with a phone in his hand, especially when he was in the LAPD's vehicle. That wouldn't look good.

He had a missed call from Maria. A new voicemail. And an email from her. He read the email first.

It was a suicide note. He checked the missed call. The email had been sent half an hour after the call. He dialed up his voicemail, pressed the phone to his ear, his other hand strangling the steering wheel, his throat cloying with the emotions that were threatening to erupt.

After the first ten seconds of the voicemail, he locked his eyes on Daryl.

Over the sound of running water, Maria told him she had gotten it all wrong. She was in a hotel bathroom, with Daryl outside. She was trapped. He was the one who had attacked her. She remembered now. Paul was innocent. Her last plea was not for help.

'You won't get to me in time. No one could. Just get this bastard. Paul told me everything, he left a message on my answering service. He's telling the truth. LeBeau must be stopped. Daryl has to be arrested. Get him. Don't let him go.'

The message ended. Dole started hammering the wheel with his fist. A black SUV pulled up outside the hotel, the valet got out of it and handed the keys to Daryl. He got in, pulled into traffic.

Dole turned over the engine of the Pontiac a few times before it coughed into life. Then he followed Daryl. He tried calling Bloch. Her phone was off. She must've been in the interview room with Paul.

Goddamn it, he knew it. He had sensed it. The mailbox had been the first clue. Someone wanted the body found – that someone wanted Paul in the frame for Maria's murder. She had survived. Now, Dole had no doubt she was dead. And he was following her murderer.

He stayed a few cars back, keeping the SUV in sight but not getting too close.

Dole took Maria's last wish, held it in his gritted teeth.

He wasn't going to let Daryl get away. He was going to stop him.

At that moment, Dole knew something else. He knew it like he knew heartache, and loss and guilt. All too familiar friends of his. He knew Daryl would be able to spin the investigation against Paul. That there was every chance Daryl could beat a charge. Maria had given him a dying declaration, but a good defense attorney could turn that into the mad ravings of a suicidal victim of a traumatic brain injury.

At that moment, he was glad Bloch hadn't picked up his call. He wasn't going to try again. He wasn't going to call for back-up. There was no justice for these victims in a courtroom.

Dole was going to stop Daryl.

But he sure as hell wasn't going to arrest him.

CHAPTER SIXTY-SIX

Two hours after he'd left the hotel room, Daryl stood in front of his bathroom mirror. The house in LA was nothing fancy. It was an old colonial. Spanish. Two floors. Three bedrooms, with a large basement. On a clear morning he could see the five-oh-one, and the traffic flowing through the early mist like ghosts.

It was late evening. Coming up on ten o'clock.

Much had changed in the last hour. Daryl had shaved his head. First with an electric trimmer, then with a razor. At the memorial service he'd sported the beginnings of a beard. Short, well kept. Now it was a goatee. Spotted with white after he had carefully bleached sections with dye and a cotton bud. He was also deeply tanned. This proved more difficult than he'd first imagined. Before, he had always visited a salon that did spray-on tan treatments. This time he'd used an expensive bottle of self-tanning lotion. It took careful application and a lot of work to spread it evenly over the skin without leaving dark patches on his neck, or on his hands.

He returned to the bedroom, dressed in sweat pants and T-shirt and then took his laptop to the study on the second floor. He opened it, read over Martha's death scene. As much as he liked that scene he knew it had to go.

Kill your darlings. Isn't that what all the best writers say?

He highlighted the text, and was about to delete it when he heard a noise.

Holding himself very still, he listened. The soft whirr of the fan in his laptop. Nothing else. Still, he didn't move. The hairs stood up on the back of his neck. Even though he could hear nothing else, he knew there was someone in the house.

Quickly, quietly, he stood and went back to the bedroom. He removed a silenced pistol from the lock box in the closet. Checked the weapon. It was fully loaded. Round in the chamber. He stepped into a pair of Nikes then made his way back to the study. While on the landing, he listened again but heard nothing.

Didn't matter. He knew someone was in the house.

CHAPTER SIXTY-SEVEN

Dole watched Daryl park in the garage of the Spanish house that overlooked the freeway. He had stayed at least three cars back from Daryl's SUV the whole way. Hardest part of the drive was keeping a respectable distance from the car in front.

He thought the LAPD pool car could've been worse. He had gotten used to it. The brakes on the Pontiac needed a lot of work. They were either on or off. There was no real margin for slowing down. You were stopping or not, and that was the way of it.

How he had avoided an accident he wasn't quite sure. But he was here now.

He waited until most of the house lights had either been switched off or muted. Dole checked his gun. Made sure he had a full clip. Then he got out of the car and approached the house. There didn't appear to be any alarms that he could see.

No boxes on the wall to tell potential intruders there was a burglar alarm. No cameras on the corners of the house.

Once he'd completed a circuit of the property, he'd noted two possible points of entry. The back-door lock could be picked, or he could try to slip through the kitchen window.

He opted for the back door. There were no rear lights on the property. Only a fence and a small yard stood between him and the back door. Climbing fences wasn't Dole's strong point. The fence was made up of wooden panels, about five feet high. At least it was solid. Dole used his arms to push himself up, then hooked a leg on top of the fence, threw his other leg over and dropped to the ground. A searing pain shot through both knees. He swore under his breath, rubbed at his joints then crept through the yard.

He knelt at the back door. Stopped. Listened.

No dogs or neighbors and no lights coming on in either this house or the one beside it. Drawing up his pant leg, he felt for the object in his boot. Found it. Drew out the picks he kept with him. There were a lot of summer homes in Port Lonely. Properties that lay vacant in the winter months. Dole had lost count of the amount of times he had to gain access to one of those homes to turn off the alarm after a raccoon had set it off. Usually the owners were four to five hours' drive away and more than happy to let the sheriff pick the lock, turn off and reset the alarm and then close the door behind him.

To this end he had become reasonably proficient with picks.

He checked the lock. A cylinder with probably six barrels. He selected the picks, worked through touch and had the door open in under two minutes.

He put his picks away, put his hand on his gun at his hip and stepped lightly into the dark house. He closed the door over, but didn't let the lock catch. He might need to make a quick exit.

Gritting his teeth against the bites of pain in his knees that came with every soft footfall, he made his way through the house. Kitchen, lounge and hallway were clear.

He glanced upstairs. The light was on in the bathroom. Another light spilled from a different room. He couldn't tell which room, but it was soft light. Probably from a lamp.

Footsteps above him.

Dole stopped. Held his breath.

He heard the sound of wood and old rollers. An unmistakable sound. Someone opening an old window. He crept further into the hall. Now he could hear sounds of traffic outside, but it was coming from upstairs. Then another sound, directly above the hallway. Someone on the roof.

Dole crept carefully up the stairs. Drew his weapon as his eye-line came level with the landing. He glanced through the bannisters, and saw a small study. A lamp burned on a desk. Beside the lamp, a window thrown fully open. Dole narrowed his eyes.

He moved quickly now. Unconcerned about the potential noise. He got to the top of the landing, made for the study, then ran in, his gun raised. The room was empty. A small bed sat behind him. He ran to the open window and looked out. His gun following his line of sight.

No one on the roof. No one on the street below. He'd lost Daryl. Dole put his gun back in his holster. He put a foot on the window, gripped the sides of the frame with both hands. He was going to climb onto the roof to see if he could get a better view of the street and the rest of the roof. Either Daryl was long gone, or he was trying to make it onto the roof next door.

Dole felt the presence behind him before the man could say a word.

'I have a gun. Don't move. You're a trespasser,' said the voice.

Dole stayed still, didn't turn around, but the Glock on his hip called to him.

'Put both feet on the floor. Raise your hands where I can see them, and then stay perfectly still,' said the voice.

Dole put his foot back down, let go of the window frame, slowly. Holding out his empty hands, Dole said, 'I'm a police officer, don't shoot.'

'Turn around, slowly, and keep your hands up,' said the voice.

Dole did as he was told, careful not to let his arms slip down even an inch. He saw a man in a crouched position behind the bed. He had his arms spread on the bed and in his hands Dole saw a silenced pistol aimed straight at him. At first he didn't recognize the man at all. He was bald, tanned. With a salt-and-pepper goatee. Then, when he looked closer, he saw the familiar jaw line, but what gave it away were the eyes. Dole would never forget those terrible eyes.

'Hi, Daryl,' said Dole. 'Or should I call you LeBeau?'

'You're a lot smarter than I gave you credit for. I want you to get on your knees.'

The weight of knowledge hit Dole like an anvil falling from the heavens. This was it. The final moments. He didn't feel afraid. He wanted to make a stand, that was for damn sure, but he knew this was only going to have one outcome.

'Before I get down on my knees, tell me one thing – you broke the mailbox, didn't you? So that the mailman would find Maria's body?'

'I was going to use the car. You know, drive over it. But I was worried about leaving a paint trace on the post, and I'd have to change my tires. Damned if you do, damned if you don't. Now get on your knees,' said Daryl.

'You killed Maria tonight, didn't you?' said Dole.

'On your knees,' said Daryl.

Dole smiled. He wasn't the best driver, wasn't the smartest in his own department, couldn't run, damn near blew out his knee getting over the fence and he probably should have pieced all of this together a lot sooner. One thing he could do was shoot.

He put in the hours. Draw and fire. Hit the target. Five rounds in under three seconds was his personal best.

Dole breathed out, went for his gun.

Dole's weapon hadn't cleared leather when he felt the first bullet. He didn't feel the second.

CHAPTER SIXTY-EIGHT

Daryl held the silencer in his hand, and with the other he twisted the pistol free.

He looked down at Dole's body.

This would be messy. He put the gun in one pocket of his pants, the silencer in the other, walked around the corpse and took hold of the feet. He dragged Dole out of the study, rolled his corpse down the stairs to the hallway. He followed after, stepped over Dole's lifeless arm then unlocked the basement door. Dragging Dole toward the open door, he saw the blood trail on the floor. He could clean it easily enough. The floor was polished wood. The whole house had the same wooden flooring. The staircase and landing too. He would only need to replace the rug in the study.

As Dole's body fell down the steep, treacherous basement stairs, Daryl heard the crack of a bone snapping.

Not that it mattered. He picked up Dole by the boots again, dragged him behind the staircase, onto an area of soft earth. Eight by ten. A shovel leant against the back wall of the stairs. Daryl set to work. The earth moved easily, and soon piled up. He left the gun in place, in Dole's holster, but took the car keys, cell phone and wallet. Lifting Dole by the torso now, Daryl shifted around and tossed him into the dirt. In a few minutes he would find Dole's car, move it to one of the less enchanting areas of Los Angeles. Leave the keys, phone and wallet in the car. It would be gone within ten minutes.

He covered him up, shovel after shovel, then smoothed down the soil, leant the shovel against the wall. In the morning he would concrete that area. Just enough to cover the grave. When he'd first bought the house that basement had a dirt floor.

Slowly, over time, Daryl brought guests to the basement. He killed them, buried them and concreted over. Looking around the basement now, he saw that there was very little of the dirt floor left. In a basement fifty feet by thirty, he'd managed to put a lot of bodies in the ground, and pour a lot of concrete. He tried to estimate how many he'd put down here.

Too many to count.

And one more wouldn't make a difference.

Then there was the house in Port Lonely. Dole hadn't checked the basement floor. Anyone who got in Daryl's way in Port Lonely or Bay City had ended up in the basement. There weren't many, just half a dozen. Not like Boston. He'd finished that concrete floor four years ago. Some of the other houses still had room though. The house in New York. Austin. Orlando. Cheyenne. His second house in Los Angeles. DC. Phoenix. Houston. And now the new house in Medina.

The Medina house had plenty of room. It was a new purchase. Five million. A modest price in Medina, whose residents included Bill Gates and Jeff Bezos. Medina was a small, secure millionaire's paradise that looked over the bay to Seattle. Daryl couldn't wait to get settled in.

CHAPTER SIXTY-NINE

'Something else has come up. We need to go over this again. I don't care how many times you've told this story. You tell me again about J. T. LeBeau or so help me God you'll never leave this cell. Dole is missing. I don't have time to fuck around.'

Paul could see spit at the corner of Bloch's mouth. She was two seconds away from leaning over the interview table and tearing out his throat. Paul had spent twenty-four hours in custody, he'd been to court and arraigned for attempted murder. He was waiting for transport back to Port Lonely when Bloch came into the holding area, told him she had to talk to him about new information. Paul didn't see any point in holding back. He knew he had to co-operate.

'I'll tell you. I don't want anyone else to get hurt,' said Paul.

He told her the story again. Same as before. He didn't leave out any details.

'Everyone I've confided in about LeBeau gets killed. You have to go and save Maria. Get her the hell away from Daryl.'

Bloch bit her lip. Dole had gone to see Maria last night. She still couldn't raise him.

'Where would we find Daryl? What other properties does he have?' asked Bloch.

'I don't know. The house in Port Lonely, he used to have a place in Manhattan, but he sold it. I honestly don't know if he has any other property anywhere.'

Bloch got up, silently, and left the interview room.

That morning Paul was arraigned on new charges in Port Lonely. Josephine Schneider had arranged a lawyer this time, and he applied for bail for Paul. The DA objected to bail and the old judge set bail at ten million dollars. He would need a tenth of that amount as a bond. There were conditions, too. He could not stay in Port Lonely – he had to find an address outside the town limits. No contact with his wife, Maria Cooper. And no contact with any potential witnesses or persons of interest in an ongoing police investigation – namely Daryl Oakes. The lawyer Schneider arranged said, 'My client will post bail this afternoon. The bond will be with the court as soon as possible.'

Sure enough, after the hearing, the lawyer said Josephine had paid the one-million-dollar bond, told him to call her. From a payphone in the holding area of the Port Lonely courthouse, Paul called Josephine.

'I've been calling like every half-hour. You okay?'

'I'm alright. Jesus, Josephine, I didn't know you had that kind of money. I can't tell you what that means to me. Thank you so much for bailing me out. Only problem is I can't stay here. I'll need to find a hotel,' said Paul.

'We'll talk about that in a second. Look, it's just so good to hear your voice. You should've called me. I haven't heard from you since you were in the Caymans.'

'I just needed some time on my own. I appreciate you helping me out. And I hate to ask . . .'

'Don't be silly, honey. That's what I'm here for. When you get out there's a Western Union a couple of blocks away. There's ten grand for you. It's traveling cash. I've got a plane ticket waiting for you at Bay City airport. I'm sorry, I just took the liberty. You see, I got you a place to stay. Somewhere you can rest for a while. Take stock of things.'

'Where?'

'I've got this new client. He's a heavy hitter. Took him on a while ago. Big money. I told him one of my other clients was having a real hard time at the moment. This guy wants to help out. He's going on tour in Europe, so his house is free. He lives in Washington State. Said you could stay as long as you wanted. The lawyer I sent has cleared the address with the judge. It's all set, you can stay.'

'That's very kind.'

'Look, it's a beautiful place. I'm going to meet you there tomorrow. I'll bring you out to the house and I'll stay for a few days. Make sure you get settled in. I'm actually quite excited about seeing the place myself. It's a mansion, across the bay from Seattle.'

'What's the name of the town?' said Paul.

'Medina,' said Josephine.

CHAPTER SEVENTY

Paul used the cash he'd picked up from Western Union to buy some decent clothes, then he checked into a Bay City hotel. He planned on resting and trying not to think about the upcoming trial. As part of his bail conditions he was prevented from making any contact with Maria. So he didn't try. There was no point anyway, he thought. Not after the way she'd looked at him at the memorial. Instead he called the Port Lonely Sheriff's Department, gave them his hotel room number and the name of the hotel – all part of his bail terms. They would check and make sure he was there. They didn't want him skipping out.

After a long shower, he wrapped himself in the hotel robe and crashed out on the bed. He couldn't put on the TV. Didn't want to risk seeing himself on the news. Instead, he drifted off to sleep.

A knocking at the door slowly roused him. He got up, checked the peephole to see who was standing on the other side of the door. He sighed, hung his head, and reluctantly let Bloch inside.

She entered the hotel room without a word. Paul noticed she was not in uniform. Black jeans, black boots, black leather jacket zipped to the neck.

'I already checked in with your department. I haven't breached my terms,' said Paul.

Fixing him with a derisory look, Bloch took an armchair in the corner of the room. Paul remained standing.

'How did you think I knew you were here? I'm aware you checked in, Paul. We need to talk.'

'Maybe my lawyer should be here for this.'

'Go ahead and call him, if you want. I'll leave. If you want to talk, it's just you and me. I think it'll be in your interest,' she said.

Running his fingers through his hair, Paul sighed, then said, 'Go ahead. What is it?'

'I hacked into Sheriff Dole's cell phone. He got a call from Maria. She left him a voicemail saying that Daryl was J. T. LeBeau. He hasn't been seen since. LAPD found his pool car burned out on the South Side. No idea how it got there.'

'Jesus, is Maria okay?' said Paul. He suddenly felt sick, a cramp took grip in his stomach and began to spread.

'I think Dole went after Daryl. He didn't call for back-up. He just called me. I told him about my father, you see. My dad covered for some guys in his precinct. Cops who were on the take, every which way. Dole knew I understood that law. Cops don't rat on cops. I think he went after Daryl, but he wasn't going to try and bring him in. I think he was going to kill him. But Daryl got to him first.'

She said this with a flat look on her face. One of loss, and disappointment. Her shoulders were hunched in the seat, but her fists were clenched. There was a rage inside of Bloch, which she was barely keeping under control.

'Where's Maria?' he said, this time Paul's voice cracked. He coughed, cleared his throat.

'It's like you said. Everyone with the knowledge of LeBeau's identity ends up dead. Help me find him. This has to end.'

'I'll help, but please just tell me. Maria is . . .' He couldn't say it.

Bloch's demeanor changed, her eyes softened, her hands relaxed. She leaned back in the armchair and spoke softly.

'I think you should sit down for this.'

He sat on the edge of the bed.

'Paul, Maria took her own life.'

Fourteen hours later, Josephine embraced Paul at the arrivals gate of the airport. It was a long, warm hug. Full of affection.

'You look far too thin. I'll have to fatten you up. Thankfully there are half a dozen great restaurants I've got lined up for us. Come on, my car is outside.'

Josephine led him into the late afternoon sunshine and a green convertible parked close to the exit. Paul put his bag in the trunk, and they took off.

He said little, preferring to let Josephine talk. She didn't mention the trial, or the money, or the litany of problems that now faced Paul. He was glad of that.

After a while they arrived in a suburb filled with huge houses. Some were traditional, some more art deco and others were positively industrial. The light was fading now, turning to a crimson dusk.

'Who would want to live in a house that looked like a factory?' she said, scoffing.

Soon she pulled off the road into a street lined with tall colonial mansions. At the end of the street a particularly old and beautiful house sat back from the others. A large oak tree grew in the garden. She parked in the driveway, and got out.

Paul fetched his bag from the trunk and saw Josephine standing in front of the house, admiring the place. The house had a classic look – wood panel siding painted brilliant white. Three brick steps led to a porch, with dormer windows stretching across the face of the building. It even had a white picket fence at one end of the front lawn.

A dream house.

'Gorgeous, isn't it, darling?' said Josephine.

Paul nodded, smiled. The old house had stood the test of time. It looked well-maintained and somehow, in the sunlight, a place where anyone could be happy.

He followed Josephine to the front door. She unlocked it with her key, and he followed her inside.

A two-story entrance hall. Massive curling staircase on the right, with a polished redwood bannister. On the left was an old oil painting – a woman who was seemingly in the clutches of a huge black swan.

'Isn't it beautiful? *Leda and the Swan*. You know, from Yeats?' said Josephine.

Paul nodded, he didn't know. There were fresh flowers on a table below the painting. They masked the slightly musty smell of the old place.

Straight ahead he saw a set of French doors leading to the kitchen, and no doubt the garden and pool beyond. To his right, just before the staircase, an alcove led to a large living room. He turned his attention back to Josephine. She was standing in front of the painting with her back to Paul. Inhaling through her nose, then breathing out slow through her mouth. As if she was drinking in the air and the painting all at once.

Paul glanced over his shoulder, saw the front door was closed. Paul breathed out. He'd lost everything that had been good in his life. And now it was time to finish this tale, once and for all.

He dropped his bag, stepped forward and grabbed Josephine's throat from behind. The fingers of his right hand locked around her slender throat. Her mouth opened, gasping.

'What are you doing?' she said, panic in her voice.

'Where is he? I know it was you who told Daryl where I was hiding. I know it. I've thought about it for a long time and it could only have been you. So where is he? Where's your new client? Where's LeBeau?'

A voice called out from the living room. It was at once familiar, and yet strange.

'Bring her in here, Paul. Don't hurt her. That would be rude.'

Paul turned around, sharply, keeping Josephine in front of him. He had one arm around her throat, keeping her close. He stepped forward. Josephine acting as a human shield.

Once through the alcove, Paul saw a grand open-plan living space. Green leather couches surrounded a mahogany coffee table. The four couches formed a wide square, with the table in the center. On the couch facing the entrance to the living room sat a man in a pale blue suit, open white shirt. He was tanned. His head must have been shaved down with an electronic razor, or perhaps the man had shaved his head some days ago, because a dark fuzz, and no more than that, passed for a hairline. It was Daryl. Only it wasn't. Daryl was just another identity. One he had changed. The man who sat on the couch was now LeBeau. His posture, skin, eyes, all had taken on a different aspect.

'Why don't you sit down, Paul? Before you do something stupid,' said LeBeau. He gestured to the couch in front of him, across the coffee table. Paul noticed a gun sitting on the couch beside LeBeau. His right hand strayed toward it, then rested gently on the grip, index finger on the trigger guard – ready to pick it up and fire.

'I'm just fine where I am,' said Paul.

'I wouldn't want you to hurt Josephine,' said LeBeau. 'She's been so helpful. I wouldn't have found you without her. Let her go, and I won't shoot. I'm glad you've come. I have something for you.'

His eyes flicked toward something on the coffee table. Paul took a moment to glance at it now. It was a bound manuscript, sitting beside a laptop.

'I have a lot to thank you for, Paul. First, for holding onto my money. Second, for giving me my latest novel. I think it's my best. I'd like you to read it.'

'Fuck you and your book,' said Paul.

'Let me go,' said Josephine.

'Shut up,' said Paul.

He couldn't take his gaze off LeBeau. The man had a feral quality that Paul found magnetic, and terrifying. It felt like being in a room with a tiger – those large eyes calculating how and when to strike. The man on the couch was a true predator.

Paul heard a click. Somewhere in the house. Out back. A door latch of some kind.

LeBeau heard it too. His eyes flicked wide, his lips drew across his face, baring his teeth, and then he moved, with incredible speed.

At once LeBeau had the gun in his hand. He stood and backed away toward the other end of the room where there was a door. LeBeau raised the gun.

Footsteps now, behind Paul. Boots running. Coming toward him from the hallway.

'Police, drop the gun,' said Bloch, as she came into the room, arms stretched into a firing pose, a Glock in her hand.

At that moment, Josephine squirmed to one side, threw a backhanded fist into Paul's groin and his grip on her broke. He felt the agonizing pain as a wave that traveled through his stomach, and sucked all the air from his lungs.

He didn't see what happened next. He dropped to the floor, two shots rang out. Bloch was suddenly there on the floor beside him, taking cover behind a couch. The air was thick with plaster dust as more shots fired over their heads into the wall behind them.

The volley of shots ended, Bloch got both feet beneath her in a crouch, then popped up, gun aimed, and loosed one shot before she was thrown backwards by another volley. She hit the wall behind her, hard, and slumped down, her head lolling to one side. Paul saw the rips in her leather jacket, as if it had been torn apart by a wild animal. The gun had fallen from her grip, and landed on the floor beside her.

From the other end of the room, Paul heard a groan, and the sound of a body hitting the floor. Bloch must have tagged LeBeau with that shot. Paul crawled toward Bloch's gun, but someone grabbed his ankle and something heavy hit him in the back. He turned over, and Josephine was on top of him. She had a heavy glass vase in her hands, raised above her head.

She was going to put it in Paul's face.

Josephine arched her back, her face contorted in rage.

And then Paul heard another bang. His face was hit with something wet. He opened his eyes and saw the vase fall backwards over Josephine's head. Her face was blank, and she had a massive wound in her chest. Her eyes rolled back in her head and she slumped off of him, and replacing her in his field of vision he saw Maria.

She had a pistol in her hand, pointed at the spot where Josephine had been. Only it couldn't have been Maria.

Maria was dead. Bloch told him she had taken her own life. And yet here she was. Dressed in blue jeans, and a black jacket. Her hair tied back. She looked at Bloch, then nodded at Paul. Paul tried to sit up, then a searing pain in his chest forced him down. He looked at his chest, put his hand there and found a pool of blood. The bullet had gone through Josephine and hit him in the chest.

Maria took the pistol from Bloch while they were out back. They had arrived on the flight before Paul's. Rented a car, and waited for him and Josephine to arrive. Maria trusted Bloch. She was the only one who knew she was still alive, that she had faked her suicide in the hotel room with Daryl.

The mansion had large gardens, and they had climbed the fence with ease. Bloch had found the back door open, and they had both slipped inside quietly. Paul was taking most of the risk. Bloch was a good person. Maria could tell. Dole was dead, of that she was sure. LeBeau was deadly. She had to end it. And Bloch had agreed.

Now things were falling into place for Maria.

She'd stood at the entrance to the living room, gun in her hand, and watched Bloch take two shots to the chest. She heard the body drop at the other end of the room. LeBeau had been hit. She saw Paul crawl toward the gun, Josephine hitting him in the back with a vase, then, when he turned over she climbed on top of him. She was about to kill him, and when she raised the vase over her head Maria had shot her without a second thought.

Paul saw her then, and he looked wild and dazed. Incredulous. And she saw the wound in his chest. The bullet had gone clean through Josephine, and hit Paul. She didn't mean it. It had been an accident. Putting her panic and guilt aside, she realized if she didn't move, she might be next to catch a bullet. LeBeau was still in that room.

She stepped into the lounge, and turned to see LeBeau lying on the floor, trying to crawl out of the door at the back of the room. The blood was thick and dark on the carpet. He had discarded his gun, and Maria knew then he had been hit badly by Bloch's round.

'Daryl, my love,' said Maria.

LeBeau stopped, turned over, his eyes wide in panic. His face soaked in sweat. His suit was a bloody mess. The bullet had taken him in the stomach, dead center.

'You're dead,' he said. 'Am I dead?'

He had a stupid look on his face. Panic making him shiver.

Maria raised the gun, pointed it at him.

'When I woke up in the hospital they told me I had vasculitis. An underlying condition. Inflammation of the veins. Said I scared the shit out of the doctors because they could hardly find a pulse. I knew if I made it look like I was dead it would fool you too. I won – you son of a bitch.'

He opened his mouth to say something more. A distraction, as he reached for the gun, just a few feet away. Maria robbed him of his words with three pulls of the trigger. First shot took him in the head. The last two in the chest.

Maria breathed out, walked back to Paul, and stood over him.

He was gasping for breath, his lips coated in blood. She knelt down, and cradled his head.

'You're alive . . . I'm so glad you're alive. I'm sorry,' he said.

Maria kissed him, told him it was okay. Everything was going to be okay. None of this was his fault.

'No . . . it is my fault. Please . . . forgive me,' said Paul.

'I forgive you,' said Maria, and she held his hand until his breath gave out, and he died in her arms.

She got up, and moved to Bloch. Gently, she touched Bloch's cheek, spoke softly to her. There was no blood on her chest. The vest had stopped the rounds but there was blood at the back of her head from contact with the wall. Slowly, Bloch came to.

'It's over,' said Maria.

Maria helped Bloch to her feet, and when she was steady, Maria let go. She put the pistol in her pocket, and picked up the laptop and manuscript from the table, tucked them under her arm.

'Go,' said Bloch. 'I'll call local police, straighten everything out.'

With that, Maria left.

CHAPTER SEVENTY-ONE

Maria adjusted the laptop. It had almost slid right off her thighs. She took a sip from the piña colada, set it back down on the sand next to her Manolo Blahnik shoes.

She focused on the screen. She was on a deadline.

Bloch had covered for her. The news on the day after the shootout in Medina was all about a brave officer called Melissa Bloch who had traced a bail jumper to Medina, and had shot him dead, but not before he had murdered two people. A man and a woman, whose names had not been released to the media.

A week after Maria had returned to Bay City, she placed a call to a man in New York named Fullerton. He worked at the publishing house that produced the LeBeau books.

'Mr. Fullerton, it's Maria Cooper. Thank you for your kindness at the memorial, but I feel so terribly guilty. I have to tell you the truth. My husband, Paul, or J. T. LeBeau, well, he left an unfinished manuscript. I'm going to finish it. I'm going to be your new J. T. LeBeau and I'd like to agree terms, but please, for now, let's make it our secret.'

Two weeks after that phone call, Maria had a publishing deal for five million dollars, a team of attorneys who were tracing the LeBeau properties, and the money. No one else was going to claim it. And Maria had the means to make it hers.

Her new novel was to be called *Twisted*. It was mostly complete when she took the manuscript from the house. A digital copy remained on the laptop, and she was able to make some small changes to it. The ending had to be rewritten, for a start. The original author had used fake names, like Martha, Saul and Darren. She changed it back to the real names of the main characters. The author's note at the beginning of the novel she left unchanged. It fitted her purpose too. No one would know what was real, and what was fiction, apart from those involved. And they were all dead, bar her and Bloch. Bloch would never tell anyone what really happened.

Maria took another sip from her piña colada, looked up at the bright blue sky over Barbados, then returned her eyes to the manuscript. She was close to the end. She read over what she had just typed.

Maria stood at the entrance to the living room, gun in her hand, and watched Bloch fire off one round before she took two shots to the chest, hit her head against the wall and then fell unconscious. She heard the body drop at the other end of the room. LeBeau had been hit, too. She saw Paul crawl toward the gun, Josephine hitting him in the back with a vase.

Josephine hadn't realized the danger she was in. Maria aimed the gun at Josephine's back and pulled the trigger. The shot stopped her instantly, and she fell dead to the floor.

Paul turned in shock, looked at Maria wide-eyed. She had saved his life. He tried to stand and Maria said, 'Stay down, Paul.'

She stepped into the lounge, only to see LeBeau trying to crawl out of the door at the back of the room. The blood was thick and dark on the carpet. He had discarded his gun, and Maria knew then he had been hit badly by Bloch's round.

'Daryl, my love,' said Maria.

LeBeau stopped, turned over, his eyes wide in panic. His face soaked in sweat. His suit was a bloody mess. The bullet had taken him in the stomach, dead center. He had a stupid look on his face. Panic making him shiver.

'You're dead,' he said. 'Am I dead?'

'Yes,' said Maria. 'You are now.'

Maria raised the gun, pointed it at him and shot him in the head. For good measure she put two in his chest.

She turned away from him, and there in front of her stood Paul.

'You're alive. I'm so glad you're alive. I'm so sorry,' said Paul.

He stood before her, his hands outstretched, his face filled with genuine regret. He was alive, and unharmed, and Maria knew then that she could never love him.

'I'm sorry too, Paul. I'm sorry I ever met you,' said Maria as she pointed the gun at his chest and pulled the trigger.

Paul fell to the floor, dead.

Maria selected the passage of text she'd just read, then deleted it.

She would need to make up something better.

The truth can be far too brutal.

ACKNOWLEDGMENTS

from the author, Steve Cavanagh

There are many people who deserve thanks for their help with this novel. The idea for this book came from my wife, Tracy. For that I am very grateful, and for her support, comments and suggestions which made the book come alive. I couldn't do anything without her.

My editors, the brilliant Francesca Pathak and Christine Kopprasch, for making the book so much better and pushing me to the limit with this story. To Emad, Harriet, Katie and all at Orion. To Amy, Bob and all at Flatiron Books. To Euan and all at A. M. Heath for your support, wisdom and expert representation.

To Luca Veste, for early reading and encouraging me to continue with this book.

To the writers who have supported me and helped me in this business.

To James Law and Quentin Bates for all their nautical assistance on sinking a boat.

To Chloe and Noah. And Lolly.

To my Dad.

To Marie and Tom.

To my family and friends.

To the booksellers all over the world who hand-sell my books to customers.

To you, the reader.

Thank you all.

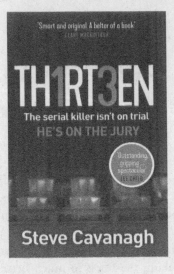

Eddie Flynn returns in the next edge-of-your-seat thriller

WHO IS DEADLIER . . .

Leonard Howell's worst nightmare has come true: his daughter
Caroline has been kidnapped. Not content with relying on the
cops, Howell calls the only man he trusts to get her back.

. . . THE MAN WHO KNOWS THE TRUTH . . .

Eddie Flynn knows what it's like to lose a daughter and vows to
bring Caroline home safe. Once a con artist, now a hotshot criminal
attorney, Flynn is no stranger to the shady New York underworld.

. . . OR THE ONE WHO BELIEVES A LIE?

However, as he steps back into his old life, Flynn realizes that
the rules of the game have changed – and that he is being played.
But who is pulling the strings? And is anyone in this twisted case
telling the truth . . . ?

**A missing girl, a desperate father and a case that
threatens to destroy everyone involved – Eddie Flynn's
got his work cut out in this thrilling new novel.
Available to buy in paperback and ebook now!**

FRAUD. BLACKMAIL. MURDER.
IT'S ALL IN A DAY'S WORK FOR EDDIE FLYNN.

'Highly intelligent, twist-laden and absolutely unputdownable'
Eva Dolan

'Steve is a fantastic thriller writer' Mark Billingham

When David Child, a major client of a corrupt New York law firm, is arrested for murder, the FBI ask con artist-turned-lawyer Eddie Flynn to secure the case and force him to testify against the firm.

Eddie is not someone who is easily coerced, but when the FBI reveal that they have incriminating files on his wife, he knows he has no choice.

But Eddie is convinced the man is innocent, despite overwhelming evidence to the contrary. With the FBI putting pressure on him to secure the deal, Eddie must find a way to prove his client's innocence.

But the stakes are high – his wife is in danger.
And not just from the FBI . .

Don't miss out – available to buy now.

Eddie Flynn has 48 hours to save his daughter . . .

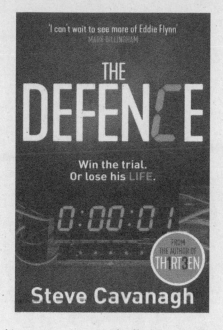

'A gripping, twisty thriller' Ian Rankin

'*The Defence* is everything a great thriller should be' Mark Billingham

It's been over a year since Eddie vowed never to set foot in a courtroom again. But now he doesn't have a choice. Olek Volchek, the infamous head of the Russian mafia in New York, has strapped a bomb to Eddie's back and kidnapped his ten-year-old daughter, Amy. Eddie only has forty-eight hours to defend Volchek in an impossible murder trial – and win – if he wants to save his daughter.

Under the scrutiny of the media and the FBI, Eddie must use his razor-sharp wit and every trick in the con-artist book to defend his 'client' and ensure Amy's safety. With the timer on his back ticking away, can Eddie convince the jury of the impossible?

Out now in paperback and ebook.